History of the Evangelical Association

Vol. I

SALZWASSER
VERLAG

W.W. Orwig

History of the Evangelical Association

Vol. I

Reprint of the original, first published in 1858.

1st Edition 2023 | ISBN: 978-3-37514-936-9

Verlag (Publisher): Salzwasser Verlag GmbH, Zeilweg 44, 60439 Frankfurt, Deutschland
Vertretungsberechtigt (Authorized to represent): E. Roepke, Zeilweg 44, 60439 Frankfurt, Deutschland
Druck (Print): Books on Demand GmbH, In de Tarpen 42, 22848 Norderstedt, Deutschland

HISTORY

OF THE

EVANGELICAL ASSOCIATION:

BY REV. W. W. ORWIG.

VOLUME I.

FROM THE ORIGIN OF THE ASSOCIATION TO THE END OF THE YEAR 1845.

TRANSLATED FROM THE GERMAN.

FIRST EDITION.

"The Lord hath done great things for us; whereof we are glad."
Ps. 126, 3.
"Ascribe ye greatness unto our God." DEUT. 32, 3.

CLEVELAND, OHIO:
PUBLISHED BY CHARLES HAMMER,
FOR THE EVANGELICAL ASSOCIATION.
1858.

View of the first Church of the Evangelical Association, at New Berlin, Union County, Pa., erected in 1816.

INTRODUCTION

TO THE

HISTORY OF THE EVANGELICAL ASSOCIATION.

A thorough acquaintance with the history of the Church of God on earth, is of the utmost importance for every true Christian; and its study ought, therefore, not to be neglected by those who take any interest in the cause of God, and the acquisition of useful information. The benefits arising from this study are many. For it not only incites the Christian pilgrim, on his journey to the heavenly Canaan, constantly to increase his knowledge, and to establish himself more firmly, in the fundamental truths of the Bible; but it also encourages him, amidst the difficulties of this life, and the manifold temptations by the enemies of God and his kingdom, to continue to fight boldly the fight of faith, and to remain steadfast in the service of the Lord to the end of his pilgrimage. Nor is this all. In its study the Christian beholds the glorious promises of God—to support and protect his servants in all their temptations, trials, and difficulties, while on their pilgrimage—literally fulfilled by many facts; and thus he becomes more thoroughly established in the belief of the Divine origin of the Bible and of Christianity. Another reason why the history of the Church ought to be studied is, it forms a very important part of the history of the Bible, which the Church received by Divine inspiration.

It would not, indeed, be safe to receive all the statements contained in the various histories of the Church, that have been written by different authors, from the times of the apostles up to the present, as infallible and in all points correct; for, in many instances, matters of great importance may have been omitted, and others misrepresented, both from want of proper information, and from prejudice and human frailty, and thus many and serious errors committed. Yet, notwithstanding this, the Church-historical works which we possess, especially those of some modern, highly gifted divines, unquestionably contain the substance of the origin, spread, experience, and fate of the Church up to the present time, as well as of her hopes for the future. Hence, a good history of the Church ought, next to the Bible, to be diligently read and studied by every Christian, especially by every minister of the Gospel.

If, then, an acquaintance with the history of the Church Universal is valuable and useful to the Christian, equally so must be an impartial account of any individual branch of the Church—provided it deserve that name—in proportion to the blessing God has bestowed upon it, and the general attention it has attracted in the world. The histories of the origin, polity, and progress of different denominations, have already been written, and are read with deep interest, and not without benefit.—Without any apprehension, therefore, of being charged with arrogance by any *liberal* sister Church, that acts in the Spirit of Christ and in conformity to the Bible, we hereby venture to present the Evangelical Association also as one of the members and branches of the Church Universal.

True, it is as yet a small and feeble twig of the great tree of the Church, of recent date, and perhaps, on account of the many large branches surrounding it, scarcely visible to dim eyes; yet, having hitherto been so signally protected and blessed by the great Head of the Church, it considers it as a sacred duty to be thankful to Him, and to increase its zeal and activity in the extension of his kingdom on earth.

In order to discharge this duty more effectually, a history of our denomination was long since felt to be highly necessary. And hence, ere this, the subject had received the attention of the General Conference, and resolutions were passed with reference thereto.

No proper arrangements having been made, however, to collect the necessary materials, the subject was postponed from time to time. Finally, at the session of General Conference in 1843, its attention was again called to the subject, and Rev. John Dreisbach was commissioned, with the assistance of our bishops, and the presiding elders of the several Annual Conferences, to commence the work. But no proper system having as yet been devised for collecting materials, Mr. Dreisbach received but little assistance in the enterprise, and until the next session of General Conference in 1847, he had collected but fifteen sheets of written matter, which he handed in, with a desire to be released from his commission. Rev. A. Ettinger was then appointed to continue the work; but as he soon after withdrew from the Society, it was again suspended till the next session of General Conference in 1851. At this time, the editors of our Periodicals were instructed to proceed with the collection of materials and the prosecution of the work, as time and circumstances would permit. But this resolution was likewise frustrated, by several changes in the editorial department during a few years, caused by the sickness and eventual demise of one of them; and nothing further was done for the time being.—In the spring of 1854, the West Pennsylvania Conference, at its annual session in York, Pa., requested the Writer to undertake the work, provided the other Annual Conferences would concur in this request. This proposition met with almost unanimous approbation at the conferences, and then the Author commenced his task, July 10th, 1854.

As there were, however, but few documents extant, relating to the origin and the first thirty-five years of the existence and progress of the Association, the Author was often greatly embarrassed in his labor. For, although he had personally visited most of the Annual Conferences, and made arrangements with them, to render him all possible aid in the enterprise; yet he failed to obtain certain necessary documents, especially from certain parts and places of the Society, during its first thirty-five years up to the appearance of the "Christliche Botschafter." That under such circumstances many a vacuum has been left in this history, and many a description become defective, is highly probable. But, whatever these defects or errors may be, it is hoped that in a second edition of the work they will be supplied and rectified.

With these prefatory remarks, the Author would commend the result of his labors to the indulgent attention of the Public, and of the members and ministers of the Evangelical Association; invoking the great Head of the Church to command his blessings to rest abundantly upon it, for the best interests of his kingdom.

W. W. Orwig.

New Berlin, Pa., August 25th, 1856.

FIRST SECTION.

FROM THE ORIGIN OF THE EVANGELICAL ASSOCIATION IN 1800, TO ITS FIRST CONFERENCE IN 1807.

The *Evangelical Association* traces its origin to the beginning of the nineteenth century, in the state of Pennsylvania, North America, and may properly be regarded as a *child of Providence;* inasmuch as its founder, the Rev. *Jacob Albright*, when he went forth to preach the Gospel, had, in all probability, nothing else in view but the honor and glory of God, and the welfare of his German brethren, without entertaining the remotest idea of ever becoming the founder of an ecclesiastical organization. For he had labored several years in the ministry, and God had already given him many souls as the seal to his mission, before he became convinced of the necessity of organizing regular classes and societies, in order that he might thereby be enabled to prosecute his labors in the Lord with greater success, and to direct the pardoned souls committed to his care, in the work of grace, and to edify them by Christian discipline, as well as by precept and example, and thus to advance their growth in the divine life. Such was, by the interposition of Providence, the origin of the Evangelical Association, without any preconceived plan on the part of its founder.

The Rev. Jacob Albright having thus been the instrument, in the hand of God, of founding this Christian denomination, its members were, at first, generally called *"the Albrights"*—an appellation that is still given them by many who either do not know better, or who wish to manifest their disregard for the same. Having, however, no reason to be ashamed of the name and character of this pious and devoted servant of God, the Society for a while acquiesced in this matter; but, not wishing to be called after the name of any mortal, they adopted, at a later period, the name of *Evangelical Association;* not anticipating that any one would take umbrage at a name in itself so appropriate for Christians, and much less that it would be considered a mark of presumption or spiritual pride.

The Society thus claiming, without hesitation, the Rev. Mr. Albright as its founder, it will not be out of place to insert here a brief sketch of his life, convertion, deportment as a Christian, his call to the ministry, etc.

Having enjoyed no advantages but those that are common to all, Mr. Albright did not, indeed, attract public attention, either by his ancestry, or his literary attainments. He was born in Douglass township, Montgomery co., Pa., May 1, 1759. His parents had him baptized in infancy, and afterward instructed in the rudiments of the German language, and the principles of the Christian religion, according to the doctrines of the Evangelical Lutheran Church, into which he was received as a member. But he seems to have fared no better than many others did, and still do, who, after their baptism, catechetical instruction, confirmation, and reception as members of the Church, continue to live in sin and ungodliness, and become worse every day, instead of reforming. Yet it appears from his own confession, that notwithstanding his frivolity, and the sinful pleasures in which he indulged with the world, his conscience was never fully silenced, and he enjoyed no peace in that condition; nay, his conscience often accused him, when he had rendered himself guilty of some sin. And although, for some time, he paid but little attention to the warnings of that monitor, yet, continuing they became stronger and more pungent, until at last he became convinced of his sinfulness, and resolved to reform. But he had, at that time, merely the power *to will* to a certain degree—*to do* the good, he was still unable. Sin and his corrupt nature had as yet full dominion over him. Meanwhile he came several times into imminent danger of death, and was, as it were, miraculously saved; whereby a feeling of gratitude to God was almost involuntarily called forth in his soul. But he at the same time felt his unworthiness to such a degree, that he almost despaired of God's grace and mercy, and was deeply humbled. During this sad state of his mind he derived great benefit from the catechetical instruction he had received in his youth. Although unable, at that time, fully to understand and realize all the great truths of religion; yet he had, in those earlier days, imbibed a lasting feeling of reverence for God; and every place where He was worshiped, appeared sacred to him. It was this feeling of reverence, which induced him to frequent religious meetings, and to listen attentively to the preached word. By this means, as well as the chastening grace of God, and sore affliction by the death of several of his children, he finally fell into a state of extreme anguish and sadness. Speaking of this state of his mind he says:—

"I was afraid of myself. The judgments of God were before my mind. My spirit was in such a state of depression, that no external allurements of the senses could dispel the gloom. The feeling of my unworthiness increased from day to day, till in my thirty-second year, in the month of July, it reached a degree bordering even on despair. I felt myself so little and unworthy, and my sins so great, that I could not conceive how a just God, who judges according to deserts, could possibly do otherwise than hurl me into the abyss of damnation! The anguish of my soul increased every moment, so that I was ready to exclaim, 'Ye mountains, fall upon me; and ye hills, cover me.'"

This knowledge of his sinfulness, and the great danger of losing his soul, led him to a deep and heart-felt repentance of his sins. "I fell upon my knees," says he, "tears of bitter sorrow rolled over my cheeks, and a long, ardent, and inmost prayer ascended to the throne of grace for mercy and the pardon of my sins." He now felt some consolation, and the assurance that God desired not his death, but waited to be gracious unto him, for the sake of Christ's merits. This encouraged him to continue in fervent prayer, and finally the happy hour of his deliverance arrived. "By and by," he says, "all anxiety and anguish of soul disappeared; happiness and a joyous peace in God filled my soul, God's Spirit bearing witness with my spirit, that I had become a child of God ; one happy sensation followed another, and such a heavenly joy pervaded my whole being, as no pen can describe, and no mortal can express—compared with which, all fullness of sensual pleasures, that I had ever enjoyed, was nothing but wretchedness and illusion. My prayer consisted no longer of mere entreaties, but the offering of praise and gratitude, mingled with tears of joy, ascended also to heaven, to the Giver of every good and every perfect gift."

From this description of his conversion, given by Mr. Albright himself, it is evident that it was by no means an artificial or merely superficial work, but a genuine and thorough change of heart. It was not barely an awaking from the sleep, and a groaning under the burden, of his sins, attended with good resolutions and a partial reformation ; but it was, at the same time, a rising from the dead, a passing from spiritual death unto divine life—a genuine renewal of the heart after the image of God, a delivery from the power of darkness, and a translation into the glorious kingdom of the Son of God.—Genuine contrition, a deep sense of his wretchedness and lost condition out of Christ, attended with painful sorrow and sadness, had preceded ; and while in this state of mind he lay at the feet of the cross, bitter tears flowing copiously down his cheeks, God granted him the assurance that there was help for him, that He would accept him for Christ's sake, and complete the work begun in him. And no sooner had he become satisfied about this *willingness* of God to accept him, than he was also enabled to believe, and the pardon of his sins, life and happiness followed this exercise of faith.—This short sketch of Mr. Albright's conversion is inserted here, from a full conviction that it was a genuine work of grace, strictly Biblical, and therefore an infinitely better qualification for the Gospel ministry, than human learning and culture ; although these are valuable also, and ought not to be neglected.—If there were such a thing as apostolical succession, it would, without the *genuine conversion* of him who enjoys this prerogative, be a mere illusion and altogether worthless ; while it is for him who is really converted, called and qualified by the Holy Ghost for the sacred office, altogether needless.—Although Mr. Albright was, as has already been remarked, an *illiterate* man, yet he was far from underrating or despising human learning and mental culture in the ministry. On the contrary, he acknowledged that after he had been called to the Gospel ministry, he deeply felt his lack of a liberal education; and many that were personally acquainted with him, assure us that it was his constant endeavor to cultivate and store his mind with useful knowledge, and that he advised the ministers under his superintendence to do the same.

As to his moral character and Christian deportment after his conversion, they were unexceptionable. His motto was, "Holiness to the Lord!"—this he strove to verify in his whole life He denied himself all illicit pleasures; and by fasting, prayer, and constant meditation upon the Word of God, he overcame his sinful propensities so completely, that he hated everything sinful instinctively, and found *his delight* in doing all possible good. Being deeply concerned for the salvation of his own soul, he also took the deepest interest in the welfare of his fellow-men, especially his German brethren, whose religious life was at a very low ebb. The German Churches of America were in those days in a wretched condition, as the ministers were, to a great extent, unprincipled and vicious hirelings, who stripped the sacred office of its dignity and influence upon the masses. The administration of Church discipline was neglected, and flagrant sins and vices were the order of the day in all the so-called Christian congregations.* This deplorable state

*As frequent mention is made in this history, of the corruption and wretched condition of the German Churches of this country, in the days of Albright and at a later period, we subjoin here, for the confirmation of what we say, the testimony of some of the ministers of these Churches.—

The Rev. J. L. Reber, a German Reformed minister, in his tract entitled, "Ein ernsthaftes Wort über den Sektengeist und das Sektenwesen." (An Earnest Word on the Spirit and Character of Sectarianism.), while speaking of Albright and other servants of God, says: "When these men arose, the Church presented a gloomy aspect. The ways of Zion were desolate, and the Church lay in a sleep of sin, almost lifeless, and for the most part godless."

When the writer was stationed at York, Pa., 1844, a Lutheran of things affected the pious man deeply, and filled his soul with intense grief. In this frame of mind he often fell prostrate on

minister, (the late Rev J. G. Schmucker,) told him, while on a visit, that he once heard Albright preach, during a synod at Lebanon, in a grave-yard there; and among other things he also remarked, that the state of things in the German Churches wore a gloomy aspect in those days, and that only a small number of the ministers, composing the synod to which he belonged, were, in his view, converted men.

In a biography of Dr. Schmucker, deceased, which was published in the "Lutheran Observer," Dr. B. Kurtz says that the departed, when he took charge of several congregations at and about Hagerstown, Md., in 1794, found the state of Christianity in a deplorable condition. After noticing the general (spiritual) ruin of the Churches, Dr. Kurtz goes on to say:—

"Sunday schools, Bible classes, prayer-meetings, weekly lectures, &c., had not yet been introduced. There were no stoves and no lamps in the Churches, and night-meetings were regarded as "new measures," and as tending to fanaticism; though for dancing, playing cards, &c., they were thought to be very appropriate. Conversion was a strange word, and revivals were unknown. Methodists indeed, and they alone, talked about conversion; and some few among them, we presume, knew from personal experience what it meant. In other Churches also, the Lord doubtless had his chosen few; but they were like the gleanings of the olive tree, two or three on the topmost branches. The cock-pit, the race-course, the long-bullet lane, the dog and the bear fight, &c., were more numerously attended than the house of God. On the whole, darkness comparatively covered the land, and gross darkness the people."—*Luth. Observer*, No. 1107.

This description of the congregations of Hagerstown and vicinity, is a true picture of most congregations of the German Churches of this country in those days. Such was the state of things in a spiritual point of view, when the Evangelical Association took its origin. Now, is it at all surprising that Albright and his followers met with opposition and persecution?

In No. 1114 of the Luth. Observer (Jan. 12th, 1855,) Dr. Kurtz remarks, with reference to the same subject:—

"Some thirty-five years ago, when God in his mercy sanctioned our poor labors with a glorious outpouring of his Spirit, and for the first time in our ministry granted us a mighty revival, the opposition of the world and the devil was almost unparalleled. A revival in the Lutheran Church was a new thing in that day: we had never heard of but one, and that was in Bro. Reck's Church, in Winchester, Va. He can testify to the bitterness, malevolence and awful wickedness which characterized the adversaries of such divine visitations in those days of ignorance, hardness of heart and spiritual blindness. It seemed as if all hell were let loose. What *was*,—what *could* be done in the face of such fierce rebellion? If in view of the work itself, it was the happiest event of our ministry; in connection with the diabolical hate and slander that enveloped it, it was one of the darkest periods of our life."

his knees, beseeching the Lord with tears, that he would bring his German brethren to the knowledge of the truth, and send them faithful servants who would preach the Gospel unto them in power, to their conversion and salvation. "Thus," he says, "I prayed daily, pleading for the conversion of my brethren; and while I was thus wrestling with God, all at once light arose in my soul—I heard, as it were, a voice whispering in my soul: 'Is it mere chance, that you take so deep an interest in the welfare of your brethren?— — — How, if God's infinite love, that wishes to bring every soul into Abraham's bosom, had chosen you to lead your brethren to the knowledge of the truth?'" It appeared to him as if God himself were addressing him thus: "Go out and labor in my vineyard," etc.

Shortly after his conversion, Mr. Albright joined the Methodist Episcopal Church, not knowing any other that appeared to be more zealous and active in the service of God. He complied with their rules, attended their religious exercises, and thus was greatly edified, and made rapid progress in the divine life: he was especially well pleased with their excellent discipline and order.

Finally he complied with the urgent requests of his brethren, to exhort now and then, and God's blessings attended his efforts. This procured him a written license to exhort in the German language, wherever he might find an opening. Naturally he was not gifted as a speaker; but when he was filled with the Spirit from on high, the divine truths flowed eloquently from his lips, so that sinners were awakened and converted, and the children of God greatly edified by his discourses. Thus he labored several years for the benefit of his German brethren in the vicinity, God richly blessing his labors; and his interest in their spiritual welfare, and that of his fellow men generally, increased all the while, so that his sphere of labor soon became too narrow to satisfy the demands of his inward conviction. Feeling an urgent call to *preach* the Gospel, he accordingly paid occasional visits to other parts; and thus from an exhorter he became a preacher. It is true, he had not been licensed by his Church to do so; but the signal blessings God was pleased to bestow upon his labors, satisfied his mind at times, that the Lord had chosen him to preach the Gospel. He lived at that time in Lancaster county, Pa., and having a family to support, it was necessary for him to attend to his farm and brick-kiln, and therefore could not devote as much time to preaching as he really desired.—In consequence, however, of his laboring thus on his own responsibility, and being frequently absent from the public services of his Church, he, as a matter of course, lost his membership there.

At that time this good man had to pass through a severe struggle, touching his call to the Gospel ministry. At times he felt, indeed, satisfied that God had called him to preach the Gospel; but then again a sense of his unworthiness, the great opposition he had to encounter, and his temporal affairs, etc., filled him sometimes with doubts concerning it.

Now, since the question whether the founder of the Evangelical Association was *divinely* called to the Gospel-ministry or not, is of the utmost importance for this denomination, and as no Christian—yea no reasonable man will call in question the legitimacy of its independent organization, if this *divine* call of its founder can be fully established: we here subjoin Mr. Albright's own statement on this subject, somewhat abbreviated. He expresses himself thus:—"Although I was fully satisfied about my *divine* call, yet my flesh raised many doubts about it in my mind, and thus I became irresolute. But this was followed by great, *great* despondency: a heavy load lay upon my mind, and I enjoyed neither peace by day, nor rest by night. I fell into a state of despondency that baffled every effort to cheer me. My peace of mind had fled, and the objection that it would be impossible for me to travel through the country for the purpose of preaching the Gospel, *alone, without reputation, without support, without the assistance of others, without being connected with any ecclesiastical organization*, could not satisfy my mind. All dangers to which I should expose myself by so doing, presented themselves to my excited imagination; and although I had the promise of God on my side, yet I trembled. But all these doubts had to give way again to the conviction which God had wrought in me—that his strength is made perfect in weakness—that he imposes on no one more than he can bear—that to whom he gives the courage to fight, he also grants the power to conquer, if they have his honor and glory for their sole object—that he possesses all power, and strengthens those that do his pleasure,—truths which I afterward often experienced in a remarkable degree, after I had submitted to his will. Thus my conviction grew stronger and stronger, finally excluding every shadow of doubt that God had called me to the great work, *to preach his Gospel to my erring brethren.* All obstacles which at first seemed to be in my way, had now disappeared from my spiritual vision; and, on the other hand, the ardent love for my brethren, with which God had filled my heart—the confidence in his powerful protection and assistance—the assurance wrought by him in my soul that he would bless my labors—the sight granted to me by God of the great reward in heaven, that awaited me if I should prove faithful,—all these were so many powerful motives which I could no longer resist, and I resolved to obey his divine call. However, to carry out this resolution, I put off from one time to another. I still imagined to see new impediments in my way. And when one was removed, another seemed to have taken its place. But for this irresoluteness and delay to obey the call of God, I was visited with a sore affliction; my whole nervous system was seized with acute pain, and all my members ached almost insufferably. My countenance changed, and scarcely anything was left of my frame but a shadow. Yet more terrible than all bodily sufferings, was the anguish of my soul, arising from the fear that I was a *reprobate.* What I suffered during this disease, in body and mind, language cannot express. While under this feeling of being a reprobate, I have shrieked sometimes so terribly, that all who saw and heard me, turned away from me with horror and dismay.

"In this chastisement I learned to see, more than ever, the finger of God; and the conviction forced itself upon me, that man cannot do better than always to submit unreservedly to the

2

will of his Maker, and obey his call. Deplorable as my condition was, during this time of suffering, yet the Lord was still merciful to me, and did not withdraw his grace entirely from me. He continued to give me strength to persevere in prayer; and I was enabled to prostrate myself at his feet, and to seek with tears the forgiveness of my sins; and I vowed solemnly unto him, that if he would raise me up once more, I would forthwith follow his call. As soon as I had firmly taken this resolution, the heavy load was taken from my soul, and peace again returned to my mind. The tranquility of my mind being thus fully restored, my bodily suffering also soon ceased—my strength returned, new life pervaded my system, and in a short time I was well again. I now prepared myself as I deemed necessary, and made everything ready to enter upon my mission. My qualification for the preaching of the Gospel, I sought only from the Lord, by persevering prayer and the constant meditation upon the Word of God. My body, too, I strove to consecrate wholly unto the Lord, so that no passion, desire or love of convenience, might arrest my course; for God had showed me plainly what a miserable and wretched condition it must be, to preach unto others the practice of virtue, and I myself be a reprobate."

Having laid these extracts from the biography of Mr. Albright before the candid reader, the writer leaves it with him to decide whether Mr. Albright was divinely called to the Gospel-ministry; being himself fully convinced from many reasons, that the founding of the Evangelical Association is the work of God, and has already contributed much to his glory, and the welfare of many immortal souls.

Under these circumstances and trials, Mr. Albright set out in 1796, to proclaim the Gospel of Jesus Christ to his fellow-men. He traveled through a great part of Pennsylvania, and some parts of Maryland and Virginia, preaching wherever he found an opening—in Churches, school-houses, private dwellings, barns, in the woods, in market-places, in church-yards, and sometimes even on public roads: God crowning and blessing his labors everywhere to the conversion of many souls.

The following letter from Brother R. Yeakel furnishes a sample of Mr. Albright's method of laboring in those parts of the country where he afterward formed his first classes.

"ORWIGSBURG, PA., Oct. 20th, 1855.

Dear Brother Orwig:—

Since I received your letter, I paid a visit to my parents at their home, and took occasion to inquire after Mr. Albright's first appearance among the Schwenkfelders. Samuel Schultz, now about 78 years of age, who is fully acquainted with the facts in the case, related to me the following:—'It happened about the year 1795,* that as a Schwenkfeld child was to be buried, a stranger arrived at the house where the corpse lay, and asked permission of the preacher (Geo. Kriebel) to give an exhortation to the assembled congregation. This stranger was Mr. Albright. Saying, as he did, that he was an evangelical preacher, who proclaimed the Gospel wherever he could, his request was readily granted by the good old preacher.

Mr. Albright, accordingly, went with the funeral procession to the meeting-house, and took a seat beside the preacher behind the table—there being no pulpit in the house. Every one was now anxious to know who the stranger might be; but this question no one could answer. When the sermon was over, Mr. Albright rose, to the astonishment of all, and exhorted them powerfully. He then asked permission to preach there, which being readily granted, he made an appointment for a certain Saturday, by day. On the day appointed, he preached to the assembled multitude with such energy, that many tears were shed. He obtained leave to make a second appointment, and a third in another meeting-house. But now the persecution of the good man began to break out. The most fictitious and abominable reports were circulated about him, representing him as a man of the very worst character. But this attracted a still larger audience, after which, however, the meeting-houses were closed against him. Yet a few private houses were

*This must have taken place one or two years later.—AUTHOR.

forthwith opened for him, in which, for a time, he continued to scatter the good seed, amidst sore persecution. At the same time, people of other denominations also gave him permission to preach in their houses, in which some conversions took place, especially in the neighborhood of Buchwalter's and Liesser's, in Berks county; and the work seemed, for some time, to prosper in spite of all opposition. But for the want of faithful assistants and some other causes, the work remained in a fermenting, germinating state, up to the years 1825–30–35, when it pleased the Lord to send his word with crowds of evangelists and with great power in those regions, so that many were converted to God, and classes were formed and added to the circuit, in the Eastern Conference.'"

Mr. Albright's sermons were plain,—well adapted to the capacities of his hearers, and generally full of unction and irresistible power. His whole soul was in the work, and God enabled him to preach the Gospel with great freedom of speech. It often happened that his hearers were carried away by his sermons as by an irresistible torrent, and were so powerfully moved and affected, that many became convinced of their lost condition, and repented; while the believers were always greatly edified and encouraged by his discourses. Opposition, slander, calumny, and persecution, were, as a matter of course, not wanting; as Satan was greatly enraged against this faithful servant of the Lord, and the world hated him because he exposed and reproved its wickedness, in his pointed sermons. Lukewarm and slothful nominal Christians, dead in trespasses and sins, read their sentence of condemnation in his sermons which reproved all injustice, sanctimoniousness, and hypocrisy; and even well-disposed Christians sometimes took offence at his unusual zeal in the cause of his Divine Master. And unconverted, carnal, mercenary preachers raised their voices, and warned the people against him. Many base and slanderous reports were rapidly circulated in every direction, and filled the ignorant multitude of lukewarm Christians with prejudice against the good man. But all this did not in the least discourage him from following his sacred calling.—He saw, however, more and more clearly, that his labors would, in a great measure, be lost, unless he would form those, that had been awakened and converted by his instrumentality, into societies by themselves, and introduce Christian discipline among them. Accordingly, in 1800 he ventured to take this all-important step. But, as the fruits of his four years' labors were scattered far and wide, he could, at first, not unite all in the manner indicated, and the societies which he actually formed, were but small. The first three of these societies or classes were formed in the counties of Northampton, Berks, and Bucks, one near Quakertown, called *Walter's class*, the other near Colebrook-Dale ironworks, called *Liesser's class*, and the third in Northampton co., called *Phillip's class*. There were, at the same time, leaders elected, who are now generally called classleaders, whose duty it is to see to it, that everything be done according to divine and human order, in the small assemblies, and to hold prayer-meetings at stated times, etc.

This, then, was the origin of the Evangelical Association.

But this step of Mr. Albright, to found a new ecclesiastical organization, was disapproved by almost every one that heard of it, even by the better disposed professors of religion; some looking upon the enterprise as an act of great weakness, while others saw in it nothing but arrogance and nonsense. Many prophesied its failure, and looked confidently for its speedy downfall; which, as a matter of course, did not fail to increase the persecution and contempt of the little band. But the Lord stood by their side, increasing their number from time to time, although but slowly at first. The membership of the Association numbered in the first and second years of its existence only about *twenty*. Yet as early as 1802, there was among that small number a promising fellow-laborer in the Word, *John Walter*, a youth, one of Mr. Albright's first converts. This young man became very soon a ready exhorter, and then commenced also to preach. He was of great service to Mr. Albright, and became in a few years an excellent preacher. He preached with uncommon energy, and could truly be called a *son of thunder*. Some that heard him preach, thought they had never heard the like before. When he was (to use a popular expression) in the right mood to preach, it seemed as if the keys to the understanding of the Holy Scriptures had been given him, whose divine precepts came like heavy showers upon his audience, and sometimes carried them away as with a torrent. He sometimes preached on great and deep texts, to the great astonishment of his hearers. He was, at the same time, an active, faithful, and humble instrument in the service of his Master, and his labors were abundantly blessed to the conversion of many. He served about twelve years as a traveling preacher, and many of the older members of the Church still remember his faithfulness and zeal. He survived Mr. Albright, and ranked for some time among the first preachers of the Society. He had, however, less ability for the management of affairs, and did not, for this reason, take as conspicuous a part in the transaction of business and the carrying on of the work, as many of his cotemporaries and successors.

On the day of Pentecost, in 1802, Mr. Albright commenced his first *general meeting*, at Samuel Liesser's, sen., which was richly blessed of God, to the edification of the believers and the awakening of many sinners.

In 1803, the membership had risen to 40, and another young man, *Abraham Liesser* by name, also one of Albright's converts, commenced to preach. Thus Mr. Albright had two assistants, though still young and inexperienced in the great and important work.

The slow increase of the Evangelical Association, during the first three years of its existence, will not much surprise any one that takes into consideration, that it had its origin in regions where Christianity was sunk to its lowest ebb, and where its professors, with few exceptions, lived in ungodliness and vice. Taking these circumstances into consideration, as well as the fact that the instruments God employed to bring about this reformation, were of ordinary descent, and illiterate men ; that they met, on all sides, with contempt and scorn, and even with threats and severe persecutions—it is, indeed, surprising that the work was not crushed in its very start, and completely annihilated. Had it not been of God, it would, in all probability, have been frustrated at that time. But the little flock strove, amidst all storms and persecutions which they had to encounter, to cling firmly to God, to trust in his promises, and to progress in the good work, in spite of all opposition by the devil and ungodly men. But, as neither an ecclesiastical government, nor articles of faith, nor, in general, any proper order and rules for the maintenance and continuation of the work had as yet been introduced, the Association deemed it necessary to hold a council, for the purpose of introducing a better regulation, which, as appears from a preserved document, took place Nov. 3rd, 1803.

Besides Mr. Albright and his two assistants, J. Walter and A. Liesser, the following fourteen brethren of the Society were present:—*Jacob Phillips, George Miller, Charles Bissey, Conrad Phillips, John Brobst, Solomon W. Friderici, Christian Brobst, George Phillips, Michæl Brobst, Samuel Liesser, Peter Walter, Adam Miller, Jacob Riedy, and Solomon Miller.* These pious followers of Mr. Albright, regarding him as their spiritual father to whom they owed, under God, their awakening and conversion, declared him now, in the name of the whole Association, *a genuine evangelical preacher*, recognized him as their teacher, and solemnly ordained him as such. Hereupon the meeting declared the Holy Scriptures of the Old and the New Testament as their *rule of faith* and *practice*, and presented to Mr. Albright a written certificate, signed by all present, containing their recognition of him as their teacher.—This is, in the writer's view, *the organization proper* of the Evangelical Association, although it had its rise three years earlier, by the formation of several societies.

If the bold usurpation of the privilege of a regular *succession* in the ministry by ordination down from the apostles were no fable, or if its existence and necessity could be proven from the Bible or the history of the Church, then the Evangelical Association would indeed have no valid claims to a churchship and the validity of its ministry. But in this respect it has nothing to fear, though there are some narrow-minded, bigoted sectarians, who envy its rapid progress and increasing influence, deny it the character of a Church, and declare the ministrations of its preachers to be null and void.—Yet, if each branch of the Church Universal had to prove an apostolic, uninterrupted, and sacred succession, in order to confirm the validity of its existence and ministry, then all would come under the same sweeping condemnation of the above mentioned arrogant sectarians, and they themselves would be compelled to lay their hands upon their mouths, and remain quiet forever. The good success which hitherto has attended the operations of the Evangelical Association, is *alone* sufficient evidence, that the ordination of its ministers is valid before God, notwithstanding all the objections that may be urged to the contrary.

During the first two years, after the organization of the Evangelical Association, Mr. Albright confined his labors principally to the three counties already mentioned, wherein he had made a beginning to gather the first societies. This may also have been the chief cause of the slow progress of the Association during that time. The ignorance and hardness of heart of the people were too great to justify the expectation of better results. But Mr. Albright's deep interest in the spiritual welfare of the inhabitants, which was still heightened by his having been born and reared there, and their wretched condition, seem to have been the principal reasons that induced him to labor there so perseveringly. But with sorrow he had to learn the truth of what his Divine Master has said, "No prophet is acceptable in his own country;" and even this induced him afterward to extend his sphere of operations, and also that of his assistants, in other directions. As Christianity was almost entirely swept away from those countries in the East, where it had first been preached, so it died out here, and the people seem to have become harder and harder, and thus their last state was worse than their first. For a long time this region lay desolate, as far as the operations of the Evangelical Association were concerned; and when, subsequently, attempts were made there to preach the pure doctrine of the Bible, the combined forces of hell, and the ungodly nominal Christians and false teachers seemed to rise in opposition against them, as the writer but too often had to experience during the first years of his ministerial labors, when he, his colleagues, and successors were sometimes in imminent peril of death. Yet the truth has prevailed at last —the ground occupied by Mr. Albright has finally yielded its fruit, and bids fair, for the future, to be second to no other part of the sphere of operations of the Evangelical Association. Mr. Albright's prayers and tears have, doubtless, like the prayers and alms of Cornelius, come up for a memorial before God, and been answered.—A more minute report of the work in those regions will be given hereafter.

In 1804 the Society numbered 60 members, nearly all of whom professed to enjoy peace with God, and to have experienced a change of heart. In this as well as the previous year, the Society's field of operations was considerably enlarged by having a new circuit added to it, which extended over parts of the counties of Northumberland and Centre, Pa.; and J. Walter and A. Liesser labored on the same, the greater part of the year. This circuit was at first called *Shamokin*, afterward, however, *Northumberland* circuit. The following were some of the first preaching places on this circuit:—Abr. Eyer's, John Aurand's, Michæl Maize's, Dreisbach's Church, Martin Dreisbach's, sen., Philip Hay's, Henry Schmidt's, Jacob Hoch's, John Swartz's, and Charles Straub's. During this year another preacher was received on probation, *Alexander Jimeson*, who came with Mr. Albright to the last mentioned circuit, in order to take the place of the two other brethren. From this it appears that the first ministers of the Evangelical Association, like the first Methodist preachers that had come over from England, did not always travel a whole year on the same circuit, but changed sometimes during the year, in order to become the sooner acquainted with the whole extent of the work, and form an acquaintance with the people.—This may, in those days, have been a wise plan to prosecute the work.

The writer has heard many old members of the Society speak of this as well as a subsequent visit of Mr. Albright to the interior of Pennsylvania, of his conduct toward the people, his powerful preaching, and his firm trust in the promises of God. His conversation was mild, affectionate, and so charming that nearly all that formed his acquaintance loved him, and recognized him as a devout man and a faithful and active servant of God. His conduct was especially exemplary for ministers. Father *Chr. Spangler*, of Brush Valley, Centre co., Pa., always spoke with particular enthusiasm of him and his labors; and he was one of the first, if not the very first, who received Mr. Albright in said valley, and gave him permission to preach in his house, for which reason he was at first greatly despised by many of his neighbors. But not only Mr. Albright, but also his assistants were kindly received on the new circuit, and their efforts were soon crowned with more or less success.

The membership of the old circuit increased considerably during this year; but likewise also the opposition, contempt, and persecution. And this persecution was not confined merely to the preachers, but extended to all that befriended them. Yet all slanders, threats, and abuses, could not prevent them from going forward in the path of their duty.—The preachers were so much despised and hated, that frequently in passing the houses of false professors of Christianity, they were assailed, in the public road, with the vilest slanders and calumnies. And this rage for scandal seems to have descended from the parents to their children, in that part of the country; for about thirty years afterward the same conduct was met with, and even violence was resorted to, which could only be stopped by the interference of the magistrates. Yet the preached word did not remain without its effects; for many assented to the truth, and experienced its gracious and saving power in their hearts. One happy result of these persecutions was, that but few half-hearted and hypocritical professors joined the Society; for it required pure gold to pass through such fiery trials.

The salary of the preachers was made up by voluntary contributions, and was, on the whole, very small. During the last mentioned year it amounted only to five pounds, fourteen shillings, and nine pence Pennsylvania money—not even twenty dollars. It is true, the ministers did not labor for money; yet they were entitled to a better support, and should have received more. The salvation of precious souls was their only object and aim—for this alone they labored.—For this reason they were not easily discouraged by the wants of support, in the prosecution of their work; and for the same reason they did not neglect those places and regions, where but little or no support was expected.—Not satisfied with those conquests which they had made by God's Word and assistance, their constant endeavor was to enlarge their fields of labor, and to enlist as many souls as possible in the cause of their Master. Oh! that this spirit to diffuse the saving doctrines of the Gospel of Christ, might be rekindled among us in general, by means of this history.

In 1805 the number of the members was but *seventy-five*, consequently, on an average, only fifteen souls per year, during the first five years of the existence of the Society. This, indeed, was not very encouraging; yet, if we take into consideration the untold value of one immortal soul, and the fact that most of these souls thus gathered were really converted and by faith united to Christ, we must admit that, even in those times, a great work had already been accomplished, and the foundation of a still greater one laid. As in everything else, so also here the beginning was difficult. But shortly afterward matters changed for the better, as the old circuit was considerably enlarged, in those regions where the work afterward progressed more rapidly. It would seem that it must have become evident to these dear men of God, that the old ground was hard to cultivate, and promised but a scanty harvest; wherefore they turned their attention to other parts. It may have been true what one of them once remarked, with regard to the ground at first occupied by them; viz., "*It seems as if the devil had here measured off a tract of ground for himself*," etc. But in this year they found open doors in the counties of Lancaster and Dauphin, Pa., and the circuit was therefore called *Schuylkill* and *Lancaster* circuit. Likewise Northumberland circuit was extended into the counties of Mifflin and Huntingdon, Pa., and about 35 souls were added to the membership during this year. As early as this year, the little flock lost one of its pastors by death—the young brother *Abraham Liesser* was called from the walls of Zion to his everlasting home. He was an humble, pious, and promising youth; and although his co-operation seemed to be so much needed by his brethren, yet thus early he had to bid them farewell. But why so soon? they may, indeed, have thought or asked. Such dispensations of Providence are hid from our view, and their real object is probably reserved to be learned in the eternal world.—Another youth, C. B., who, under the superintendence of Mr. Albright, had already made some progress in preaching, was, being yet a minor, by force suddenly torn away from the Society, by his guardian, and apprenticed in a place remote from Christian friends, where he was like a sheep among wolves, by whom, in a spiritual sense, he was actually torn to pieces—yet he is said to have been plucked as a brand from the burning, before his death. God grant that this may be so! But to repair this loss, the Lord gave to the little flock, who trusted in Him, another assistant, *George Miller*—a man full of holy fire, zeal, and indefatigable activity in the service of his Master, and who afterward became a strong pillar in the Society, as will appear from the sequel.

Encouraged by the more rapid increase of membership and the providing care of God, the preachers and their little societies continued to pray for a further outpouring of the Spirit, and to labor incessantly, being fully persuaded that under the guidance of Him who cannot err, the work would ultimately prosper, as it was now perceptible that a process of considerable fermentation was going on in the minds of the German population. Yet the enemies of light and truth still indulged in the expectation, that this straw-fire, as the work was called by many, would soon be extinguished; and hence they continued to predict its speedy downfall, with unabated boldness. But some time after, this their prediction was changed into the words: "We must defend ourselves better, or else these

Strawelet will prevail, and take away from us both our place and nation." The origin of this opprobrious term—straweler—formerly so often applied in this country to Methodists, the members of the Evangelical Association, and other zealous Christians, we have not been able to trace. But it is, in all probability, of American origin, and derived from the German word Strappeln, signifying *to struggle with the feet*, etc. Enemies and scoffers of zealous and active Christians may have taken occasion to apply this term to them from the fact that in the meetings, under the powerful preaching of the first Methodist preachers in this country, as also of the preachers of the Evangelical Association and others, sinners were often seized with fear and terror, and being wrought upon by the power of God, frequently fell involuntarily to the ground; and under a deep sense of their lost and wretched condition and danger, like many on the first day of Pentecost, under the preaching of Peter, they exclaimed—what they must do to be saved, and would then wring their hands, struggle with their feet, and make other strange gestures, and when it pleased God to remove from them the burden of their sins, and to give them peace and consolation, they would sometimes leap for joy, burst out into shouting and praising God, and give vent to the joy of their hearts by clapping their hands. Now, such wrestling, similar to that of Jacob with the Angel of the covenant, to enter in at the straight gate, such tears of penitence, like those of backslidden Peter, or of the great sinner at the feet of Jesus, and others being under a sense of guilt, appeared to an ignorant Church populace and their blind leaders, as not only foolish, but even absurd and blasphemous. Hence, like blind Saul, they thought to do God service, by despising, slandering, and persecuting his children and followers. Yet it sometimes happened that some of the greatest scoffers and persecutors were seized, and, before they were aware of it, were so completely overpowered, that they fell, as if struck by lightning, to the ground, and were unable to rise again, until after a severe struggle and earnest prayer by faith in the Son of God, they had obtained the pardon of all their sins, whereupon they praised God with joyful hearts, to the utter astonishment and confusion of their former comrades and associates. Such occurrences then gave rise to the foolish notions of some, who believed that the preachers of these people understood magic, and were able to charm persons by looking at them, especially those of weaker constitutions, and particularly females; because they, as a general thing, are neither so obdurate and hardened, nor so rebellious as men. Others fancied, that the preachers secretly scattered a certain charming powder over the hearers, whereby the weaker were made to fall down, to cry out, to struggle, to clap their hands, to leap, jump, etc. Others, again, being ashamed of these foolish notions of the vulgar, especially some carnally-minded *clergymen*, and some *medical wiseacres*, accounted for that phenomenon on other principles. They either ascribed it at once to the agency of the devil and wicked spirits, or else represented it as an effect of hypochondriasis and hysterics! But admitting this explanation, another difficulty would arise, viz., the fact that most persons with whom the phenomenon in question has taken, and still takes place, had never before been affected with these diseases! Such quacks in spiritual matters might indeed have been fitly answered in the words of our Saviour, addressed to the Sadducees: "You err and know neither the Scriptures, nor the power of God."

Both history and experience teach us that similar phenomena took place, to a greater or less extent, during all great and truly religious revivals, especially in this country. This was the case during the great revival in New-England, in the times of President Edwards; during the great awakenings brought about by the first Methodist preachers in Virginia, Maryland, and the two Carolina's, as well as that in the Presbyterian and Baptist Churches; and it still occurs in our times. Especially did this take place under the powerful preaching of Messrs. J. Wesley and Whitfield. And even in *those* German Churches of our land, in which revivals were suffered to take place, great care had to be taken, or, rather, the Spirit of God had to be forcibly quenched, in order to prevent such phenomena.

But then the consequence of such proceedings was, that these revivals, because conducted after the rules and regulations of men, were therefore superficial and of short duration, and did more harm than good. For this reason also they have come into great disrepute, and are now carefully avoided in said Churches.

Far be it from us, to justify all such demonstrations and bodily exercises, either during revivals or other religious meetings. It is highly probable that, to the injury of the genuine work of the Spirit, spurious elements have at all times mingled with it; but he who is too much afraid of "*wild fire*," is in danger of mistaking the *genuine* for such, and to come to *that* zone of the moral heavens where he must *freeze* to death. Notwithstanding this, preachers and officers cannot guard too carefully against everything spurious and excessive, during revivals and other religious meetings.

In 1806, the Society numbered 120 members, and 4 itinerant preachers, namely, Jacob Albright, *elder;* John Walter, *deacon;* Alexander Jimeson, and George Miller, probationers —the first of the last two named in the second, and the latter in the first year of his office. From the documents that are still extant, it cannot with certainty be ascertained how these ministers were stationed. But this much we learn from the record, that Mr. George Miller traveled alone on Northumberland circuit, for the greater part of the year; and that Mr. A. Jimeson located during the year, on account of his family circumstances. Hence it may be inferred, that Messrs. Albright and Walter had charge of the old circuit. Yet they assisted Brother Miller during the year in holding a number of general meetings. As has already been mentioned, the preachers in those days did not confine themselves exclusively to their designated circuits or spheres of labor, but rather accommodated themselves to the times and circumstances. On the old circuit, the work increased considerably during this year. Glorious revivals took place near the Muehlbach, Tulpehocken, and in a place called Swamps; and several respectable classes were formed; so also in Packston, near Harrisburg, where likewise a class was formed.

Brother Miller's labors on Northumberland circuit were also greatly blessed. To him may be applied, to some extent, what is written of his Divine Master: "He taught as one having authority, and not as the scribes." Hence a great stir and agitation used to follow, wherever he preached. Nor will this appear strange to any one who becomes acquainted with his manner of commencing and continuing his labors on his circuit. Anticipating the difficulties on his new field of labor at his arrival, he resolved to commence the work in good earnest. Speaking of this time, he says in his auto-biography: "I resolved, therefore, to commence the work with fasting and prayer, relying on the help of God, and to preach the truth of the Gospel unfeignedly, even if no man should be pleased with my preaching, if only God be satisfied with it. Hence I often wept during my journeyings from one preaching-place to another, that I might be acceptable to God, and useful to my fellow-beings." No wonder that, under these circumstances, he could afterward say to the praise of God, that his labors had not been in vain. He who commences and continues in such a frame of mind, and with so deep an interest in the salvation of his fellow-beings, surely his labors in the vineyard of the Lord cannot fail to prosper.

During this year the brethren held a general meeting in Buffalo Valley, at father Martin Dreisbach's, the narration of which, in this place, is expected to be welcome to the reader, and deserves to be held up as a model for similar meetings in our days. It commenced Oct. 25th, 1806; and how deeply this servant of the Lord was concerned that something might be done for the glory of God, and the welfare of immortal souls, appears from the following extract from his auto-biography. He says:—

"I expected that the penitent and newly converted souls on the circuit, of whom I had united about 40 into classes, would meet there. Therefore I prayed much on their account unto the Lord, and that He would be pleased to bring the Brethren Albright and Walter, clothed with power from on high, to the meeting.—The appointed day came, and my wishes were realized; for both preachers and members, together with a large number of penitents, were present. My feelings on that occasion cannot be described, for I was sad and joyful at the same time, and experienced in my own soul the powerful words of our Saviour: '*Blessed are those that mourn; for they shall be comforted.*' While humbled before God, praying that sinners might be converted, the happiest feelings of consolation and divine favor filled my heart. I had to preach the opening sermon, and during the delivery the power of God came in such torrents upon the congregation, that many fell upon their knees, and prayed with tears to the Lord for the pardon of their sins. Albright and Walter preached so powerfully and pointedly, that the congregation was visited with showers of divine grace, and in every room the cries of penitent sinners were heard, and many souls were converted. The voice of praise and thanksgiving unto the Lord could also be heard everywhere in the house, and there was great joy in the Lord among the brethren."

"Soon after this meeting," he continues, "conversions occurred everywhere on my circuit, and no malice of man could hinder the work any longer, so that after two months the number of conversions exceeded 80. The Lord gave me also, at this time, some assistants, who exhorted in fervency of spirit and with power."

After the close of this meeting, these three men of God renewed their league with each other in writing, to prosecute the work of the Lord with increasing zeal and earnestness; and Mr. Albright exhorted and encouraged the two others to continue courageously and boldly in the work commenced, and to win as many souls to Christ as they possibly could. At the close of Mr. Miller's time of labor on that circuit, which had been but 7 or 8 months, the number of converts exceeded 100, and the prospects for the future were very encouraging. The circuit extended over parts of Buffalo, Dry, Middlecreek, Mahontonga, Penn's, and Brush Valley, &c. The first class was formed in Dry Valley, and extended as far as New Berlin; its leader was Mr. Michæl Maize, who afterward became a local preacher. The second was formed near Jack's creek, in the neighborhood of Lawer's, and was called *Thomas' class*, *Frederick Herbster* its leader, who likewise afterward became a local preacher. The third class was formed in Millheim, Penn's Valley; the fourth in Buffalo Valley, *Martin Dreisbach* its leader; the fifth in Brush Valley, *Christopher Spangler* the leader, who afterward became a local preacher, and has continued as such to this day (July 21, 1854); he is now about 90 years of age; the sixth in Lewisburg, Union co., *Christian Wolf*, the leader, who also afterward became a local preacher.

Beside the three traveling preachers of this year, there were also four local preachers in the Society; namely, *Charles Bissy, Jacob Phillips, Solomon Miller, and John Dreisbach*, the last of whom went out the following year as a traveling preacher, and became, in subsequent years, one of the principal leaders of the Society, and has collected a great portion of the materials for this history, for the first twenty-five years of the Association.

During this year a voluntary contribution, called subsidiary contribution, was introduced, the object of which was to establish a fund for the incidental expenses of the traveling ministers, and the relief of the poor of the Society. It was also resolved, that hereafter a regular *Annual Conference* be held, which had hitherto not been the case.

SECOND SECTION.

FROM THE FIRST ANNUAL CONFERENCE TO THE SESSION OF THE SECOND IN 1809.

First Conference.

In the year of our Lord 1807, Nov. 15th and 16th, the first regular conference of the Society was held in a place called *Muehlbach*, then belonging to Dauphin, but now to Lebanon co., Pa., in the house of Mr. *Samuel Becker*. It is true, in 1803 a similar meeting had been held, as above stated, which was, however, not considered a conference. It appears that up to this time, Mr. Albright had superintended the whole work, and made such rules and regulations as seemed good to him. It was left with him to transfer the preachers from one place to another, and he generally made these changes at general meetings, at which, in those days, nearly all the preachers were always present. But, as already stated, the ministers did not, in those days, travel a whole year on their circuits, but were often changed about, every 6 or 8 months. Yet it appears from the conclusion of the first section, that Mr. Albright by no means acted arbitrarily, but consulted at their meetings, probably at their general meetings, the other preachers, leaders, and most experienced members, and with their consent made new rules and regulations for the best interests of the Society; as, for instance, the rule that in future an Annual Conference shall be regularly held.

This first conference was of considerable importance for the Association, and contributed greatly toward its consolidation and prosperity. It consisted of all the officers of the Society; namely, the traveling and local ministers, the classleaders and exhorters—28 in all: 5 itinerants, three local preachers, and twenty classleaders and exhorters. We can easily imagine what a joy it must have been for this little band of brethren, to be thus assembled in singleness of heart and in the fear of the Lord, for the purpose of deliberating upon the best means to prosecute, successfully, the work committed to their charge. But we can also in some measure conceive, how great their embarrassment must have been, to transact their business without any rules as a guide, and without experience in such matters. It seems, however, they were led, in their arrangements, mainly by circumstances and exigencies; and as they had deeply imbibed the principle, that *every thing depends on God's blessing*, they looked up to him full of confidence, and prayed that He would assist and prosper them in their work. One of the most important resolutions of this conference was, that Mr. Albright should draw up *articles of faith* and a *discipline* for the Association, in conformity with the teachings of the Bible. Although the council of 1803 had declared the books of the Old and New Testaments as the only *rule of faith and practice* for the Association; yet experience seems to have taught them, that a systematic explanation or statement of the principal doctrines of the Bible, the duties of Christians, and rules for Church government, were indispensably necessary to the future prosperity of the Society, notwithstanding the fact that the canonical books of the Bible contain everything that a Christian must believe and practice in order to be saved. It is true, that even in those days certain fellow-believers declared themselves against such articles of faith and Church discipline, slandering them as works of the devil; and others have done so since. Yet some of them have long ago seen their folly, and returned to sound reason. But, although Mr. Albright expressed his willingness to undertake this difficult and important task, if God would prolong his life, and give him the necessary strength and health; yet he did not carry it out, as his health failed, and he died six months after this conference. By his death the drawing up of articles of faith, etc., was postponed, but afterward undertaken by Mr. George Miller; and the result of his labors was printed in 1809. The conference enjoined upon the ministers, to have personal interviews with their hearers, and to examine them on the subject of experimental religion after every sermon, if practicable, especially in those places where classes had been formed. It was also resolved, that the licenses of the local and traveling preachers be annually renewed by the conference, and signed by the president and secretary; and that the circuit preachers should give the appointed exhorters written certificates. Moreover, Mr. Albright was elected *superintendent* (bishop), and Geo. Miller *elder*, and Jacob Frey and John Dreisbach were received as traveling preachers on trial.

The number of members at this conference was 220, that of traveling preachers, the two newly received included, five, and that of the local preachers, three.—The minutes of this Conference say nothing of the stationing of the ministers, and it is, therefore, probable that no changes were made. The business being finished, all united in prayer, and then separated in peace and harmony.

By this conference a new impulse was given to the work, and afterward it increased and prospered more and more.—Although many things were still very defective in the arrangements of the Association, and most of the preachers and officers of the different societies had but little experience in building up the kingdom of God; yet they were neither wanting in courage, nor confidence in God, on which two qualifications much depends in all religious enterprises. Mr. Albright's health, however, declined from day to day. But yet he continued his travels, and visited the societies, preaching and exhorting among them as much as he possibly could. During the winter he occasionally accompanied Mr. John Dreisbach who was yet young and inexperienced, on the old circuit. Yet notwithstanding his youth and inexperience, it would seem that Mr. Albright loved and esteemed him in a high degree; and it is probable that he accompanied him for the purpose of preparing him the better by his example and instructions, for future usefulness. Brother Dreisbach writes of this, as follows:—

"I derived great benefit from his paternal instruction and pious example, as well as from his fervent prayers, childlike confidence in God, and his humble resignation to his holy will. All this made deep impressions on my mind, and was highly useful to me afterward in my calling as a Christian and minister of the Gospel. O, what a blessing it is for a young minister to have such a guide and instructor!"

George Miller and John Dreisbach were stationed for this year on the old circuit which extended partly over the counties of Dauphin, Lebanon, Lancaster, Berks, Bucks, Montgomery, Northampton, Lehigh, and Schuylkill, and numbered about 30 appointments, some of which were from 20 to 30 miles distant from each other. No special revivals took place during this year, yet some souls were converted here and there, and in Millerstown on the Conestoga, a considerable number embraced religion, so that the class there had an increase of twenty members. Among the new converts was *John Erb*, who afterward became an itinerant preacher.—On Northumberland circuit also, some conversions took place during that winter, and the believers increased in the divine life.

On Easter, in 1808, a general meeting was held in Albany tp., Berks co., Pa., at John Brobst's, where Mr. Albright changed the preachers for the following year. He stationed John Walter and Jacob Frey on the Lancaster and Schuylkill or *old* circuit, and G. Miller and J. Dreisbach on Northumberland circuit. This was the last time that Mr. Albright stationed the preachers; for one week later, at a general meeting in the house of P. Radenbach, near Linglestown, Dauphin co., Pa., G. Miller and J. Dreisbach shook hands with him for the last time. Mr. Dreisbach writes, "His last words to me were:

'Kämpfe bis auf's Blut und Leben,
Dring' hinein in Gottes Reich.'
(Resist and fight, even unto blood;
Enter by force the kingdom of God.)"

From this place the brethren traveled to their new fields of labor, and the first news of Mr. Albright was the intelligence of his *death*. The last two mentioned general meetings were richly blessed with the outpouring of the Spirit of God; the believers had a glorious waiting upon the Lord, and a number of sinners were converted to God.

Mr. Albright traveled and preached as much as he could, till finally he was compelled by too great weakness, about four weeks before his death, to resolve to go home and remain quiet. But his disease had already made such progress that he was obliged to remain with Christian friends, near *Muehlbach*, Lebanon co., Pa., where he also expired, May 18th, 1808, in the fiftieth year of his life, after being confined to his bed but a few days. His earthly remains were interred two days after, May 20th, when a great concourse of people from all directions, especially such as had been converted by his instrumentality, formed his funeral procession. As the congregation there, had as yet no grave-yard of their own, his remains were deposited in a private burial-place, close by where a few years ago a church was erected to his memory, called the "*Albright's Church.*" He left a widow and three children. His funeral sermon was preached by his assistant, John Walter, from Daniel 12, 3.

Mr. Albright's early death was caused, as is believed, by his many and hard tours, and great exertions in preaching. He would never spare himself, so that his strength became exhausted, and the foundation of a consumption was laid, which soon put an end to his earthly career. Why this good and pious man was called away so early, after he had been but twelve years engaged in preaching the Gospel of his Master, when the Society, which had been gathered by his ministry, was yet so weak and small, and his services seemed to be so much needed in order to carry forward the work—why he was under such circumstances called away, has often been asked by many of his followers. To the writer it seems probable, that both Mr. Albright and some of his first followers impaired their health by *over-exertion* in the discharge of their duties, and thus fell victims to an early death; while others, through the same cause, became disqualified for active service in the prime of life. But as it was done with a good intention, and for the want of experience and a better insight into matters, there can be no doubt that it was for the best interests of those faithful servants of God and their successors, and always will be so.

His followers in general, but especially the ministers, felt the death of this good man very keenly. Its remembrance often made them burst into tears; and their grief would have been insupportable, had not God's promises been their support and consolation, and the thought, that he is now, after having borne the burden and heat of the day, enjoying the sweet and promised rest in heaven, comforted them in their bereavement. Of the enemies of Mr. Albright and his followers, after his death, Mr. G. Miller, in his biography, says: "Our enemies exulted and rejoiced, that they had become rid of this *acid salt;* for they hated it. They also indulged in the belief that his work was now entirely undone, and that no one would trouble them any more; wherefore they would exultingly exclaim:—"*They are now fallen—Albright is dead, and they are undone,*' etc. But in this they were greatly mistaken; for although Mr. Albright was dead, yet God was stilla live, who had sanctioned this good work, and who also knew how to preserve and enlarge it."

Since the short biography of Mr. Albright, that is extant, is known only to few persons, it is presumed that it will gratify many readers of this history, to find here some particulars of his life, his ministry, and especially of his dying moments. His biographer, when speaking of them, says: "His sermons and prayers in public were powerful, penetrating and convincing—after a child-like manner, not couched in high sounding words of human wisdom, but in power, and full of the unction of the Holy Ghost, which was felt in all his conversation. He was always filled with a universal love to his fellow-men, which enabled him to pray fervently for his enemies and persecutors; and he left no opportunity unimproved, to advance their spiritual interests, and to point out to them the path of truth. His gestures, mien, and motions frequently indicated the presence o God's Spirit in his breast, so that the hearers were often deeply affected, without his using many words. And at times, he would so completely forget himself, and the Spirit of God operated so powerfully in him and upon him, that, while speaking, he would go from his stand into the midst of the room, without himself being aware of it. After such powerful agitations, heavenly joy beamed from his countenance, and the praises of God resounded from his lips. — — —

"In the discharge of his official duties, he was diligent and scrupulously exact. He never failed to fill his appointments, when the state of his health permitted him to do so; and he attended to his official duties, not only from a feeling of duty, but with joy and cheerfulness.

"He was constantly laboring to draw closer the bond of union among his brethren; and he watched with paternal anxiety over them and their whole conduct, always setting them the very best example. For his highest aim was, to incite them to real holiness of heart, and to keep it pure and undefiled.

"All persecutions and sufferings, which he had to endure for the sake of God and his Gospel, he bore with patience, opposing to them nothing but meekness, and counting them but little; because he considered the grace which God had bestowed upon him, as so great a blessing, that compared with it, all sufferings of this life were nothing. He therefore remained steadfast in the doctrine of Christ, to call sinners to repentance, and to urge them to believe in Christ, and to edify and exhort the believers to pursue holiness. Thus he was a chosen instrument in the hand ot God to revive true godliness, and God's grace was evidently with him.—None of his adversaries were able to harm him in the least, although they strove to do so with all their might; for his uniform aim in his whole conduct was, to promote the honor and glory of God. This was a firm and unchangeable principle with him, guiding all his actions, and which he inculcated on all his followers. Therefore he gave to his brethren who labored with him in the vineyard of the Lord, when he saw them assembled for the last time in this life, the following good advice: '*In all you do or intend to do, let it be your aim to promote the honor and glory of God, and to promulgate and exalt the operations of His grace, both in your own hearts and among your brethren and sisters; and be faithful co-workers with them in the path which the Lord has shown unto you, and He will grant you his blessing.*'"

The excellency of this last advice of our highly esteemed Mr. Albright to his brethren, and, consequently, to all his followers, must be obvious to all who are acquainted with the Bible. It is greatly desirable, that it may be followed by all at all times. If this were done, the Evangelical Association would have no equal among all the branches of the Church Universal, and would prosper before all others. And why should not all who are connected with it, carry out this noble principle, since it involves not only no impossibility, but is an express command of the Most High? "Ye eat or drink, or whatever ye do, do it to the glory of God." This is a commandment given to all believers, and whoever desires to please God and save his soul, must observe the same. May then every reader, and especially every member and preacher of the Evangelical Association, take this good advice to heart and carry it out!

"As his life had been, so also was the death of this pious man. He retained his self-consciousness to the very last moments of his life. A tranquillity of mind beamed from his countenance, such as only a good conscience, a true interest in the merits of Christ, and the consciousness of having spent his life in a useful and God-pleasing manner, together with a lively hope of eternal life, can give. In this happy frame of mind, he bade to all who were present at his death-bed, an affectionate farewell, exhorting them with him to praise God who would now speedily take his ransomed spirit to himself. All were deeply affected, and every one was edified, wishing sincerely that his own death might be like that of this just man."

With regard to the work of reviving true godliness among his German brethren, which had been begun by his ministry, he was, indeed, very anxious that it might be properly continued in the name of the Lord; yet it would seem, that he was at a loss whether the little flock, that had been gathered by himself and his fellow-laborers, should continue as a separate organization or not. Yet it does not appear that this gave him any particular trouble; for he had not the least intention to acquire great fame by founding an independent ecclesiastical organization. Such vanity could find no place in his heart, which he had consecrated to God. As above stated, his only aim and object were, to promote the honor and glory of God, and the welfare of his fellow-men. What is said in this paragraph, is confirmed by some remarks of Mr. John Dreisbach, in his collections for this history. He writes of it as follows:—

"About two or three months before Mr. Albright's demise, I once traveled with him, and we were speaking of the work of God in our midst, when I expressed to him my great desire, that he might be enabled to draw up the projected articles of faith and discipline. His reply to me, which I remember distinctly, was: 'Brother John, if it is God's will for you to be and remain an independent organization, he will take care of you also in this particular; there will appear men among you, who will accomplish what I am unable to do. The matter is in the hands of God; it is his cause, and he will also take care of it.' This, says Mr. Dreisbach, was at that time very remarkable to me, and is even yet to-day, since it appears clearly that he was still in doubt as to the continuation of the Association as a separate body. Notwithstanding this, he labored incessantly, according to the best of his abilities, as a faithful servant of Christ, and left the final issue with God."

This, then, was an eventful year for this young organization. Mr. Albright had been not only its founder, but, under God, also its principal pillar; and his death was a loss the more painful, as there was but little prospect of getting his place supplied. It is true, Mr. G. Miller proved himself a worthy successor of him, and, in a practical point of view, was but little, if at all, inferior to Mr. Albright. Yet he was not *Albright*, and therefore did not command that universal confidence which Mr. Albright had enjoyed, even if he did deserve it. Mr. Albright had, shortly before his death, once more changed the ministers. But as no conference was held that year, no report of the number of members is extant. But the labors of the brethren, on the two circuits, were crowned with abundant success, although, in addition to the death of Mr. Albright, Mr. G. Miller's health also failed so much toward the close of the year, that he was compelled to go home. Meanwhile, however, two young laborers, namely, *John Erb* and *Matthew Betz*, made their appearance in the vineyard of the Lord. John Erb was associated with J. Walter on the old circuit, and Jacob Frey was sent to York county on the other side of the Susquehannah, to explore the country for the purpose of forming a new circuit; but marrying shortly afterward, he resigned the office of an itinerant minister. J. Walter and J. Erb labored with great success, the Lord blessing their labors abundantly, so that sinners were awakened and converted, and the children of God greatly refreshed and advanced in the divine life.

After G. Miller had been taken sick, J. Dreisbach was alone on the extensive Northumberland circuit; and being very young in years and experience, it was with difficulty, as he himself acknowledged, that he discharged the many and onerous duties of his calling. But he trusted in God, and continued to pray, and wrestle with God to bless him, and make him useful in his service. His prayers were answered and his labors richly blessed, so that the number of new members, whom he received during the year, was considerable. Shortly before the next conference, M. Betz, above mentioned, came to assist him, to the inexpressible joy of both the preachers and the members. This young brother afterward became a very useful minister, and his labors were crowned with abundant success—Bishop *Seybert* is one of his spiritual sons in the Lord.

At the close of this year, shortly before conference, *Henry Niebel* of this circuit, joined their number, went with them to conference, and accepted an appointment. The following year, after harvest, he entered upon the duties of the itinerancy, and served for a number of years as an acceptable itinerant of the Society. Mr. G. Miller, after he had returned home from his circuit, at the instance of his brethren, especially J. Walter, commenced to frame articles of faith, and to draft a constitution and discipline for the Association, since Mr. Albright had been prevented by death from accomplishing this work assigned him by his brethren. But he encountered great difficulties in this enterprise; both because he was an unskilful writer, and because he had to struggle against bodily disease and strong temptations. He speaks in his auto-biography of these difficulties, as follows:—

"It is impossible to describe the many inward and outward temptations, into which the devil led me, while engaged in this work; but all of which I overcame with the help of God. At times I prayed and wrestled with God till after midnight. I would often lie on my bended knees on my couch, and deprive my worn-out body of rest, although protracted meditation on the subject had exhausted my strength. It would often appear to me as if this work could not possibly be finished. Yet the Lord enabled me to get through with it, and prolonged my life, so that it became also a guide even for myself."

At this time a powerful storm of opposition, persecution, and calumny arose against the Association, and all those who preached and labored in the same way. The storm, it is true, was principally directed against the *Methodists*, who increased very rapidly in those days; but the people generally, at that time, understood by "*Methodists*" also the Evangelical Association, "*the United Brethren*," and all those who held the same religious views. The Evangelical Association was then already, and at a later period still more so, called "*the German Methodists*;" because the Methodists, at that time, confined their labors exclusively to the English portion of the community, and were, on that account, not so much annoyed, as was the Evangelical Association, by those German Churches that were destitute of vital piety. Now, though this storm of persecution was nominally directed against the Methodists, yet it principally hit the Evangelical Association, and other German Christians of the same religious sentiments.—As already stated, the German Churches of this country had, at that time, as is even acknowledged by some of their own ministers in later times, fallen into a state of lifeless formality. Experimental Christianity and religion of the heart had become almost unknown terms, and even the *outward appearance* and *form of godliness* were comparatively rare. Sin and vice were in most of the congregations the order of the day; the most impudent and hardened sinners were frequently consecrated as officers of the Churches, because there was not much danger that such characters would rebuke the ungodliness of either members or preachers, and there was still less danger that they would be deceived and apostatize from the faith, i. e. go over to the "*fanatics.*" Many of the clergymen themselves were notorious drunkards, and given to other vices; while the greater part of the rest were satisfied with an outward morality. This being the state of things, it was not more than natural that all who would oppose, expose, and rebuke such hypocrisy and daring impiety, would be calumniated, hated, and persecuted; and as this was done more boldly and unsparingly by the first preachers of the Evangelical Association, than perhaps is done by their successors in our times, the unconverted preachers and their blind and hardened followers were roused up against them, and induced to slander and persecute them.—But this was not the only cause of the general hatred and persecution of the Evangelical Association, and its ministers especially. Their pointed preaching of the truth would frequently break through the more than Egyptian darkness, and diffuse some light here and there; so that many a deluded Church member had thus his eyes opened, to see his lost and wretched condition; and his carnal security being thereby disturbed, he would search the Scriptures and reform his life, and become punctual in the discharge of outward duties, and sometimes also experience the necessary change of heart. Such members either left their Church at once, or they attempted to remain in it, and lead a new and holy life; but they were generally so much slandered and persecuted, that they saw themselves compelled to leave the Church of their fathers, and join the so-called "*deceivers.*" In this way those carnal ministers lost not only many a member of their congregations, but also many a *nice dollar.* And as the purse is with many persons a very delicate point, these preachers were also unpleasantly affected by their losses; and in order to take revenge, they would scold and abuse the Methodists and so-called "*Albrights,*" both from their pulpits and in private; and to give effect to their words, they represented these people as innovators, as dangerous to both Church and state, that ought therefore to be exterminated. The ministers, especially, had all the shafts of malice directed against them; they were represented as false prophets, wolves in sheep's clothing, and deceivers, who were given to extreme lewdness, and committed the most unnatural crimes, especially at their *night* and *campmeetings*, and thus gave to others a chance to sin and commit similar excesses—and even in our own days many still oppose these meetings thus unjustly and foolishly, for the same pretended reasons.

In addition to these slanders and calumnies from the pulpit and other places, the press was also resorted to, by these enemies of light, truth, and experimental and practicable Christianity, in order to bespatter these people with the filth of their malicious hearts, and to slander them. One of the most respected of this kind of clergymen, as is believed, composed a *lampoon* or *libel* of the worst kind, and his ministerial brethren assisted him in circulating it among their people. And as many looked upon this libel as containing the truth, they believed themselves authorized to persecute these people as much as they could; and some declared their readiness to take up arms against them, and to exterminate them, if this were not against the laws of the country. "If it were lawful," said one of them, "I would just as soon shoot a '*straweler*' *preacher*, as I would a mad dog." Another, who on account of his advanced age was exempt from militia service, said, if the militia were called out, for the purpose of exterminating these people, he would be one of the first to shoulder his musket against them. These are facts which cannot be denied. Such a murderous spirit was engendered and fostered among their people, by the clergy of those days. Moreover, they did not fail, at the same time, to warn their people most energetically against apostatizing from the faith, against hearing these "deceivers and false prophets"—in other words, against forsaking their Church, and going over to the Methodists.

These things are mentioned in this history, not from a feeling of hatred or revenge against any Church or sect, nor for the purpose of casting reproach on the modern clergy of those Churches. Nor do we wish to convey the idea, that there were no exceptions among the congregations and clergy o. those days, to such characters as we have described. Far from it. There were always praiseworthy exceptions, both among the *laity* and the *clergy*, who were truly sorry for this sad and melancholy state of their Churches, and who did their best to bring about a better state of things. At the same time it cannot be denied either, that in those days, and even later, some preachers of the Evangelical Association and others, in their denunciations of the *abuse* of high schools, the ministry, catechetical instruction, confirmation, as well as of the sacraments of the New Testament, did not act as prudently as they might have done, denouncing with the *abuse* often the *proper use* of these things, at least not discriminating carefully enough between the two. Because the Churches and preachers in question, laid too much stress, as a general thing, upon these points, their assailants frequently went too far in the opposite direction, thereby exposing themselves to just censure. This may have increased the malice of carnal clergymen and their mobs, and may have been one of the causes to keep up and strengthen the prejudices and slanders against the ministers of the Evangelical Association, and others. As we have already said, we do not refer to these things here, for the purpose of bringing reproach upon any of our sister Churches; but we mention them, because they are facts and must be stated in order to throw the proper light upon the history of the Evangelical Association. The following incident, which took place at that time, is here inserted in order to confirm what has been said of the opposition to, and slander of, the Evangelical Association, and to give, in general, a portraiture of the religious state of things in those times.

It was in the month of August, 1808, when John Dreisbach returned from a general meeting near the Muehlbach, accompanied by a young brother, *Andrew Wolf*, in order to fill an appointment that evening in Jonestown, Lebanon co., Pa.; but as he had been disturbed while preaching there before, on his way to said general meeting, it was his intention to preach to the friends there, without giving public notice of it. From fear, not of the Jews, but of heathen-like Christians, the doors had been locked, and the window shutters fastened inside, before the services commenced. After singing and prayer, the sermon commenced; but as the exercises had, in all probability, been heard by some of the adversaries, a mob gathered in a short time, and forcing the doors and shutters open, they rushed with a dreadful noise and with still more dreadful imprecations into the house, and thus put a stop to the exercises. The preacher then took a light, and went among the crowd, to restore order, but was seized by several ruffians and dragged toward the door, at the same time treating him very roughly, and extinguishing all the lights in the house. Those who were dragging him, hallooed to their companions, who were outside: "*Boys, open the door, we have got him!*" They replied: "*Give it to him; kill the priest!*"

The preacher was justly apprehensive of still worse treatment, if they should succeed in getting him out of the house; but how to get out of their hands, he knew not. All at once it flashed upon his mind, as if God had revealed it to him, that if he would jerk himself up with all his might, and then suddenly fall down like a log, he might get out of their hands. He did so, and thus got rid of them, although he was still among the crowd in the dark. Now, as the ruffians were groping for him, they got hold of each other, letting torrents of blows descend on one another, each fancying that he was giving it to the "*priest*." But while they were thus regaling each other, to their hearts' content, with blows and pushes, he managed to get out of the crowd, and the mob got outdoors. Alarmed for the minister, some of the friends hastened out also, but were seized and very much abused by the mob. The landlord, father *P. Walter*, was so much hurt, that the blood gushed from his mouth and nose. A sister was knocked down, and carried into the house for dead. And several more friends were likewise very roughly dealt with.

This is *one* of the many examples of persecution and ill-treatment, which the first ministers and members of the Evangelical Association often experienced. Similar occurrences took place 20 and 25 years later, in different places in the counties of *Berks* and *Schuylkill*, Pa.

On the following day, the ringleaders of the Jonestown mob, 7 in number, were legally indicted by the brethren, and afterward delivered over to the county court. But they also brought charges against Mr. Dreisbach and some other brethren, vainly hoping to gain some advantages thereby; and when the case was tried by the court at Harrisburg, it seemed at first, as if they would really be benefited by it. But after all, they did not gain their end: the jury found them *guilty*, and acquitted the brethren. After the suit, the brethren remitted to their persecutors all their costs, thus showing them that they had not brought the suit against them from malice or revenge, but merely to teach them that the Evangelical Association enjoys the protection of the laws not less than all the other religious denominations of the Union, and that they were determined to hold their meetings without being disturbed.—The favorable issue of this prosecution had a very salutary influence on the public at large, benefiting other denominations as well as the Evangelical Association. Prior to this prosecution, tumults and disturbances of religious meetings were very frequent; but after this, they were, for years, much rarer and less outrageous.

It may not be out of place, to notice here that one of the twelve jurors, who tried the case in question, *Philip Breidenstein*, who lived not far from Lebanon, was shortly afterward converted and joined the Society. He became a useful local preacher, and remained in the connection, faithfully serving his Master to his very end. He afterward declared, that during that trial he had become satisfied that these despised people were Christians and children of God. Thus this slander and persecution of the brethren by the world and ungodly nominal Christians, served, after all, to promote the best interests of the cause of God and its followers.

This year, though one of sore trials, was, on the whole, a very prosperous one for the Association. It struck deeper roots, and gradually spread in various directions; while the older societies advanced in grace, knowledge, and numbers, and gained an increasing influence.

THIRD SECTION.

FROM THE SECOND CONFERENCE IN 1809, TO THE SEVENTH IN 1814.

Second Conference.

In the year of our Lord 1809, our membership amounted to 426. In the month of April of the same year, the second regular conference of the Association, was held in the house of Rev. G. Miller, in Albany township, Berks co., Pa. The following six itinerants were present; namely, George Miller, John Walter, John Dreisbach, John Erb, Math. Betz, and Henry Niebel, the last two on trial. The session was opened with prayer to God, for his blessing and assistance in their proceedings. G. Miller was nominated chairman, and J. Dreisbach secretary, after which the transactions of business progressed as circumstances required, and the brethren understood it, having no special rules to guide them. J. F. was, for certain offences, expelled from the Association; the brethren J. Walter and J. Dreisbach were set apart for the office of elder, but were not ordained until sometime after. The preachers were stationed, as follows: Northumberland circuit, John Walter and John Erb; and Lancaster circuit, John Dreisbach, Math. Betz, and Henry Niebel. G. Miller was instructed to travel and preach as much as his enfeebled health would allow; he was also to write a religious work for the Association, and to publish, at his own expense, the *Articles of Faith* and *Church Discipline*, as drawn up by himself. This conference gave the Association the name: "*The so-called Albrights;*" it also instructed J. Dreisbach to publish the catechism, which he had translated from the English, to be used as a guide for the instruction of the young, which he did. *Jacob Phillips*, one of local preachers, had died during this year, and entered into the joy of his Lord.

The ordination of G. Miller, as ordered some time before, and that of J. Walter and J. Dreisbach, as ordered by the last conference, took place some time after, at a general meeting in the house of Henry Eby, near Lebanon, Pa.

This was the first formal ordination in the Evangelical Association, and it has ever since been regularly continued. It was a solemn and refreshing time for the brethren, confirming and encouraging them to be faithful in the service of their Lord and Master, and in the discharge of the duties of their high calling. Whatever objections may be urged against the validity of the ordination of the Evangelical Association, these brethren felt assured that the Lord owned them as his servants, having blessed their labors to the salvation of many precious souls. And this was, indeed, a better confirmation of their divine call to the ministry, than any consecration through an uninterrupted apostolical succession could have given them. At all events, the success of their and their successors' ministry is conclusive evidence of God's approbation.

This year was, generally, a very prosperous one for the Association; five new classes were formed, and a considerable number of souls converted to the Lord. During the winter, extensive revivals had taken place, especially on the Schuylkill and Lancaster circuit; near the Tulpehocken, where *Lewis Henky* and *George Lanz* were among the new converts, both of whom were afterward received as local preachers; likewise near the conflux of the great and the little Conestoga, a considerable number of souls were converted to the Lord. *David Thomas* and *John Rueply* among them, both of whom afterward became preachers—the former served for some time as an itinerant. Near Manheim, also, several were awakened and felt the need of a change of heart, among whom were *D. Boyer* and *John Seybert*, who afterward joined the people of God, in order to work out their souls' salvation; they both became ministers of the Gospel, God's blessing attending their labors. Revivals also took place in Oley, Berks county, where D.

Bertolet and others were converted, and became willing to suffer affliction with the people of God. On Northumberland circuit, the Brethren Walter and Erb labored likewise with great success; a considerable number of souls were brought to the fold of Christ, and the circuit was considerably enlarged. Thus the work became every year more established, extending far and wide, so that the little band of believers greatly rejoiced in God, and felt encouraged in their Christian career.

Third Conference.

The third conference took place April 18, 19, and 20, 1810, in the house of George Becker, near the Muehlbach, then Dauphin, now Lebanon county. G. Miller was again chosen chairman, and J. Dreisbach secretary. Each session was opened with prayer. The Society now numbered *seven itinerant* and *ten local preachers*, and 528 members. The preachers were closely examined as to their conduct and discharge of duties, and information was gained concerning the state of the different societies. *Michæl Becker* and *David Yerlitz* were received into the itinerancy, and J. Erb and M. Betz were ordained to the office of deacon. The circuits were allotted to them as follows; Schuylkill and Lancaster circuit, J. Walter, H. Niebel, and M. Becker; Northumberland circuit, J. Dreisbach and D. Yerlitz; and J. Erb and M. Betz were appointed what is now called missionaries, to form a new circuit or missionary field in the counties of York, Adams, Cumberland, and Franklin. The Evangelical Association, indeed, had in those days neither a missionary society nor a missionary treasury as yet; but itself was, in fact, nothing else but a missionary society, and all its ministers were missionaries. The conference ordained likewise, that J. Erb and J. Dreisbach should, during the year, relieve the last two mentioned brethren, or rather exchange places with them, a measure from which great benefit was derived. G. Miller was requested, as he had been the year before, to travel according to his discretion and strength, to visit the members, to preach, and to write. J. Walter received permission to publish a small hymn-book, and G. Miller having written a biography of Mr. Albright, was authorized to publish it, at the expense of the itinerants. Conference also resolved to hold, during this year, two camp-meetings, which were, accordingly, the first held by the Association.

This year, also, was eminently blessed. Said two camp-meetings were held, one in the forepart of summer, the other after harvest. The former was held on the land of Michæl Maize, near New Berlin, Union co., Pa., commencing May 10, 1810; the second took place on the land of Rev. G. Miller, in Allemangle corner, Berks co., Pa., in the month of October. These two meetings caused a great stir among the people, and induced many to come within the sound of the Gospel trumpet, who had never before attended the other meetings of the brethren. For these camp-meetings were quite a novelty to those people, in whose midst they were held. The members had come from all directions; some from a distance of 80 miles, with their wagons, tents, provisions, etc. The preaching of the Word made deep impressions upon many, and a considerable number repented of the error of their ways, and were converted to God, while others were wounded by the Spirit, so that they had no more rest until they gave themselves up to the Lord. The believers were greatly edified and encouraged, and returned to their homes rejoicing in the Lord. How the brethren and friends felt at these their first camp-meetings, as they had not the least experience in conducting them, may easily be imagined. But what a joy they experienced, on the other hand, by the new acquaintances they formed by their Christian intercourse with each other, and by the rich outpouring of God's grace and Spirit during these meetings, may readily be imagined by all the friends of camp-meetings. It is highly desirable that the same spirit and courage to attend such meetings, would prevail more generally in our own days! But alas! there are now too many who lack self-denial and zeal for the cause of God to such an extent, that they but rarely make their appearance at these meetings, to say nothing of bringing their tents with them. But even admitting that the many protracted and other meetings in spacious and convenient meeting-houses or Churches in our days, have, to some extent, taken the place of camp-meetings, and made these less necessary now; yet experience still teaches that well arranged and properly conducted camp-meetings are of great benefit everywhere, as they advance the believers in the divine life, and prove a blessing to the neighborhood where they take place; although, as a general thing, they neither cause any more that agitation, nor make that impression on the people, as was the case when they were yet new and less frequent.

The Brethren J. Erb and M. Betz, who had been appointed to form a new circuit in the above named counties, labored with glorious success. Considerable revivals occurred in various places under their superintendence, especially in the counties of York and Franklin, and a considerable number of precious souls were converted to the Lord, and several classes formed. Thus the Society's field of operations continued to enlarge, and the prospects became more encouraging. On the old circuits also, the brethren labored with great success; the number of preaching places and members had increased, and a great many converts professed to have found the pearl of great price. Upon the whole, there had been fourteen new classes formed during the year, and the membership increased by 200.

This success of their labors convinced the brethren more and more, that the hand of the Lord was in the work, and that He had called them to revive true and experimental religion among the degenerated German Churches of this country. But they attracted also more and more the attention of the Laodicean clergy, and were increasingly hated and slandered by them; for many of their Church members listened to the pure and artless preaching of the Word by our itinerants, and thus were led to see their lukewarm state and fatal condition, and expressed their dissatisfaction with the sad state of things in their Churches; yea, not a few of them bade farewell to their former pastors, and united with the despised "*so-called Albrights.*"

But it was especially the doctrine of purity of heart and life, as preached by our ministers, which the said Laodicean clergy hated, censured, and represented as erroneous and dangerous —saying that it was impossible to keep the commandments of God, and to lead a holy life in this world; although the whole Word of God insists on it, and makes it the condition of salvation on the part of man, excluding, however, all meritorious claims to heaven. Some declared openly, that in this life none could keep the commandments of God; that even the holiest of men sinned daily in *thoughts*, *words*, and *deeds;* and that whoever fancied that he could become free from sin here on earth, was fatally mistaken. And whoever opposed, or refused to receive, this perverted doctrine, tending to lessen the merits of Christ, dishonor Christianity, and to console and strengthen men *in* their sins, was decried by them as self-righteous, sanctimonious, and as a Pharisee or hypocrite.—Many of their followers gladly received this doctrine, so pleasing to man's corrupt nature, consoling themselves that they could be good Christians, and, at the same time, sin daily in thoughts, words, and deeds—and, as may well be supposed, their conduct was in perfect agreement with this their belief. The dispute about this doctrine, as well as about some others, lasted for years, and is to this day not yet settled in some places; for even in our days, this doctrine has still its advocates and followers. However, it cannot be denied, that the light of truth has driven this error, as well as many others, into the back-ground, and in some places exterminated the same altogether, which happy result is in no small degree contributable to the instrumentality of the Evangelical Association.

During this year a conversation took place between Mr. John Dreisbach, and Bishop *Asbury* of the Methodist Episcopal Church, which it may be interesting to mention here. Mr. Dreisbach on his journey down the Susquehanna river, met the bishop and his companion, H. Boehm. After conversing with Mr. Dreisbach freely on various topics relating to Christianity, the bishop, in order to enlist him for the M. E. Church, made him an offer, which is here given in Mr. Dreisbach's own words, only somewhat abbreviated:—

"After we had, for some time, freely conversed on various Christian topics, the bishop made me a very liberal and respectable offer, on certain conditions, to unite with his Church. I was to withdraw from the Evangelical Association, and go with them to Baltimore to attend their conference; there to join them, and to travel a year with *Jacob Gruber*, who was then presiding elder, for the purpose of better acquainting myself with the English language, wherein Brother G. might be very useful to me, that I might then be able to preach, according to circumstances, both in German and English; and I was to receive my salary as if I had traveled on a circuit, etc. Moreover, the bishop remarked that, by being able to preach in both languages, I could make myself so much more useful, and that among them there would be less danger of my becoming self-conceited, and to fall away, than in my present position, etc.—But however enticing the offer and truthful the statement of the bishop was, yet I could not determine in my mind to take such a treacherous step toward the Evangelical Association. I therefore told the bishop, that we considered ourselves called of God to labor principally among the German population, and that thus far our labors had not been in vain. To this he replied, that the German language could not exist much longer in this country, etc. I rejoined, that if this should ever be the case, it would then be time enough to discontinue preaching in German, and gave it as my opinion, that this would not very soon occur, but that the German language would rather increase, at least as long as the immigration from the old world would continue. I then gave him my views, in which I expected my brethren to concur, and made him the following offer: 'If you will give us German circuits, districts, and conferences, we are willing to make your Church *ours*, be *one* people with you, and have one and the same Church government.' 'This cannot be—it would not be expedient,' was the bishop's reply."

After passing some more remarks on this subject, they finally took, not far from Harrisburg, an affectionate and cordial leave of each other, when the bishop presented Mr. Dreisbach with

Fletcher's Portrait of St. Paul, embraced him, and bade him Godspeed in his work.—This conversation took place August 2d, 1810, and afterward these brethren never saw each other again. Whether the advice of the bishop, or the offer of Mr. Dreisbach, if carried out, would have promoted the interests of the kingdom of God, cannot with certainty be decided; but it is a well known fact, that many ministers and members of both parties have since wished, and still wish, a union of the two Churches. It is, however, very probable that many would have opposed this union; and if attempted, it might possibly have done more harm than good.—These two Christian denominations have always lived in harmony and peace, and agree in doctrine, manner of operation, and Church government nearly in every point. In this respect there would be no impediment to a union. And there are, perhaps, no two Christian denominations which, on the whole, manifest to one another so much friendship and confidence, as the Evangelical Association and the Methodist Episcopal Church.

Shortly before this time, the Articles of Faith and Church Discipline, drawn up by G. Miller, appeared in print, and made a very salutary impression both on the members and the ministry.—

Before this, it would seem that not only irregularity, but even disorder, caused by difference of opinions, had prevailed sometimes at the sessions of conference. Touching this subject, Mr. Miller writes in his auto-biography, as follows: "The opposite views of the members of conference, and the disputes arising therefrom, caused me much inward suffering. The principal cause of this lay in the fact that for the transaction of business by conference, we had as yet no fixed rules for each member to observe. Hence, necessity compelled me to draw up rules for the transaction of business by conference, and God blessed the undertaking; for we were now enabled to transact our business according to established rules, supporting by a majority of votes whatever was good, and suppressing what was evil, without hurting each other's feelings or offending weak brethren. From this time our conferences were like antechambers of heaven, by which all of us were edified and profited."

With reference to the publication of the Articles of Faith and Church Discipline, and the effect produced thereby, he makes in another place the following remarks: "The work seemed to be connected with great difficulties, for want of support, yet matters soon took a turn, perhaps altogether different from what any one had expected; for when this compendium of our articles of faith appeared in print, our Association was so well pleased with it, that the expenses were easily defrayed.—The effect of the new Discipline upon the Association was, that all took new courage to continue their union with God and among themselves, and many others were induced to unite with us, and to work out their souls' salvation, according to this regulation."

The conference of the preceding year had by resolution made it obligatory on all itinerants, to present at each conference a correct report of their income and expenses. The support of the preachers, however, was still very small, and by no means adequate to their wants. In this year each received but *thirty dollars*. In these days no arrangements had yet been made for the support of the families of the ministers, and single and married men received almost the same salaries. Now, as *thirty dollars* do not even suffice to keep an itinerant in clothes, during all seasons of the year, and as most of them were poor, it may easily be imagined why most of those who had families, located so soon and followed some secular business. This had a very pernicious effect on the Society, as in this way they were from time to time deprived of the services of the more experienced itinerants, and the majority of the preachers in actual service were young and inexperienced men. As long as the first zeal for the Lord's honor and work continued, it might do, and the so-called *hirelings*, who are even in our days still too numerous, could be properly inveighed against; but at length the preachers themselves felt (although it was not wrong to expose those who trafficked with religion and the ministerial office,) that it would be very convenient and advantageous, while discharging the duties of the ministry, to receive also a sufficient support for themselves and families. Yet it was a very long time till the ministers of the Evangelical Association received a somewhat more adequate support. This neglect was doubtless one of the main causes why the Society for so many years made such slow progress, and its membership, instead of increasing, sometimes decreased. There was too great a want of practiced and experienced itinerants, and their insufficient support prevented a more rapid increase of their numbers.

Fourth Conference.

At the fourth conference, which took place April 9, 10, and 11, 1811, near the Muehlbach again, the Society numbered 740 members, 8 itinerant and 12 local preachers. Mr. Miller presided again, and Mr. Dreisbach was re-nominated secretary. *Leonard Zimmerman* was received into the itinerancy, and H. Niebel ordained to the office of deacon. The preachers were appointed by a committee, as follows: Schuylkill and Lancaster circuit, J. Walter, M. Betz, and D. Yerlitz; Northumberland circuit, J. Erb and L. Zimmerman; Franklin and York circuit, J. Dreisbach, H. Niebel, and M. Becker.

At this conference the first resolution was passed for the itinerants to introduce and impart regular instruction to the young, on their respective circuits.

Unlike some of the preceding years, this one had, on the whole, not been as prosperous; for although over 200 new members had been received, yet the increase amounted only to 21. The Society must, therefore, have lost many members during the year, in some way or other. Notwithstanding this, the brethren had extended their spheres of labor considerably, by taking up many new preaching places in different parts of the country. A camp-meeting held in May (1811), on the land of Philip Breidenstein, near Lebanon, Pa., and a number of general meetings, were abundantly blessed of God during this year. As the Society had in those days neither bishops nor presiding elders, the brethren used to inform each other of the time and place of such meetings, and to assist one another.

During this year, a glorious work of grace, that had already begun in the preceding year, took place near Strassburg, York co., Pa., and in other parts of said county, and extended as far as Maryland. Brother Dreisbach and his colleagues labored with great success, and were permitted to see the fruits of their exertions. Among the families that came under the influence of divine grace, and were gained for the kingdom of God, were those of Jacob Kleinfelter, Jacob Baley, Lukas, Dick, Frueh, Dehoff, and others. From these families, there arose afterward several laborers in God's vineyard; namely, the brothers *John* and *Jacob Kleinfelter*, *Adam Kleinfelter*, *John Frueh*, and the two brothers *John* and *Moses Dehoff*, and still later *Joseph Dick*.—Conversions likewise took place in the vicinity of John Seitz and J. Reber, above Strassburg. Above Dover on the Conewago, several doors and hearts were opened by the Lord, and the brethren were also received by the family of the German Reformed minister Ettinger, and afterward most of them united with the Evangelical Association. Three of the sons, viz., *Adam*, *Benjamin*, and *Jacob*, became ministers, and the first two served some time in the itinerancy, and were useful laborers in the vineyard of the Lord.—In Cumberland county near Shippensburg, in the families of Buchman, John Vandersal, and others, the preached word yielded an abundant harvest; A. Buchman and John Vandersal, who subsequently became ministers, were from these families. It is a remarkable fact, that so many of the new converts of this circuit became preachers. It is therefore no wonder, that Satan and his servants raised so powerful an opposition, and strove to impede the work by slanders and calumnies.

On the other two circuits, also, the brethren had considerable awakenings, especially the brethren Erb and Zimmerman on Northumberland circuit—more than 100 new members had been added to the Society. In Centre co., Pa., on Pottersplain, a considerable class had been formed, which included the families of John Dauberman and father C. Dillman in part, and others. The societies at Millheim and Lewisburg and vicinity, had increased considerably. In the neighborhood of John Walter, near Swinefordstown, a glorious work of grace had taken place. The Brethren Walter, Betz, and Yerlitz, on Schuylkill and Lancaster circuit, had also been permitted to see fruit of their labors, especially on Turkey Hill in Lancaster co., and in a place called the Swamp, near Shaferstown.

Mr. Miller had attended the general meetings during the year as much as he had been able, and had preached generally with good effect. In this year he wrote his "Practical Christianity," a little work that has edified many, and is still read with great profit. The salary of the preachers amounted this year to $50, which was more than usual.

Fifth Conference.

This conference was held April 2 and 3, 1812, in the house of Martin Dreisbach, Union co., Pa.; the number of itinerants present, was twelve, and the membership of the Association amounted to 761. G. Miller presided again, and J. Dreisbach acted as secretary. *Fr. Shauer, Abr. Huth, Mich. Deibler,* and *Robert M'Cray*, were received on trial into the itinerancy, and John Erb was ordained as elder. Some of the old circuits were divided, and the formation of a new one in the state of New York was resolved upon. A committee, consisting of G. Miller, J. Walter, and J. Dreisbach, stationed the preachers for the ensuing year, as follows: Schuylkill circuit, H. Niebel and A. Huth; Lancaster circuit, J. Erb and M. Deibler; York circuit, M. Betz and M. Becker; Franklin circuit, J. Walter and D. Yerlitz; Northumberland circuit, L. Zimmerman and F. Shauer; for the mission in the state of New York, John Dreisbach and R. M'Cray. Thus the Society now numbered *five* circuits and one mission. This conference also resolved, that on Schuylkill and Northumberland circuits arrangements should be made, to build or buy suitable dwelling-houses for the families of the poor itinerant preachers; but this was not carried into effect. It was likewise resolved, that, in conformity to a former conference resolution, the preachers should not neglect to instruct the youth in their respective circuits, as much as possible.

This conference year seems to have been one of sore trials for the Association. Misconceptions and ill feelings among ministers, faithlessness and apostasy on the part of some, and disorders that had found their way into some of the societies, had made it necessary to make many changes of the ministers during the year, whereby the progress of the good cause was greatly impeded. Although 129 new members had been received during the year, yet the real increase amounted only to 35. As in the preceding year, so also in this, many of the members had left the Association; judging from the state of things, either by falling away, or by expulsion. Want of extensive experience on the part of many of its members and also some of its preachers, was an especial cause of many difficulties and sore trials for the Society in those days; however, similar things we meet with in the histories of nearly all Christian denominations in their incipient state, to a greater or less extent. From a desire to extend and increase the work as speedily as possible, all such as showed the least qualifications for the ministry, were urged to be obedient to the divine call, and to set out as heralds of the Gospel. Thus it came that frequently young men without sufficient experience, firmness, and fidelity, entered upon the ministry, who were afterward unable to withstand the many temptations, allurements, inconveniences, and dangers, to which an itinerant is exposed, and thus became either discouraged or fell away, to the great injury and impediment of the good cause. Against such difficulties and obstructions the Evangelical Association had to struggle a number of years; nor have they entirely disappeared in our days, although the number of immoral preachers is now much less, than it formerly was. Yet the Society was never guilty of the crime of sparing and suffering in its connection immoral or faithless preachers. The office of the keys of the kingdom of heaven was, at all times, properly and rigidly exercised—offenders were tried and dealt with, according to their deserts, both preachers and laymen.

Notwithstanding the above mentioned difficulties and sore trials, awakenings and conversions took place in various places on the different circuits, and the limits of the Society were somewhat extended. The brethren were gladly received in the Triangle, (between the eastern and northern branches of the Susquehanna river,) in the vicinity of Danville as far as Berwick and Williamsport, as well as in Whitedeer and Nippenose Valley, and on the large Island, etc. But the mission in the state of New York for the present failed. It is true, the brethren John Dreisbach and R. M'Cray set out immediately after conference for their new field of labor, and soon arrived there in safety at Brother Christian Wolf's, who was a local preacher, and had with some other friends emigrated from Pennsylvania to Seneca co., N. Y. Highly delighted with the arrival of the brethren, the few members there had anticipated glorious times from their ministry. But they were disappointed, as the missionaries remained but a short time with them. Discouraged by the great distance of the mission from the central point of the work and by the small number of Germans, who lived there, and taking into consideration that they might do more good by laboring in places nearer the centre, the brethren came, after due deliberation, to the conclusion to leave the mission with Brother Wolf, and return to Pennsylvania. Brother Wolf continued his labors as a local preacher with great success, till at length help was sent him by conference, and a circuit was formed.—The brethren on their return from New York sought and soon found admittance in the above mentioned places along the two branches of the Susquehanna, but toward the fall of the year their services were needed on the old circuits, in consequence of those occurrences that had made it necessary to change a considerable number of ministers. Northumberland circuit was allotted to J. Dreisbach, and R. McCray was associated with H. Niebel on Schuylkill circuit. This change of ministers during the year was made by the elders, and seems to have given general satisfaction, and advanced the best interests of the Society. In addition to the general trial and sifting of the Association during this year, Mr. Dreisbach had to undergo quite a peculiar test, that proved almost too much for him. A great weakness had come over his body, which very much affected his mind, so that he was almost disqualified for preaching, without knowing himself, what really ailed him. His sermons lacking their usual energy, some of the brethren suspected him of being tempted by the love of the world; and a rather rough and offending censure, administered unto him by an older ministerial brother, who mistook his circumstances, made his condition still worse. Speaking of this severe struggle, Mr. Dreisbach says: "I had to pass through the most formidable struggles and trials. Being almost on the point of despair, I often feared that I should have to yield—that my frail bark would sink. 'My harp was turned to mourning, and my organ into the voice of them that weep.' Yet my deliverance came, for which the Lord be praised! And these sore trials and struggles were followed by the most glorious victories.—'Our help is in the name of the Lord, who made heaven and earth.'"

Mr. Dreisbach had now arrived at a period that was important both to himself and the Association. The Brethren Miller and Walter, who had been the main pillars of the Society since Albright's death, were, on account of indisposition, unable to superintend the work much longer, and therefore much depended on Mr. Dreisbach's deep interest in it, as he was not only one of the oldest and most experienced, but at the same time one of the most talented and influential ministers of those days. Hence the sore trial, through which he had to pass, may have been intended as a school to prepare him for greater responsibility and usefulness in the Church. The narration of this circumstance here, may perhaps be useful and instructive to some in our time.

It deserves also to be noticed here, that agreeably to a former resolution of conference, regular catechetical instruction had been introduced in the Association for some years past, and was regularly attended to. Mr. Dreisbach had published a catechism for children, whereupon the conference of 1811, had made it obligatory on the itinerants, by a formal resolution, to introduce catechetical instruction on their respective circuits, which was renewedly insisted upon at the conference of the following year.—Now although this good cause was not generally attended to, for the following reasons; viz., because the societies were in those days yet small and scattered far and wide; partly also, because the preachers, on account of their very extensive circuits and long journeys, had not sufficient time to introduce it at every preaching place; and partly also because many of the ministers were yet young and inexperienced; still it is evident from the arrangements and resolutions of conference in those days, that catechetical instruction is no new thing in the Evangelical Association, and that, therefore, the charge of some who say that the Association had, until lately, been opposed to the use of the catechism and to catechetical instruction, is not founded on truth, but is a slander.

That some preachers as well as laymen, in their protestations *against the abuse of catechetical instruction and the confirmation of the young in their unconverted state,* by which rite they were received as members into the Churches, and then declared as believers and true Christians, without having experienced a change of heart,—as well as in their censures of other abuses, were not sufficiently careful in the choice of their expressions, has already been admitted; and that, at times, a short-sighted individual condemned catechetical and other useful instruction without reserve, may likewise be true; for there have always been more or less enthusiasts and fanatics in the Evangelical Association, as well as in all other denominations. But to say that the Association as a body censured and rejected the proper use of these reasonable and necessary things, is an unfounded charge.

When the writer was received as a member into the itinerancy of the Association, in 1828, he found in the Discipline of the Church the following among the duties of an itinerant, "*that he shall by no means neglect to impart catechetical instruction;*" and two years later, when he took charge of a circuit, it afforded him much pleasure to attend to this duty. The children met in the afternoon during the week in a convenient private house, where after singing, prayer, and a short address, they were instructed from the catechism, by explaining and practically applying to them the questions and answers they had committed to memory. The result of this was, that in the course of a few months, most of them became concerned for the salvation of their souls, and many were converted to God.

But it must be acknowledged, that in those days only a minority of the preachers attended to this duty in the manner specified. The method of imparting instruction not being defined in the Discipline, some contented themselves with merely conversing with the children on religious subjects in the family-circle; and even this was, and is yet, too much neglected, to the great injury of the cause of religion! Familiar, religious intercourse with the children of all the families under a minister's charge, whether they are grown or small, converted or unconverted, is one of his most sacred duties; and the alarming neglect of it, is doubtless the reason why our young people, generally, remain unconverted, and are thus lost to the Association. The commission given by the great Shepherd to Peter, "*Feed my lambs*," is addressed to every apostle, and every preacher of the Gospel.

When catechetical instruction was introduced in the Evangelical Association, about 1810, several of the preachers were greatly interested in it, among whom was John Erb, whom the writer often heard remark, that this exercise had afforded him great pleasure, and that much good had resulted from it. Since the late revival of this subject in the Society, the same blessed results have been experienced.

Sixth Conference.

This conference was also held in Buffalo Valley, Union co., Pa., in the house of father M. Dreisbach, April 21, 22, and 23, 1813. G. Miller presided, and J. Dreisbach acted as secretary. A. H. and M. B. were, on account of immoral conduct, deposed from the ministry and expelled from the Society. J. Erb obtained permission to locate, on account of bodily infirmities. Adam Hennig, Abr. Buchman, John Kleinfelter, Jacob Kleinfelter, John Stambach, and John Walter, jr., were received on trial into the itinerancy. D. Yerlitz and L. Zimmerman were ordained as deacons, and M. Betz and H. Niebel as elders. The committee of last year again stationed the ministers, as follows: Schuylkill and Lancaster circuit, John Walter, Jacob Kleinfelter, and John Walter, jr.; Northumberland and Centre circuit, M. Betz, R. M'Cray, Abr. Buchman, and John Stambach; Franklin circuit, H. Niebel and M. Deibler; York circuit, L. Zimmerman and Fr. Shauer.—John Dreisbach and A. Hennig, D. Yerlitz and John Kleinfelter, were instructed to form new circuits west of those already existing. The number of itinerant preachers amounted to 15, that of the membership, to 796.

This was, on the whole, a very prosperous year to the Society, so that it extended and increased considerably, although it was not without its trials. On the old circuits, especially those of York and Northumberland, considerable awakenings took place, and the brethren who had been sent out to form new circuits, labored also with good success. J. Dreisbach had been instructed to visit, during the year, several circuits in the eastern part of the conference district, and to assist the brethren at general and camp-meetings, as there were as yet no presiding elders. Toward the latter part of August, they held a general meeting at Jacob Kleinfelter's on York circuit, which was remarkably blessed, so that some souls were converted, and the believers greatly edified. On the 1st of September they commenced a campmeeting on Turkey Hill, Lancaster co., Pa., and on the 8th, another near New Berlin, Union co., at M. Maize's. Both were crowned with awakenings and conversions, and the children of God were greatly encouraged; the former particularly so. A great many persons had assembled, who, on the whole, listened attentively to the preached word, and many were deeply impressed by what they heard, while others actually sought and found peace with God. In those days campmeetings were yet a novelty among the German population, and were generally very numerously attended.

The four brethren appointed as missionaries, proceeded as follows: D. Yerlitz and John Kleinfelter chose for their field of labor the counties of Huntingdon and Bedford, east of the Alleghany mountains; where they were gladly received, formed several classes, and thus gathered a very considerable number of converted souls, and such as were anxious to be saved, during the year. One of these classes was near Bedford, the other near Eckstown (now Williamsburg). In the following year, this new circuit was added to the western part of Northumberland circuit, and called *Bedford circuit*, but in the second year it received the name *Centre circuit*. Among the first classleaders of Bedford circuit were, Jacob Eck and John Rickel, the latter of whom afterward served for some time as an itinerant, and for many years as a local preacher. J. Dreisbach and his colleague, A. Hennig, broke the ice *to* and *across* the Alleghany mountains into Somerset and the adjacent counties; and as they met with the greatest success in Somerset co., they called their new circuit Somerset circuit. They received during the year nearly 60 members, and formed three classes; the first in the Glades near Laurel Hill, H. Wieand leader,—the families of Herbach and Puttman were some of the first members; the second in Brother's Valley, H. Meyer leader—both these leaders afterward served as preachers, the former for some time as an itinerant; the third class below Stoyestown, Jacob Paul leader, who was but 15 years of age when he was chosen, but acted his part as a man and proved faithful.

In this way the first ministers of the Evangelical Association had to go to work in order to extend their field of labor. Not as is frequently the case now-a-days, when members settle in new parts, and cordially bid their preachers welcome at their arrival, and provide a good home for them. They had to *break ground*, and often encountered great opposition and persecution. The roads in many places were yet new and rough, leading over steep mountains and deep valleys—the dwellings of the new settlers were small, inconvenient, and frequently so well aired, that the ministers could by night on their couches see the stars, and feel the falling snow, as well as wind and cold. This required self-denial and humility—but in many instances was also injurious to their health. Yet it could not be expected otherwise in this work; and if such a spirit of self-denial, enterprise, and earnestness, and such a zeal for the spread of the kingdom of God, had kept equal pace with other improvements in the Society, how much more rapidly it would spread in our days, and how many precious souls could be saved, that alas! are probably lost—and who will be held responsible for it?

Now, as this year was in these respects greatly blessed, so also it had its afflictions. The active and beloved laborer, *Math. Betz*, was during this year called from Zion's walls to his home in heaven. Although his services seemed so greatly needed, especially in this year, there being those young brethren under his superintendence, who looked up to him for advice and encouragement, yet he had to bid his brethren farewell. He had been a pious, humble, and very useful minister, and had served about five years as an itinerant when he suddenly departed this life, after an illness of but a few days. He died of inflammation on the chest, in the house of Brother Steffe, near Boalsburg, Centre co., and his remains rest in the Presbyterian grave-yard, near a place which was then called, Slab-Cabin Meetinghouse. This was a heavy stroke and a mysterious providence for the brethren. But this was not the only trial—the experienced J. Walter, whose services seemed almost indispensably necessary, was, in consequence of bodily infirmities, compelled to discontinue the office of an itinerant,—M.'C. was deposed from the ministry, on account of faithlessness,—and J. Walter, jr., who had been received at the last conference, had traveled but a short time when he retired from the field. Thus the conference which had been weak before, lost in this one year four of its members. Yet the brethren were not discouraged, but continued their labors in the name of the Lord, and he also smiled upon and blessed their efforts.

FOURTH SECTION.

FROM THE SEVENTH CONFERENCE TO THE FIRST GENERAL CONFERENCE IN 1816.

Seventh Conference.

The seventh conference was again held at father Dreisbach's, in Buffalo Valley, April 13, 14, and 15, 1814. J. Dreisbach presided, and H. Niebel was secretary. *Thomas Bruer, Michæl Walter*, and *Henry Staufer* were received on trial, and Fr. Shauer, A. Buchman, A. Hennig, and J. Stambach were ordained as deacons. This conference elected the first *presiding elder*, viz., John Dreisbach. The stationing committee consisted of G. Miller, J. Dreisbach, and H. Niebel. The appointments were, as follows: Conference district, J. Dreisbach, presiding elder; Union circuit, H. Niebel and John Kleinfelter; Bedford circuit, D. Yerlitz and M. Walter; Franklin circuit, Fr. Shauer; York circuit, J. Stambach and Thomas Bruer; Lancaster circuit, L. Zimmerman and H. Staufer; Schuylkill circuit, A. Hennig; Somerset circuit, A. Buchman and Jacob Kleinfelter. The membership as reported at this conference amounted to 1016, consequently an increase of 220 during the year; the itinerants numbered 13.

The election of a presiding elder at this conference, was not only a wise, but a very necessary step, and was crowned with good success. As already remarked, the conference still consisted mostly of young and inexperienced men; and yet the field of operation was already too extensive to enable most or all of the ministers to attend every general or campmeeting as heretofore had been the practice; hence it was of the utmost importance to appoint a man of greater experience and influence, to superintend such meetings, and to assist the brethren in every emergency. As J. Walter and G. Miller could no longer serve as itinerants, on account of bodily infirmities, choice was wisely made of the eldest of the other itinerants, J. Dreisbach, who in qualification was inferior to none of his brethren.

During this year general peace prevailed within the bounds of conference, and both the ministers and the laymen excelled by being faithful; yet the increase was not as large as it had been in some of the preceding years. Mr. Dreisbach writes: "We held *four* campmeetings, *fourteen* general meetings, and *eight* watch-nights, all of which I attended, and nearly all of them were crowned with conversions, and an advance of the children of God in the divine life. The campmeetings especially were times of refreshing from the presence of the Lord," etc. One was held in York co., Pa., near A. Ettinger's at the Conewago; another in Oley, Berks co., on the land of D. Bertolet; the third at John Buechler's, between Mifflinburg and Hartleton, Union co., and the fourth at G. Schwartz's, near Millheim, Centre co. At some of these meetings, especially that in Oley, Berks co., considerable disturbance was caused by mobs, for which occurrences, however, the friends of such meetings were generally prepared. At that time the members and ministers were yet in the habit of attending camp and general meetings from great distances; and as such meetings were as yet something new to most of them, they took a deep interest in them, and were generally greatly edified and encouraged. Now, as among the crowds that assembled at such meetings, there were also many enemies of the truth and blasphemers of the Holy Spirit, who there heard and saw many things that were strange and unintelligible to them; and besides, being filled with the very worst suspicions, even before they came: such meetings served not only to make the Society more rapidly known, but also to increase the contempt and hatred against it. The enemies of the cross circulated some of the most abominable lies, concerning these people; and the farther they spread, the more they increased, each one, through whose lips they passed, adding his part thereto. Thus it happened, that persons of some parts of the country, who knew these people merely from hearsay, dreaded their coming into their neighborhood as much as pestilence itself. In these their fears they generally were yet confirmed by their pastors, who represented the itinerants unto them as the false prophets and deceivers who were to come in the last times, and with all their might warned their congregations against them as the most dangerous men. In consequence of this, many well disposed and even religious persons had become filled with prejudices against them, who afterward, upon closer acquaintance, acknowledged them as God's people, and subsequently joined the Society.

As the sermons on such occasions were usually very plain and pointed, a great number were generally deeply impressed, many of whom were at once made acquainted with their lost condition, and turned unto the Lord; while others went to their homes, deeply wounded in their consciences, and found no rest, until they sought it in the blood of Christ. Such glorious results established the propriety and usefulness of such meetings beyond a doubt, and the friends were thus encouraged to continue them from time to time, in spite of the persecutions and disturbances which were generally in their train.—But we do not deny that imprudent, ignorant, or hypocritical persons, may sometimes have given just cause for censure, by their improper conduct during the exercises. And that such offensive conduct, which proved very detrimental to the good cause, was too often overlooked, partly from fear of hurting the feelings of the innocent, or for want of better insight into the great injury arising therefrom, cannot be denied either.—But it is strange that religious organizations, as well as individuals, should make so much ado about isolated cases of extravagance and hypocrisy, regarding them as certain evidences of the spuriousness of the entire work of such as are annoyed and grieved by these unpleasant occurrences; while they themselves have so many proofs of hypocrisy continually staring them in the face, of a great majority of their own Church members, attending public worship in all its parts the year round, with impenitent and worldly hearts; while others devote themselves openly to the service of the devil, to the world, and sin. Yet so it is, men always see the splinter in their neighbors' eyes much sooner than the beam in their own.

What made the censure and opposition by the fickle crowd

of nominal Christians and their lukewarm indolent pastors so general in those days, was the *effects* of the doctrine preached by our ministers, insisting on immediate conversion and a holy and godly life; namely, *many real conversions from darkness to light and from the power of Satan to God;* with their repeated egressions from those corrupt and lifeless Churches, and uniting with the Evangelical Association.—By the simple and powerful preaching of the word, candid hearers were generally soon brought to see the fallacy and untenableness of their religion, founded upon the mere literal and outward observance of baptism, catechetical instruction, confirmation, confession and the Lord's supper, going to Church, and other religious exercises; and if, as further instructed, they continued to plead before the throne of grace, in true contrition of heart, weary and heavy laden, renouncing all sin, and truly believing in Jesus Christ as the only and all-sufficient Saviour of mankind, they learned by actual experience, the *truth of the doctrine concerning man's justification by faith in the Son of God*, and, enjoying comfort and peace, life and happiness, and the witness of the Spirit, they rejoiced in hope of the glory of God. Having made such an experience, they could not possibly harmonize any longer with the dead, secure, and obdurate children of this world or nominal Christians. Neither could they be silent concerning what the Lord had done for them, or wink at wickedness and hypocrisy: and then, if they did not leave the wicked of their own accord, they were expelled by them as fanatics, disturbers of the peace of the Church, and as misguided wretches. As long as they indulged with them in acts of frivolity, tippling, or even cursing or swearing, they passed for good Christians, provided they defended their Church bravely, attended public worship regularly, paid their share toward the preacher's salary, and, above all, knew how to rail against the "*fanatics;*" but no sooner did they begin to feel and confess their sins and helpless condition, and to inquire after the way of salvation, than they were persecuted. These are facts which cannot be successfully contradicted. Thus matters stood, and thus, alas! it is yet in some places.

The preachers of the Evangelical Association were, in a classical point of view, *unlearned men.* Many of them had perhaps never read any other religious books besides the Bible, when they set out to preach. Some could not even read correctly. But these things we do not state here to their *praise;* for they certainly were not the cause of the good effects of their preaching. Nor do we wish to be understood, as if it were our opinion that men with so limited a knowledge of theology, history, and other useful sciences, were able to explain the fundamental doctrines and deep passages of the Bible, and to defend them against scoffers and infidels, or to labor in every manner for the kingdom of God, in which the *learned,* pious, and devoted minister can work. But this was not their call and object. Christianity among the people, where they lived and labored, needed not so much a thorough explanation and defence of its *deep* and *mysterious doctrines,* as a *revival.* To explain its *theory* was less necessary than to enforce its *practice.* The great desideratum was, to show to the sinner his lost and dangerous condition out of Christ, in his natural state—to convince him that the observance of the external duties of Christianity, without regeneration or a change of heart, is insufficient for salvation,—to convince him that he must come as a condemned sinner, penitently, prayerfully, and believingly, to the great Friend and Saviour of sinners, in order to be pardoned and adopted into the family of God. This simple plan of salvation they had learned by their own experience, and could therefore preach it with the joyful assurance of having themselves an interest in Christ, and amid the attending influence and unction of the Holy Ghost. And herein lay the secret of the success of their labors. Hence the common people, who at that time were still more ignorant than they are now, understood their sermons much better than those of well educated preachers. And being able, plainly and impressively to explain to the sinner the way of obtaining peace with God, as they had themselves experienced it; so they understood also, successfully, to explain to, and inculcate on, believers the doctrines of Christ and his apostles, with reference to watching and praying, self-denial, growing in grace and the knowledge of our Lord and Saviour Jesus Christ, perfecting holiness in the fear of God, the practice of love to God and our fellow-men, perseverance in hope, faith, and charity, etc., as well as that with regard to future rewards and punishments. And was not this the method of the apostles and all their successors everywhere, except *then* and *there* where circumstances required more? And where this was the case, the more experienced and talented among our preachers were, by the grace of God, soon qualified for this also. By preaching almost daily, many of the ministers made rapid progress in qualifying themselves for a proper discharge of the duties of their calling; and those who persevered in *reading* and *searching*, as well as in daily prayer, were soon able to compete, in this respect, with most of the educated preachers of those days. And as to spirit, power, life, and effect, they were, on the whole, by far their superiors: hence the glorious results of their labors.

Eighth Conference.

This conference was held April 4, 5, 6, 1815, in the house of Jacob Kleinfelter, in York county, Pa., near Strassburg. H. Niebel was president, and John Kleinfelter secretary. The following brethren were received into the itinerancy: David Thomas, James Bruer, and John Dehoff; the following were ordained as deacons: John Kleinfelter, Jacob Kleinfelter, and Thomas Bruer. D. Yerlitz located. At this session the conference district was divided into two presiding elder districts, and H. Niebel was elected the second presiding elder. One of these districts was called *Canaan*, and the other *Salem* district. The conference committee of this year consisted of H. Niebel, John Erb, and L. Zimmerman, who stationed the 15 preachers present, as follows:—

Canaan district, John Dreisbach, presiding elder. Franklin circuit, T. Bruer and J. Dehoff; York circuit, A. Buchman and D. Thomas; Lancaster circuit, John Kleinfelter and J. Bruer; Schuylkill circuit, L. Zimmerman.

Salem district, H. Niebel, presiding elder. Union circuit,

J. Stambach and Jacob Kleinfelter; Bedford and Centre circuit, Fr. Shauer and H. Staufer; Somerset circuit, A. Hennig and M. Walter.

The membership at this conference amounted to 1108, consequently an increase of 92 members during the previous year.

This session changed the time of conference meeting from April to June, in consequence of which the following conference year was two months longer than usual. After this, conference met for a number of years regularly in June.

This was one of the most blessed years of those times. All the circuits, with the exception of Schuylkill, had extended their bounds, and increased considerably in membership. On some of them great revivals had taken place; but Schuylkill circuit had hitherto generally been weak, and had lost 15 members this year. Nor was there a change for the better, until the great revival in Orwigsburg and vicinity took place, in the years 1823 and 1824; when in the following year, 1825, this circuit numbered 312 members, and was thus, in point of numbers, superior to every other.

The six campmeetings that were held during that year, had generally been crowned with glorious success. The word had been gladly received in many houses and regions, and many hearts had experienced its happy influence. At some of these meetings, especially that in York co., on the land of John Seitz, and another near Manheim, Lancaster co., Pa., on the land of John Seybert, the brethren had encountered great opposition and disturbance by mobs. At the first, an occurrence took place which deserves to be mentioned here. A very daring scoffer, on the upper end of the tent-ground, was struck to the ground by the power of God, where he lay helpless and appeared frightful, surrounded by his companions, who were as if seized by the terrors of the Lord. Nearly all who saw him, recognized in his visitation the finger of God.—Another wicked man, overcome by anger, commenced to bellow like an ox during the sermon, and hurried out of the meeting like a madman.—The word had similar effects, when preached by Jesus himself: some were moved and drawn by it, but others became *full of wrath*, so that they would gnash with their teeth, foam with anger, and would have destroyed everything, had it been in their power. During the meeting near Manheim, one Sunday night, a great disturbance was made. There came a gang of about 40 persons, who were armed with clubs, their shirts' sleeves rolled up, and ready for the attack, threatening to break up and scatter the meeting; in which, however, they were disappointed, although they made some disturbance. At one time, as is believed, they were put to flight by the united prayers of the children of God, and the next time they were put down by taking prisoner and securing one of their leaders.—The campmeetings in those days were always kept over Sunday, and this may have contributed much to increase those disorders and disturbances, as the people met on Saturdays and Sundays in still greater crowds than they do at present, because at that time the thing was yet a novelty. Nevertheless there was a great deal of good accomplished through these meetings. One of them held during this year, which was under H. Niebel's superintendence, in Somerset co., Pa., is said to have been remarkably blessed and victorious. Another was held in Buffalo Valley, Union co., Pa., on the land of M. Dreisbach, which was also greatly blessed; and another near Jonestown, Lebanon co., Pa., on the land of father Faber, where likewise the arm of the Lord was revealed. "Here," says Mr. Dreisbach, "our dear Brother Walter preached once more for us, from 1. Tim. 2, 8., to the great edification of the members."

The general meetings and watch-nights had also been richly blessed during this year. The former generally began on Saturday at 1 or 2 o'clock, P. M., and were continued over Sunday. On Sunday, after the morning services, the Lord's supper was administered. At campmeetings, this was generally done on Saturday morning, followed by an experience meeting, in which the children of God related their experience before all the congregation, whereby the membership were greatly edified and encouraged, and even unawakened souls were often deeply impressed. It is to be regretted, that these experience meetings have in many places come out of use, at camp-meetings. Great care, however, is necessary, to make them generally useful and edifying. Imprudent persons have sometimes done more harm than good, by their confessions; and this may be one of the reasons, why this practice has become comparatively rare. Yet by proper instruction this evil might be prevented in most instances.—The watch-nights were generally commenced in the evening, and lasted with but few interruptions during the greater part of the night. After one or two sermons, sometimes also after one sermon and a few exhortations, the rest of the night was mostly spent in singing and praying, and very often also in laboring with mourners. These meetings were in those days, proportionably, much more frequent than in our days, and generally proved very edifying and encouraging to the members.

During this year, Mr. Dreisbach visited Philadelphia several times. The first visit he made in the month of May, the second in November, and preached there three times: the first time on a Sunday, May 7, (1815,) in a masonic hall, four doors from Poplar lane, North 2nd st.; the second sermon he preached in the house of a certain George Fisher; and the third, at his second visit in 3rd, near Green st., in the commissioner's hall. It is remarkable that during Mr. Dreisbach's first visit in Philadelphia, his first sermon was preached in the same quarter and neighborhood, where our preachers, 25 years later, again found admittance, and soon gathered a society; and where a few years after the first Church edifice of the Association in that city was erected, which has since proved a blessing to many already, and bids fair for the future.

But, although this was a very prosperous year for the Society, yet it also brought its trials. Death appeared in the midst of the small band of ministers, and took away one of its principal pillars—the active *George Miller*, who had taken so deep an interest in the prosperity of the Society, and who had, not only by his preaching and ability to conduct the work, but also as the author of several small works which had been printed, become renowned and highly esteemed in the Evangelical Association. G. Miller was in several respects a peculiar man, and a powerful instrument in the hands of God, to awaken and convert sinners, as well as to edify and advance the faithful. In his younger days, before he was 16 years of age, he had perused the Bible studiously and with great devotion, while its divine contents had often affected him deeply, and made him desirous of becoming a pious man. While he was being catechized and received the rite of confirmation, in his sixteenth year, he was deeply concerned for the salvation of his soul, and groaned to be delivered from the burden of his sins. But this time passed away without his becoming really converted, and the good impressions gradually wore off, so that, as he himself confesses, he fell into open sins and transgressions, in which state he continued for several years. At length, however, he again resolved to reform his life; but it was not until his 28th year, in 1802, that through the instructions of Mr. Albright, he obtained the assurance of his acceptance with God. In 1805, after he had gone through the severest struggles and trials, he set out as a traveling preacher under the superintendence of Mr. Albright, and in this capacity he served four or five years with great success; but was then, in consequence of bodily infirmities, obliged to withdraw from the itinerancy. Nevertheless, he continued to take the deepest interest in the prosperity of the Society and the spread of the kingdom of God, preaching as much as his health and circumstances would allow. He composed the first Church Discipline of the Evangelical Association, a short biography of Mr. Albright, and a small work called "Practical Christianity."—His main object during this time was, to advance professors of religion in the divine life, a task for which he was eminently qualified. He also took great pains to encourage his brethren in the ministry to follow holiness, and assisted them every way he could, both by word and deed. His great zeal for the Lord and his kingdom made him very bold in his sermons, denouncing sin under every form and shape with great severity, both publicly and in his private conversations, and very rigid in the application of the Discipline; and as a consequence, he frequently met with strong opposition, and sometimes even gave unintentional offence. All well disposed persons, however, could easily overlook this trait, as he was so upright and active in the service of his Master. His disease was consumption, which caused him great pain during the last three months of his pilgrimage; but he was richly comforted by the Lord during this time, and awaited his death in the full hope of everlasting life. He departed this life April 5, 1816, and his last words were: "I know that I go to heaven." His residence was at that time in Union county, Pa., a few miles east of New Berlin. His remains were deposited in the New Berlin graveyard of the Society, the spot being marked by a beautiful tomb-stone, with proper inscriptions. Many a visitor here, has already been solemnly impressed, by calling to mind the life and death of this faithful servant of God, and desired at the same time, that his own death might be like that of this just man. H. Niebel delivered his funeral sermon, from Rev. 3, 10. This faithful and successful servant of God only reached the age of 42 years and not quite two months, and thus in the very prime of his useful life entered into the joy of his Master. Why was this, to the Society so indispensably necessary man not permitted to live longer? and why was it, that *Albright* and *Walter* died so early? These questions have often presented themselves to the writer, and the only answer he could ever return was, "*The Lord has done it.*"

Ninth Conference.

This conference was held at father Abraham Eyer's in Dry Valley, Union county, Pa., June 11, 12, and 13, 1816. John Dreisbach acted as chairman, and H. Niebel as secretary. The following brethren were received into the itinerancy: John Frueh, Philip Schmidt, Moses Dehoff, Adam Ettinger, John Shilling, Benjamin Ettinger, John Rickel, Fred. Kaltreiter, and Andrew Wolf. The following were ordained as deacons: D. Thomas, M. Walter, John Dehoff, and S. Miller; as elders: Fr. Shauer and L. Zimmerman.—A. Buchman, Th. Bruer, and H. Staufer, located on account of bodily infirmities.

The conference committee: J. Dreisbach, H. Niebel, and L. Zimmerman, made the following appointments for the next year:—

Canaan district, J. Dreisbach, presiding elder. Franklin circuit, J. Bruer and F. Kaltreiter; York circuit, L. Zimmerman and A. Ettinger; Lancaster circuit, D. Thomas; Schuylkill circuit, J. Frueh and B. Ettinger; Lake mission, Jacob Kleinfelter.

Salem district, H. Niebel, presiding elder. Union circuit, J. Kleinfelter and M. Dehoff; Columbia circuit, P. Schmidt; Centre circuit, J. Stambach; Bedford circuit, J. Dehoff and J. Shilling; Somerset circuit, M. Walter and J. Rickel; Canton mission, A. Hennig; Scioto mission, Fr. Schauer.

The membership amounted to 1401, showing an increase of 293 members during the past year.

By comparing the proceedings of this year's conference with those of the preceding one, it appears that not only 3 missions had been taken up, but also several of the old circuits had been divided and their number increased; and that in consequence of the great increase of itinerants, conference was also enabled to supply all these places. It is however to be regretted, that not all of the ministers remained at their posts to the end of the year.

This conference was also compelled to depose two of its members from the ministry, as transgressors. Moreover, the following resolutions were passed:—

1. That the presiding elders shall visit the missions during the year.

2. That the ministers shall hereafter be entitled to $56 salary, besides reasonable traveling expenses, provided the state of the treasury will allow it.

3. That the local preachers shall henceforth, after a trial of six years, and at the recommendation of 12 itinerants, be entitled to receive the ordination as deacons.

4. That J. Dreisbach and H. Niebel shall during the conference year, have preachers' licenses printed, for the use of conference.

5. That J. Dreisbach and H. Niebel shall make a proper collection of hymns for the Society, and improve the present Discipline of the Church.

6. That the first General Conference of the Society shall take place in October next.

J. Dreisbach having at his last visit to Philadelphia, during the past year, purchased, at his own expense, the necessary materials for a small printing establishment and book bindery for the Association, which was afterward set up at New Berlin, Pa.; therefore this conference elected a committee of seven, viz., J. Dreisbach, H. Niebel, S. Miller, A. Ettinger, D. Bertolet, P. Breidenstein, and Chr. Spangler, to superintend the affairs of the printing establishment and book bindery, and to carry on the business, as the wants of the Society might require, and to report to conference from time to time.

The following members of conference were elected delegates to the General Conference; namely, J. Dreisbach, H. Niebel, John Walter, L. Zimmerman, J. Erb, J. Stambach, J. Kleinfelter, S. Miller, J. Dehoff, D. Thomas, A. Ettinger, and J. Frueh—*twelve*.

From the foregoing statement it appears that an unusually large amount of business was transacted at this conference; for, as the Discipline, at that time, contained as yet no limits to the power of conference in their doings, the conference transacted at its annual sessions all the business that seemed necessary to the furtherance of the work entrusted to their care. Hence, without any one interfering, this conference transacted some business that in our days could only be done by the General Conference.

During this year the work had again extended considerably; not as much though, as in some preceding years, at least in point of numbers. Some of the old circuits, indeed, had increased somewhat, but others again had lost considerably. This happened, in all probability, mostly by expulsion, as the Discipline was, generally, pretty rigidly enforced. This was then, and is yet a cause of the slow increase of the Society. If from the beginning all, or nearly all, that were received as members, had, as is done by many denominations, been retained in Church, without regard to their conduct, the Evangelical Association would have increased more rapidly, and might perhaps at this time number half as many more. For, not only hundreds, and even thousands of members were lost to the Society, by expulsion for immoral conduct, continued neglect of duty, disobedience to the Discipline, etc.; but also many awakened and even partly enlightened persons joined with other denominations, in preference to the Evangelical Association, which, for this very reason, was shunned by many, and by some called *the rigid and bigoted "Albrights."*

Although the increase of membership during the past year had not been so great, yet the bounds of the Society had been considerably extended, two of the new circuits or missions having greatly prospered. At different places on the Lake mission in the state of New York, conversions had taken place, and some new classes had been formed, so that, at the close of the year, the mission, together with the classes formed by Brother Wolt, numbered 42 members. J. Dreisbach, as instructed by conference, had visited the mission during the year in the capacity of presiding elder, and labored with great success. A general meeting on the mission, held on Christmas at father Jacob Riegel's, had been particularly blessed. Here in Fayette, Seneca co., was the principal point of the mission, whence the work extended, from time to time, into all directions, till at length it became a presiding elder's district, and is now a conference district. Yet for many years it increased but slowly, and at times it almost seemed as if it would fail altogether; but it always recovered again, till it was finally placed on a permanent footing. During this tour, Mr. Dreisbach also traveled westward as far as Buffalo, the Niagara Falls, and Canada, preaching as he went with good effect. In Canada he preached six miles above the Falls, at the house of a certain Jacob Miller, also at John and Jacob Buck's, near Burlington; and on the American side, in the neighborhood of Jacob Schopp, about 12 miles from Buffalo, and at P. Bluecher's near Buffalo—also in another place at Chr. Thomas'. The Germans, as a general thing, were at that time very thinly scattered in those parts of the state of New York; yet afterward they increased considerably, so that in some places large German societies could be gathered.

The first attempt to extend the work to the state of Ohio, was made in this year by founding two missions, or, as the missionary operations of the Evangelical Association were then called, by *seeking* two new circuits. But one of these missions (that in *Scioto*) failed this year, as the preacher (F. S.) stationed there, proved unfaithful to the Society, and united with another denomination. The other, however, *Canton* mission, succeeded well by the labors of its missionary, A. Hennig. Although the country was yet new, to a great extent, and the people mostly lived in log-houses, and were but poorly prepared to entertain strangers, yet Brother Hennig very soon found many open doors, and in a very short time had formed a circuit of 32 preaching places.

In a letter to the writer, Brother Hennig, with reference to his labors there, among other things remarks: "When I arrived at my new field of labor, four miles west of New Philadelphia, I met with a family of our dear friends, that had just arrived the day before. O how they rejoiced that their preacher had followed them to that wilderness! They immediately made arrangements for preaching at a neighbor's house, and that evening I had a log-house full of hearers from various denominations, who were greatly pleased to have German preaching, and requested me to continue it. My text was, 1. Peter 4, 8., and the word seemed to be well received." He then goes on to say, that the country had been but thinly peopled, especially by Germans, many of whom had but shortly settled in the dense forests, and had neither stables nor fields for a horse, so that he was frequently obliged to tie a bell round his horse's neck and drive it into the woods, to seek its food during the night. The bell was intended to enable him by its sound to find his horse again, the next morning. "The roads," he continues, "were in some places very bad. I frequently met with dangerous swamps and deep bridgeless rivers, across which

I had to swim my horse, at the risk of my life. Some of the inhabitants were as rough and wild as the country itself; yet I also met with such as had a disposition to hear the Gospel preached in the German language."

A large portion of the new circuit was in Stark county, about the town of *Canton*, for which reason it was called "*Canton* circuit." However, it extended also over the counties of Tuscarawas, Wayne, and Richland, and was about 400 miles in circumference. Brother Hennig mentions, that he frequently preached two or three times a day, and completed his round on his large circuit in about 3 or 4 weeks. But no sooner had sinners been awakened and converted to God, than opposition and persecution arose. The work was declared to be fanaticism, and the people were warned against deception. Toward the fall of that year, the presiding elder, H. Niebel, visited the new field of labor and brought an assistant to Brother H., namely J. Shilling. These two brethren labored during the winter with great success, formed several classes, and reported favorably of the new country at the next conference. The membership amounted already to 55.

This was the beginning of the Society's operations in the state of Ohio; and as the emigration of members from Pennsylvania had already commenced and increased annually, and considerable revivals soon took place, the good work progressed so rapidly, that subsequently the 2d Annual Conference of the Association was formed in that state. Among the first families there, that received the preachers of the Society and united with the Church, were the following: M. Reidinger, P. Strayer, A. Shilling, P. Oberlin, A. Rausch, C. Dillman, D. Williams, P. Stroh, J. Schwartz, P. Hennig, etc.; some of whom, however, had been members of the Society before they emigrated to Ohio. Not until the third year, did the first general meeting of our brethren in the West take place at A. Shilling's, and in the fourth year the first campmeeting, on the land of W. Weiss, 7 or 8 miles north of Canton, which was richly blessed.

A remarkable instance of the vindictive justice of God took place during this year, near the village of Dover, York county,

Pa. The brethren and friends there had for a considerable length of time been disturbed in their religious services, and grossly insulted with slanders and calumnies, by a gang of Belial's sons, headed by one named *Sharp*.—Once, while the brethren were engaged in worship, this gang went so far in their impiety as to celebrate a mock-communion with sweet-cakes and whisky, close by in the street. On their knees, they received the cakes and the whisky from the hand of their ringleader Sharp, blasphemously repeating the words of the institution. Shortly afterward a horse-race took place in the neighborhood—Sharp was one of the riders on the ground, but fell from his horse and expired a few minutes after! The Bible truly says: "*Be not deceived; God is not mocked.*" After this tragic scene the disturbances of public worship subsided somewhat in that vicinity, but without being followed by any great change for the better.

FIFTH SECTION.

FROM THE FIRST GENERAL CONFERENCE OF THE ASSOCIATION IN 1816, TO 1823.

First General Conference.

Various causes at this time had, in the opinion of the brethren, rendered it necessary to hold a *General Conference*, which, accordingly, took place at father M. Dreisbach's, in Buffalo Valley, Union co., Pa., October 14–17, 1816. To promote the interests of the printing and book establishment, started by the brethren, and to deliberate on a *union* of the "Evangelical Association" and the "United Brethren in Christ" into *one* Church, seem to have been the main objects of this conference. Several of the brethren and members of both denominations were greatly in favor of this union, especially *J. Dreisbach*, on the part of the Evangelical Association, and father *Chr. Newcomer*, on the part of the "United Brethren;"

which brethren had, on former occasions, already consulted on this measure, and were the leaders of the movement. Brother Dreisbach assures us, that their motives were perfectly pure, considering, as they did, that such a union would be highly advantageous to the prosecution of the work of God among the Germans of this country.

Pursuant to the resolution passed by the last conference, the chosen delegates met at the above mentioned time and place, together with Bishop Newcomer, and some other ministers of the "United Brethren." Conference being opened with prayer for the blessing of the Most High, the regular organization took place, by electing J. Dreisbach chairman and H. Niebel secretary.

The first item claiming the attention of conference, was the appointment of a General Book Agent and an Assistant. Although the printing establishment was then but a small matter, yet a beginning having been made, some one had to attend to it. Bro. S. Miller was, accordingly, elected General Agent, and H. Niebel Assistant.—The next topic was the proposed union. What was said in favor and against it, is not recorded in the minutes; but there is reason to believe, that the two sides of the question were duly considered. Bishop Newcomer and the ministers of the "United Brethren," who had come with him, took an active part in the discussions, and both parties agreed on making an attempt at said union. Hereupon a conference was appointed, to consist of ministers of both denominations, to be called "*Social Conference.*" On our part, the following brethren were chosen delegates to said conference: J. Dreisbach, H. Niebel, S. Miller, John Kleinfelter, D. Thomas, and A. Ettinger. This Social Conference was to meet February 14, 1817.

The German hymnbook (Das Geistliche Saitenspiel), compiled by J. Dreisbach and H. Niebel, was approved, and 1500 copies were ordered to be printed. This was the first hymnbook of the Evangelical Association, and was very favorably received by the membership at large. The "*Articles of Faith and Discipline,*" better arranged and improved by the same brethren, was likewise approved by General Conference. Its publication was however deferred, on account of the proposed union; but in case of its failure, 1500 copies of the Discipline were also forthwith to be printed.—The annual salary of an itinerant, fixed by last conference at $56, besides traveling expenses, was raised to $60. It was likewise resolved, that the Society shall hereafter be called "THE EVANGELICAL ASSOCIATION," instead of "The so-called Albrights."

These were the business transactions of the first General Conference of the Evangelical Association; after which the brethren bowed once more in humble supplication before the throne of grace, and having commended themselves and their cause to the protection of God, conference adjourned.

The Social Conference.

At the appointed time, the delegates of the Social Conference met at *Hen'y Kumler's*, in Canogechigg, Washington co., Maryland, near Hagerstown; but the delegation of the "United Brethren" not being properly authorized, as soon appeared, to act finally, their General Conference having reserved to itself the right of final action on the resolutions of the "Social Conference," contrary to their previous understanding: our delegation was greatly disappointed in their expectations. The delegation of the "United Brethren" consisted of the following individuals: Bishop C. Newcomer, Joseph Hoffman, Jacob Baulus, Abraham Meyer, Christian Berger, and Conrad Roth. —Although this delegation was not constitutional, yet these brethren insisted on a union; and the delegates of the Evangelical Association would readily have agreed to it, if it could have been done in a proper manner for the promotion of the cause of God.—But there were still other impediments in the way: the plan of a regular itinerancy had not yet been generally recognized and approved by the United Brethren. Some of their members and even ministers had opposed it; neither had they a printed discipline, and its introduction was yet doubtful, as they held opposite views on the subject. Even one of their delegates expressed himself more against than for a discipline. "Notwithstanding this," says Mr. Dreisbach in his report on this Social Conference, "they insisted on our uniting with them, in spite of all these difficulties. But we said: No! For we considered it unreasonable under these circumstances, and consequently could not agree to it." Thus ended this Social Conference, without having accomplished its object. "Yet," continues Mr. Dreisbach, "we prayed with and for each other, preached and exhorted alternately, bade each other Godspeed in our operations, and pledged ourselves to treat one another as Christians and children of God."

Mr. Dreisbach, in conclusion on this subject, says: "The failure of this attempt to bring about a union of these two denominations, displeased many members of both parties; yet, I believe, it grieved none so much, as it did father Newcomer and myself."

The good intentions of the projectors of this union, no one will be disposed to call into question: both parties expected to profit by it, and to promote their Master's cause.—As both denominations were yet feeble and small in point of number, and the opposition and persecution by the world and nominal Christians were great, their union would have given them more respectability and influence, and also lessened the burden. But how the brethren could hope, that such an enterprise would succeed, can be accounted for only by the fact that they were conscious of their upright intentions, and had overrated each other's disinterestedness. After the discussion was over, they saw very plainly, that under existing circumstances the contemplated union was impossible. Human nature being so weak, selfish, and corrupt, a union of two independently organized denominations, is, in our view, not only impracticable, but even not desirable, since such a union would scarcely last for any length of time, as the history of the Church of all times so amply testifies.

The *branching out* of organized religious societies into two or more parties is, indeed, no rare occurrence in the Church Universal, and sometimes cannot be prevented,—yea, it may even, in some cases, promote the best interests of the Church.

But to merge two denominations in *one*, and to prevent the rise of new ecclesiastical communions, is indeed no easy task, especially in a country of religious and political liberty.—Now, although such a state of things often brings the different sects of a country into collision, yet almost every one will admit that in countries where the Church is divided into many denominations, the state of religion, as a general thing, is fully as good, if not better, than in those countries where the so-called sects are oppressed and persecuted by the state and the established Churches, and consequently cannot prosper. May we not, then, justly take it for granted, that this division which, on the whole, refers only to non-essentials, impedes the cause of vital and practical Christianity and the spread of the pure Gospel among all the nations of the earth far less than the great torpor, degeneracy, and corruption of the Church in countries where there is more unity in its outward organization? And is not this outward unity less calculated to rouse the corrupt Church out of its lethargy, than the many denominations into which it is divided in other countries? In short, is not competition in spiritual as well as in worldly matters, the *nerve* of life, and thus serves to promote the prosperity and more rapid spread of Christianity? Who would deny this in the face of countless facts? Do not some of the older Churches of this country openly admit, that they have been roused out of their torpid state by the competition of more recent orthodox parties? And if others are not willing to admit this, yet they cannot deny it consistently with truth.

Our modern anti-sectarians are generally the greatest sectarians themselves, who would make of all sects proselytes to their *own sects* or denominations, if they had the power, as appears so plainly from all their writings and efforts. No one has experienced this more than the Evangelical Association. Yet in spite of the many charges, slanders, and wrongs, heaped upon it by its enemies from its very start up to this day, on account of its existence, doctrines, and mode of operations; it has the satisfaction to know, that by the grace of God, it has been contributing its share toward the reformation of the German Churches of this country. None can deny that wherever the Society had an opportunity of exerting its influence on the people, their moral condition was greatly improved. Many parts of the country have, through its influence, been entirely changed, civilized, and moralized, and, to a great extent, led to vital piety.

Erection of the first Printing Establishment, and of the first Church of the Evangelical Association.

During this conference year, the printing establishment and bookbindery, already mentioned, and the first church of the Society, were erected, both on the same lot, at New Berlin, Union county, Pa.: the church at the northern, and the printing establishment at the southern end of the lot. These two buildings are standing yet, an engraving of which is given in front of the title-page. The church is a log-frame, 38 by 34 feet, and one story high. It has been repaired and altered several times, and is now weather-boarded and painted white. Its inside has been entirely remodeled, furnished with a new pulpit, small steeple and a bell. Its first pulpit was, to some extent, like the pulpits of the old Churches in this country, high, rounded in front, and very inconvenient. It was consecrated March 2d, 1817: Mr. Dreisbach delivered the dedicatory sermon from Ps. 27, 4. It was a precious season, and both the ministers and members of the Society felt, as did Jacob when the Lord revealed himself unto him on his journey, namely, that it was none other but the house of God, and the gate of heaven. In this church the truth of God's word has already achieved many a victory, in awakening and converting sinners, and advancing the children of God in their spiritual life. Several considerable revivals took place in it, although the society there never was very numerous.

The printing establishment is a frame building, 26 by 20, and one story and a half high. It was used ten or twelve years for said purpose; but as the Society was yet too young and feeble to sustain such an establishment, it soon failed. The brethren sold the materials, and from that time had their printing and binding done by G. Miller, who, from the very start had been their printer and binder, till the second establishment was erected. As they were deeply involved, and the business proved by no means lucrative, it required a number of years till the debts were paid; and when the second establishment was erected, in 1837, exactly 20 years after the erection of the first, there were scarcely a few hundred dollars in the treasury, without any dividend having ever come to the conferences. The old printing office was afterward used for various purposes; then fixed up, and used for our Sabbath school; and finally sold to the school-directors of the borough for a school-house.

Tenth Conference.

This conference was held from June 2—7, 1817, at New Berlin, in the new church of the Society. H. Niebel was chairman, and John Kleinfelter secretary. Two members, the one an itinerant, the other a local preacher, were expelled from the Society as transgressors; and three more deposed from the ministry, for neglect of duty. D. Thomas, A. Hennig, and P. Schmidt withdrew from the itinerancy and located, the first two on account of bodily infirmities, the last because of family concerns. Five young men were received into the itinerancy on trial; viz., James Barber, Adam Kleinfelter, Samuel Muck, Henry Weiand, and Benjamin Boeshor. J. Bruer and A. Ettinger were ordained as deacons, and John Kleinfelter, Jacob Kleinfelter, and J. Stambach as elders. The conference committee: H. Niebel, John Kleinfelter, and J. Dreisbach, stationed the itinerants, of whom there were 21, as follows:—

Canaan district, J. Dreisbach, presiding elder. Franklin circuit, M. Walter; Berkley circuit, J. Bruer; York circuit, Jacob Kleinfelter and B. Boeshor; Lancaster circuit, A. Ettinger and J. Barber; Schuylkill circuit, J. Frueh and S. Muck; Lake circuit, J. Shilling.

Salem district, H. Niebel, presiding elder. Columbia circuit, L. Zimmerman; Union circuit, B. Ettinger and Fr. Kaltreiter; Centre circuit, M. Dehoff; Bedford circuit, J. Rickel; Somerset circuit, J. Stambach and H. Weiand; Lancaster Ohio circuit, John and A. Kleinfelter; Canton circuit, J. Dehoff.

As the Printing Establishment had been erected, and was publishing several works at that time, conference elected in addition to the aforesaid Book Committee, a number of agents, who were called Book Commission men, to whom the books were sent, and from whom the ministers received them. These agents had to account to the General Book Agent for all the books they received, and the ministers in their turn to these agents for their books. This was the business arrangement of the Society in those days.

The membership of this conference amounted to 1493: consequently an increase during the year of but 92.

Although one of the ministers in Ohio had failed last year, yet this conference sent two other ministers to that field of labor, and called it *Lancaster Ohio circuit.* The two brethren labored with great success, and reported to the next conference 55 members. Canton circuit increased by 10, and the Lake circuit by 17 new members. Some of the old circuits increased considerably; but although about 400 members were received, the increase did not much exceed 200. The Society was, comparatively, still losing many members every year, so that its increase was but slow. From the statistics of the converts and newly received members, it appears that in those days many more were received who proved faithless to the Society, than in later years. The contempt and persecution being in those days greater than more recently, it is probable that every year many of the newly received members left again, being unable without divine grace to suffer persecution. This as well as the expulsion of the offenders, at that time not less than now, was, and is yet, in all probability the cause of the slow increase of the Society.

However, this year was, on the whole, a prosperous one: the preachers were faithful and zealous in the discharge of their duties, and the Lord owned and blessed their labors to the conversion of many souls. The believers grew in grace and in the knowledge of Christ, and the work gained, on the whole, a firmer footing. Its enemies now abandoned most all expectations of an entire failure, and hence did their best to impede its progress.

Brother Dreisbach makes mention of a particularly blessed and victorious campmeeting, which was held immediately after conference, on the land of father John A. Hennig, at the lower end of Penn's Valley. This, it seems, was the first German campmeeting in this and the adjoining Brush Valley, which have since become so famous for campmeetings. "Never," says father Dreisbach, "did I hear the brethren deliver better, more instructive and energetic sermons, than at this campmeeting. Sinners were awakened and converted, and the children of God greatly edified and advanced in the work of grace."

Eleventh Conference.

This conference was also held at New Berlin, from June 1—5, 1818. J. Dreisbach was chairman, and H. Niebel secretary. J. Frueh, A. Ettinger, H. Weiand, and J. Bruer left the itinerancy, the first two on account of bodily infirmities, and the last two because of family circumstances.—*Henry Hassler*, *John Breidenstein*, *Samuel Witt*, and *John Peters*, were received into the itinerancy on trial. J. Frueh, J. Rickel, M. Dehoff, B. Ettinger, Fr. Kaltreiter, J. Shilling, and J. Barber, were ordained as deacons. This conference like the preceding, numbered 21 itinerants. J. Dreisbach and H. Niebel were reelected presiding elders, and their districts changed. The two presiding elders and John Kleinfelter were the conference committee, who stationed the preachers as follows:

Canaan district, H. Niebel, presiding elder. Schuylkill circuit, M. Dehoff and A. Kleinfelter; Lancaster circuit, J. Shilling and B. Boeshor; York circuit, John Kleinfelter and John Breidenstein; Franklin circuit, H. Hassler; Berkley circuit, Jacob Kleinfelter; Lake circuit, F. Kaltreiter.

Salem district, J. Dreisbach, presiding elder. Union circuit, J. Stambach and J. Dehoff; Centre circuit, L. Zimmerman and J. Peters; Bedford circuit, J. Rickel; Somerset circuit, J. Barber and S. Witt; Canton circuit, M. Walter; Lancaster Ohio circuit, B. Ettinger and S. Muck.

Columbia circuit was re-united with Union circuit, and there was, consequently, one circuit less than the year before. At this conference the number of itinerants was 21; that of local preachers 32, and that of the membership 1707: an increase of 214 during the past year.

The salary of the preachers, traveling expenses included, was, on an average, $59,03½, and at the last conference it had been $56,40. Never before, nor for many years afterward, the salary of the ministers was as high as these two years. These sums, however, were not the real salaries of each of the ministers; some received more, others less, according to their circumstances. In the following year the salary was again $44,-59, and then sank every year till it was as low as $28, and not till 1831 it again rose to $50. Under these circumstances, it was no wonder that so many of the preachers, after a trial of several years, saw themselves compelled to return to their handcraft, in order to be able to support themselves and families decently. Many served but *one* year. Those who were single or had means of their own, which they were willing to sacrifice besides their time and strength, could of course stand it longer. The small and inadequate support of the ministry was, unquestionably, one of the main reasons why the number of itinerants increased so slowly, and the work did not spread more rapidly.

This year was, on the whole, not as prosperous as the preceding one. Yet some of the circuits increased considerably, especially Canton circuit in the state of Ohio. Brother Dreisbach visited the two circuits in that state during the year, and assisted in holding two blessed protracted meetings on each of them. —On Lake circuit, in the state of New York, the minister proved faithless, and did more harm than good, which was grievous to the friends and offensive to the world. This kind of preachers caused the Society a great deal of trouble in those days: almost every year some of them, both *itinerant* and *local preachers*, were deposed from the ministry, on account of immoral conduct, and others were expelled. This was evidently owing to the fact, that in those early days of the Society, men were frequently received into the ministry, who lacked the necessary experience and moral firmness. It is pleasing, however, to perceive that under these circumstances, the Discipline of the Church was faithfully executed. As soon as a minister proved himself unworthy of his sacred office, he was called to an account and censured, or deposed from the ministry, or even expelled, according to the nature of his offence.

In order fully to show the anxiety of the brethren of those times, to prevent the spread of every evil, and of every thing that was in their view conformity to the world, and also their position to the Methodist Episcopal Church, with regard to receiving of their members into the Society; we give below some more of the resolutions of the last conference, as being also a part of the history of the denomination. These resolutions are:—

1. "That every preacher be forbidden to wear gloves *during summer*, or to use any of the following articles at any time of the year, viz., silver-plated stirrups and bridle-bits, loaded whips, and large watch-keys."

2. "That it shall be considered a transgression for any one of our ministers to receive members of the Methodist Episcopal Church into our connection, without the consent of the preacher having charge over them; except in cases where they move from the bounds of their Church into those of the Association, or have been regularly dismissed by their Church."

From these resolutions it appears, that the things forbidden therein either threatened to become fashionable, or had become so already; and that the brethren looked upon them as foreboding harm. Although the articles mentioned in the first resolution, may appear trivial to some, and any ecclesiastical enactment with regard to them, as being weak and even fanatical; yet such an enactment, provided it is not abused by excess, can easily be reconciled with the conduct of the apostles themselves. Peter and Paul did not deem it beneath their dignity, to warn the faithful against wearing luxurious apparel, gold and pearls, plaiting the hair, etc. Yet in reference to this, we must be guarded against both extremes, and great care is necessary, lest we judge others harshly, on account of their different dress: a practice which among Christians, and especially among members of the same denomination, is productive of more injury than the evil itself, against which it is directed.

Resolutions against the use of tobacco and strong drink, then so universally in vogue, both among professors of religion and others, we do not find in the protocol of the conferences of those days. This was, in all probability, owing to the fact, that the so-called *moderate use* of these articles, was not then considered an evil. In later times, the Society protested against both these evils, and the ministers and members were unqualifiedly forbidden to use strong drinks as a beverage.

In reference to the last quoted resolution of this conference, we would merely say, that it would have been desirable, if the principle it embodies, had been mutually regarded. Many a temptation, annoyance, and ill feeling would thus have been prevented, and the cause of the Lord much better served.—It is still worthy of being recommended to the consideration of both Churches.

During this conference year, the Society lost another of its first and most able champions by death, viz., the renowned *John Walter*. As Mr. Albright's first assistant in the ministry, he has already been partly portrayed, and he still lives in the memory of many of the older members. He was converted when quite young, through the ministry of Mr. Albright, under whose superintendence, also, a few years later, he went forth as an itinerant, proving himself a faithful servant of the Lord, till in 1813 he was compelled, by bodily infirmities, to quit the field and locate. He served the Church about 12 years as an itinerant, distinguished himself everywhere by his piety and humility, and was universally loved and respected. While preaching he generally put forth the most strenuous exertions, and often preached for hours with the greatest enthusiasm. In consequence of this, he was frequently hoarse, especially toward the close of his ministry; and it is probable, that his health was greatly impaired by his over-exertion in preaching.

J. Walter was born August 21st, 1781, near Quakertown, Bucks co., Pa.; and when he was almost full-grown, Mr. Albright preached in his father's house, at which time he & some others were converted. A few years after his conversion, he became an itinerant preacher, and labored on many circuits, to the conversion of many souls and the edification of the believers. His last circuit was Schuylkill, or rather, as it was then called, *Schuylkill* and *Lancaster circuit*, which the conference of 1812 had assigned him, together with two other brethren, as their field of labor. In this year he commenced to spit blood, but did not leave his field of labor till he began to bleed freely from his throat and became very sick. From this time he was sickly and never able again to serve as an itinerant; yet notwithstanding his weakness, he frequently attended general and camp-meetings, and his preaching was blessed. Sometimes he was confined to his bed, and then again he could walk about, but was too weak to labor much. At the time of the first appearance of his disease, he lived in a place called "the Swamp," in West Cocalico township, Lancaster county, Pa., where he owned a house and a few acres of land. But subsequently he sold this property and bought another house and some acres of land in Hanover township, Lebanon county, near the residence of his parents and brothers and sisters.—He was indigent and unable to support himself, and therefore sometimes received the kind assistance of his neighbors and friends.—Three weeks before his death, he became confined to his bed, but enjoyed great peace and tranquility of mind. He bore his five years' sickness with great patience and submission to the will of God, always enjoying a firm hope of everlasting glory. He said: "*I know that my Redeemer liveth*," and exhorted his wife and relatives, not to mourn for him, assuring them that death would land him in the haven of everlasting bliss. In this full hope of eternal life, he expired December 3rd, 1818, aged 37 years, 3 months, and 6 days. On the 5th, his earthly remains were buried near his house, and

David Thomas preached an affecting funeral sermon from Heb. 13, 17., before a pretty large audience. Thus this faithful servant of the Lord closed his earthly career, and now rests in peace in the enjoyment of the inheritance of the saints in light.

Twelfth Conference.

This year (1819), conference was again held in New Berlin, and continued from the 7th to the 11th of June. J. Dreisbach acted as chairman, and H. Niebel as secretary. B. B. and Fr. K., itinerants, and T. B. a local preacher, were expelled for misdemeanor, and H. Niebel and J. Rickel located on account of bodily infirmities. *David Wolf, Jacob Peters*, and *Jacob Baumgartner* were received on trial into the itinerancy; the former two, however, had traveled for some time the year before; also J. Frueh and J. Frey re-entered the itinerancy. The conference committee consisted of J. Dreisbach, H. Niebel, and John Kleinfelter, who stationed the preachers as follows:—

J. Dreisbach, presiding elder for the two districts. Schuylkill circuit, J. Shilling and J. Baumgartner; Lancaster circuit, L. Zimmerman and S. Muck; York circuit, M. Walter and M. Dehoff; Franklin circuit, J. Frueh; Berkley circuit, B. Ettinger; Lake circuit, John Kleinfelter; Union circuit, H. Hassler and J. Breidenstein; Centre circuit, J. Stambach and Jacob Peters; Bedford circuit, S. Witt; Somerset circuit, A. Kleinfelter and John Peters; Canton circuit, Jacob Kleinfelter and J. Frey; Lancaster Ohio circuit, J. Barber and D. Wolf.

In order to enable the reader to make a correct estimate of the numerical strength of the respective circuits, we here subjoin the statistical report of this conference, as we find it in the old protocol. In Pennsylvania: Union circuit, 239; Centre circuit, 304; Lancaster circuit, 277; York circuit, 194; Somerset circuit, 204; Franklin circuit, partly in Maryland, 93; Schuylkill circuit, 93; Bedford circuit, 43.—In Ohio: Canton circuit, 139; Lancaster Ohio circuit, 90.—In N. York: Lake circuit, 59.—In Virginia: Berkley circuit, 160.—Altogether 1895; increase during the last year, 188.

All the circuits, with the exception of the one in Virginia, were almost exclusively German; although English preaching was expected in some places from the preachers, and it is probable, that the Society would have increased in numerical strength, and spread much more rapidly, had this been done. But the brethren believed that the Lord had called the Evangelical Association for the express purpose of helping to revive Christianity in the German Churches of this country; for which reason English preaching found at that time, and for some time after, but little favor, and was neglected within the Church. The main objection to the introduction of English preaching was as follows: The Methodists preach everywhere in the English language the same doctrine, as is taught and believed in the Evangelical Association, and they labor in the same manner for the conversion of mankind; hence it is quite needless for us to introduce English preaching. Whether this conduct was justifiable, the English being the language of the country, we leave for the present with our readers to judge.

From what has been said, it appears that, although conference lost four of its itinerant members by expulsion and location, yet the circuits were all supplied, but had only one presiding elder, whose health began to fail at this time, for which reason he could not visit the circuits in Ohio and New York at all, and the rest but irregularly. This was very injurious, preventing the spread and increase of the good work, and several of the circuits lost considerably in point of numbers, especially Union, Centre, and Canton; and some scarcely retained their number. This was, consequently, the beginning of a time of sore trials for the Society. Yet it appears, that the brethren did not lose their courage, but prosecuted their labors in humble reliance on help from on High, and in some places their labors were crowned with good success. Somerset circuit had an increase of 50 members, and old Schuylkill circuit began to stir, as if it were already feeling within itself the great reformation which was so near at hand. Thus the brethren were not without hope and comfort, although some dark clouds were spreading over their horizon.

The financial matters of conference, were as yet very deficient, besides being connected with many difficulties. The subsidiary contributions, which have already been mentioned, were hitherto retained in the hands of the trustees, until they were drawn by the ministers with an order from conference. This gave rise to serious difficulties in settling with the ministers at conference, and hence the last session supplied the superintending preachers with written orders on the trustees, to send in such contributions, in case they could not attend conference in person. This custom being continued in future, contributed much to remove the former difficulties, in settling with the ministers.

In this year the Society was again called upon to mourn the loss of one of its most valuable men, viz., *Solomon Miller*, who was removed by death. He was a brother to the well known and sainted George Miller, and they both had experienced religion about the same time. Solomon was one of the first local preachers of the connection, and as such was present at the first conference, and afterward, while living in New Berlin, he took an active part in the work, and since the erection of the Book and Printing Establishment at that place, he served the Society as General Book Agent.

Thirteenth Annual Conference—and the Second General Conference.

In 1820, conference met again at New Berlin, and the session continued from the 5th to the 9th of June. As this was the fourth year since the session of the first General Conference, therefore the Annual and General Conferences were held simultaneously; although but few items of a General Conference nature were transacted, and these had reference chiefly to the book and printing affairs of the Society. Hence no delegates had been chosen, as was the case at the first General Conference; but all members of the Annual Conference, who had a right to vote, had a voice in the proceedings. From this time henceforth, until the introduction of the regular delegate system at the General Conference of 1839, every minister, in the office of elder, had a right to attend General Conference, and was entitled to a vote.

J. Dreisbach and H. Niebel, as in several of the preceding years, were again the officers of the conference.

J. Dreisbach was chosen General Book Agent in place of the deceased S. Miller, and he with H. Niebel and J. Stambach, were constituted the Standing Book Committee for the investigation of such works as were to be published, etc.

J. Stambach located on account of bodily infirmities; and J. Peters, S. Witt, and J. Fry, on account of family circumstances. *Daniel Middlekauf* and *George Lanz*, and the following brethren that had traveled before, viz., J. Erb, J. Rickel, and J. Dehoff, entered the itinerancy. John Erb was elected presiding elder, in place of H. Niebel, for Canaan district. H. Hassler, J. Breidenstein, D. Wolf, and G. Lanz, were ordained as deacons; and M. Walter, J. Barber, M. Dehoff, J. Frueh, B. Ettinger, and J. Shilling, as elders. The conference committee, consisting of J. Dreisbach, J. Erb, and L. Zimmerman, stationed the preachers as follows:—

Canaan district, J. Erb, presiding elder. Schuylkill circuit, B. Ettinger and Jacob Peters; Lancaster circuit, John Kleinfelter and D. Wolf; York circuit, J. Barber and J. Dehoff; Franklin circuit, L. Zimmerman; Berkley circuit, J. Frueh; Lake circuit, S. Muck.

Salem district, J. Dreisbach, presiding elder. Union circuit, A. Kleinfelter and G. Lanz; Centre circuit, J. Shilling and J. Baumgartner; Bedford circuit. J. Rickel; Somerset circuit, M. Walter and M. Dehoff; Canton circuit, H. Hassler and M. Middlekauf; Lancaster Ohio circuit, Jacob Kleinfelter and J. Breidenstein.

At this conference, the Society numbered 22 itinerants, 50 local preachers, and 1992 members; consequently an increase of 97 during the past year. The preachers' salaries, besides traveling expenses, amounted to $36,30 each. All received the same amount, whether married or single.

The year before, as already intimated, the work had begun to *stagnate;* this year it began to *retrograde.* Although the Society, for the last few years, had annually increased somewhat, in point of numbers; yet its boundaries had been enlarged but little if any, having formed no new circuit since the last four years. This year it *decreased* in point of numbers. This indeed was not encouraging; but taking into consideration, that the more experienced preachers had during the last years left the itinerancy, and that their places had been filled with men who had no experience, and some of whom were also deficient in other respects; this result need not surprise us at all, for under such circumstances nothing else could be expected.—Some of the preachers had families to support, and received nothing for them from the societies. Some made the trial to travel *one* or *two* years, but located then "*on account of family circumstances.*" No wonder! Others, it is true, did the same "*on account of bodily infirmities;*" but whether even in some of these cases *family circumstances*, or in other words, *the impossibility of living on the wind*, were not the real causes of their locating, is still a question. Those who had property to sacrifice, or were blessed with wealthy and sympathizing relatives, who were willing to help them along, could stand it longer; but even in their case it would not do for ever. Cares, not for riches, but for their very existence, undermined both their *spiritual* and *natural lives*. Temptation became too powerful, and the consequence was that many of the men and youths, who had come to conference with the firm conviction that God had called them to the ministry, after *one* or *several* years' trial, returned to their secular business in order to be enabled to support their families as the Scriptures require. If they had not done this, they would have been compelled, either to contract debts without any reasonable prospect of paying them, or to suffer want, except God had supported them in a miraculous manner, as he did Elijah and the widow of Sarepta. It is true, the number of preachers was too large in proportion to the number of members, their being less than one hundred members to one preacher; yet if the members had annually contributed but *one dollar* each, toward the support of their ministers, there would either have been no want at all; or if any, it would have been less grievous and injurious. But the contributions toward the support of the ministry, did not, on an average, amount to even more than *fifty cents per member!* Yet in justice to the Society, it must be added, that the duty of liberality was not so well understood in those days among Christians generally, as in modern times, especially not in the Evangelical Association. Nor is it improbable, that it was, to some extent, the fault of the ministers themselves, that they were not better supported; partly because they did not wish to be called *hirelings*, and therefore neglected to explain and enforce the duty of liberality, with that stress as they did the duty of *watching* and *prayer;* and partly also, because the proper means were not adopted to realize this end. That this cause, with perhaps some others, had, to a great extent, discouraged and paralyzed the ministry in those days, must appear evident to all who examine its circumstances and affairs. There was not that enterprising spirit in the ministry, to spread and push forward the work, that had before characterized that body, and characterized it again in subsequent times. In short, for some reason or other, the work had begun to stand still and to retrograde.

Fourteenth Conference.

Conference met this year at New Berlin again, and held its sessions in the church, from June 4—8, 1821. J. Erb was chairman, and Jacob Kleinfelter secretary.

On account of misconduct, two of the itinerants were deposed from the ministry, and two local preachers excommunicated. *Seven* located on account of *bodily infirmities*, viz., J. Dreisbach, J. Rickle, J. Frueh, S. Muck, J. Shilling, L. Zimmerman, and G. Lanz! Mr. Dreisbach, writing on this subject for this history, says: "*Almost one third* of the itinerants of last year," as if he meant to say, that this was really too bad.

It is not our object to cast any reflections upon these esteemed brethren; yet we cannot pass by this circumstance, without calling attention to the fact that the desertion from the ranks of the itinerancy of such a large proportion in one year, besides the number who had located during several of the preceding years, notwithstanding that some of them were really unwell, and may perhaps have been almost unable to travel, cannot easily be reconciled with the high calling and the important work which they had commenced in the name of the Lord. Death by starvation would surely not have been their lot, although they might not have been under any obligations to their salaries for it; and that, under the circumstances in which the work was at that time, they left the itinerancy without any better reason than a slight indisposition, and thus by their withdrawal increased the danger and imperiled the very existence of the Church, we do not know how to justify, however well disposed we might be to do so. With our view of the call to the ministry, we cannot justify a cessation of the discharge of the regular official duties, unless that minister should devote in an equally effective manner, both his time and talents to the cause of God. But in no case of accidental indisposition, where perhaps not even any serious debility has taken place, is such a course justifiable—nor is it less censurable where real want of support has been the cause, if such a relation is continued after these obstacles are removed, whether it be by his own efforts or otherwise. To resign the sacred office, because it is deficient in prospects for a proper provision in old age or for accumulating wealth for children or posterity, would be base and a denial of the faith once delivered to the saints.

This state of things affected conference for several years to an alarming extent. To *locate*, either on account of bodily infirmities or of family circumstances, had, as it were, become the order of the day, at the sessions of conference; and yet the evil, it seems, was not properly understood, nor were effective measures taken to remove it, or to arrest its progress.

While contemplating these unfavorable circumstances of conference, it is, however, refreshing to see that there were always others, though generally inexperienced men, ready to take the places of those who had withdrawn; and that many of the older brethren, who had withdrawn for the assigned reasons from the ministry for some time, afterward re-entered its ranks, and spent many years of usefulness in the service of the Church, some even to this day.

But to return to conference, we notice here that, although nine members had left the itinerancy, partly by location and partly by expulsion, the ranks were entered by six new applicants, viz., *John Seybert, John Vandersal, Frederick Glasser, Jacob Bixler, John Stoll*, and *John Eisenberger*.—J. Baumgartner, J. Vandersal, and Christian Wolf, were ordained as deacons; and J. Dehoff and A. Kleinfelter, as elders. The conference committee, J. Erb, J. Kleinfelter, and J. Dreisbach, stationed the preachers for the following year, as follows:—

Canaan district, J. Erb, presiding elder. Schuylkill circuit, Jacob Kleinfelter and J. Bixler; Lancaster circuit, J. Breidenstein and J. Eisenberger; York circuit, B. Ettinger and J. Vandersal; Franklin circuit, J. Baumgartner; Berkley circuit, J. Dehoff; Lake circuit, M. Walter.

Salem district, John Kleinfelter, presiding elder. Union circuit, J. Seybert and Fr. Glasser; Centre circuit, D. Wolf and M. Dehoff; Somerset and Bedford circuit, J. Barber and D. Middlekauf; Canton circuit, H. Hassler and Jacob Peters; Lancaster Ohio circuit, A. Kleinfelter and J. Stoll.

But the districts were too large, to be properly taken care of by two presiding elders; which seems to be the reason why some of the circuits are given in the protocol of conference by themselves, and not like the rest, as belonging to the districts.

The membership this year amounted to 1974; consequently a decrease of 18 during the past year.—The salary of the preachers amounted to $28,66;—all who had traveled the whole year, received this amount, besides traveling expenses which varied from $2,25 to $25,52. The sum total that was distributed among 21 preachers, amounted to $554,03, thus each member contributing on an average 28½ cents during the year! Speaking of this time and these circumstances, Mr. Dreisbach says: "The wives and children of the itinerants of those days were not supported by conference, for which reason so many preachers were obliged to locate, to enable them, as honest citizens, to support their families decently." This, then, was the *real cause* why so many of the preachers withdrew from the itinerancy; and yet it does not appear in the conference minutes of those days, that any proper measures were taken to present this subject in its proper light to the membership, and thus to check the progress of this alarming evil!—Viewed in the light of truth or reason, this must be regarded as a gross neglect of duty. If this subject had been properly explained to the members, every one's duty with regard to it pointed out, and plainly indicated and enforced, there is little room to doubt, that the salary of the preachers might even then have been increased by one half; which would have been not only more honorable for the Society, but also contributed greatly to its more rapid spread, its increase in numbers and influence. But in this, as in many other things, great indulgence must be exercised, for the want of knowledge and experience in those days: considering that the Evangelical Association could not become in a few years what it is at present, and that even now it has much to learn and in many respects to reform. The ministers were certainly not lacking sincerity, but intelligence and a proper spirit of enterprise. Painful as it is to the writer, to mention this sad state of things in the Church of his choice, to which under God he owes his spiritual experience to a great extent, yet as a *faithful* historian he must record them.

Equally unsatisfactory and discouraging were the affairs of the Printing Establishment in those days. In speaking of this, Mr. Dreisbach says: "In the last year (1819) the New Testament (in German) was printed and bound in our establishment, but the edition was much too large for those times and circumstances; for, in consequence of an extraordinarily large importation of books from Europe, during the previous year, the prices had been much reduced, and having other German books yet on hand, and the number of our patrons being comparatively small, our books found a slow sale, and thus the establishment suffered. Hence we were compelled to curtail our printing operations, and to confine ourselves to the publication of some few tracts."—Speaking of this conference year, he says: "It was resolved by this conference, that the Standing Book Committee shall, if possible, let out the Printing Establishment, if not, the work to be carried on according to the means in hand; or, if deemed best, to be suspended altogether."—This was about the *last* of the *first* Printing Establishment of the Evangelical Association. The committee let it out for three years; afterward it was sold, and G. Miller did all the printing and binding of the books for the Society until, as already stated, the second establishment was erected in 1837. The general Book Committee of the Society was, however, always retained, and the book-trade carried on as circumstances required, and finally all the debts of the Establishment were discharged.

In concluding this subject, we will add what father Dreisbach says of the year 1826, in his closing remarks on it: "Although our book affairs terminated in this manner, yet we were not without consolation, for we were assured that the purest motives had prompted us to engage in the work, viz., the honor and glory of God, and the welfare of our fellow-men; and in the next place, we were glad that we were not insolvent, but had, after all debts were paid, still some means left for carrying on the business in future."

From this it appears, that the time under consideration was one of sore trials for the Society, especially the year just described, and also the following. It seemed as if pitchy clouds were spreading over the whole horizon of the Society, and the powers of darkness triumphing over the newly risen light for a season.—Of particular persecutions in those days there are no records extant, and it appears as if the violent storm had abated, and the enemies of light and truth had dismissed their apprehensions with regard to this small band of believers. But this state of things was not to last long: the temptation was not to exceed the possibility of endurance, but was to terminate in such a manner as "to make a way for escape." A few years after this time,—when the fury of the conflict with the powers of darkness had reached its highest pitch,—signs of better times became perceptible. The light of truth commenced to penetrate at different places, and tokens of the favor and approbation of the Most High became more and more visible, until at last help came out of Zion to this small Israel of God, and glorious revivals occurred in various places, as the sequel of this history will show.

Fifteenth Conference.

In the year 1822, conference held its session again at New Berlin, commencing June 3rd. John Kleinfelter was chairman, and J. Erb secretary. B. Ettinger and M. Walter located on account of bodily infirmities, and M. Dehoff on account of family circumstances.—*Joseph Long, Philip Wagner, John M. Walter, Abr. Becker, Fred. Borauf,* and *Wm. Sholty,* were received into the itinerancy.

The following brethren were ordained as deacons: John Seybert and D. Middlekauf; as elders: D. Wolf, J. Breidenstein, and H. Hassler. The conference committee consisted of J. Erb, John Kleinfelter, and Jacob Kleinfelter, who stationed the preachers as follows:—

Canaan district, J. Erb, presiding elder. Union circuit, J. Barber and J. Eisenberger; Centre circuit, D. Middelkauf and J. Stoll; York circuit, Adam Kleinfelter and W. Sholty; Lancaster circuit, J. Vandersal and J. W. Miller; Schuylkill circuit, J. Breidenstein and F. Borauf; Lake circuit, J. Dehoff.

Salem district, John Kleinfelter, presiding elder. Franklin circuit, Jacob Kleinfelter and A. Becker; Berkley circuit, Fr. Glasser; Somerset circuit, J. Baumgartner and Jos. Long; Canton circuit, J. Seybert and P. Wagner; Lancaster Ohio circuit, D. Wolf and J. Peters; H. Hassler, to seek a new circuit.

The membership at this conference amounted to 1936, consequently a *decrease* of 28 during the past year; the number of itinerants was 23; that of local preachers, 41. The salary of the preachers amounted to $35,61. This was another year of sore trials. Most of the circuits lost in number, some considerably, especially York and Lancaster; only Canton circuit, in the state of Ohio, increased considerably. J. Seybert was the only preacher on this circuit for the greater part of the year, his colleague having been transferred to the Lancaster Ohio circuit, in place of J. Peters who had been taken sick. Toward fall a camp-meeting was held on the land of Mrs. Jolly, a widow. John Kleinfelter was presiding elder and preached powerfully, so that many hearts were moved. Some were anxious to give themselves up to the Lord, but the mob dragging them away, not much good resulted from this camp-meeting.

The decrease in point of numbers during this year, was the greatest, but also the last, which the Society thus far suffered. —On Schuylkill circuit, where the foundation of the glorious reformation, which broke out in the following year, had been laid several years before, the work gradually progressed during this year. Brother J. Breidenstein preached several times to deeply attentive audiences in the court house of Orwigsburg, and some of the hearers were awakened and enlightened, and assented to the word of truth. Some had, as it were, already become secret disciples, but were still afraid to confess it openly before men. Thus many of the place and vicinity were nigh to the kingdom of God, but no conversions occurred during this year. On the whole, the circuit numbered at the close of the year 129 members, 1 less than the year before, although 16 new members had been received during the year.

The numerous withdrawals from the itinerancy for several years, seem not only to have kept the ministry in a state of feebleness with regard to numbers, but to have discouraged them and the membership more or less. A considerable number of the oldest and most experienced members had withdrawn from the itinerancy, among whom were *J. Dreisbach* and *H. Niebel.* After Albright, Miller, and Walter, these two brethren had, for a number of years, been the leaders of the Society: the former especially had excelled as a general of the small evangelical army of the Lord. His services were almost indispensable, and it would have been of uncalculable benefit to the Church to have enjoyed them still longer. But, although Brother Dreisbach had, in his younger years, been an active and robust man, yet his health had during his fourteen years' itinerancy suffered so much by exposures, fatigues, and excessive labors, both by preaching and traveling, that scarcely any one, who is acquainted with his circumstances, will censure him for locating.—For a number of years afterward, he was altogether unable to preach; and if at the urgent request of his brethren, he undertook it, his sufferings would generally be greatly enhanced thereby for some time. Yet it is a gratifying thought to his friends to know, that this aged father, after a location of about 30 years, has re-entered the itinerancy, and still labors with success. Several of the other brethren, who located at this time, at a former or subsequent time attempted to serve as itinerants again—among whom was H. Niebel, as will appear from the sequel—and some of them made themselves very useful. But others never returned to the field.

SIXTH SECTION.

FROM THE YEAR 1823, TO THE FOURTH GENERAL CONFERENCE IN 1830.

Sixteenth Conference.

Our history, which has been for some time of a rather discouraging nature, is now taking a turn for the better. The storm, or rather the calm—for the right kind of wind did not blow—had, during the last year, reached its acme, and the following begins with brighter prospects for the future.

Conference met this year (1823) in Strassburg, York county, Pa., and held its sessions in the new church from June 2—4. This church edifice had shortly before been erected by our friends jointly with the Methodists, and was the second of the Society. J. Erb was chairman, and John Kleinfelter secretary.

As usual, after conference was organized, the character, life, and conduct, as well as the administration of each preacher, was closely examined, while the one, whose case was being examined, withdrew from the presence of the conference during the inquiry. This was the rule then, and has been so ever since: one withdraws after another, and while he is absent, his case is examined—if complaints are brought against him, he is called in and required to make his defence. These examinations generally take up the greater part of the first day of the session: at times, when complaints were brought against individuals, the investigation lasted for two or three days.

At this conference seven preachers again withdrew from the itinerancy, viz., J. Erb, J. Vandersal, D. Wolf, J. W. Miller, and J. Eisenberger, on account of bodily infirmities; and H. Hassler and W. Sholty, on account of family circumstances. Only five were present to take their places, viz., *Conrad Kring*, *Jacob Foy*, *Thomas Buck*, *Benjamin Bixler*, and *John Conrad Reisner*, the last of whom, however, had traveled already the greater part of the previous year. The following were ordained as deacons: J. Stoll, Fr. Glasser, J. Frey, and W. Sholty; as elders: J. Barber and A. Kleinfelter. The conference committee consisted of the presiding elders, J. Erb, and Jacob Kleinfelter, who stationed the preachers as follows:—

Canaan district, John Kleinfelter, presiding elder. Schuylkill circuit, J. Seybert; Lancaster circuit, Jacob Kleinfelter; York circuit, B. Bixler and C. Kring; Franklin and Berkley circuit, J. Long and J. C. Reisner.

Salem district, J. Barber, presiding elder. Union and Centre circuit, J. Breidenstein, J. Foy, and A. Becker; Somerset circuit, J. Dehoff and T. Buck; Lake circuit, Fr. Glasser.

Ohio district, A. Kleinfelter, presiding elder. Lancaster Ohio circuit, J. Stoll and P. Wagner; Canton circuit, J. Baumgartner; Jacob Frey, to seek a new circuit.

The number of itinerants this year was 19, that of local preachers 59, and of members 1854—consequently a decrease of 82 during the past year: the salary of the preachers was $31,66. Speaking of this conference, and the circumstances of the Society, father Dreisbach says: "Although we now had three districts, yet we numbered 4 itinerants and 138 members less than in 1820. This was indeed discouraging, yet we did not despond; but looking upon this state of things as a trial of our faith, we took courage, and in humble reliance on God's promises, that he would make us fruitful, extend our borders and give us many more souls, we continued our labors, and we were not disappointed. Praised be his holy name!"

In this year began the glorious awakening and revival at Orwigsburg and vicinity, in Schuylkill co., Pa.; and as this was one of the greatest and most extensive revivals that ever took place in the connection, we here subjoin a somewhat circumstantial report of it, being fully persuaded, that it will not only be interesting to the majority of our readers, but even edifying and encouraging. The revival continued for years, and extended more and more in various directions, to the salvation of many souls. Not only the neighborhood, but also many other regions experienced its salutary influence. Some of the new converts wrote to their relatives, friends, and acquaintances in distant parts of the country, or visited them, relating what great things the Lord had done for them. Or when they were visited by them, they scattered, by their confessions, exhortations, fervent and believing prayers, as well as by their fear of God and their godly walk, the good seed richly into their hearts. Those of our preachers, who were invited from other circuits to attend the general and camp-meetings here, as well as those in charge of the circuit, during the years of the awakening, were seized by the fire of the unfeigned love to God and man, that was burning there, and extended the work in all directions, so that almost the whole Society was more or less affected by the fruits of this revival. However, we go back and consider first the moral condition of this place and vicinity, prior to this revival, and then its origin, progress, and results.

Schuylkill, Berks, and several of the adjacent counties, were long before noted for their immorality, their adherence to the old ecclesiastical institutions, their abhorrence of all innovations, and their hatred of the sects. In some places, when a new minister was to be called, little or no inquiry was made concerning the candidate's moral or religious character; but the question was, whether he was opposed to such innovations as Sunday-schools, Bible, Tract, and Missionary societies, prayer-meetings, etc. If this was the case, he was the man for these people. Some parts of these countries had by their opposition to education, learning, and improvements of every kind, become a by-word almost throughout the entire country. All kinds of sin and vices reigned in all the so-called Christian congregations; and when now and then a person was found, who saw the corruption to some extent, and ventured to censure it and to disapprove the spurious service of God, he was considered and despised as a fanatic. The few individuals that were better disposed and anxious to save their souls, living among these ungodly crowds of nominal Christians, were suppressed and had but little influence on their rough fellow members. Such was the condition of Orwigsburg and vicinity, prior to the great revival in question.

The main source of our information in this matter is a document of eight sheets, written by father *John Hammer*, of Orwigsburg, embodying partly his own observations, partly extracts from the journals of Bishop Seybert. To this are added the writer's own observations, which he made as an eye and ear witness, when the awakening had been progressing about 18 months, and was perhaps in its best state, before himself had experienced the saving influence of divine grace, but had partly learned its necessity.

Father Hammer's document begins with the aborigines of this region, and their cruelties committed against the white settlers. But by and by, he goes on to state, the region was peopled, and its inhabitants were considered a moral people; although one could not hear a word about true Christianity among them, nor about the necessity of the new birth. The nature and necessity of conversion was something entirely unknown to them, though some seemed to have an instinctive feeling, that, to inherit eternal life, man must experience a change of heart. But these impressions of the Holy Ghost were, as we may well infer, generally opposed and quenched by the fatal consolations of false teachers, who comforted their people with the assurance that the observance of various religious rites and ceremonies, and a correct external deportment was sufficient for salvation. Thus men generally lived in indifference, and walked in darkness.—At one time Mr. Albright came to that part of the country, and preached in a church near Orwigsburg; but as Satan soon found his agents willing to circulate the foulest reports concerning him, he was forbidden to repeat his visit. Thus also a certain Methodist minister preached several times in the house of a church-elder, near Orwigsburg; but when the preacher of the place heard of it, he violently inveighed against it, and the elder did not dare to admit the strange minister into his house again. Other offers of pious preachers were likewise declined, and thus matters went on till the year 1817, when it pleased God to work powerfully, and soon after to awaken a man named *Daniel Focht*, proprietor of an iron-forge near Orwigsburg, who was thoroughly converted the following year, by the instrumentality of the Evangelical preachers A. Kleinfelter and M. Dehoff. This man, soon after his conversion, felt a divine call to preach the Gospel, and clothed with power from on high, he stood up in the name of the Lord as a real boanergis—son of thunder,—preaching with power, denouncing sin and vice of every description unmercifully, and producing a considerable sensation among the people. He insisted on repentance and faith, representing Christ as an impartial and perfect Saviour, and assured all, that if they would come to him in true contrition of heart and in faith, they would be accepted. God blessed his labors, so that in the course of a few years, a nice little band had gathered around him, who were resolved to serve the Lord. But, as might be expected, persecution soon followed; however, instead of allowing this to discourage him, he made still greater efforts, faithfully improving every opportunity to advance the salvation of his fellow-men and to do good. In 1822 he once requested and obtained permission to preach in the court-house of Orwigsburg. God granted him strength and power from on high, so that a considerable portion of his audience were powerfully affected and thoroughly awakened. But on a certain clergyman, who happened to be present, the word made quite a different impression. He was filled with wrath, went his way, and endeavored to circulate slanderous reports about Brother Focht; effected however but little with his machinations.

Shortly after this meeting in the court-house, a camp-meeting was held on the land of Brother Focht, which was richly blessed of God. Some of the citizens of Orwigsburg, among others R. Rickert and Joseph Zoll, were awakened and enlightened, who in their anxiety to save their souls, invited J. Breidenstein, then preacher in charge of Schuylkill circuit, to come and preach in their neighborhood. Mr. Breidenstein accepted the invitation, and preached several times in the court-house of Orwigsburg, to the entire satisfaction of many of his hearers. On one occasion, the court-house was not opened at the proper hour, when he resorted to and preached in the school-house of the place. Many heard him gladly, and some even received and entertained him at their homes. But as usual, the preachers were again his principal enemies, who by slanderous reports endeavored to blast his reputation, and thus to alienate the hearts of the people from him; but again they failed. Next they assailed his doctrine, maintaining that men could not in this life be freed from sin; that even the holiest and most devoted persons were sinners as long as they lived on earth, and could not keep the commandments of God, etc. Mr. Breidenstein refuted these errors, representing Christ as a perfect Saviour, who saves such as submit to him in true repentance and in faith, from all sin, and makes them *free indeed.* God blessed his preaching abundantly to the awakening and enlightening of many souls, who then commenced to search the Scriptures and inquire for the way of salvation.

In 1823, as may be seen from the minutes of conference of that year, Brother Seybert was appointed to Schuylkill circuit, and found the field white for the harvest. The seed of the divine word had not only germinated and struck deep roots—it also began to bear fruit, but had not yet come to a perfect development. Brother Seybert commenced preaching regularly in and about Orwigsburg, in the court-house, in school-houses, private dwellings, and sometimes also in woods under the canopy of heaven. In the month of September he had an appointment in a school-house, 3 miles from Orwigsburg; but when he arrived at the spot, he found the school-house locked. A poor colored man named Wilson, who lived in a tenant's house, opened his door to him, and he preached from the words John 1, 12. 13.: "He came unto his own," etc. The locking of the school-house proved a blessing in this case, as during this sermon God opened the hearts of many, as he once did the heart of Lydia by the preaching of Paul, and henceforth some of them found no more rest, till by penitence and faith, they had obtained the forgiveness of their sins. The meetings continued to increase in earnestness and importance, and at this time Bro. Seybert made the acquaintance of Christopher Wagner, who kept a hotel two miles below Orwigsburg, and was, with his family, to some extent awakened and inquiring for the way of salvation. On the 30th of November Mr. Seybert preached for the first time in his house, from Acts 3, 22. 23. Speaking of this meeting, Brother Seybert says: "An uncommon weeping and wailing broke out here, and awakened sinners were heard to exclaim, '*lost! lost!*'" On the next day he held a prayer-meeting with the anxious inquirers, and the following Sunday the slumbering elements of conviction broke forth during a meeting in the house of said Wilson, where Brother D. Focht preached, having been requested by Brother Seybert by letter, as the latter was obliged to meet other appointments on that day. Accordingly, he came with several other friends and preached; and they continued laboring with the penitents till evening, when seven of them were permitted to taste God's pardoning grace. This, then, was the first complete victory in this reformation, and part of Wagner's family, and some persons from Orwigsburg, were the first fruits of it. The pardoned souls seem to have been thoroughly filled with the divine life and with heavenly joy, so that a mighty shouting and praising of God took place among them. In noticing this occurrence, our informant says: "Among them there was a woman of Orwigsburg, who wrestled and prayed so violently in her anguish of soul, and was then so richly filled with the love of God, that her husband, B. N., who witnessed the scene, was so much affected and moved, that he too made up his mind to take hold of the work, and to surrender himself to God. The next day he wrestled in an upper chamber of his house 3 or 4 hours with God, when light burst upon his soul, and he was so much filled with divine love, that he with his wife greatly rejoiced in God. Soon afterward we held meetings in his house." It is also mentioned, that about the same time an extremely affecting and melting meeting took place in R. Rickert's house, one of the two men who had invited Breidenstein to come and preach in their vicinity, and that the weeping of the whole congregation at this meeting was such that it might have been taken for that of one man.

During the winter of 1824, there was a great stir among the people, and a number of precious souls were awakened and converted to the Lord. Brother Seybert writes, that on the 17th and 18th of January, S. Rickert, Joseph M., and Jacob Saylor were converted, all of whom afterward became preachers of the Gospel; subsequently many more promising men and youths were converted, who became useful preachers of the Gospel, some of whom are still in the itinerancy, while others have entered into the joy of their Master. This region furnished, on the whole, a comparatively large number of candidates for the ministry, most of whom became very useful. The first class consisting of 25 members, was formed here by Brother Seybert on the 23rd of January, 1824. B. Dreher, jr., was appointed leader, and B. Neff assistant. Toward the close of this conference year in June, the number of converts amounted to 40, and many more were in a state of anxious inquiry, who, with many others, were happily converted at a later period. But unfortunately the first classleader, soon after his appointment, suffered himself to be frightened and overcome by the enemy, so that W. Wagner was elected in his stead. But when the work took such a glorious turn, Satan and his followers rose to oppose it by slanders, lies, and calumnies: the consequence was, that in many cases parents were set against their children, and children against their parents, husbands against their wives, and wives against their husbands, so that the words of our Saviour, "Henceforth five in one house will be at variance, two will be against three, and three againt two," etc., were literally fulfilled. Yet, where the children of God remained faithful, the opponents were generally gained over to the truth.

Soon after this, Hammer's, Reifshneider's, and some more influential families, were awakened and converted; and as the heads of several of them were officers in the respective Churches of the place, and enjoyed a high reputation, it caused a great deal of excitement. This raised the indignation of the selfish clergymen of these Churches to the highest degree; but the work being from God, they were unable to arrest its progress. For several years the work continued to extend and deepen in its influence, because these salutary effects upon the morality of Orwigsburg and vicinity could not be mistaken; and that a great moral reformation had taken place, could not be denied. Not only such as submitted to the influences of the Spirit, reformed their lives, but even those who refused, were compelled to change their external conduct for the better, to sustain their reputation, as those who obstinately persisted in their sins and vices, were respected no longer.—In several families the work of grace commenced with a child ten or twelve years of age, and continued until all the members of the family had become willing subjects of divine grace. Not unfrequently it occurred that one or more members of a godless family were arrested and converted, who would then attest by their pious and godly lives, that their conversion was a genuine change of heart, and not a mere outward change of life. In short, people of every age and every rank espoused the cause of God; from the child of ten years to the gray-haired sire, some of whom had belonged to the most honorable, and others to the most degraded classes of society.

In the 2nd year of the revival, J. C. Reisner and J. W. Miller were the regular ministers of the circuit, during which time the work was in its best state and the number of converts was doubled, so that at the end of the year two new classes were formed, of which father J. Hammer and Fr. Hoffman were appointed leaders. During this year the first camp-meeting was held in that neighborhood, on the land of Christopher Wagner, which was richly blessed with God's grace and the conversion of many precious souls. This meeting is represented as having been so eminently blessed, that its equal is not often found.

Toward the close of this conference year, in the month of May, the writer, with his sainted mother and some other relatives, made a visit of several weeks to this part of the country, where he was an eye and ear witness of the great work of grace. The work itself was something entirely new to him, having never before enjoyed the privilege of witnessing anything similar. His mother was a member of said Wagner's family, who were at this time burning with the ardor of their first love, and naturally felt a deep interest in the salvation of their children and relatives, sparing no efforts to gain them over to the cause of God and his kingdom. Nearly every evening there was preaching or prayer-meeting somewhere in the neighborhood, and two or three times divine service on Sunday, which opportunities were diligently improved during our stay. The exercises were, on the whole, very lively and powerful: a great deal of shouting, leaping, and praising of God; and in all probability matters were sometimes carried too far, as is generally the case at great revivals. Yet the writer did not then as much as suspect any thing of the kind; and although he understood not the nature of the work, yet he deemed everything holy and pure.—Such were the exercises of the new converts during preaching and prayer-meetings generally, with the exception of leaping, which was confined to comparatively few, and by-and-by it disappeared altogether. The writer would also remark here, that this visit of his mother and himself, was the occasion of introducing the work into his home in Union county, where it spread considerably, and has continued to flourish to this day.

In the third year of the revival, C. Kring and J. Erly were the preachers of the circuit, and the work continued and spread farther and wider in various directions.

In 1826, the first church of Orwigsburg was built, which was the third of the Association. From this time, almost every successive year some souls were converted to God, though cases of backsliding and other adversities did also frequently occur. Yet Orwigsburg and vicinity have ever since been one of the principal points of the connection, and many who had been awakened and converted there, removed to other places, especially the states of Ohio and Illinois, where not a few of them have been an honor to the Society to this day.

A considerable part of the first fruits of the work have long since been set free from all struggle, and in the triumphs of faith have entered into the joy of their Master. Some of them were already advanced in years, when they entered into the vineyard of their Lord, and hence their time of labor was short; but others were called to their home in the prime of life. May those, who are still engaged in the noble struggle, imitate them in their good works!

During this year some doors and hearts were likewise opened to the truth in some other parts of Schuylkill circuit, especially in the tps. of Bern and Heidelberg, Berks co., beginning in the families of Klein, Tobias, Loos, Deppen, and others. Some of the other circuits also increased somewhat in point of numbers; but on most of them they continued decreasing, so that at the close of the year, the increase in all was but small.

Seventeenth Conference.

In 1824, conference held its session again in Strassburg, York county, Pa., from the 7th to the 10th of June. John Kleinfelter was chairman, and Jacob Kleinfelter secretary. J. Breidenstein located on account of bodily infirmities, and J. Frey and J. Baumgartner on account of family circumstances, and J. Kleinfelter in part, visiting but a few circuits during a portion of the year, as presiding elder. Thus the circuits of York, Franklin, and Berkley, had no presiding elder this year. *Henry Wissler* and *Daniel Manwiller* were received into the itinerancy, and J. Bixler and Fr. Borauf were received a second time, having been in the itinerancy before. J. Long, A. Becker, P. Wagner, and J. C. Reisner, were ordained as deacons, and J. Seybert as elder. The conference committee consisted of John and A. Kleinfelter, and J. Barber, who stationed the preachers as follows:—

Canaan district, John Kleinfelter, presiding elder. Schuylkill circuit, J. C. Reisner and J. W. Miller; Lancaster circuit, W. Sholty and A. Becker.

Salem district, J. Barber, presiding elder. Union and Centre circuit, P. Wagner, C. Kring, and T. Buck; Somerset circuit, J. Stoll and Fr. Borauf; Lake circuit, Fr. Glasser.

The following circuits had no presiding elder during the year, but were supplied with preachers as follows:—

York circuit, J. Seybert and J. Bixler; Franklin and Berkley circuit, Jacob Kleinfelter, B. Bixler, and H. Wissler.

Ohio district, A. Kleinfelter, presiding elder. Canton circuit, J. Foy; Mansfield circuit, J. Dehoff; Lancaster Ohio circuit, J. Long and D. Manwiller.

The young preacher Jacob Peter had died during the past year; but as the writer knows nothing of his character, qualification and manner of operations, he must pass him by, merely mentioning his decease.

The preachers' salary for this year, besides traveling expenses, was $35,88.

The membership amounted to 1878, consequently an increase of only 24. Yet a change for the better had taken place, and during the year considerable revivals had occurred on Lancaster, York, and Centre circuits, besides Schuylkill. In the southern part of Berks county, between Womelsdorf and Reading, where the work was still new, it continued to progress gradually, and toward the close of this conference year the memorable camp-meeting,—known as *Ernst's camp-meeting*—was held in that vicinity, which was broken up in a terrible manner, by a godless mob, headed by their preacher. Bishop Seybert, who was present, furnishes a report of this tragical event, which is now before the writer, and after a few abbreviations, is subjoined here almost literally. The report is as follows: "At last Ernst came to be in earnest, so that he consented to have a camp-meeting on his land, which began on Monday, May 29th. On Wednesday and Thursday, the last of May and first of June, there was a great stir, awakenings and conversions taking place on the camp-ground. Amongst others a poor cripple, who had but one arm, was converted during the meeting, and confessed that he had been hired by the mob to stone us. But when he became convinced of his malice and sinfulness, through the powerful preaching of the word of God, the stones in his pockets became too heavy for him, and pulled him, as it were, down on his knees for prayer. The preaching at this meeting was eminently powerful and full of unction, and at length the grace of God became so overwhelming, that sinners fell fainting to the ground. These effects were so entirely new, and so little understood by the ignorant rabble, that some of them were raised to such a pitch of malicious frenzy, that, like famished beasts of prey, they fell upon those under conviction, and dragged them from the camp-ground to a house close by, where they had an ungodly physician at hand, in order to cure and restore their sin-sick hearts, by bleeding, and sprinkling water over their faces, and to heal wounds that were inflicted by the sword of the Spirit. There was also an ungodly Reformed clergyman present, by the name of B. Boyer, who endeavored to quiet and console the awakened souls in their sins. Around this pastor, an impudent, impious mob of his followers had gathered, roaming over the woods, while armed with clubs and other murderous weapons. These club-men the worthy pastor called his sheep, saying that he had come to the meeting for the purpose of watching them. But he also several times threatened to whistle for his *hounds*, to chase the foxes to their holes. Thus his Church-members were, by his own confession, both his sheep and his hounds at the same time.—On Thursday afternoon and evening, this mob became very numerous. The dismal and terrible night had set in, and the sons of Belial, being well instructed by their leader in reference to the attack, some armed with clubs, and others in the rear with dung-forks, as I afterward learned, were now ready to commence their work of destruction. At this time their leader was in the rear, fully assured that his commands would be faithfully executed without his presence.

"Brother D. Manwiller commenced preaching from Ps. 7, 12–14; but before he came to the conclusion, the mob of clubmen ushered in through the passage between the preachers' stand and the tents, uttering dreadful oaths and threats, and tore off the boards from the lower part of the stand, after which a terrible shower of stones and clubs followed, so that no one's life was safe any longer. Divine service was at once broken up, and the devil and his vassals took possession of the camp-ground. The fire-places for illuminating the ground, were torn down, and it was altogether impossible to keep order. Entreaties and remonstrances seemed but to increase their fury. The mob continued to rave and roar all night, more hideously than wild beasts. Sometimes they would bellow like cows and calves; then crow like roosters; then curse and swear, damning their souls to hell, while uttering the most terrible imprecations!—Reader! these were mostly members of one or the other of the Protestant Churches, and gloried in the genuine faith!—O how we longed for the light of the day, during that night! We would often say, as did the prophet of old: 'Watchman, what of the night? watchman, what of the night?' But there were also some decent persons on the ground, and these gathered around us and about the tents. On Friday morning, part of the mob left the ground, when the tumult subsided.—Brother *Ernst*, on whose land the meeting was held, was that night mercilessly beaten with a club, and Brother D. Loos had one thrown with such force against his breast, that for some time he was unable to breathe; and others were severely stoned. Yet God had mercifully protected us, so that no lives were lost, which, under those circumstances, was almost a miracle.—Some of the friends advised to close the meeting at once; while others preferred to have another sermon preached—the latter course was adopted. I preached, accordingly, from Ps. 43, 3., and Brother Breidenstein added a powerful exhortation: God's grace worked mightily, and the enemies raved violently. Toward noon we broke up—one day sooner than we had intended."

Thus, at this camp-meeting, a violent storm of persecution had arisen against the Society.—Shortly after this, on a Sunday, some of the friends visited a widow, who was deeply concerned for the salvation of her soul, in order to pray with her. Pastor Boyer preached on that day not far off, and at the close of the sermon, news reached the congregation that the *fanatics* were at widow Kaufman's, for that was her name. Immediately a crowd, some on horseback, others on foot, hastened to her house, armed with clubs and their shirt sleeves rolled up, in order to drive away the *fanatics*. But when this infuriated mob reached the house, most of the friends had left already, and the rest escaped this time without any injury. At another time, during a meeting at Brother D. Loos', the windows of the first and second stories were broken by the mob. And some time after, a great disturbance took place during a meeting at Jacob Klein's, where about 200 club-men—although baptized and nominal Christians—had congregated.

When it had come to this, that the members of the Society could hold their meetings only at the peril of their lives, they claimed the protection of the law: they prosecuted some of the ring-leaders of the persecutors, together with their preacher. And when these saw what the consequences were likely to be, they agreed to compromise the matter without a judicial decision, pledging themselves not to disturb our religious meetings hereafter. But the pastor alone was not satisfied with this, and afterward brought a suit against our friends, claiming damages for his character, which, however, was discovered before the court in its true light. He lost the suit and had to pay the costs, which almost ruined him. In consequence of this, he lost his influence, fell out with his parishioners, was dismissed by them, and thereby reduced to abject poverty. —But the reader will be astonished to learn, that about twenty years afterward, the writer saw this same parson, Boyer, at a camp-meeting in Dry Valley, Union county, Pa., with other poor penitents, prostrate on his knees around the altar, crying to God for mercy and pardon. But it appeared as if he lacked the proper contrition of heart, and whether he ever became a partaker of divine grace, the writer does not know, but heartily wishes it to be so.

But after all, this persecution served to promote the best interests of the believers in those parts of the country. It stirred them up to greater activity and zeal in the service of their Master, and the work increased from time to time, and has prospered to this day. The history of this persecution, and what happened at a later period in Berks and some adjacent counties, will fully confirm what has been said in this history, of the moral condition of these counties, and the character of some of the preachers of those times.

Eighteenth Conference.

This conference held its sessions at New Berlin, and commenced June 7th, 1825. Adam Kleinfelter was chairman, and J. Seybert secretary. Wm. Sholty was expelled from the Society, and S. M. deposed from the ministry. J. Stoll and J. Bixler located on account of bodily infirmities, and John Kleinfelter, Jacob Kleinfelter, B. Bixler, and Fr. Glasser, on account of family circumstances. *Joseph M. Saylor*, *Jacob Erly*, *John Hamilton*, *George Reich*, *George Schneider*, and *Benjamin Becker, M. D.*, were received into the itinerancy; C. Kring, J. W. Miller, J. Foy, and T. Buck, were ordained as deacons, and J. Stoll was ordained as elder. The preachers were stationed by the presiding elders as follows:—

Canaan district, J. Seybert, presiding elder. Schuylkill circuit, C. Kring and J. Erly; Lancaster circuit, T. Buck and Dr. B. Becker; York circuit, J. C. Reisner and J. M. Saylor; Franklin and Berkley circuit, P. Wagner and Fr. Borauf.

Salem district, J. Barber, presiding elder. Union circuit, J.

W. Miller and G. Reich; Centre circuit, J. Foy and D. Manwiller; Somerset circuit, A. Becker and J. Hamilton; Lake circuit, to be attended by the local preachers, Chr. Wolf and Fr. Glasser.

Ohio district, A. Kleinfelter, presiding elder; Lancaster circuit, J. Long and G. Schneider; Mansfield circuit, J. Dehoff; Canton circuit, H. Wissler.

At this conference the membership amounted to 2039, consequently an increase over the preceding year of 161. It is true, a great many more members had been received during the year; but owing to the continual and comparatively great losses the Society sustained, the number thus remained small.

For several years the annual small salary of the ministers had been about the same, and yet no special efforts were made to increase it. It appears as if the brethren considered it neither prudent nor expedient, to say much on this subject in public, nor to explain and enforce the duty of liberality to the members in private; although the many locations that occurred every year, plainly demonstrated to them and to every one the insufficiency of their support. How was it possible, that a man, on whom devolved the support of a family, could, for any length of time, live on a salary of from $35 to $40 annually, unless he had other means of support? This, however, was not frequently the case, nor is it so to-day. Although the Gospel expressly says, that a laborer is worthy of his hire, and that he who preaches the Gospel, shall also live by it; yet these men were compelled to earn their living *in some other way*. It should be remarked, however, that during those years, when the preachers' salary had sunk to the freezing point, the monetary affairs of the country were in a very unsettled condition, and that provisions were then very cheap, so that *one* dollar would go as far as *two* or *three* had done before or did again afterward. Hence the support was, after all, as good in those days as it was afterward; with this difference, that preachers who had traveled five years or more, did subsequently draw twice the amount, that single itinerants received for their support.

In this year the work spread chiefly on the circuits of Schuylkill, Lancaster, York, and Somerset. The other circuits were either increasing but slowly, or else decreasing, which was particularly the case with the three western circuits of Ohio. The former impediments to the spread of the work, had not yet been fully removed on all the circuits; yet, generally, matters took a better turn by and by, though some of the circuits failed almost entirely, and recovered only in later years.

Conference resolved, that an edition of 1000 copies of the smaller Hymn Book of the Society, called "Die Geistliche Viole," with an appendix of eight hymns, shall be published.

Nineteenth Conference, and the third General Conference.

In the year 1826, the Annual and the General Conference were held the second time, simultaneously, at New Berlin, beginning June 5th. The last General Conference had taken place in 1820, there was consequently an interval of six years between the two conferences. The first two had been four years apart, from which it appears that there was no fixed time yet for holding the General Conference, but that it was held as circumstances required. John Seybert acted as chairman, and J. C. Reisner as secretary. The doings of General Conference were chiefly as follows:—

1. "Resolved, That hereafter an Annual Conference of local preachers be held on every presiding elder district, in order to inquire into the conduct and doctrine of every local preacher." These conferences were always to be held shortly before the Annual Conference, and an exact report of their minutes was to be laid before the latter body. But it appears, that these conferences were never generally introduced, as it was scarcely practical to bring all the local preachers of a presiding elder district together annually. Afterward these conferences were ordered to be held on every circuit, and this has been the practice to this day.

2. The formation of the second Annual Conference of the itinerancy out of the Ohio presiding elder district. The great distance of that district from the places where the Annual Con-

ference usually met, and the inconvenience to its preachers, to take so long and expensive a journey, in order to attend the sessions, were some of the principal reasons for forming a new conference there. This conference was then called the "*Western Conference*," and the former the "*Eastern*," which names they retained until the formation of the third conference. As the new conference numbered at first but few itinerants, which the "Eastern Conference" was still required partly to furnish, it remained for years in a state of dependency on the latter body, transmitting through a delegate a copy of its annual minutes for revision, at the same time drawing an amount of funds from the older conference, which enabled it to place its members on an equal financial basis with the members of the old conference. Not until 1836, the dependency of the "Western Conference" was discontinued, with regard to its minutes, and not before 1843, with regard to its funds. In all other reports, the Western Conference had all the rights and privileges of an annual conference, conformably to the Discipline in those days. It kept a record of its minutes, although the Eastern Conference recorded them also. During the period of its dependency, the new conference always held its annual session one month prior to that of the parent body, so that its minutes might be prepared and laid before that body in due time.

3. A resolution that on every circuit, wherever practicable, a parsonage be built or bought, by voluntary contributions.—This had been recommended once or twice before, but the former resolutions, as well as the present, remained unheeded. Of late years this recommendation has been repeated and carried out to some extent, but up to this day much remains to be done in this matter.—In consequence of the want of proper residences for itinerants having families, they were often compelled to hire houses that were either too *large* or too *small*; sometimes only a few rooms, and at times they could not get even these. This was the principal reason why some of the preachers, who were able to do so, purchased residences, thus hoping to escape the difficulty in question; but instead of

succeeding, they frequently only increased their inconvenience, as they could not always receive their appointments near their respective homes, so that they were subjected to a great loss of time by going to and coming from their fields of labor. Moreover, the work itself was made to suffer by this cause, as preachers with families, in order to favor them, were often not sent to places where their talents were more particularly required. On several districts, some were changed for years in succession on a few circuits, which were close by their homes, till in some cases they had been three, four times, and even oftener, on the same circuit,—an arrangement with which the members were not always pleased.

The business of the Annual Conference was at this meeting transacted according to the usual routine.

Jacob Foy located on account of bodily infirmities; J. Dehoff, Fr. Borauf, and Dr. B. Becker, on account of family circumstances.—*Francis Hoffman* and *Samuel Tobias* were received on trial. The following brethren were ordained as deacons: H. Wissler, D. Manwiller, and M. Hassler; as elders: P. Wagner, J. C. Reisner, and J. Long. The conference committee consisted of J. Seybert, J. Barber, and J. Long, who stationed the preachers as follows:—

Canaan district, J. Seybert, presiding elder. Schuylkill circuit, T. Buck and G. Schneider; Lancaster circuit, J. W. Miller; York circuit, A. Becker and J. Bruer; Franklin and Berkley circuit, D. Manwiller and J. Hamilton.

Salem district, J. Barber, presiding elder. Union circuit, J. C. Reisner; Centre circuit, P. Wagner and S. Tobias; Somerset circuit, H. Wissler, G. Reich, and J. Frey; Lake circuit, J. Erly.

Ohio district, A. Kleinfelter, presiding elder. Lancaster circuit, C. Kring and J. M. Saylor; Mansfield and Canton circuit, J. Long and F. Hoffman.

The membership this year amounted to 2207; the increase was consequently 168. The preachers' salary was $38,46.

This also had been a highly blessed year, and most of the circuits had increased considerably, with the exception of Centre,

Somerset, and Lake circuits, and some of those in Ohio. In the preceding conference year, Bishop Seybert, at that time presiding elder, explored Mahantango and Leikens Valley, and sought out the first preaching places there; and in this year he secured some in Deep Creek Valley also, where he formed a class shortly afterward. These and the surrounding valleys were, at that time, generally in a very dark and deplorable moral condition; and the work of grace met at first with great opposition, but extending more and more, it finally effected a general reformation among the inhabitants.—Since that time many a flourishing class has been formed in these valleys, and many a new church erected. Darkness has since, to a great extent, given way, and the morality of the people is raised to a higher standard.

During this year, old Union circuit also revived in some places and extended its boundaries somewhat, after it had, as it were, been checked or even gone back for some years. In the preceding conference year, the Brethren J. W. Miller and G. Reich had already found some openings in Hartley and West Buffalo townships, which had resulted from the glorious revival in Orwigsburg some years before, and their preaching made deep impressions on many, some of whom were awakened and enlightened. But in this year they were brought to a decision by the powerful preaching of J. C. Reisner, and quite a number were brought into the liberty of the children of God, and a considerable class was formed. Amongst the families there, who first received the preachers, and joined the Evangelical Association, were those of A. and G. Orwig, and that of J. Brickley, sen. and jr., and some others soon after. The writer, too, was among the first of the redeemed of the Lord in that neighborhood.—Afterward the work of grace extended still farther, and furnished three itinerant and two local preachers, besides a considerable number of useful laymen, many of whom have since died triumphantly in the Lord. Also in some other parts of the circuit, some awakenings took place.

During this year the first class of the Society at Lebanon, Pa., was formed by J. Seybert.—This town and vicinity had formerly been very corrupt and ungodly. All descriptions of sins and vices were the order of the day, with few exceptions, both among professors and non-professors of religion; the teachers as well as members of the Churches were worldly-minded, living in a state of impenitency, after the fashion of this world. Two years previous to the formation of the first class there, a considerable revival had taken place, of which Father Felix Licht, a Mennonite preacher, Father P. Breidenstein, and his son John, were the principal instruments. Many were roused out of their lethargy, and began to inquire earnestly for the way of salvation. For some years they kept aloof from all Christian denominations, having been warned most emphatically against uniting with any of them by certain preachers, who were known as *Liberty men, Universals*, etc.

But finally some of them discovered, that without an organization, and the introduction of a good Church Discipline, the work could not possibly flourish for any considerable length of time, and therefore expressed a desire to unite with one of the Christian denominations. But others protesting violently against it, no one ventured to take the initiatory step, till J. Seybert made the attempt and formed a class of 12 members, who elected H. Fisher as their leader. The members of this class were: H. Fisher, George Reinoehl and wife, Henry Bauman and wife, John Marland and wife, David Fisher, Elias Stoever, Jacob Borkert, Barbara Riegel, and Frœnica Licht.—Subsequently this class increased from time to time, gaining a firmer footing and has existed to this day. Among the first there, who received the Evangelical preachers, were A. Licht, sen., and George Reinoehl. The former was a Mennonite, a man of considerable property and influence; and, though he never united with the Society, yet he was its friend, and the preachers always found a pleasant home under his roof. He lived at a small distance from town: George Reinoehl lived in town. In 1830, the first church of the Society there was built, and consecrated on the 26th of September. H. Niebel preached the dedicatory sermon from Ps. 93, 5., speaking 2½ hours with great perspicuity and effect. From this time the work progressed rapidly, and extended more and more.

J. Vandersal, formerly an itinerant, and John Schneider, a local preacher, finished their earthly career in the Lord, during this year. Both had been pious and useful men in the Church.

The Year 1827.

In this year, for the first time two annual conferences were held in the connection, the "*Eastern*" and the "*Western*," and this was annually continued till the third conference was formed.

The Western Conference began its first session May 5, 1827, in the house of *H. Rauch*, Wayne co., Ohio. A. Kleinfelter was chairman, and J. Long secretary. Six itinerant and seven local preachers, who had traveled before, were present. On the whole, the new conference already numbered ten elders, four deacons, and ten probationers, together twenty-four, most of whom, however, had emigrated from Pennsylvania. The membership amounted to 523.—C. Kring was ordained as elder, and J. M. Saylor as deacon. As conference elected no presiding elder for this year, it resolved, that J. Long should attend the general meetings during fall, and A. Kleinfelter during spring, instead of presiding elders.—J. M. Saylor and F. Hoffman went to the Eastern Conference, brought a copy of the minutes of the Western Conference, and remained hereafter in connection with the former conference.

(As the Eastern Conference, for yet a number of years, continued to send some of its preachers to the Western, almost every year, and as some of these returned again, it will be best to give the appointments of the preachers always together.)

This year the Eastern Conference held its annual session at Orwigsburg, Schuylkill co., Pa., in the new church, erected during the year, beginning June 4. J. Barber was president, and J. C. Reisner secretary. M. H. was deposed from his office for misconduct, and B. Becker located on account of bodily infirmities.

The following were received on trial: *George Mattinger*, *George Enders*, and *Wm. Stoll*; the following were ordained as deacons: G. Reich, J. Hamilton, and D. Focht; as elders:

T. Buck and J. W. Miller. P. Wagner was chosen presiding elder. The presiding elders were the conference committee, who stationed the preachers as follows:—

Canaan district, J. Seybert, presiding elder. Schuylkill circuit, J. C. Reisner and H. Wissler; Lancaster circuit, J. M. Saylor and W. Stoll; York circuit, T. Buck and J. Bruer; Franklin and Berkley circuit, J. Hamilton and F. Hoffman.

Salem district, P. Wagner, presiding elder. Union circuit, B. Ettinger and G. Mattinger; Centre circuit, J. Barber and G. Schneider; Somerset circuit, D. Manwiller, S. Tobias and J. Allen; Lake circuit, G. Reich.

Western Conference district.—This conference, consisting of *one* presiding elder district, had no officer of this kind during that year. The circuits were assigned the preachers, as follows: Canton circuit, J. Long: Wooster circuit, C. Kring; Sandusky circuit, A. Kleinfelter; Lancaster circuit, J. M. Miller and G. Enders. The last two were from the Eastern Conference.

The membership amounted to 2567, the increase consequently to 360. This was the greatest increase of any year up to this time. The salary of an itinerant amounted to $43,44. During this conference year, however, matters went, on the whole, very unpromisingly. The new Western Conference numbered at the close of the year 22 members less than it had at the beginning; and in the Eastern Conference also, some circuits lost in point of numbers, others with difficulty retained their own, and only the circuits of Schuylkill, Lancaster, Somerset, and especially Centre, made considerable progress.—On this last circuit a very blessed and victorious camp-meeting was held during the year, on the land of J. A. Hennig, at the eastern end of Penn's Valley, where a considerable number of persons were awakened and converted, especially in that neighborhood. Likewise in George's Valley, and in some other parts of the circuit, awakenings and conversions took place. The increase on that circuit during the year, was between 60 and 70; although the number of new converts was considerably greater. On Schuylkill circuit also, especially at Orwigsburg, the work continued to prosper.

While writing this history, I cannot but mention a few of my observations with regard to revivals.—It has been observed from the minutes of the conferences, that some of the preachers, who were for many years in the itinerancy, never reported a large *increase*, but often a *decrease* of membership, on their respective fields of labor, at the Annual Conferences. Among that number were frequently such as were considered *great preachers*, although the majority of them, as far as the writer is able to judge, were not entitled to that name. Others again had considerable revivals almost every year on their fields of labor, extended them by obtaining new preaching places and members; and those were often of the *middle class* of preachers, as far as talents and eloquence were concerned.—Judging from these facts, it would seem that, in order to prosecute the work of God successfully, and to be instrumental in awakening and converting many souls, more depends on God's grace and the unction of the Holy Ghost, and the earnestness, faith, and activity of the preacher, than on his natural gifts and talents. Especially much seems to depend on a preacher's making it his *aim* and *object*, to exert every power, to win as many souls as possible for the kingdom of God, and to preach the Gospel in every place; or in other words, if he knows and feels the importance and responsibility of his calling and the worth of immortal souls, so as to deny this perishable world and himself, and consecrates himself exclusively to God and his work, devoting all his time and strength to the discharge of his duties. In this way one sometimes accomplishes more in *one* year, than others all their lives long.—Especially has this proved true with regard to the Evangelical preachers, from the beginning of the Society, and appears more evident every year.—Those who had the unction from on High, were industrious and active, always labored with good success, and were permitted to see the glorious results of their labors; while the powerless, indolent, and indifferent, never effected much at any time or place, no matter what were their gifts and talents; and the writer is grieved to say, that the Society has had such individuals as preachers in its connection almost from the very beginning. To conceal this, would make a historian guilty of unfaithfulness and partiality. It would be desirable indeed, that this part of our history had no foundation in facts, in which case the Evangelical Association would, doubtless, have spread much more rapidly, and done more toward the building up of the kingdom of God on earth.

The Year 1828.

In this year the writer of this history entered the itinerancy, and will, henceforth, be obliged to make frequent mention of his own name, and his various relations and labors in the Association, which, however, he will do with as much modesty as will be consistent with the truth of history. But he has now also the advantage of describing things pertaining to this history from personal observation and acquaintance, and can therefore furnish a more minute detail, especially from the time when, after the expiration of nine years subsequent to his entrance into the itinerancy, he was chosen officer of the Book Establishment of the Society, in which capacity he has spent the greater part of his time ever since, and has consequently had opportunities of observing every remarkable event, movement, or enterprise, that took place in the connection, which he hopes will be of much benefit to him in the further prosecution of this work.

The Western Conference met at Uniontown, Stark county, Ohio, May 5th, 1828. J. Long was chairman, and J. W. Miller secretary.—J. F. was expelled from the Church for immoral conduct, and F. Shower received again as deacon. As most of the preachers intended to go to the Eastern Conference, and as there were no new candidates for the ministry; therefore no preachers were stationed by this conference which only required that J. Long should act as much as possible in the capacity of presiding elder for the district.—The stationing of the preachers was then left to the Eastern Conference, merely on two conditions, viz., that A. Kleinfelter be received as a member of the conference committee, and that at least three ordained preachers be stationed on the district;

which conditions were readily complied with by the Eastern Conference.

The Eastern Conference held its session again at New Berlin, beginning June 2nd. J. Seybert was chairman, and J. C. Reisner secretary. In examining the preachers, J. Allen and W. Stoll were deposed from the ministry. J. C. Reisner and J. M. Saylor located on account of bodily infirmities, and B. Ettinger on account of family circumstances. *W. W. Orwig, J. H. Yambert, Elias Stoever*, and *Jacob Hoock*, were received on trial into the itinerancy. Fr. Hoffman and J. G. Conser were ordained as deacons, and D. Manwiller and J. Bruer as elders, and T. Buck was chosen presiding elder. The preachers were stationed as follows:—

Canaan district, J. Seybert, presiding elder. Schuylkill circuit, A. Kleinfelter and J. W. Miller; Lancaster circuit, C. Kring; York circuit, J. Hamilton and J. H. Yambert; Franklin and Berkley circuit, G. Reich and J. Hoock.

Salem district, T. Buck, presiding elder. Union circuit, Fr. Hoffman and G. Enders; Centre circuit, J. Barber and W. W. Orwig; Somerset circuit, J. Bruer and G. Mattinger; Lake circuit, P. Wagner.

Western Conference district, Joseph Long, presiding elder. Canton circuit, D. Manwiller and S. Tobias; Lancaster circuit, H. Wissler and E. Stoever; Sandusky circuit, G. Schneider.

The membership amounted to 2677, which shows an increase of only 110 during the previous year; the salary of the preachers was $41,76.

This conference resolved, that hereafter married preachers having traveled five years or longer, shall draw as much salary for their families as for themselves, or in other words, as much again as a single itinerant; and it was enjoined on them, at the same time, to exert themselves to have the contributions toward the support of the ministers increased.

These two enactments were of great importance to the itinerancy of the Society, and contributed a great deal to its increase and strength.—During the last twelve years, since 1816, the itinerancy had gained but *one* preacher in point of numbers, and during the last eight years none at all. In 1816, the number of itinerants was 21, in 1820 22, and in 1828 likewise 22. During this period, the work had, *geographically*, increased but little, although somewhat in point of *numbers*. But from this period, evidently a change for the better took place. Only three years afterward, the Society numbered 34 itinerants, and 3580 members, giving an increase of 12 preachers and 903 members in three years; while in the eight years from 1820 to 1828, the number of itinerants had remained the same, and the increase of the membership had been but 685.—We are, indeed, not prepared to attribute this better success exclusively to the better support of the ministers; yet we doubt not, that this measure met with the approbation of the Most High, and caused his richest blessings to rest upon the work.—Under this new arrangement, those of the married preachers, who lived very economically and met with no accidents and losses, were at least enabled to get along without involving themselves into debts, or sacrificing their private property, if they had any; for the salary soon increased somewhat, the preachers frequently received some presents, and provisions were very cheap in those days. But yet, not all succeeded so well; and hence there were still many compelled to follow some secular business in connection with their high calling, in order to procure a livelihood. This, however, proved detrimental to them in the discharge of their duties; for, it not only took up *that portion* of their time, which they should have devoted to reading and searching, but it also frequently gave offence to some. Others, again, desired to mend matters by *locating for one or two years*; but these one or two years frequently grew into five or ten, while others clung to their secular employment all their lives long, so that they never again made their appearance in the itinerancy. This circumstance has ever been a great impediment to the Society, both with regard to its own spread, and the increase of its itinerancy.—But on the other hand, it can scarcely be denied either, that many left the field and returned to the world, not so much for want of an adequate support, as for worldliness and a want of faith and the spirit of self-denial. Thus it happened, that some would preach a year or two, and then locate; and so on to the end of their lives: accomplishing, in this way, but little either in the world or in the kingdom of God.—Those, on the contrary, who esteemed their honorable and important calling higher than all honors and conveniences of this world; who, under all trials, manfully persevered in self-denial, fidelity, and activity, and, like St. Paul, suffered not poverty, want, hunger, or nakedness, either to hinder them from the discharge of their duties, much less to drive them from the field,—these, I say, fared best, on the whole, and secured the greatest renown. Another disastrous consequence was, that they were unable to purchase proper libraries, to foster that spirit of reading and research, so indispensably necessary to the minister of the Gospel, in order to store his mind with useful information, and to enable him at all times to bring forth *things new and old*.—In consequence of this inadequate support, it was in earlier days not a rare case, that our itinerants had, besides the Bible, Hymn Book, and Discipline, scarcely a few dollars' worth of good books; and, as some of these were, nevertheless, generally able to preach at least *powerfully*, others seemed to have imbibed the notion, that a preacher's reading and searching were of little or no importance to him, provided he prayed diligently and earnestly for divine grace; forgetting that each can do this, without being necessitated to neglect the other; and likewise forgetting, that ministers, whose minds are well stored with useful information, are not only the most acceptable, but also the most useful and efficient servants of God.

The unmarried ministers who, besides their horses, were kept by the friends the whole year, without charge, did not feel the effects of the low support so keenly, and for this reason would sometimes generously distribute their salary among their more indigent brethren, being satisfied with food and clothing. Under these circumstances, but few preachers were able to set their societies an example with regard to liberality, although many of them contributed largely in proportion to their means, and even beyond them, to the support of every good cause; especially since the building of churches has become more general in the connection, and the missionary cause has received its due share of attention. With very few exceptions, there is perhaps no other body of clergymen to be found in Christendom, who contribute more liberally in proportion to means and circumstances, than the itinerants of the Evangelical Association,—though some of them are *very poor*, yet they generally give largely.—Many improvements, however, have since been made in the arrangements of the Society, so that at present the support of the preachers is generally such that scarcely any need leave the field for want of support—though there is still room for improvements.

During the year under consideration, the new small conference in the West made very rapid progress, adding 147 to its membership; while the Eastern Conference had a much smaller increase of members. It was especially on Canton circuit, where the work of the Lord prospered so mightily, under the pastoral care of D. Manwiller and S. Tobias. Among the papers of Father Dreisbach, in his collection for this history, we found, for the year in question, the following report of this circuit, which, to judge by the diction, seems to have been penned by Bishop Long. It is as follows:—

"The preachers entered on their large field of labor in humble reliance on the help of God, and with the resolve to labor for his glory and the welfare of their fellow-men, and, if possible, to bring about a better state of things on the circuit, as not a few of the members were in a state of lukewarmness. Hence they began to denounce that cold formality in public worship, and to exhort the membership to fulfill their duties zealously, and to be diligently engaged in every good work. Manwiller is said to have once made use of the following expression: '*By the help of God, I am determined, if possible, to bring the circuit into a better state.*' Thus they continued preaching the word of God faithfully and in its purity, till the camp-meeting was held on Brother J. Hegarman's land, in Wayne county, Ohio, where God's grace was so powerfully manifested, that a glorious revival of religion took place. The excitement was uncommonly great. One evening during an exhortation, almost the whole assembly was deeply moved, and penitent sinners came from all directions to seek in prayer the forgiveness of their sins; and there was such a flame of sacred love kindled in all Christian hearts, but lately so lukewarm, that from that moment to its close, the meeting was remarkably blessed. The holy fire then spread over the whole circuit, and the consequence was that the meetings everywhere became interesting, and many a precious soul was hopefully converted to God. Among these subjects of converting grace, was *John Roesner*, who afterward became an itinerant, and as a faithful servant has since entered into the joy of his Lord."

On the other circuits of this district likewise, the brethren labored with great success during this year; also on several circuits of the Eastern Conference, especially those of Schuylkill, Lancaster, and York. At the close of this year, Schuylkill circuit numbered 473 members, and had, in point of numbers, thus reached its climax. A new circuit being formed the ensuing year, a considerable part of Schuylkill circuit was cut off. Lancaster and York circuits almost equaled Schuylkill, in numbers. These three circuits added together, numbered over two hundred members more than all the circuits of the Eastern Conference together.

Brother John Stambach, who had formerly been an itinerant, closed his earthly career during this year. He was a pious, humble man, and his ministerial labors were greatly blessed. The writer saw him several times shortly before his departure, but did not become intimately acquainted with him, nor did he receive any further report concerning him. Also Brother Jacob Kleinfelter, a local preacher, died during this year.

The Year 1829.

The Western Conference held its annual session in Tuscarawas township, Stark county, Ohio, beginning May 4th. J. Long was chairman, and H. Wissler secretary. J. D., a local preacher, was expelled from the Church for immoral conduct. *John George Zinser* was received on trial into the itineraney, and George Schneider, S. Tobias, and E. Stoever, were ordained as deacons.

The Eastern Conference began its session June 1st, at New Berlin. T. Buck acted as chairman, and J. Seybert as secretary. Two preachers were deposed from the ministry, and one of them expelled at the same time, and J. W. Miller located on account of family circumstances. *George Brickley, Joseph Ebbert, Solomon G. Miller, Jacob Schnerr,* and *Wm. Ray,* were received on trial by conference. Also Bro. H. Niebel re-entered the itinerancy at this conference. The preachers were stationed as follows:—

Eastern Conference.

Canaan district, T. Buck, presiding elder. Schuylkill circuit, C. Kring and J. Ebbert; Lebanon circuit, H. Niebel and W. W. Orwig; Lancaster circuit, J. M. Saylor and G. Enders; York circuit, D. Manwiller and S. Tobias; Franklin and Berkley circuit, J. Hamilton, J. Bruer, and W. Ray.

Salem district, J. Seybert, presiding elder. Union circuit, J. Barber and J. G. Zinser; Centre circuit, Fr. Hoffman and S. G. Miller; Somerset circuit, H. Wissler and G. Brickley; Lake circuit, G. Reich.

Western Conference.

J. Long, presiding elder. Canton circuit, A. Kleinfelter and E. Stoever; Lancaster circuit, J. H. Yambert and G. Schneider; Sandusky circuit, G. Mattinger.

The membership this year was 2862, consequently an increase of 185 during the previous year. The number of itinerants at this conference was 26, and the annual support of each amounted to \$42.18.—This year the married preachers, for the first time, drew salaries for their families, i. e., those of them who had traveled five years, besides their traveling expenses; but among the 22 itinerants of the last year, there were but four who were entitled to draw for their families, nearly all the rest being single.

At this conference, a new circuit was formed called *Leba-*

non circuit, from parts of Schuylkill and Lancaster circuits, comprising, to some extent, those parts where Albright had been raised and formed the first societies of the Evangelical Association, and extending northward and westward beyond the borough of Lebanon. This circuit prospered remarkably well, outstripped in a few years all other circuits in point of numbers, and was afterward divided into several circuits.—At this conference, T. Buck was elected trustee or treasurer of all the proceeds from the book trade of the Society, and J. Seybert trustee of all legacies that might be bequeathed to the same. Some property had then already been bequeathed to the Association, and there have been other individuals since, who have devised considerable sums to it for the support of our poor superannuated itinerants, and of the itinerant preachers generally, that fall short of their due salaries.—The Missionary Society of the Association, also, afterward received some fine legacies; and it is very desirable, that a great many more such benefactors might be found, who make to themselves friends of the mammon of unrighteousness.

This was again one of the most blessed years for the Society, up to that time. All the circuits reported at the next conference considerable numbers of newly received members, especially the circuits of Lebanon, Centre, and Berkley in the Eastern, and those of Canton and Lancaster in the Western Conference.—During this conference year, the revival in Upper Milford township, Lehigh county, Pa., began, which afterward extended gloriously, proving a blessing to many souls.

Of those families in that neighborhood, who first received our preachers, and joined the connection, were: George Yeakel, David Schubbert, Peter Wist, Daniel Wieand; and near Millerstown: John Hittel. At J. Hittel's there had been preaching already the year before; but in that part of country, where the work principally began, the first sermon was preached by the writer, accompanied by C. Hammer, in the barn of D. Schubbert, on a Sunday afternoon, September 13th, 1829, and made a deep impression on many of the hearers. On the 15th of November following, there was preaching for the first time in the house of G. Yeakel, and at this time the work of conversion began to spread, but with it arose opposition and persecution also. A fine class was formed there during this year, and at its close a great many souls were awakened and convinced of the necessity of a change of heart, some of whom were afterward converted and joined the Church.—This section of country lies nearly in the centre of the first three classes, formed by Mr. Albright, and not far from the place where he was born and brought up.—Also in the townships of Heidelberg and Lower Heidelberg, in Berks county, the work progressed finely, especially at Womelsdorf and vicinity, and at Lebanon.—On Centre circuit the work spread gloriously, especially in Penn's and Brush Valleys. Many precious souls were converted and gained for the kingdom of heaven.

On Canton circuit, in the Western Conference, the work likewise extended considerably, especially in the neighborhood of Greensburg, Summit county, Ohio. A goodly number of souls were awakened and converted there, especially during a camp-meeting on the land of Brother Kreutz, out of which number the Lord afterward called some to the ministry. The other circuits of the Western Conference were also extended during the year, and the new conference commenced to gain a firm footing; at this time it received considerable increase from Pennsylvania, many members emigrating from that state to Ohio.—During this year, the preacher in charge of Lancaster circuit made the first visit to the south-western part of the state of Ohio, whither several old members of our Church had emigrated, and they expressed a strong desire to be regularly visited by our preachers. Although the prospects were then not as promising, with regard to the extension of the work in that section, as in many other places, yet it spread gradually and extended over the counties of Montgomery, Warren, Butler, Preble, and at last over Miami and Dark, as far as Wayne co. in the state of Indiana, till finally a circuit was formed there.

In this year Bro. Henry Meyer, a local preacher, died. He had been one of the first members of the connection on Somerset circuit.

The Year 1830.

This year the Western Conference held its annual session in Plain township, Stark county, Ohio, beginning May 3rd. J. Long was chairman, and A. Kleinfelter secretary. The latter located on account of bodily infirmities. *Absalom B. Schæfer* and *Christopher Aubel* were received as local preachers on probation, and *Wm. Ræhrig* as an itinerant; L. Henky and M. Kibler were ordained as deacons.

The Eastern Conference held its session at Orwigsburg, Schuylkill county, Pa., beginning June 1st, 1830. T. Buck was chairman, and J. Seybert secretary. One itinerant and three local preachers were deposed from their office. J. Hamilton, H. Wissler, and J. M. Saylor, located on account of bodily infirmities, and F. Hoffman and J. Ebbert on account of family concerns.—*Charles Hammer*, *Daniel Kehr*, *John S. Himmelreich*, and *Robert G. Hunter*, were received into the itinerancy on trial.

The preachers were stationed as follows:—

Canaan district, T. Buck, presiding elder. Schuylkill circuit, E. Stoever and J. G. Zinser; Lebanon circuit, W. W. Orwig and Charles Hammer; Lancaster, circuit, H. Niebel and J. Schnerr; York circuit, G. Brickley and J. Bruer; Franklin circuit, C. Kring and R. G. Hunter; Berkley circuit, W. Ray.

Salem district, J. Seybert, presiding elder. Union circuit, G. Schneider and S. Tobias; Centre circuit, J. Barber; Somerset circuit, S. G. Miller and W. Ræhrig; Lake circuit, Fr. Glasser.

Western Conference, J. Long, presiding elder. Canton circuit, J. H. Yambert and D. Kehr; Lancaster circuit, G. Mattinger and J. S. Himmelreich; Sandusky circuit, G. Enders.

The number of members reported at this conference, was 3245; consequently an increase of 383 during the past year. This was the greatest increase of any year up to that time. But as the number of the newly received members during the year was 720, the Society must either have lost 337 members, or those who changed their residences, must have been counted as new members; and this is much more probable than that so many should have been lost in one year, by expulsion or withdrawal from the Church; although the Discipline was rigidly enforced in those days, and not only many members, but also a number of preachers, were expelled most every year. Nor can it be denied, that then, and even afterward, offenders were often *too rigidly* dealt with. Had more patience and forbearance been exercised, no doubt many members and preachers could have been saved, who might have been of valuable service to the Church. The apostle's command: "*Put away from among you every wicked person,*" was often too rashly carried out, and not conformably to other biblical commands. To bear patiently the infirmities of the *weak*, and to restore the *erring* in the spirit of meekness, was too often neglected. In order to avoid the curse of the Most High, incurred by retaining the *wicked* and *incorrigible*, that treatment of the accused was often neglected, which might have reclaimed them from the error of their ways. The motives were generally good, but not always the consequences.

The salary of the preachers this year was but six cents higher than the year before; but conference passed a very rigid resolution with reference to the increase of the contributions toward the support of the preachers. It had often been the case, that preachers had not collected that amount of contributions, which they might and ought to have collected, had they discharged their duties faithfully in every respect; and as they were entitled, according to the system at that time, which put all the preachers on an *equal* footing with regard to salary, to draw equal shares with those who had been more faithful; therefore conference resolved, that those preachers who, by neglect of this duty, did not collect that amount of contributions, which, in the opinion of conference, they might have raised, should suffer a diminution of their salaries. This neglect of duty on the part of some, was one of the principal reasons which were afterward urged against the *system of equality*, with regard to the salary of the preachers.

It was contended, that those who either from indifference or from an unwillingness to bear the cross, neglected to raise their proportion of contributions, should also suffer the consequences themselves, and not their faithful brethren. This and the fact that in some parts of the country provisions cost much more than in others, led to changing this rule so as to make the conferences independent of each other, with regard to contributions: which change, however, was highly disapproved and deplored by some of the older preachers.—For these and similar reasons, most of the conferences subsequently made their circuits and stations independent of each other, in reference to the support of the preachers; with the exception, however, that those who fall short of their due, shall be assisted by raising a general collection for them at the close of each conference year, and out of the avails of the Printing Establishment, and by the "Charitable Society" of the Association, as far as practicable.

The Eastern Conference, as the older of the two conferences, being authorized by the Discipline of the Church to do so, resolved that a General Conference be held, to begin on the first Monday of November following.

This year was, on the whole, another very prosperous one. Most of the circuits were blessed with awakenings and conversions, and some more than usual, especially those of Union, Lebanon, and Somerset in the Eastern, and that of Canton in the Western Conference.—The awakening that had begun the previous year in Upper Milford, on Lebanon circuit, made rapid progress, and more and more hearts and doors were opened to the truth. But opposition and persecution increased proportionably also. Hitherto the enemies of truth and light had still flattered themselves with the hope that the work would either not last long, or at least not spread very widely; but now seeing themselves disappointed in these their expectations, they commenced to oppose it in good earnest, at first with calumnies and slanders, then by violence and force. It is true, those who had recourse to violence, were but the outcasts of society; but being assisted and encouraged by some of the most respectable nominal Christians, and by some clergymen in the neighborhood, they became so bold, that only by the intervention of the law, they could be restrained from carrying their wicked designs into effect. They had frequently *disturbed* the services by being noisy, and by other acts of frivolity; but now they *broke* one *up*. On the 16th of November, 1830, there was evening service in the house of P. W., but the preaching was disturbed several times by a gang of wicked fellows, and at last the whole service was stopped. After several ineffectual attempts to restore order, the friends found themselves compelled to surrender the house to the gang, and to suffer them to act out their wantonness. A scene now followed which beggars all description: for about two hours these monsters raged, cursed, swore, and threatened without intermission, in the house; jumping, howling, singing, and leaping all the while, so that as many demoniacs could scarcely have acted worse—nearly all the benches of the house were broken and knocked to pieces. After they were prosecuted and fined, tranquility was restored for some time, and the work spread more rapidly. At the close of this conference year, a great number of the inhabitants were awakened, and about 50 professed to have experienced a change of heart and to have found peace with God. In subsequent years the good work continued to spread as far as Allentown, and beyond it in the county of Northampton, and the eastern part of Bucks, and even at this day it is still spreading in those directions.

During this year, Bro. J. Seybert, who was then the presiding elder of Salem district, found open doors in Blooming Grove, Lycoming county, Pa., also in Blockhouse settlement, Tioga county. In Williamsport a family named Rothrock, had ere this received our preachers; and afterward H. Hartman opened his house to them also, and together with his wife joined the Society. For a number of years the congregation there was very small; but afterward increasing somewhat, they built a convenient little church.

In Blooming Grove there was great opposition, Brother Seybert being looked upon as a magician; in order to get rid of his magic, a number of certificates of baptism and a German copy of the New Testament, which had been bought of him, were *burned*. But in later times our preachers gained a firm footing there; many assented to the truth, and a good society was formed, which has been in a prosperous condition ever since.

In Blockhouse settlement S. Hartman was the first who received Brother Seybert into his house, and permitted him to preach there. This section of country was at that time very bad, in a moral point of view; vices of all kind, especially that of drunkenness, were the order of the day. The people indeed had churches and preachers, but the latter were like the people—*godless*.—Seybert's preaching soon made a great stir in the neighborhood; sinners were awakened and converted, houses and churches were opened to him, and persecution arose against the work.—He paid several visits to this neighborhood during this and the following conference year, founded a flourishing society, which he added to the circuit, and thus laid the foundation of a very good and lasting work, that has been progressing to this day. The first families that fell in with the movement, were those of Hartman, Koegel, Sindlinger, Knodel, Dier, Essig, Welti, Schick, Schambacher, Rupp, Glœckler, Landis, Deibler, and others. — Afterward several families moved to other parts of the country, where they received the preachers of the Society; others exerted a salutary influence on their friends and relatives, who lived scattered about; and thus Blockhouse settlement became a renowned place in the Evangelical Association, although it is somewhat remote, and the country rather rough and wild.

In this year, Brother D. Mauwiller closed his earthly career, after having served six years as an itinerant with very good success.

SEVENTH SECTION.

FROM THE FOURTH GENERAL CONFERENCE IN 1830, TO THE SIXTH GENERAL CONFERENCE IN 1836.

Fourth General Conference.

General Conference met pursuant to the resolutions of the Eastern Conference of June last, at the house of John Adam Hennig, Hains township, Centre county, Pa., in the eastern part of Penn's Valley, on Monday, November 1st, 1830. It was optional with every elder, as it had been before, to attend or not; but there were only eight preachers present who were entitled to a vote, and these constituted the General Conference, viz.: J. Dreisbach, H. Niebel, J. Seybert, J. Barber, J. Long, T. Buck, C. Kring, and H. Hassler. Joseph Long was chairman, and John Seybert secretary. The writer, with some other preachers, was several days in attendance, as a probationer, and remembers very distinctly the great difficulties arising from the improvement of the Articles of Faith and the Discipline of the Church, for which purpose General Conference had principally met, as a new edition of the work was to be published and translated into English. But as the minutes of conference do not specify the changes, which were made by that body, we here subjoin a short report on that subject, by Bishop Long. It is as follows:—

"1. *The Articles of Faith.* The first article had already been changed in 1816, and the expression, '*three persons*' changed into, '*a trinity.*' The articles 2, 12, 13, 14, 15, 16, and 18, were changed as follows: In the 2nd article for: 'In order thus to reconcile the Father to us,' the words: 'In order to reconcile the *justice of the eternal Father* to us.' In the articles 12, 13, 14, and 15, the words, '*sacrament*' and '*sacraments*' were erased, and the following substituted, '*Baptism, Lord's Supper, means of grace, representation,*' etc., and thus a whole sentence in the 14th article was dropped, viz., 'that only *two sacraments* have been instituted by Christ.'

2. The General Rules and Instructions in the Duties of this

Association, were changed and considerably abbreviated, as they are at present.

3. The power of the bishops was so restricted, that they were eligible only for two terms of four years each in succession. Formerly they had always been eligible, and this was afterward made the rule again. The formula for the ordination of bishops was dropped.

4. It was ordained by this body, that hereafter only itinerants shall be members of the Annual Conferences, as at present; before this, local preachers also had been members.—The power of the bishops to station the preachers, was likewise annulled, and it was ordained that the bishop, in connection with two elders to be elected by conference for this purpose, shall attend to this business. Yet, in the opinion of some, no bishop ever had this power in our Church.

5. Among the duties of the preachers in charge, the following changes were made, viz.: 1. With regard to classmeetings, that it be left to their discretion, to admit or exclude persons that are no members of the Society.—2. The following order to receive new members was laid down: 'Let them be addressed as follows: 'Art thou,' etc.

6. The duties of the presiding elders were so changed, that each of them became the sole book agent of his district, thus dropping the body of book agents on every district.

7. The *responses* in the form of ordaining elders were somewhat abbreviated, and the word '*sacrament*' left out. The forms of baptism for infants and of solemnizing matrimony, were also changed.

8. The word *deacon* was changed into *minister;* and the articles against antinomianism and on the final perseverance of the saints, were left out.

"These," says Brother Long, "are the principal changes of the Articles of Faith and the Discipline of the Church, that were made by the General Conference of 1830, as far as I can remember."

John Seybert and Thomas Buck were appointed a committee, to prepare the improved and altered Articles of Faith and

Discipline for the press; and J. Dreisbach and H. Niebel were added to the committee, to examine the whole thoroughly before publication. A. Ettinger and J. Dreisbach were appointed to examine the English translation of the Discipline.

As the Western Conference still was to a great extent dependent on the Eastern, General Conference ordained, that hereafter a presiding elder of the Western Conference attend annually the session of the Eastern Conference as a delegate, in order to bring the necessary documents from one conference to the other, and to assist in transacting the mutual business of both. This arrangement was to last till the next General Conference.

Another important act of this conference, must not be overlooked here. Some years before this conference, several men had been received into the itinerant ministry, who preached exclusively in English, and hence could travel only on a few circuits, the others being nearly all German; and as fears were entertained, that the English language might prevail, this conference ordained, that the itinerant ministry in general confine their labors to the German portion of the population, and that no more preachers be received into that body, who had not, at least, some knowledge of the German language.

This resolution vexed and discouraged the English brethren a great deal; and its consequence was, that the English work suffered and languished, till finally it died out almost entirely. Thus many parts of the country were and remained closed against the Association, as by far the most states of the Union were almost exclusively, and the few remaining for the most part, *English.* Herein the Evangelical Association fared like most of the other German Churches of this country, i. e., it learned a lesson by sad experience. In many parts they lost a considerable number of useful members; and even many of their own sons and daughters, besides a great many others, for this reason joined other denominations, who would otherwise have preferred to remain in the Evangelical Association. These are facts which no one can truthfully deny, and which were afterward deplored by many of the preachers and members. By a resolution of a later General Conference—that of 1843—this resolution was not only repealed, but conference also ordained, that our Association shall hereafter labor both for the English and German portion of our population, etc.

The Year 1831.

This year the Western Conference held its session in Green township, Stark county, Ohio, beginning May 2nd. Jos. Long was chosen chairman, and he appointed John H. Yambert secretary. M. K. was deposed from his office and excluded from the Society. *Michæl Miller*, *Christian Leitner*, and *John Ræssner*, were received on trial into the itinerant ministry.—At this conference there were reported 9 itinerants, some of whom, however, went to the Eastern Conference, 27 local preachers, and 963 members.

The session of the Eastern Conference was held at Lebanon, Pa., beginning June 6th. T. Buck was chairman, and J. Seybert secretary. J. F. and G. L., local preachers, and R. Hunter, itinerant, were deposed from the ministry, on account of immoral conduct; and J. Hamilton, an itinerant, was also deposed, because he had, in the opinion of conference, promulgated unscriptural doctrines. S. Tobias located on account of bodily infirmities. The following brethren were received on trial into the itinerant ministry: *Daniel Brickley*, *George Anstein*, *John P. Leib*, *Wm. Wagner*, *Charles Hesser*, *Jacob Borkert*, *John Campbell*, and *Henry Fisher*.—The following were ordained as deacons: J. G. Zinser, S. G. Miller, J. Schnerr, and W. Ray; and E. Stœver was ordained as elder. H. Niebel was elected presiding elder, and John Rank as General Book Agent.

This conference formed a new presiding elder district, called "*Zion district*," and passed among others the following resolutions: 1. That no preacher of the connection shall be permitted to publish any book or pamphlet, which has not been examined and approved by his conference. 2. That J. C. Reisner shall make an extract from G. Miller's biography, and prepare a report of his last sickness and death; and that this work shall then be examined by T. Buck, H. Niebel, and A. Ettinger, and, if approved, published.—The passage of the first of these resolutions, had been occasioned by a pamphlet, published and circulated by J. Hamilton; which was also the cause of his being deposed, as he refused to acknowledge and retract the errors contained therein.

The membership at this conference amounted to 3580; consequently an increase during the previous year of 335. The salary of an unmarried preacher was $55,68, and that of a married man twice that amount, provided he had served five years or more as an itinerant.

The preachers were stationed as follows:—

Canaan district, H. Niebel, presiding elder. Schuylkill circuit, J. Sehnerr and J. Young; Lebanon circuit, J. G. Zinser and J. P. Leib; Lancaster circuit, E. Stœver and H. Fisher.

Zion district, T. Buck, presiding elder. York circuit, W. W. Orwig, D. Brickley, and J. Rœssner; Franklin circuit, G. Brickley and J. Borkert; Berkley circuit, G. Enders; Somerset circuit, C. Kring, B. Bixler, and G. Anstein.

Salem district, J. Seybert, presiding elder. Union circuit, J. M. Saylor and W. Wagner; Whitedeer circuit, J. Barber and C. Hammer; Centre circuit, P. Wagner and C. Hesser; Lake circuit, G. Schneider and J. Campbell.

Ohio Conference district, J. Long, presiding elder. Canton and Wooster circuit, G. Mattinger, J. S. Himmelreich, and M. Miller; Sandusky circuit, J. H. Yambert and Chr. Leitner; New Lancaster circuit, S. G. Miller and D. Kehr.

This was another prosperous year. With the exception of Franklin and Berkley, most of the circuits had a considerable increase; especially those of Lebanon, York, Centre, Lake, and Canton and Wooster. The awakening in Upper Milford spread more and more, and the number of believers increased considerably during this year. The Brethren J. G. Zinser and J. P. Leib found open doors near Allentown also, in the house of a very respectable man, named David Mertz, who, with his family, soon after obtained the forgiveness of his sins, joined the Church, and exerted a very salutary influence on the surrounding country, by his example. A few years later, a glorious work of grace was in progress there, which spread extensively. During this year a glorious revival took place also on York circuit, in Canadochley. Before this, there were but few families there, who received our preachers; and, in a moral point of view, the country was, on the whole, very rough and wild. But as several influential families there embraced religion during this year, the work obtained a firm footing, and subsequently extended considerably. J. G. and H. Thomas, and their families, and in the following year H. Burg, J. A. Jacobs, and other families, found the remission of their sins. At the close of this conference year, a very blessed general meeting was held in Seitz's school house, near Strassburg, which lasted from Friday evening till Sunday after midnight, during which time 25 souls professed to have found peace with God. The writer never attended a meeting that surpassed this in point of victorious power.

On Centre circuit, in Brush Valley, and especially in a south-western direction of Millheim, in Penn's Valley, conversions occurred at different places, and the circuit was considerably enlarged during the year. In Nittany Valley an extensive revival took place, resulting in the conversion of the families of *Best*, *Brown*, and others, who subsequently became strong pillars of the Society.

On Lake circuit, in the state of New York, 160 members were received during the year; but the writer does not know precisely in what parts of the country the work took place. A report by S. Weber says, that George Schneider and John Campbell, who traveled on that district, came to Erie county, N. Y., this year, found many open doors in the vicinity of Father Schopp, and thus laid the foundation of the Buffalo circuit of that state, which was formed the following year by C. Kring and J. Bell. Jacob Schopp, S. Fleischer, P. Schneider, and Joseph Rieser, were among the first there, who received our preachers.—Joseph Rieser was the first classleader on Buffalo circuit.

On Canton and Wooster circuit, in the state of Ohio, 105 members were received during the year.

In Orwigsburg, on Schuylkill circuit, great difficulties arose about this time. The time of sifting had commenced a few years before, as by the great draught during the preceding years, more or less bad fishes had been drawn to shore, which must now be separated from the good. In addition to this, some respected and influential men arose in the society, who preached perverse doctrines, and drew over a considerable number of credulous souls. The leader of this schism was *George Kimmel*, who was in other respects an upright man and of unblemished reputation, but very prone to innovations and fanaticism, and, at the same time, inflexibly stubborn. In spiritual and divine things he considered himself wiser than all his brethren, refused to be set right by any one, and bade defiance to all who did not agree with him. His principal error was, that he considered a literal observance of feet-washing, as described John 13., indispensably necessary to salvation, denouncing all that did not practice it according to his interpretation, as disobedient to Almighty God. His brethren bore patiently with him a long time, endeavoring to reclaim him from his errors—but all to no purpose—he clung to his opinions, advocated them on every occasion, and strove to draw over to his side as many members as possible. At last he imbibed still more erroneous opinions, and caused so much disturbance among the brethren, that they could bear with him no longer. —J. Hamilton also, who had been deposed from his office by the last conference for having circulated erroneous doctrines, made an attempt to cause a schism in the Association, and was very sanguine in his expectations of success. His pretense was, to re-establish the *old foundation of Mr. Albright*, and to found a *scriptural Association*, and not *a sect;* and it is said, that he really appointed a conference, and expected the attendance of 12—18 ministers; but none appearing, he was obliged to hold his conference alone, or rather to drop it entirely. At first it appeared as if some of the English brethren would side with him, but at last all of them left him. He was in other respects a talented and popular preacher, and in later years united with the Lutheran Church. As Hamilton had been the leading man among the English brethren, and most of them had at first adhered to him, but afterward left him and scattered; therefore the operations of the Society in the English language ceased almost entirely. J. Bruer, an old preacher and well versed in both languages, favored him for a time, yet did not dare go with him; but afterward falling into erroneous opinions, he withdrew from the connection. The principal error of J. Bruer was, that a perfectly sanctified person had nothing more to do in this world, and consequently the moment he obtained perfect sanctification, would be called from time to eternity. This doctrine he preached at a camp-meeting in Morgan county, Virginia, which was held under the superintendence of the writer; and as he was called to an account for it, and complained of at the same time, he withdrew during this meeting, and died shortly afterward. It is said, however, that he humbled himself before his death, and departed, it is hoped, in the triumphs of faith.

The Year 1832.

The annual session of the Western Conference again took place in Green township, Stark county, Ohio, beginning May 7th, 1832. J. Long was president, and J. H. Yambert secretary. W. Roehrig and J. D. were deposed from their office. The following brethren were received on trial: *John Lutz*, *Elias Sichly*, *David Poorman*, *Aaron Yambert*, and *John C. Kopp*.

The Eastern Conference held its session at New Berlin, Union county, Pa., beginning Monday. June 4th. T. Buck was elected president, and he appointed J. Seybert secretary. The examination of the preachers was unusually difficult this time, as many charges were brought in, and consequently *ten* preachers deposed from office; viz., *six* for immoral conduct; *three* for not preaching; and *one*, because not qualified for the office. In addition to these, two more were put back on trial. This was, as already intimated, a time of very strict government in the Society; and there is reason to fear, that at times too little indulgence was shown. Yet, on the whole, it may have been for the best interests of the Church; for, before this, they had for years been troubled with preachers of a loose character, who did much more harm than good.—Bro. T. Buck, who is known to have been a man of great rigor, exerted a great influence on the ministry at this time, often contrólling his brethren according to his discretion. Many a brother who had been tempted, was wavering or in error, might have been saved by a little more patience, forbearance, and kindness; but being treated with too great severity, they were lost to the Society.

H. Fisher, G. Enders, J. Bruer, and B. Bixler, located on account of bodily infirmities. The following brethren were received on trial into the itinerant ministry: *Jacob Bell, Henry Bucks, Christian Thomas, Samuel Baumgartner, Daniel Fichtner*, and *Joseph Harlacher*. The district and circuits were allotted to the preachers for this year, as follows:—

Canaan district, H. Niebel, presiding elder. Schuylkill circuit, W. W. Orwig and D. Brickley; Lebanon circuit, J. Schnerr and J. P. Leib; Lancaster circuit, G. Brickley and F. Hoffman.

Zion district, T. Buck, presiding elder. York circuit, J. G. Zinser, J. Rœssner, and H. Bucks; Franklin circuit, Jos. M. Saylor and J. Borkert; Shenandoah circuit, G. Schneider and Chr. Thomas; Somerset circuit, D. Kehr and Jos. Harlacher; Indiana circuit, E. Stœver and A. Frey.

Salem district, J. Seybert, presiding elder. Union circuit, S. G. Miller and C. Hesser; Centre circuit, P. Wagner and S. Baumgartner; Lycoming circuit, J. Barber and J. Young; Lake circuit, J. S. Himmelreich and J. Campbell; Buffalo circuit, C. Kring and J. Bell.

Western Conference. J. Long, presiding elder. Canton circuit, G. Anstein and J. J. Kopp; Wooster circuit, C. Hammer and Chr. Leitner; Sandusky circuit, G. Mattinger and E. Sichly; New Lancaster circuit, J. H. Yambert and M. Miller.

The membership at this conference amounted to 3921, which shows an increase of 341 during the previous year. The salary of a single preacher was $52,29.

It was also resolved at this conference, that a *fund* be established for the support of superannuated poor itinerant preachers, and their widows and orphans. John Rank, of Union county, Pa., was elected trustee, to administer this fund. This was the beginning of the *charitable funds* of the Evangelical Association, for the administration of which a society was afterward formed, and incorporated according to law.

As it appears from the minutes of the conference, there was but little done in the book line at that time. The conference in question ordered, for instance, that 1500 copies of the "*Biography of Albright* and *G. Miller*," and 1000 copies of the Discipline (the latter work in English), be published. These small editions show that the book trade was still in its infancy in the connection. During this year the work made but indifferent progress; the increase was not quite as large as the year before, yet more uniform than usual—nearly all the circuits increased somewhat. York circuit reported the highest number of newly received members, and then followed Wooster, Canton, and Centre circuits. This year Schuylkill circuit had to pass through its severest trial, as a final separation of the two antagonistic elements took place. G. Kimmel and his party, which, however, was but small in point of numbers, withdrew from the Society; and thus tranquillity was restored, and immediately the work began to make new progress. A camp-meeting, which took place in August that year, on the land of G. Rickert, near Orwigsburg, is said to have been, on the whole, the best ever held in that section of country. It was believed that not fewer than 100 souls were converted during that meeting. From that time the work gained a firmer footing, and the societies in the neighborhood increased annually.

As already stated, Buffalo circuit in the state of New York was formed this year. For many years the Society had but one circuit in that state, Lake circuit; and this was often on the point of total failure.—When the annual allotments at conference were read, *Lake circuit* was always a subject of considerable apprehension to the preachers; and those to whom it was allotted, were frequently seen to blush. Several of the preachers left it at different times, before their time of service had expired: some went over to other Churches, and a few failed entirely. Thus this circuit was for a long time in no great repute among the preachers. The cause of it was the great distance from the other circuits. The brethren at that place had generally to deny themselves, during the whole year, the society of their ministerial brethren, except when the presiding elder visited them; and even this did not happen regularly. By the formation of Buffalo circuit, this state of things was changed. There had often been but *one* preacher sent there, but now three or four were generally sent. Hereby the work was raised and strengthened, and thenceforth it progressed every year, till about ten years afterward it was formed into a conference.

The Year 1833.

This year the Western Conference held its annual session in Pleasant township, Fairfield county, Ohio, beginning May 6th. J. Long was chairman, and J. H. Yambert secretary. J. P. was deposed from office for neglect of duty. G. Anstein and Chr. Leitner located on account of bodily infirmities, and Joseph Long on account of family affairs.—*Daniel Tobias, Peter Gates, John Shreffler,* and *Henry M'Bride,* were received on trial into the itinerancy.

The Eastern Conference held its session at Orwigsburg Pa., beginning June 3rd. T. Buck was again chairman, and J. Seybert secretary. J. C. and P. S. were deposed from the ministry, and J. S. Himmelreich and J. Borkert located on account of bodily infirmities. The following were received on trial into the itinerancy: *John Sensel, Isaac Deppen, Michæl F. Maize, Solomon Altimos, Jacob Boas,* and *Daniel Miesse.* The preachers were stationed as follows:—

Canaan district, T. Buck, presiding elder. Schuylkill circuit, J. P. Leib and J. Deppen; Lebanon circuit, J. Schnerr and J. Sensel; Lancaster circuit, J. Rœssner and J. Lutz.

Zion district, W. W. Orwig, presiding elder. York circuit,

J. G. Zinser and Jos. Harlacher; Gettysburg circuit, E. Stœver and H. Bucks; Franklin circuit, J. Barber and S. Baumgartner; Shenandoah circuit, J. Bell and M. F. Maize.

Salem district, J. M. Saylor, presiding elder. Union circuit, J. C. Reisner and Fr. Hoffman; Lycoming circuit, G. Schneider and G. Brickley; Centre circuit, C. Hesser and J. Young; Somerset circuit, D. Brickley and A. Frey; Indiana circuit, S. G. Miller and J. Boas.

Carmel district, P. Wagner, presiding elder. Lake circuit, D. Kehr and S. Altimos; Mohawk circuit, Fr. Glasser; Buffalo circuit, J. H. Yambert; Erie circuit, J. Seybert.

Western Conference, H. Niebel, presiding elder. New Lancaster circuit, C. Hammer and E. Sichle; Sandusky circuit, M. Miller and P. Gates; Wooster circuit, J. J. Kopp and A. Yambert; Canton circuit, C. Kring and D. Tobias; Miami circuit, G. Mattinger and J. Shreffler.

The increase during the past year was 331, and the whole membership 4252. The salary of an unmarried preacher was $48,48.

This conference resolved to publish an English hymn book for the Society; and J. M. Saylor and J. P. Leib were appointed a committee to make a collection; to which committee W. W. Orwig, A. Ettinger, and Joseph Hammer were added the following year, in order to revise and prepare said collection for the press. It consisted of 333 hymns, of small size; about ten years after it was considerably enlarged, and published in a larger size.—It was likewise resolved, to revise the smaller German hymn book, and T. Buck, W. W. Orwig, and J. C. Reisner, were appointed a committee to carry this resolution into effect. The former editions of this small hymn book had been in larger type and of larger size, but without any division of the hymns into their proper departments. By this revision some of the hymns were changed, shortened, divided into two or more, some left out, and a considerable number of new ones added, especially morning, evening, and funeral hymns. At a subsequent revision and enlargement of this little volume, however, most of these hymns, with several others, were embodied into the larger hymn book, while some hymns of the larger work were added to the smaller one.

From the minutes of this conference it appears, that four new circuits and a new presiding elder district were formed, and the boundaries of the connection considerably enlarged. For several years past, the number of itinerants had increased more rapidly than ever before; and as the several circuits were, therefore, better supplied and attended to than before, some had become so extensive by this time, that a division was necessary. There were also men at hand to seek new circuits, or to take up missions. The Society had recovered from its former sore trials, and taken a turn for increased activity in its high calling. The ministry embodied a considerable number of experienced, firm, and heroic men, who made it their business to enlarge the bounds of their fields of labor, and to enlist as many souls in the service of God, as they possibly could. Most of them, with few exceptions, preached *daily*. The circuits were generally very large: it required *four*, and on some even *six* weeks, to make a round; and many of the preaching places were *ten, twenty*, and some even *thirty* miles apart. Some of the circuits were from *two* to *four* hundred miles in circumference, and the districts accordingly. These, then, were signs of better times; nor did they fail to come.

This was one of the most blessed and prosperous years of the Association, and never before had the increase been so large. The brethren labored with remarkably good success on Lebanon circuit, which extended partly over the counties of Lebanon, Berks, Lehigh, and Bucks, numbering over 500 members. In Upper Milford, Lehigh county, the work spread increasingly, as well as in other places of the circuit.

During this and the preceding year a great revival took place in Brush Valley, Centre circuit, which resulted in the conversion of the families of Gramling, Beck, H. Moyer, and others; and in Nittany Valley, the families of Rissman, Heldman, etc.

Franklin circuit, extending over parts of the counties of Franklin, Cumberland, and Perry, enjoyed a glorious revival this year. A few miles east of Carlisle, at the Leathart Spring, a considerable awakening took place, and a very promising class was formed there. David Kutz, Christian Ruhl, John Kratzer, and partly their families also, were among of the first members in this vicinity. Also in Fishingcreek Valley, Perry co., awakenings and conversions took place. But above all others, did the new Erie circuit prosper, which was formed this year by J. Seybert. He reported at the next conference 100 new converts, and 121 members in all. This was one of the most blessed missions that was ever undertaken by the Society. Its principal places were: the neighborhood of the borough of Erie, Erie county, Pa., and Warren, Warren county. In these two places glorious revivals took place, and each of them had three flourishing classes at the end of the year; there was also a small class of three members, George Muck leader, in the county of Crawford, at the Canneaut lake. The first leaders of the three classes in Erie were: John Hershy, Samuel Heiss, and Jacob Long; and of those in Warren: Martin Esher, Henry D. Grunder, and John Ott. In Mercer county too, there was, during this year, the foundation of a good work laid in the families of Blank, Meyer, Bernhart, Eberhart, and others; likewise in Butler county, at Zelienopel, Harmony, etc. Mr. Ziegler, the principal man of Harmony, received Brother Seybert kindly, although he afterward opposed the work. In different places he found open doors among the Methodists, Mennonites, Baptists, Lutherans, and Reformed, preaching in churches, school-houses, private dwellings, barns, and in the woods, with great success. In some places, especially at Warren, public morality was at a very low ebb, and sins and vices of many kinds were predominant. Some parts of the country had no preachers at all; while others had such bad ones, that they would have fared much better without any. These rose with their followers against the strange itinerant, and did their best to drive him out of the country, by slanders, lies, and calumnies, calling him a good-for-nothing fellow, who had left his wife and children in the East, etc. But several of these *curates* fell into the pits themselves, which they had dug for Brother Seybert—they lost their places, and were compelled to leave those parts of the country. We here subjoin the following extracts from a report of this mission by Seybert himself. He says:—

"I reached my mission on Friday, July 12th, 1833, and lodged with Mr. Gingrich, ¾ mile south of Erie. The following day I looked about for preaching places, and the Lord opened hearts and doors to me. Sunday, 14th, I preached three times, the Lord owning and blessing my humble efforts. Among those who first received me in Erie, were the following persons: John Hershy, Jacob and John Long, Jacob Miller, Gimber, Metzler, Brown, Ripple, Kurtes, Hidler, and toward the close of the year, also Heiss's family. The German settlers of Erie county were partly Romanists, partly Lutherans, Reformed, Baptists, and Mennonites; some of whom may have been in a state of grace, while others perhaps were convinced of the necessity of a change of heart—but the great majority lived in impenitency and indifference."

As already stated, at the close of the year a flourishing society was formed in this part of the country, consisting of three classes. Afterward it increased from time to time, exerted a salutary influence upon other parts of the country, and also furnished a considerable number of candidates for the ministry, several of whom became useful men. Speaking of Warren, Bro. Seybert says:—

"The German (European) population were in a state of gross darkness, and addicted to such vices as cursing, swearing, tippling, etc. As to their religion, they were for the most part Catholics and Lutherans. Their preacher was a drunkard. A German, who had served in Napoleon's army, was their player; but instead of playing the fiddle, he used to whistle: afterwards he too became a subject of converting grace.

"October 10th, I paid the second visit to Warren, remained four days, preached three sermons, and held prayer-meetings. The beginning of the work of grace was now made: a respectable man, named Gross, fell to the ground during the sermon, as if struck by lightning, and continued to wrestle and pray, till he had obtained the pardon of his sins and the new life in God.—I visited the healthy and the sick, the wealthy and the poor; who then came to my meetings, and many of them were convinced of the necessity of conversion, and some were really converted. My family visiting and praying with the people in their houses, it appears to me, contributed more to bring about this glorious work of grace, than my preaching.—January 17th, I visited Warren the fourth time, remained six days, preached nine sermons, and held four prayer-meetings. This time a powerful work of grace took place. Scoffers, persecutors, and blasphemers broke down, like trees that are uprooted by a mighty hurricane, and were happily converted to the Lord; and many of a more respectable class, also became the blessed recipients of divine grace. Children from ten years old, and aged persons from forty to sixty years old, were powerfully affected and brought to repentance and conversion.—Now, as the tippling minister could do nothing to hinder the work of grace, the above mentioned whistler commenced to assemble his fellow tipplers and dancers at the same time when the converts and anxious inquirers met for prayer, in order to keep them away from the religious meetings, and thus prevent their conversion. But at a later period, this whistler also came to my preaching once, and was so powerfully affected and aroused from his lethargy, that he cried in great anguish of soul—'*Seybert, pray for me!*' This was an astonishing miracle of divine grace, and made a deep impression upon the whole audience. The dancing and playing at this place had now come to an end, as the whistler had embraced religion. *Hallelujah!*—Another man, who belonged to the more respectable class, came with some of his neighbors, for the purpose of disturbing me while preaching. I was dwelling on God's eternal love and mercy in Christ Jesus, and the persecutor was so powerfully affected during the sermon, that he was roused from his carnal security and melted to tears. He afterward came to meeting as a penitent, fell down upon his knees in great distress before the whole assembly, and prayed to God for forgiveness. His wife and children followed his example, and all were translated into the liberty of the children of God. Two of his sons are now useful preachers.— — — On the 24th of April, 1834, I took leave of my mission, after I had traveled 3011 miles, preached 218 sermons, and formed seven classes."

Through this mission, the foundations of the operations of the Society in the north-western part of Pennsylvania were laid, where subsequently several good circuits and promising stations were formed, and many souls enlisted in the service of God. Some time after, several of the members of the Warren society removed to the state of Illinois, and were there among the first who received the preachers of the Evangelical Association. The Warren society has been a regular station for years, and is now in possession of a very good spacious church.—In the borough of Erie, a society has also been formed, which has a church and is in a prosperous condition; and in some more places which had been gained by the mission, societies were subsequently formed, and churches erected.

Mohawk circuit in the state of New York, east of lake Erie, which was likewise formed this year, and served by Fr. Glasser, did not do so well, and was dropped the following year for some reason unknown to the writer. With reference to this, Brother Hummel in his first quarterly report of Mohawk mission, in the year 1839, writes as follows: "It is to be regretted, that the work once begun here by our brethren, was not continued. Many souls still in darkness might have been saved." From the glorious results of the mission, it may be inferred that the brethren, in this case, had been discouraged too soon. Jacob Riegel, the preacher in charge, was yet young and inexperienced, and this may have been one of the reasons why the circuit was dropped so soon. During this year the Society lost four preachers by death, all of whom had been useful men, and in former years two of them had served as itinerants; viz., Chr. Wolf, Fr. Borauf, J. W. Miller, and H. Young.

The Year 1834.

The Western Conference held its annual session this year in Lake township, Stark co., Ohio, beginning May 5th. H. Niebel was chairman, and C. Hammer secretary. C. L., J. M., and D. B., were deposed from office, and the last was excluded from the connection. J. J. Kopp and E. Sichle were ordained as deacons; and *Peter Wist, Samuel van Gundy*, and *Jacob Frey*, were admitted on trial.

The Eastern Conference held its session again at New Berlin, beginning June 2nd. W. W. Orwig was chairman, and J. Seybert secretary. The examination of the preachers this time was very difficult and tedious, as many charges were urged against a number of them. A presiding elder was deposed from his office, another itinerant put back on trial, and six local preachers were deposed from the ministry: some because disqualified for the office, some for neglect of duty, and some for immoral conduct, and three of them expelled from the Society. —T. Buck, J. H. Yambert, and S. G. Miller located on account of family concerns; and D. Miesse, J. Borkert, and J. Rœssner, on account of bodily infirmities. The following brethren were admitted on trial: *John Noecker, Jacob Saylor, Daniel Berger, Jacob Riegel, John Riegel*, and *John M. Sindlinger.*

The preachers were stationed by the presiding elders, as follows:—

Canaan district, J. Seybert, presiding elder. Schuylkill circuit, J. P. Leib and J. Sensel; Lebanon circuit, J. M. Saylor and J. Riegel; Lancaster circuit, H. Fisher and Jacob Saylor.

Zion district, W. W. Orwig, presiding elder. York circuit, J. Schnerr and M. F. Maize; Gettysburg circuit, D. Kehr and J. Noecker; Cumberland circuit, C. Hesser and A. Frey; Shenandoah circuit, S. Altimos and J. Schimp.

Salem district, J. G. Zinser, presiding elder. Union circuit, J. Young and D. Berger; Lycoming circuit, G. Brickley and S. Tobias; Centre circuit, Fr. Hoffman and J. M. Sindlinger; Somerset circuit, H. Bucks and G. Schneider; Indiana circuit, J. Lutz and P. Gates.

Carmel district, P. Wagner, presiding elder. Lake circuit, J. Harlacher and J. Boas; Mohawk circuit, J. Riegel; Buffalo circuit, D. Brickley; Erie circuit, E. Stœver.

Western Conference, Ohio district, H. Niebel, presiding elder. Lancaster circuit, S. Baumgartner and G. Mattinger; Wooster circuit, E. Sichley and D. Tobias; Sandusky circuit, J. J. Kopp and A. Yambert; Canton circuit, C. Hammer and S. van Gundy; Miami circuit, C. Kring and P. Wist.

This year the membership amounted to 4689, 1312 of whom belonged to the Western Conference. The increase during the past year had therefore been 437, and the salary of an unmarried itinerant was $50,12.

This conference ordered a second edition of the larger hymn book, then called "Saitenspiel," and appointed J. G. Zinser, J. Seybert, and W. W. Orwig a committee, to correct the typographical and doctrinal errors contained therein.—This was another highly blessed and prosperous year to the connection. Some of the circuits extended their bounds considerably, and in others glorious revivals took place. Schuylkill circuit, which then extended as far as Millersburg, Dauphin county, was especially revived during this year, particularly the western portion of it.

Lebanon circuit also continued to extend, in a north-eastern direction, beyond Allentown as far as Easton, but was subsequently divided into two, and the eastern end called *Reading circuit.*

On Buffalo circuit, in the state of New York, formed two years before, a glorious revival took place during this year in the town of Boston. Daniel Brickley traveled on the circuit and labored with marked success. Jacob Yanz and Geo. Eis were the first there to receive our ministers. The following year the first class was formed, and G. Eis became its leader.

The Year 1835.

This year makes an important and interesting epoch in the History of the Evangelical Association. For, not only did the work progress finely, the bounds extend themselves, and the membership increase; but the General Conference, which was held during this year, introduced a number of new means and measures, to advance the work of God. It resolved to publish the "*Christliche Botschafter*," requested all preachers in charge of circuits to introduce German *Sabbath-schools* into our societies wherever practicable, founded the "*Charitable Society*," besides making other improvements.

The Western Conference held its annual session in Greentown, Stark county, Ohio, beginning May 4th. H. Niebel was chairman, and C. Hammer secretary. H. W., G. A., J. K., and G., were deposed from the ministry; and a charge pending against J. S., he withdrew. J. Rœssner located on account of bodily infirmities, and G. Mattinger because of family concerns. Jos. Ebbert was ordained as deacon.

The Eastern Conference held its session at Lebanon, Pa., beginning June 1st. W. W. Orwig was chairman, and J. Seybert secretary. During the examination of the preachers, B. L. was deposed from the ministry; and S. Tobias and D. Kehr located on account of bodily infirmities. Ten applicants were admitted on trial, viz., *Sebastian Mosser*, *Henry Thomas*, *John A. Jacobs*, *Fred. Miller*, *Daniel N. Long*, *John Poorman*, *Henry Kegel*, *Jacob Kehr*, *Samuel Friess*, and *George Suger*. The following brethren were ordained as deacons: J. Boas, H. Fisher, J. Sensel, J. Lutz, A. Frey, M. F. Maize, and S. Altimos; as elders: C. Hesser, J. P. Leib, and D. Brickley.

The preachers were stationed as follows:—

Canaan district, J. Seybert, presiding elder. Schuylkill circuit, C. Hammer and S. Mosser; Lehigh circuit, J. M. Saylor and Jacob Riegel; Lebanon circuit, C. Hesser and H. Thomas; Lancaster circuit, Jac. Saylor and John Riegel; Philadelphia, J. Schnerr.

Zion district, W. W. Orwig, presiding elder. York circuit, F. Hoffman and H. Fisher. Gettysburg circuit, S. G. Miller and J. A. Jacobs; Cumberland circuit, J. P. Leib, G. Schneider, and Fr. Miller; Shenandoah circuit, J. Schimp and D. N. Long.

Salem district, P. Wagner, presiding elder; Union circuit, J. Sensel and J. Poorman; Columbia circuit, D. Berger and J. M. Sindlinger; Centre circuit, J. Brickley and H. Kegel; Lycoming circuit, J. Young; Lake circuit, M. F. Maize and J. Kehr; Buffalo circuit, J. Harlacher and S. Friess.

Carmel district, J. G. Zinser, presiding elder. Somerset circuit, J. Lutz, A. Frey, and G. Seger: Indiana circuit, S. Altimos and J. Boas; Erie circuit, D. Brickley and J. Noecker; Canton circuit, E. Stœver and P. Gates.

Western Conference, Ohio district, H. Niebel, presiding elder. Canton circuit, Jacob Frey; Wooster circuit, H. Bucks and P. Wist; Mansfield circuit, J. J. Kopp and S. van Gundy; Sandusky circuit, S. Baumgartner and A. Yambert; Lancaster circuit, C. Kring and A. Eby; Miami circuit, E. Sichly.

The membership at this conference amounted to 5119, the increase during the past year to 430; the salary of a single preacher was $51,60.

Up to that time the minutes of the Western Conference were recorded by both conferences. But henceforth this practice ceased, although the minutes of the Western Conference were still sent to the Eastern body. A few years later, General Conference ordered, that the two conferences should hereafter send each other copies of their minutes. This was done in order to draw the bond of union closer between the two bodies, to enable one conference to learn from the other, and the better to watch over each other. Up to that time the minutes of the Western Conference were subject to the revision of the Eastern body, which could approve or reject them. Afterward however, in this respect the conferences became independent of each other, and each was subject to the General Conference.

Thus far the writer has recorded in this history the names of all the ministers, as they were received, deposed from office, expelled, ordained, appointed, or located; because the minutes of the conferences never appeared in print before this time, either in part or in whole, in consequence of which but few of the later preachers and members are acquainted with them to any extent. Although this part of the History may have but little interest for the majority of the readers, yet it is presumed that it will be welcome to the preachers generally. But as these items appeared from 1836, together with other extracts from the minutes of the conferences, in the "Christliche Botschafter," they will hereafter be omitted.

As may be seen from the minutes of the conferences, the number of itinerants increased for several years more rapidly than it had ever done before; although there were still more or less locations taking place every year, either on account of bodily infirmities or family concerns. It is, however, but too probable, that some located more for want of a spirit of self-denial and of love to the life of an itinerant, than on account of bodily infirmities or for other substantial reasons. Yet in proportion to the number of itinerants, locations were far less frequent now than formerly. The support of the preachers, it is true, was still very low; but as those having families, were now entitled to draw something for them from conference, and as in addition to their regular support, they were sometimes presented with clothing and provisions for their families,—those who knew how to economize, and met with no losses, nor incurred heavy expenses by sickness, enjoyed a competency. But those who understood not frugality, or whose families could not accustom themselves to a simple and frugal living, would still fall back.—Moreover, the districts and circuits were from time to time made smaller and more convenient, so that the journeys and labors of the preachers became easier, and consequently there was not so much occasion for locating on account of bodily infirmities, although *daily*, or almost daily, *preaching* was still the order of the day. Healthy, stout men were expected to do this; and those who were both able and willing to do so, were, on the whole, the best and most efficient preachers. By *daily preaching*, their whole attention was engrossed, and the mind preserved from worldly thoughts: a taste for reading, searching, and praying was cultivated; their faculties were more rapidly developed, and their usefulness was thus proportionably increased. And even in our days, those who, on the extreme boundaries, in thinly settled conferences, travel on extensive circuits, preaching almost daily, seem to be, if not the *greatest*, yet, on the whole, the most *useful* preachers of the Society. Those, on the contrary, who have but few appointments, which they can fill on Sundays, seem to make, as a general thing, the slowest progress in their calling, and to accomplish the least. As the circuits were in former years too *large* and *difficult*, to the injury of some of the preachers; so many are in our days (1855) too small and too convenient, likewise to the injury of many preachers.—

In the same ratio in which the number of itinerants increased, so likewise the increase of the membership went on more rapidly. Some of the circuits were enlarged, others divided and new ones formed, and thus many parts of the country were explored and occupied, which for want of preachers, had not been visited before. The conference year from spring 1835 to 1836, was again very prosperous, and in reference to increase of membership exceeded every previous year. The work of God spread especially in the East, more particularly again on the upper part of Schuylkill circuit, in Mahantango Valley, where during this year the first camp-meeting was held in that vicinity, on the land of *Henry Heppler*, which was a very good meeting; also in Leikens Valley, on Reading circuit in Lehigh county, Upper Milford, and near Allentown at Mertz's, and farther east.—In Philadelphia also, where one of our preachers was stationed this year for the first time, the prospects for gathering a large congregation continued to brighten; the society there increased considerably during the year, and at its close numbered 72 members.—The efficient Sabbath-school, which has existed there ever since, was established during this year. On Cumberland circuit, formerly called Franklin circuit, near Carlisle, where the gracious work had begun some years before, it also spread gloriously this year; the number of believers increased considerably: those who had been converted in former years, were strengthened in their faith; and some of those in other parts, who had grown lukewarm, were filled with new zeal. Also on the circuits of Union, Lycoming, and Centre, the number of believers increased considerably during this year; likewise on Buffalo circuit, in the state of New York.

In short, the work spread, with but few exceptions, on all circuits of the Society in a glorious manner, and its prospects were, on the whole, brighter than ever before.

Fifth General Conference.

As General Conference had hitherto not been held regularly every fourth year, but only whenever the Eastern Conference deemed it necessary; the intervals were sometimes more, sometimes less than four years. The fourth General Conference took place, as already stated, in 1830, in Nov.; and the fifth was held in May, 1835, four years and a half after; while the sixth took place in Nov., 1836, after an interval of only eighteen months.

Pursuant to a resolution of the Eastern Conference of 1834, the General Conference assembled May 25th, 1835, at Orwigsburg, Schuylkill county, Pa. As the system of *delegates* had not yet been introduced, each elder had still the privilege to attend and to vote, as a member of conference. The following elders were present: H. Niebel, J. G. Zinser, J. Seybert, W. W. Orwig, P. Wagner, J. Barber, J. Breidenstein, J. C. Reisner, J. Long, C. Hammer, J. H. Yambert, C. Kring, J. Schnerr, D. Kehr, S. G. Miller, G. Brickley, F. Hoffman, E. Stœver, and J. M. Saylor,—in all 19.

After reading a portion of Holy Writ, singing a hymn, and invoking the blessings of the Most High, conference was organized by H. Niebel being elected chairman, who appointed J. G. Zinser secretary.

A much larger amount of business claimed the attention of this body, than had been the case at any former General Conference; the most important items are here subjoined.—The presiding elder districts were, to some extent, changed, and the conference districts divided differently. The circuits of Somerset, Indiana, and Erie, were cut off from the Eastern Conference, and added to the Western; they were, together with Canton circuit of the Western Conference, formed into a new presiding elder district, called *Carmel* district. Thus the Eastern Conference numbered three districts, viz., *Canaan*, *Zion*, and *Salem*; while the Western numbered two, viz., *Carmel* and *Ohio*.—But in the following year, the Western Conference formed *three* out of its two districts, and called the new one *Tabor* district. The conferences of those days seem to have had a strong predilection to *figurative names* for their districts; which, however, represented nothing more than the land, and certain mountains and cities of the Israelites of old, without indicating, in the least, their geographical position; subsequently, however, the conferences took this point always into consideration, in naming their districts. The time of session for the Annual Conferences was also changed, the month of March being fixed on instead of May and June.

This body also enacted a law, requiring a book to be kept on every circuit and station, for the purpose of recording therein the minutes of the quarterly conferences; and to hold local preacher conferences on every circuit, containing several of them; and prescribing the rules and routine of business for their sessions, as they are contained in the Discipline. The enactment of this conference, requiring *German Sabbath-schools* to be introduced into our societies, wherever practicable, and making it obligatory on the superintending preachers to take an active interest in this matter, was seasonable and very wholesome for the connection; but the word "*German*" had afterward to be struck out, because it gave rise to misunderstanding, some contending that the introduction of English or partly English Sabbath-schools was forbidden thereby. Henceforth it seems there had not been a single Sabbath-school established within our borders; although many of our members sent their children to the Sabbath-schools of other denominations, and patronized them. But shortly after this conference, these *nurseries* of the Church arose in various places within the Association. The good cause, however, in some places met with opposition, by members of the Church. Partly for the want of better information, partly from prejudices, strengthened by false reports as to their end and object, some in other respects well disposed persons looked upon Sabbath-schools as dangerous and as belonging to *Babel;* and so likewise afterward with regard to the cause of missions, when its claims were urged on the attention of the Society at large. Yet, the second number of the "*Christliche Botschafter,*" dated February, 1836, contains the following remarks, setting forth the manner in which this enactment of General Conference had been received by the Church at large, and expressing strong hopes that it would be universally carried out:—

"We are pleased to learn, that in compliance with the injunctions of General Conference, measures are taken nearly throughout the Evangelical Association, to introduce Sabbath-schools.— — — — Our preachers on their respective circuits, have exerted themselves, and succeeded without meeting with great opposition, in making a promising beginning in this good cause. It is true, the cause does not yet command that general attention, to which, in our opinion, it is so eminently entitled; but it is progressing, and we hope to see ere long, at least *one* Sabbath-school established in each class of every circuit, throughout the entire Association."

Although this hope has hitherto not been realized, yet the cause has taken a good start, and is still moving onward. But it is to be regretted, that so many members of the Church, though they declare themselves in favor of Sabbath-schools, take no part themselves, either in establishing or conducting them; and yet they cannot assign any sufficient reason to justify their inactivity. How such persons can read the passage of Scripture, "*To him that knoweth how to do good, and doeth it not, it is sin,*" without feeling compunction, is difficult to explain, except they are ignorant or reprobates.

It is indeed a small matter, in which place the first Sabbath-school of the Association was established, yet New Berlin seems to claim this honor; while others are of opinion that it is due to Lebanon, Pa. At all events, it is certain that in these two places, as well as in Orwigsburg and Philadelphia, the first Sabbath-schools of the Society were established. The first report of the Philadelphia Sabbath-school was published in the "Botschafter," Vol. I. No. 3., page 20. At first the main object was to establish *German* Sabbath-schools. This was, however, soon found to be impracticable, as not only many members were in favor of putting the English on an equal footing with the German; but in some places a sufficient number of *German teachers* could not be found, and in others none at all. The English language was then introduced, and is now, in some places, in the ascendency. Yet in the maritime cities, where the congregations consist almost exclusively of European German members, and in some places in the North and West, the Sabbath-schools are still exclusively German. The scarcity of proper German Sabbath-school books, was at first another great obstruction to German schools; but this evil was soon after remedied, in part at least, by the Book Establishment of the Society.

The founding of the "*Charitable Society*" of the Evangelical Association, was another useful measure of this conference. The object of this society is, to take charge of all legacies which have been or may still be bequeathed to the Society, to relieve the poor superannuated itinerants, and after their death, their widows, and orphans under 14 years of age; to loan them out on lawful interest, with sufficient security, and to divide the yearly proceeds among the several Annual Conferences of the Society, for the purpose aforesaid. This was the original object of said legacies; but as the proceeds from the funds were formerly rarely or never altogether used for this purpose, permission was granted to apply the surplus to the support of the itinerants in actual service.—The society consists of *nine trustees*, and is lawfully incorporated for the management of said funds.—As it may be interesting to some of the readers, to become more fully acquainted with said society and its mode of doing business, we insert its constitution, beginning on the following page.

CONSTITUTION

OF THE CHARITABLE SOCIETY OF THE EVANGELICAL ASSOCIATION.

Be it known, that John Seybert, Jacob Hammer, Joseph Hammer, Eli Hammer, Samuel Rickert, John Rickert, John P. Leib, William Wildermuth, and Andrew Schwalm, all citizens of the Commonwealth of Pennsylvania, have formed themselves into a society, for the purpose of creating and establishing a fund for the relief and support of the itinerant superannuated ministers, their wives and children, widows and orphans, of the Evangelical Association, in the United States of America; and being desirous to acquire and enjoy the powers and immunities of a corporation or body politic in law, agreeably to an Act of Assembly, passed the sixth day of April, 1791, entitled an Act to confer on certain Associations of citizens of this Commonwealth, the powers and immunities of corporations or bodies politic in law, have agreed upon the following articles for their government:—

ARTICLE 1. The name, style, and title of this corporation shall be "*The Charitable Society of the Evangelical Association*," and shall be located in the borough of Orwigsburg, in the County of Schuylkill, and Commonwealth of Pennsylvania; and shall be managed and conducted by *nine trustees*; *five* of whom shall at all times constitute a quorum, for the transaction of business, and the present trustees shall consist of all the members of this society, to wit., John Seybert, Jacob Hammer, Joseph Hammer, Eli Hammer, Samuel Rickert, John Rickert, John P. Leib, William Wildermuth, and Andrew Schwalm, they and their successors, qualified and appointed as is hereinafter mentioned, are hereby vested with full powers for carrying into effect the benevolent and charitable purposes in this instrument mentioned and declared.

ARTICLE 2. The said trustees and their successors, by the name, style, and title aforesaid, shall be able and capable in law to take, receive, have, hold, possess, and enjoy, all and all manner of lands, tenements, rents, annuities, franchises, and hereditaments, and any sum or sums of money, and any manner and portion of goods and chattles, given, granted, or devised unto them, or their successors, by any person or persons, bodies politic or corporate, agreeably to the intention of the donors respectively, and according to the objects, articles, and conditions in this instrument mentioned and declared: Provided that the clear yearly value or income of the messuage, houses, lands and tenements, rents, annuities, or other hereditaments and real estate of the said corporation, and the interest of money by it lent, shall not exceed the sum of two thousand dollars; and by the name, style, and title aforesaid, shall be able and capable in law, to sue and be sued, plead and be impleaded, in any court or courts, before any judge or judges, justice or justices, in all manner of suits, complaints, pleas, causes, matters and demands whatsoever, and all and every matter and thing therein to do in as full and effectual a manner as any other person or persons, bodies politic and corporate, within this Commonwealth, may or can do.

ARTICLE 3. In case of the death, resignation, or expulsion from membership, according to the rules and discipline from time to time adopted by the itinerant ministers of the said Evangelical Association in the General Conference assembled, of any or more of the members of the said corporation or their successors; then and in such case it shall be the duty of the remaining trustees, to nominate double the number of those whose seats may have been vacated, as aforesaid, and to make a representation thereof in writing to the itinerant ministers of the said Association in their next General Conference assembled, whose duty it shall be, then and there to proceed and choose, and by a majority of votes, appoint one or more persons, as the case may be, out of the whole number of those nominated by the trustees, as aforesaid, to fill such vacancy or vacancies, in order to keep up the number of nine trustees forever; and upon every such choice and appointment, a certificate shall issue from the said General Conference, signed by their president, and countersigned by their secretary, and directed to the trustees of the said corporation, containing the name or names of the person or persons so chosen and appointed; which said certificate shall be registered in the books of the said corporation; and the person or persons thus chosen and appointed, shall be vested with all the powers and immunities of a member of the said corporation: *Provided* nevertheless, that no person or persons shall be eligible as a trustee or trustees of the said corporation, who has not been a member of the said Evangelical Association according to the rules and Discipline thereof, as aforesaid, at least one year next preceding his or their election and appointment, as aforesaid, and who shall not be at least twenty-one years of age.

ARTICLE 4. The said corporation shall meet at least once in every year, for the dispatch of their necessary business, at such time and place as a majority of them may judge most convenient and proper; when so met, they shall have power to make such by-laws, rules, and regulations, for their government in the management of their affairs, as a majority of them may judge necessary; and also at every such annual meeting, they shall proceed to choose, and by a majority of votes appoint two of their own number, to act, the one as president, and the other as secretary to the said corporation, who may continue them in office from year to year, as a majority of the said corporation may think proper.

ARTICLE 5. It is provided and declared that, if at any time hereafter a majority of the trustees should deem it expedient, by deed or otherwise, to grant, bargain, sell, convey, or otherwise dispose of any part or parcel of the estate real or personal of, and belonging to, the said corporation, or charge or encumber the same; then and in such case it shall be their duty to make a representation thereof in writing to the itinerant ministers of the said Association, in their next General Conference assembled, who shall then and there judge of the necessity or expediency of such proposed sale; and if two-thirds of the ministers assembled as aforesaid, shall consent and agree thereto, a certificate shall issue from the said General Conference, signed by their president, and countersigned by their secretary, declaring such approbation and consent, and specifying the kind and amount of the property to be sold or otherwise to be disposed of, which certificate shall be transmitted to the said trustees, who shall cause the same to be recorded in the books of the said corporation: *Provided* always, that the moneys arising from such licensed sale shall be vested by the said trustees as soon as conveniently may be, in such other securities and property as in the judgment of a majority of them will be most productive and safe; and, *Provided* further, that the annual interest and income arising from the money so vested, shall be exclusively applied in the manner and for the uses and purposes in this instrument mentioned and declared.

ARTICLE 6. The annual rents, interest, and income of the estate real and personal, which now does, or at any time hereafter may, belong to the said corporation, and their successors, shall by them be held subject to the exclusive order and control of the itinerant ministers of the Evangelical Association in the United States, in their General Conference from time to time assembled; and the said ministers thus assembled, are hereby vested with full powers, to appropriate and point out the mode of applying the same to the objects under the limitations, and for the uses and purposes herein mentioned and expressly declared.

ARTICLE 7. The object and design of the fund hereby intended to be established, is expressly for the purpose of relieving the distresses, and supplying the deficiencies of itinerant and superannuated ministers of the Evangelical Association in the United States of America, who remain in connection with, and continue subject to, the order and control of the General Conference, as also for the relief of the wives and children, widows and orphans, of such ministers, and for no other use, intent, or purpose whatever.

ARTICLE 8. No sum exceeding fifty dollars, shall in any one year be appropriated and applied to the use of an itinerant superannuated single minister; also that no sum exceeding one hundred dollars in any one year shall be applied to the use of an itinerant superannuated married minister; and that no sum exceeding fifty dollars in any one year shall be applied to the use of each widow of such ministers, as are herein before mentioned and described; and also that no sum exceeding twelve dollars shall be applied in any one year to the use of each child or orphan of such ministers as are herein before particularly mentioned and described.

ARTICLE 9. No sum or sums of money, under any pretence whatever, shall be drawn from the fund hereby intended to be established, other than for the uses and purposes, and under the limitations and restrictions herein before expressly mentioned and declared: *Provided* nevertheless, that the trustees of the said corporation, and their successors, shall have power to draw and apply from time to time as much money belonging to the said fund, as in the judgment of a majority of them may be wanting, to defray all the necessary expenses of conducting the business of the said corporation.

ARTICLE 10. It shall be the duty of the trustees, to cause regular and fair accounts to be kept, in books to be provided for that purpose out of the funds of the said corporation, as it respects the kind and amount of the capital stock, and of the annual interest and income thereof, as of all and every sum or sums of money which shall from time to time be drawn therefrom, for the objects under the limitations, and for the uses and purposes herein before particularly mentioned and declared; and further, it shall be the duty of the said trustees and their successors, at every General Conference of the ministers as aforesaid, to prepare and lay before them a statement of the affairs of the said fund, for their inspection and examination, which said statement shall be signed by the president, and countersigned by the secretary of the said corporation, certifying that the same is fair and correct.

In testimony whereof we have subscribed our names hereto.

John Seybert,	Jacob Hammer,
Joseph Hammer,	Eli Hammer,
Samuel Rickert,	John Rickert,
John P. Leib,	Wm. Wildermuth,

Andrew Schwalm.

From this constitution of the society it appears, that it was not the object of its founders to grant to poor superannuated itinerants or their widows and orphans their entire support, but only part of it every year. It is presumed, that the persons in question will support themselves, if able to do so; but if their means are insufficient, they are entitled to some support from the conferences to which they belong. Respecting this Charitable Society, people are divided in their opinions. While some regard it as very good and even necessary, others call its usefulness into question, as being calculated to blunt the zeal of some individuals to support themselves, and to induce them to keep themselves always in such circumstances as to be entitled, by the rules of Discipline, to some support from their respective conferences. Those who entertain this view, are of opinion that it would be better to allow the preachers better salaries, while in actual service of the Church; and when they quit it, to let them look out for themselves, as also other poor people are compelled to do. Moreover, according to the rules of Discipline, they say, even such preachers as have never been of much service to the Church, but rather a burden to it, as well as their families, can claim support from the Church.—Be this as it may, the Society has hitherto had but few of the kind mentioned to support, as most of them were determined to provide for themselves; and some would rather live in indigence and deny themselves the necessaries of life, than apply to the conferences for support, as long as these are not able to give their ministers in actual service a respectable support.

The rule with regard to the salary of the preachers was also changed by this conference. Hitherto the married preachers, who had served five years or more as itinerants, had received, irrespective of the number of their children, equal salaries, i. e., twice as much as an unmarried preacher. This rule was now changed as follows: a married preacher without children was to receive three halves of the salary of a single man; and he who had *one* or *two* children, seven-fourths; and he who had *three* or more children, double the amount of the salary of an unmarried preacher. By this change, married men who had either no children at all or not more than two, suffered a considerable diminution of their salary, while that of unmarried men, who needed it the least, was considerably increased; for this reason the rule was soon after repealed. In the next place, it was resolved that a preacher having been married two years previous to his entering the itinerancy, should after two years be entitled to an allowance for his family, according to the above rule; but a newly married preacher was to be put on an equal footing with a single one, i. e., he was to travel five years before he should be entitled to any allowance for his family. The latter clause of this rule was afterward changed from five to *four* years. Many young preachers, indeed, have already complained of this rule; but it has thus far remained in force, being considered just and wholesome. Its object is, as every one knows, to prevent young inexperienced preachers from burdening the societies, which they may be called to serve, with the maintenance of their families; or rather, to induce a young man, who is called to the ministry in single life, to remain in that state, till by his usefulness he gains the confidence of the Church. and acquires some practice and experience in his office. And experience has also taught, that those young men who travel a number of years before they marry, become the most useful and efficient preachers, and usually maintain their posts as heralds of the Gospel the longest. But the most important measure of this conference, was the resolution for publishing the "*Christliche Botschafter*," a measure which proved much more important than had been anticipated. This enterprise, however, like all others, met with considerable opposition even from an influential party of conference itself—yet a great majority was in its favor.—A religious paper had long before been felt to be a desideratum in the Church; but this feeling had not been general, but confined to comparatively few. The German Churches of those days were, in general, unacquainted with this kind of literature; and only those members who were in the habit of reading similar English papers, were prepared to appreciate its value and importance. Some attempts of the kind by other denominations, had failed; and even some English religious papers were but meanly patronized, while others from want of support failed altogether. Add to this, that some considered the enterprise a dangerous innovation, similar to *Sabbath-schools*, the *temperance cause*, etc.—For these and similar reasons it required a great deal of persevering efforts to procure the number of 700 subscribers, as stipulated by General Conference. Some apprehended that the paper in question would make the Society proud and worldly-minded; that its members would attach too much importance to mere *literary attainments*. Others said they had the *Bible*, with which they were satisfied, as the contemplated paper would scarcely be better than that. General Conference appointed a committee from the Eastern Conference to publish the paper in the manner prescribed, as soon as the above mentioned number of subscribers could be procured. The superintending preachers, all of whom had been constituted agents for the Periodical, went to work in a spirited manner, and early the next fall it appeared that the enterprise could be carried out, according to the conditions laid down. The Brethren A. Ettinger, of York county, Pa., and G. Miller, of New Berlin, who was a printer, were charged by said committee with the publication of the paper, and thus its first number appeared in January, 1836: during the first four years of its existence, it appeared but once a month. The first number was anxiously looked for, and was received and read with delight by many. Although defective, both with regard to arrangement, order, contents, and external appearance; yet its friends became more and more satisfied of its usefulness and advantage for the Society, so that the number of its patrons increased every month, till at the close of the second year, they had risen to 1500. At first, it had but few correspondents, and these kept themselves as much as possible in the back ground, as their names appeared but rarely; perhaps they were afraid of giving offense, or of becoming proud by seeing their names so often in print. But in course of time matters changed, and the names of correspondents were given more frequently, especially with reports. Although the contributors were mostly inexpert, and their diction imperfect; yet the Periodical became more and more popular, and exerted a very salutary influence on the Association.—The reports of revivals and new openings to the cause of the Gospel, and its progress generally—the times of meeting of the conferences, and their minutes in extract—deaths and other important events, described in simple, yet enthusiastic and glowing language—such and similar subjects filled the columns of the Periodical, and the results brought about thereby, were glorious: the Association learned to know itself and others better—its various parts became more closely and intimately united—the interest in the general welfare was rapidly increased—unanimity in the application of the most efficient means and measures for the advancement of the Redeemer's kingdom was promoted—the talents and energies of the connection were called into healthful action, and thus its prosperity and more rapid increase were effectually secured. The establishment of this Periodical was, therefore, one of the best measures the Society ever took to develop its strength, extend its borders, enhance its influence, and to increase its usefulness among sister Churches.

Brother Ettinger's residence being at a great distance from New Berlin, where the Periodical was printed by G. Miller, he resigned his editorship already in the first year; and thus the paper came, after it had existed 15 months, into the hands of the writer of this history, who edited it nearly seven years in succession, during which time both its circulation and usefulness greatly increased, although there was still room left for improvements.

In addition to this, conference resolved to have an edition of 4000 copies of the smaller hymn book printed; a committee was also appointed to examine "Fletcher's Appeal," and to decide about the expediency of getting this work translated into German. Several more resolutions were passed in reference to the book trade of the Society, which was still in a very prostrate condition; as without a printing establishment of its own, the profits, as a matter of course, were quite limited. These, together with a few items of less importance, were the doings of the fifth General Conference, the consequences of which, as appears from what has been stated, have already proved a great blessing to the connection, and we trust, will continue to do so in future.

In consequence of the change of the times for the conference sessions, the conference year of 1835–36 was shortened by two months; it had, notwithstanding, a greater increase than any former year, viz., 509. The membership of the entire Association at the end of this year, was 5628.

Since for the reasons already given, the minutes of the conferences will hereafter be omitted, the order of the history will now be somewhat changed, and the annual increase and the whole membership given at the close of every conference year, instead of at the opening of the following year.

The Year 1836.

Both conferences held their annual sessions this year in March, the Western beginning the 7th, and the Eastern the 28th of that month: the former in Jackson township, Wayne county, Ohio; the latter at Rebersburg, Centre county, Pa. Four of the itinerants located, and eight new applicants were admitted on trial. The Eastern Conference numbered 30, the Western 25 itinerants, in all 55. Ten years before, in 1826, the entire number of itinerants had been 21.—

During this year, the Association prospered more than it had done in any previous year. Although the preceding year had a greater increase than any former one, yet this year the same was more than doubled. Nearly all circuits of both conferences had a considerable increase of members; in several places glorious revivals took place, and many circuits enlarged their borders by taking up new preaching places, and forming new classes. The Eastern Conference received 747, the Western 673 new members; in all, 1420. The old Union circuit of the Eastern Conference had a considerable addition this year, the result of an extensive revival, that occurred along the Susquehanna below Selinsgrove, under the superintendence of D. Berger and C. Holl. During a camp-meeting, which was held there in August, a considerable number of precious souls had already been awakened and converted. Toward the close of December, and in the beginning of January, a protracted meeting was then held there in private houses, one day in this, the next in another place, which resulted in a number of conversions, some of which were of a very remarkable character.—The Strickler's family, on the island in the Susquehanna, opposite the section of country under consideration, were converted this year, and afterward added to Schuylkill circuit.

In the city of Philadelphia also, the work made glorious progress this year. Divine service was held there in a large school-house, near the spot on which the church of the first society was afterward erected, between North 2nd and St. John's streets, near Poplar lane. Toward Christmas a glorious revival began, which continued nearly all winter, with but few interruptions. The society was strengthened thereby, and its influence greatly increased. At the close of the conference year, in March, 1837, the society numbered 124 members, and the prospects for the future were flattering. During this revival, the writer, accompanied by Brother Seybert, came on a visit to Philadelphia, when one evening a woman, 94 years of age, made her appearance with others at the altar of prayer, and at the close of the service, professed to have found peace with God, rejoicing in his love. This, indeed, was an entering into the vineyard of the Lord at the *eleventh hour*.

The Brethren J. G. Zinser and C. Hammer visited Upper Canada this year, the former *once*, the latter *twice*. These were the first visits there by preachers of the Evangelical Association, since Brother Dreisbach's visit in 1816. In several regions of that province of the English empire lived a great many Germans, who, for the most part, had emigrated thither from Pennsylvania, and were, in a religious point of view, in a very neglected condition, having either no preacher at all, or only such as were not worthy of the name of an evangelical preacher. The brethren were cordially received and found many attentive hearers, who were anxious to learn. By these and some later visits from other brethren, as well as by the information concerning the Evangelical Association, gained by some families who had emigrated to the state of Ohio, embraced religion there, and written back to their relatives and acquaintances in Canada, the longing of the people after regular preaching by our ministers continued to increase, and the invitations became more urging, till at length the Eastern Conference, at its session in 1839, established two missions there, the *Waterloo* and the *Black Creek* mission, both of which have prospered.

In order to give the reader a better insight into the religious condition of the German population in Canada in those days, and the views of the brethren who had visited that country, we here insert a few extracts from their letters, which they had published in our Periodical. Brother J. G. Zinser, in a letter dated June 28th, 1836, among other things says:—

"I have also taken a journey to Canada this summer: I remained there nine days, preached five sermons in different places, and had attentive hearers every time, nearly all of them Germans, by whom this section of the country is thickly settled. But as for the means of grace, these people are in a very bad condition. As far as I came, the Mennonite societies are the most numerous of the Germans professing religion. There are, however, many persons professing nothing at all; but their outward appearance is evidently very plain. It is very desirable, that faithful ministers of the Gospel be sent thither, believing that the Lord would gather a large congregation there to Himself. Ought we then not to pray to the Lord of the harvest, to send laborers into his vineyard?—I could not but with compassion and grief look upon the condition of these people, being like sheep without a shepherd. There are indeed, as it appeared to me, a great many persons anxiously engaged to save their immortal souls, in their own way, which consists principally in their appearance, which is very plain and lowly; but about the new life in God they know nothing, yea, many of them being taught so by their wretched and lifeless preachers, deny and reject true holiness altogether. The abominable doctrine, so favorable to the devil's kingdom, viz., '*that a man must all his life long remain a poor sinner, and can not become free*,' is spread in Canada as well as elsewhere."

Brother C. Hammer writes in a letter, dated January 27th, 1837, of his two visits to Canada as follows :—

"Since our last Annual Conference, I have also paid two visits to Upper Canada, where I met a great many Germans, who were very anxious to hear the word of life preached to them in their vernacular tongue. I made my first journey thither in the month of October last, remained ten days, and preached nine sermons to attentive audiences. The second journey I took in the beginning of this month. I traveled about 100 miles into the northern part, and found a great many Germans, both Americans and Europeans, who appeared to me like sheep without a shepherd. Preaching in the German language seemed to be a novelty there. I do not remember of ever having been in any part of country where the hearers manifested a greater desire to hear the word of God than here. It is true, I had no time to remain long ; yet I preached eight sermons before I left, two each day ; and I have reason to believe that my labors were not in vain, for many hearts were so powerfully affected by the word that tears flowed freely. O! how it rejoices the servant of God, to see that the hearers manifest a true desire to hear the Word of God ; then preaching is a pleasure. Strange emotions filled my heart when I left this region, pondering within myself that many of the Germans are so entirely forsaken, having no true teacher to point out to them the way to heaven. I also thought, if they had the opportunity to hear the Gospel preached in its power, as many have it in the United States, not a few would become obedient and bow to the mild sceptre of Immanuel. O! that the believers would pray to the Lord, to send laborers into his vineyard ; for the harvest is great, but the faithful laborers are few."

About this time the so-called "*protracted meetings*" were introduced into the Evangelical Association. Before this, the general and quarterly meetings usually lasted not longer than *two* or *three* days; although several other Christian denominations, especially the Methodists, had introduced this kind of meetings long before. The reason for their introduction was, as follows: It was often found, that not until the close of two or three days' meetings, the audience became quite awake and affected, and that then, if the meeting had been continued for a few days longer, many would, in all probability, have been converted; as the experience had often taught at camp-meetings, which generally lasted five, six and even eight days.—Some of the brethren tried this method, and met with very good success. But like every other new measure, this also found its opponents in the Society. It was objected, that if there would be preaching in one place every day for weeks, other parts would necessarily be neglected; that it would be a burden to the neighborhood, where these meetings were held, as vagabonds would thus have a chance to be fed for weeks by others, etc.—But as the good results of several such meetings were published in the Periodical, they were soon advocated and tried by other brethren, who had similar good success.—Brother Boas was among the first who introduced these meetings, and published the first report of the result of such a meeting in our Periodical, part of which is here inserted. The report is dated, Erie county, Pa., June 27th, 1836, and among other things, contains the following:—

"We had an eight days' meeting in a settlement, about four miles south of Brighton, near the Conneaut lake. It began May 27th; the Lord was present and wrought so powerfully, that I had never witnessed the like before. During the first few days there was but little stir; yet the word of God often reached the hearts of the hearers, so that they melted and bewailed their sins. On Sunday we had very blessed meetings; in the evening some persons prayed for pardon. On Monday we again assembled three times, and God granted us his blessing, especially in the evening, so that sinners implored God's mercy and pardon, and their faithful prayers were answered. On Tuesday there was preaching at 10 o'clock, A. M., and in the afternoon we held an experience meeting, when God's power was revealed to us, and the hearts were softened and melted. In the evening of the same day, a great many persons obtained pardon.

On Wednesday, June 1st, the meeting continued prosperously. In the evening we had such powerful times, that before I commenced preaching, the place was almost shaken, and sinners commenced to cry out for mercy. I then gave a brief exhortation, and God accompanied the word with power to the hearts of the hearers, so that a mighty shaking of the dry bones ensued. There lay many stricken and wounded souls; but God be praised! some of them found the good physician (Jesus), who can heal all diseases, and who delivered them from the load of their sins, translating them into the liberty of the children of God. There was life, and the praises of the Most High resounded through the place. On Thursday we again had a happy season. A considerable number of penitent souls were pardoned, and the meeting lasted all night. We could joyfully exclaim with Peter, '*Lord, it is good for us to be here.*'

On Friday I preached two more sermons, and a few more penitents found Christ precious to their souls. In the evening after the sermon, I called on those persons who had found peace during the meeting, and knew that they had passed from death unto life; whereupon from 25 to 30 persons were not ashamed to rise, testifying thereby that they had found peace with God during that meeting.

At the close of the meeting, I gave an invitation to those who were willing to unite with us, and a considerable number of the new converts gave me their right hands, to go with us to heaven.

Two years ago we had not a member in this part of the country, but now we have a society of about 50 members in a prosperous condition. It is true, persecution has been very sore since our meeting; yet the Lord is with his people, and to them that love God, all things work together for good.

In my opinion, more good could generally be accomplished on our circuits, if more such protracted meetings were held. For it is often the case, that when meetings of two or three days are held, the effects do not begin to show themselves until at their close; and then perhaps but little good has been accomplished, and the labors of the servants of God are sometimes almost entirely in vain. But had such meetings been kept up longer, many precious souls might have been saved. Add to this, that many go home under the load of their sins, grow cold and insensible, and perhaps never again come to a true knowledge of themselves.—O brethren in the Gospel! let us work diligently in the vineyard of the Lord, and make use of all good means, that souls may be saved, and the kingdom of God extended!"

Another report of such a meeting, in the state of New York, by Brother Jacob Riegel, who a few years ago entered into the joy of his Master, dated, Lake circuit, Sept. 20th, 1836, contains the following:—

"Several years ago, our preachers found entrance in Howard Town, Steuben co., and regular preaching has been kept up there ever since, but without any important results, until lately. We had appointed a two days' meeting, which began August 20th; but instead of *two*, it lasted *sixteen* days, with but little interruption. The Lord so blessed his word, that on the first evening, after an invitation had been given, quite a number of mourners came forward to seek the Lord, and to be prayed for. On Sunday, the 21st, there was preaching thrice, and the word made so deep an impression that tears flowed freely. In the evening the whole assembly were visited with such a powerful outpouring of God's Spirit, that parents with their children fell on their knees, crying to God for mercy and the pardon of their sins. On Monday evening, the power of God was again so great in the meeting, that nearly the whole assembly melted into tears: some cried to God, till they found peace, and could rejoice in the Rock of their salvation; others became so disquieted, that they had no rest day or night, till turning in faith and contrition of heart to the Lord, they found mercy.—On Tuesday and Wednesday, the 23rd and 24th, preaching was discontinued; but on Thursday, the 25th, the meeting began anew and lasted till Saturday night, the fourth of September; during which time the Lord wrought so powerfully, that some found peace in the meeting, others at home.—On Sunday, the last day of the meeting, we commemorated the Lord's sufferings and death; which was the first time that this ordinance of the Lord was observed in this place among the Germans, and we had a blessed time.—In all, we have formed during this meeting a class of 25 members, nearly all of whom profess to have found the pardon of their sins and peace with God."

This report of Brother Riegel was followed, in the same number of our Periodical, by a communication of the writer of this history, on the same subject. An extract from it is here subjoined:—

"Brethren, permit me to say a word on the same subject, treated of by Brother Boas in the 8th number of the Periodical, namely in reference to protracted meetings. It has long been the opinion of some of our preachers, that it would be much better, and that considerable more good could be accomplished, if our general meetings were continued, instead of from 2 or 3 days, to 8, 10, 12, or even 14 days; especially in towns, and such places where we have church edifices; and these views have also been confirmed by reports from different parts of the country, where such meetings have been held with glorious success. It is often the case, that meetings are closed when they begin to be interesting; but if they were continued, no doubt sometimes many souls would be converted to the Lord, who, as the meetings are brought to a close so soon, remain unconverted, and—perhaps are lost!—Should we not, therefore, make it a practice, to continue our general meetings, whenever practicable, for a longer time than has heretofore been the case? Other Christian denominations are, in this respect, far ahead of us, and why shall we remain in the rear? It is perhaps objected, that our districts and circuits are too large, to arrange matters thus. This is true; some of them are almost too large; but it would be better not to appoint so many general meetings, and to keep them up longer, even if there should not be regular preaching every two weeks at each preaching place of our circuits. * * * * * I am of opinion, that if we are in earnest to save souls, we should make use of every imaginable means, in order to gain our object. The above stated communication of Brother Riegel, furnishes a new proof of the usefulness of such meetings as are continued for several weeks.

I do not now urge that this should be done everywhere, yet in many places it should. Even if we would continue the exercises sometimes only 5, 6, or 8 days, more good would undoubtedly be accomplished, than has hitherto been the case by our regular routine of business. It might perhaps also be better, that only the friends of one or more classes should meet, than that so many should convene in a place as to overburden those who receive the meeting."

In consequence of these and other reports and commendations of such meetings, they increased rapidly, and in the course of a few years became pretty general in the connection, proving a blessing to hundreds and thousands of souls, and contributing much to the rapid increase of the Association. In several instances they lasted from *four* to *six* weeks, and were richly blessed of God.—It cannot be denied, however, that they were, and are still, sometimes abused, to the great detriment of the good cause; for some preachers spend nearly all their time, or at least the greater part of it, by holding such meetings, and accomplish comparatively but little, at the same time neglecting to enlarge their fields of labor, to take up new preaching places, and to fill their distant appointments. Others sometimes appoint a number of such meetings in advance, allowing for each the space of several weeks; and if the prospects are not very promising at the very outset, they bring them to a close, and then have no appointments for the rest of the time, and, as a matter of course,—*go home*. Thus, in many instances, a great deal of time is lost, and but little accomplished. The work at such meetings, is also sometimes too much *forced;* and, as a general thing, these meetings have of late not been as successful as formerly—especially in such places where they are often repeated. Their novelty has worn off, and their impression is not as strong any more as it used to be. For this reason some have opposed these meetings, while others have dropped them entirely.—It is true, the earlier mode of operation has thereby been changed somewhat. At first it was the object of every service and prayer-meeting, to persuade mourners to come out and get converted, which was often accomplished. But now this is in too many places put off to the protracted meeting, and even then sometimes but little is done. The good "*old measures*" ought never to be dropped; and it should be our aim to use, in connection with them, the "*new ones*" to the greatest possible advantage of the whole Church.—That protracted meetings may sometimes be abused, to the great detriment of the cause of religion, both in the Evangelical Association and other denominations, is no reason against their *proper use.* And the assertion, that such meetings are often followed by times of a *spiritual drought,* is, to some extent, true; but this drought is no necessary consequence of them. Such a consequence is, as experience has often taught, always the fruit of the mismanagement of such meetings: overdoing the exercises, dismissing the meeting at too late hours, exhaustion, bluntness, etc.; and after such meetings are over, neglect of the regular services and of the conscientious use of the ordinary means of grace.—Under these circumstances, a re-action is quite natural and unavoidable; but for this the *protracting* of the meeting can never be blamed.

In a similar way, the camp-meetings also have in some places lost their influence and effect, and, as a consequence, their credit to a great extent. This, however, is no reason why they ought to be given up; on the contrary, people ought to return to the old simplicity and activity during the same, from which they have deviated; which, alas! has also been done in too many places of the Evangelical Association. For although they may in such places especially, where they are an old and well known thing, and where the societies have large churches, in which they hold almost every year one or two protracted meetings, be no longer as effectual as they used to be; yet we still hear occasionally of *old fashioned* camp-meetings in the Association, some of which are held even in places, well provided with church edifices.

The membership at the close of this conference year, was 6665; the increase during the past year, consequently 1035.—This was very encouraging and inspired the ministry with new zeal to prosecute the work of God; it likewise confirmed their belief, that the new measures adopted by the last General Conference, had met with the approbation of the Most High, and warranted the hope that they would continue a blessing to the Society.

Brother John Rœssner, a useful preacher of the Association, closed his earthly career this year. In 1828 he was converted, in the state of Ohio, and afterward joined the Church. In 1831 he came to Pennsylvania to attend the session of the Eastern Conference, and was received into the itinerancy. The writer had him and D. Brickley for his colleagues that year, on York circuit, and thus had the best opportunity of becoming acquainted with him.—He was of slender stature, about six feet high, of a sanguine temperament and witty, and almost universally beloved on account of his affability. For want of practice and because he had read but little, his preaching was at first feeble; but by perseverance in reading and searching, he made rapid progress and soon became a very useful preacher. He was always active in his calling, and was especially intent on seeking new preaching places, for which he was particularly qualified by his philanthropy and courageousness. Revivals were his element, and he delighted in working with the mourners at the altar.—But he impaired his health by over-exerting himself in his exercises, and exposing himself too much to the weather. Thus he once almost froze to death on horseback, on a very cold winter day. On dismounting and entering a house, he fainted away. There he probably contracted his disease which was consumption.

He traveled for two years in succession on York circuit, and was generally beloved. In 1833, he served on Lancaster circuit of the Eastern Conference; but could no longer attend to his duties properly, on account of an increasing cough and debility of the breast. At the next conference session he located. He then returned to the state of Ohio, made an attempt to travel again, but it was only for a short time. His disease became worse, till in 1836 he was confined to his bed, and after a great deal of severe suffering, died in peace and happy in the Lord, January 5th, 1837, in the county of Wayne, Ohio.

EIGHTH SECTION.

FROM THE SPECIAL GENERAL CONFERENCE IN 1836, TO THE REGULAR GENERAL CONFERENCE IN 1839.

Sixth General Conference.

Some of the preachers having for several years, prior to this General Conference, looked upon the re-opening of a printing establishment and book-bindery of our own as practicable and advantageous; and as the publication of the "Christliche Botschafter," the introduction of Sabbath-schools, and the more rapid increase of the Association, which enhanced also the demand for books, seemed to make this measure really necessary; therefore, the Eastern Conference, at its session in March, 1836, appointed a *Special General Conference*, to be held in November next, mainly for this purpose. Each elder in the ministry had still a right to attend General Conference, and was entitled to a vote; but notwithstanding this, only a comparatively small number were in attendance.

Conference met on Monday, Nov. 14th, 1836, in the house of *John Ferner*, in Somerset township, Somerset county, Pa., and closed its session on Saturday following, Nov. 19th. According to the directions of our Discipline, it was opened with reading a portion of the Word of God, singing, and prayer; and organized by electing Henry Niebel chairman, who appointed C. Hammer secretary.

The following brethren were in attendance: Henry Niebel, C. Hammer, Samuel Baumgartner, Solomon G. Miller, John G. Zinser, Elias Stœver, Henry Bucks, John Young, Jacob Schnerr, Charles Hesser, John Seybert, W. W. Orwig, Philip Wagner, Daniel Brickley, George Brickley, Francis Hoffman, John J. Kopp, John P. Leib, and Daniel Kehr, 19—just as many as had been present at the last General Conference, although not the same men throughout.

The printing and book establishment for which this conference had been called, claimed and received its main attention. But although principally convened for this object, yet the proposition to create a printing establishment and book-bindery of our own, met with great opposition: it is true, this opposition proceeded from but few members, but they wielded a powerful influence. They pronounced the enterprise to be premature, unsafe, and impracticable—called to mind the former attempt in the matter and its failure, sparing no efforts to induce conference to drop the subject, which almost succeeded. Even the warmest advocates and friends of the enterprise, at one time vacillated somewhat during the discussion; but soon recovering they then maintained the practicability and advantages of the undertaking with all possible arguments at their command, and with the greatest assurance of final success. At last, after protracted debates, it was resolved by a majority, that the year following a printing office and book-bindery be established at New Berlin, Union county, Pa.; and if sufficient money could not be raised to purchase a lot and erect a suitable building thereon, it was resolved, that a building be rented for the purpose, and to proceed in the matter as well as they could.

P. Wagner, John Rank, and the writer, were elected trustees, to superintend the founding and managing of said establishment. The writer was, in addition to this, appointed agent to solicit contributions for said purpose, within the district of the

Eastern Conference; he was also elected Editor of the "Christliche Botschafter," and General Agent of the establishment. He could, however, not enter upon the duties of the latter offices before April, 1837, as he had to devote all the time up to that period to the collection of funds. This accumulation of duties, imposed upon him in founding and managing the establishment, he looked upon, to some extent, as a punishment for his enthusiasm in the enterprise. The presiding elders and superintending ministers were also requested to assist in collecting, in those parts which the agent might be unable to visit.

Simultaneously with the publication of the resolutions of this conference, concerning the Printing Establishment, the following Editorial appeal to the entire membership for a liberal support of the enterprise, appeared in the Periodical of December, 1836:—

"While we lay before our friends the principal resolutions of General Conference, we would make the following suggestions with regard to their resolutions and propositions, to establish a printing office and book bindery of our own. That such an enterprise will involve heavy outlays, all can readily imagine; and that the Evangelical Association has no funds on hand to meet these expenditures, is likewise known to all. Those therefore, who look upon such an establishment as useful and necessary, will not deem it strange to be called upon for help, which, we trust, they will feel disposed to impart: and this the more so, if they will bear in mind, that what they contribute toward this object, is in reality the same, as what they are in the habit of giving toward the support of the Gospel; for, besides the benefit derived from good books, to be printed in the Establishment, the entire avails arising therefrom, will be applied toward the support and further spread of the Gospel. Hence we confidently expect that our brethren and friends, who have always been ready to support every good cause, will in the present instance also have open hearts and hands, that the kingdom of God may be built up everywhere, and his honor promoted."

A subscription for said purpose was immediately opened at the session of General Conference, and the majority of the brethren subscribed very liberally, considering the times and their circumstances, and most of them *paid down* their full amounts subscribed.—On Christmas following, the agent commenced to solicit subscriptions among the membership, during a general meeting in Rebersburg, Centre county, Pa., and $264 were subscribed. The following four days he traveled in Penn's Valley of the same county, preached every evening, and $200 more were subscribed. During the watch-night on the last of December, in Buffalo Valley, he received $50; and during the following five weeks he traveled throughout the counties of Schuylkill, Lebanon, Berks, and Lehigh, as far as Philadelphia, and over $1000 were subscribed. The friends, both rich and poor, generally manifested great readiness to support the enterprise; and it seemed as if the Lord directed them in so doing. Orwigsburg, Lebanon, and their vicinities, and Upper Milford, especially excelled by their liberality. Also in the counties of York and Cumberland, which the agent, on account of indisposition, could not visit, the preachers received many liberal contributions, as well as in many other places within the Eastern Conference. In the Western Conference no general efforts were made in the matter; yet some of its circuits contributed liberally toward it, especially that of New Lancaster.

But before much had been done by way of collecting, and ere it was known how the agent would succeed, the trustees purchased a house and lot, in Water street, New Berlin, near the church of the Association, for three hundred dollars, at a sheriff's sale. But when it was ascertained that the support of the enterprise would outstrip the most sanguine expectations of its friends, said property was exchanged for a spacious brick building in New Market street, and $1600 were given to boot. This was a bold, unexpected step, which was approved by many, but also censured by not a few. Those who did not favor the enterprise and gave nothing toward it, were loudest in their censures. The trustees, however, were not discouraged thereby, but purchased the necessary materials, and prepared the house both for carrying on the business, and for the General Agent and the printer to live therein, both of whom moved into it the following spring: toward the close of the same year, the new Printing Office went into operation. As has already been stated, the printing and book binding was done, from the failure of the first Printing Establishment up to this time, by *George Miller*.

With regard to the Editor of the "Christliche Botschafter," it was resolved, that he shall in future always be elected by General Conference, be eligible only for two terms in succession, each of 4 years, and that his salary shall be as much as an itinerant actually receives, not what he is entitled to by Discipline, and the sum of an unmarried itinerant's salary for his board. Thus his salary was, at first, from $90 to $110, besides from $45 to $55 for his board. But, as it was impossible for him to subsist on this small allowance, he received additions of from $25 to $35 several times, and at the close of seven years, another addition of $100 from General Conference. During the first two years he also filled the office of General Agent; but as afterward a General Agent was elected, he received the same salary General Conference had fixed upon for the Editor. The other workmen in the Establishment were paid the usual prices for their labor.—In consequence of this economical arrangement and administration, the Establishment soon yielded considerable profits, which were partly distributed among the conferences, partly applied to the increase of the business stock,—something which had never before taken place, while the printing and binding had been done elsewhere. These results satisfied all, that the possession of a printing establishment was a great advantage, and thus all opposition ceased.

This conference resolved likewise that an edition of 2000 copies of J. C. Reisner's German school book shall be published. This book has since passed through several improved editions, has lately been stereotyped, and is held in very high reputation; also a new edition of 4000 copies of the smaller hymn book was ordered to be printed.

These are the principal business items with regard to the Printing Establishment, that were transacted by General Conference. But in addition to these, some others of great importance claimed and received the attention of that body; they were briefly as follows:—

It was resolved, that the two Annual Conferences shall hereafter be independent of each other in their proceedings, the contributions for the support of the preachers alone excepted. Up to this time, the Western Conference had been entirely dependent on the Eastern in its proceedings; the latter body having the power to approve and to reject them, as it deemed best.—The contributions toward the support of the ministers, however, remained the joint property of the two conferences, and were equally divided between them, in proportion to the number of itinerants composing each conference; as the support was still less in the Western than in the Eastern Conference, and therefore a certain amount was sent every year from the latter to the former, to make up their deficiency. Yet the conferences were required to send each other copies of their proceedings annually. It was also resolved, that the Western Conference shall annually send two delegates to the Eastern, to compose, with three members of the latter body, a committee whose duty it shall be, to examine the books that may be laid before it, for publication.

The rule in our Discipline, requiring the superintending minister to give recommendations to those members, who move from one circuit to another, was also established by this General Conference, and perfect liberty of conscience granted to the members of the Society, with regard to baptism, both as to *who* are the proper subjects for baptism, and *how* this rite is to be administered.

C. Hammer was elected presiding elder, in the place of the writer; and S. Witt was ordained as deacon.

The time of meeting for the next General Conference was, for the first time, fixed upon by this body—a practice which has been adhered to ever since. It was to convene in Centre co., Pa., in March, 1839.

The acts and proceedings of this General Conference were of great importance and value to the connection, especially its act with regard to the Printing Establishment and Book-bindery. The effects of this measure have been highly beneficial to the Society, and contributed much to promote its increase.—During the first years, the press was almost constantly in operation. Besides our hymn books, Discipline, a number of Sabbath-school books, etc., the following larger works were also printed at a subsequent period in our Establishment, namely, a German pocket Bible, Rambach's German translation of Collier's Introduction to the Sacred Scriptures, and several works of considerable size for private individuals. In a few years hundreds of thousands of books had proceeded from our establishment—more, alas! than could be sold. Notwithstanding this, there was sometimes a want of some kind of books in certain places. This, however, was not owing to the Establishment being unable to meet every want of the Church in this respect; but it was the consequence of the unequal spread and distribution of the books; too many being sent to some places, and not enough to others, in consequence of the very deficient book system of the Association in those days. Especially was the cause of Sabbath-schools furthered in the connection, by the Establishment, which supplied them with the most necessary books. It distributed also at as early a period as the close of the first year of its existence, $500 of its income to both conferences, for the support of the indigent itinerants, and their poor widows and orphans. This removed the prejudices against the Establishment, which had yet been lingering in many a mind, and secured, in general, a fair reputation for it. At the close of 16 years of its existence, it had distributed *eighteen thousand dollars* among the conferences for said purposes, and increased its own capital to more than *thirty thousand dollars*. Thus, the success and usefulness of the Establishment exceeded by far the most sanguine expectations of its founders, warmest advocates and friends. During this period of sixteen years, the writer was connected with the Establishment, as an officer, nearly twelve years, and as such had the best opportunity to observe its progress and efficiency. Truly, the Society ought to be thankful to Almighty God for his rich blessings vouchsafed to this Establishment, and to rejoice that he has done great things for them also in this enterprise.

The following is an engraving of the building of the Establishment in question.

The Year 1837.

The Western Conference held its annual session this year in Green township, Stark county, Ohio, from the 6th to the 11th of March; and the Eastern at New Berlin, Pa., from the 27th of March to the 3rd of April. Three preachers located, and five applicants were received into the itinerant ministry. The salary of an unmarried preacher was $56,40.

In the Eastern Conference two new circuits were formed, viz., *Leiken's* circuit, out of the western end of Schuylkill, and *Dansville* circuit, out of the western end of Lake circuit. Although the increase of membership was not as great this year, as in the previous; yet the work made visible progress, and the Association extended its borders considerably.—At this time there was a remarkable spirit at work among the ministers, to extend and to enlarge the boundaries of the Church: many of the preachers made it their business to seek new preaching places, and to extend their sphere of labor more or less every year, no matter how large it was already.—Although they had a sufficient number of appointments to fill, every two weeks; yet they were not satisfied, unless they took up a number of new preaching places annually, in new parts of the country.—The presiding elders especially, exerted themselves to obtain new preaching places; and above all, Brother Seybert who then served the Church almost continually as a presiding elder. His example herein, stirred up many others to follow his steps. His district extended over several of the eastern counties of Pennsylvania, and was considerably enlarged during his four years' service there. In order to give the reader a clearer view of the state of things, we here insert his own report on the subject, which was published in No. 5, Vol. III. of the Periodical, and is as follows:—

"As the time is fast approaching, when I must bid farewell to Canaan district, I feel myself inwardly constrained to publish in the "Botschafter" a few of those things which the Lord has wrought for us, during the last four years. When I took charge of the district, I found three circuits, viz., Schuylkill, Lebanon, and Lancaster. In Philadelphia there was but a slight beginning of a work of grace.—The circuits of Schuylkill and Lebanon, I found in a good condition, and the prospects for conversions were fair; but on Lancaster circuit matters looked gloomy in most of the preaching places, except those in the eastern end, where the prospects for conversions were favorable. As the district was small, I devoted during the first two years part of my time to seeking new preaching places, in the dark regions toward the East and North-east; and God crowned my efforts abundantly, so that our borders were soon enlarged about sixty miles. We then united everywhere, to enlarge our borders, till we succeeded, by the help of God, to extend them to such a degree, that there are now six circuits, where four years ago there were but three; and in Philadelphia, where there was but a slight beginning of a work of grace among the Germans, there is now a flourishing, considerable society, and a numerous Sabbath-school; and the whole district, on which four years ago but seven itinerants were traveling, is now numbering fourteen. We have now succeeded, by the help of God, to penetrate far and wide into the formerly so dark counties of Bucks, Northampton, Lehigh, Monroe, as far as Wayne, and have found entrance. At Allentown, Lehigh county, the work of grace has also made a beginning, and the prospects for future conversions are good; in Monroe county two new classes have already been formed. Here we had another illustration of what can be accomplished, if the itinerant and local preachers unitedly strive to enlarge their borders, to seek new preaching places, and to proclaim the pure doctrine in dark regions. O that the Lord would increase the zeal of all his anointed servants among us, and in all other Christian denominations, to discharge their duty, until *the earth shall be full of the knowledge of the Lord, as the waters cover the sea!*"

The following extract from a report of Somerset circuit, on which three ministers traveled during this year, furnishes another proof of the zeal of the ministers to extend their boundaries. It was published in No. 1, of Vol. III. of the "Christliche Botschafter."

"Last spring, when we arrived on this circuit, two of us set out at once for Virginia, in order to obtain new preaching places, as there had not enough appointments been given out for us. On our journey, we called at a house and were told by its inmates, that their house was open for religious meetings. We left an appointment, continued our journey, and found entrance at two more places. On our return we preached in the first mentioned house to a large audience. The next time, one went to Virginia through Maryland and found open doors; also in other places, at which we called, we were received. Some entreated us during the meeting, to preach in their houses also; and others sent us requests from a distance, so that we have already taken up sixteen new preaching places.—We also rejoiced, when a number of persons came to our meetings during harvest on week-days, from a distance of 7 or 8 miles; and a certain man once said to his laborers, '*Come, let us go to meeting; that is better than making hay.*' In these new places some seem to have been wounded deeply, and others have begun to seek the Lord in prayer. Although we met with great opposition from ungodly, unconverted teachers, yet the prospects for conversions are now favorable. The Lord was with us in our journey, so that the word preached was better received than in those places where it has become a trite subject, and the people do not deem it worth while any more to travel a short distance to hear it.—But also some of the old places are in a prosperous condition."

Many more such examples might be given; and it is greatly desirable, that this spirit to extend the kingdom of God and to promote the best interests of the Society, would be rekindled among us, and become more general than it has ever been.—It is true, there have always been some in our midst, who were filled with this spirit; but they were generally only the minority.

In Philadelphia the work progressed remarkably well during this year, under the charge of the beloved and esteemed *C. Hesser*. More than a hundred members were received, and notwithstanding the many cares and troubles arising from the building of a new church, everything prospered. Brother Hesser labored there for two years in succession very satisfactorily; and after an absence of a little more than a year, nearly two years again. But this year was the most prosperous of his time of service there. The church was dedicated to the service of God on the 1st of October, and Brother Seybert made the following remarks on it in the "Botschafter":—

"On Sunday, Oct. 1st, our church in Philadelphia was dedicated. The services were continued during the week, and a number of attentive hearers were always in attendance, some of whom were awakened and converted.—The house is 60 by 36; it is built very plain, but well and conveniently arranged.

The basement is divided into a large room for holding prayer-meetings and the Sabbath-school, and two smaller rooms for class-meetings; the upper story forms a very spacious and convenient hall for preaching."

On Lebanon circuit, especially in the town of Lebanon, a glorious revival took place this year, under the charge of F. Hoffman and J. Vogelbach. With regard to the work in the town, J. V. makes the following remarks in a report published in the "Botschafter":—

"We held a protracted meeting at Lebanon, from Nov. 24th to December 5th. Here the light of truth has shone for some time in brightness; had the inhabitants made room for it and followed out their convictions, most of them would now have the love and life of God in their hearts. But the conditions which Jesus lays down for his followers, *to forsake everything*, were too hard for many; yet the truth was too powerful, the light too bright, to go backward. The motto finally was, *forward!* Arrangements were made in churches and school-houses; one step more was taken. May God help to move still more onward! The struggle between light and darkness has come to a happy issue; now it is between life and death, and O that *life* may prove victorious! Our meeting now fell in the time of the special gracious visitation of God, and we had heavenly times: the believers were melted together in fervent love; they supported the work of God with all their might, and the Lord gave the increase, so that daily such were added as are saved. The number of new converts rose as high as 45. We were often on the point of giving out, under the pressure of our continued exercises which lasted till midnight; yet the nearness of our God was so refreshing to our souls and bodies, that we could endure it. On Tuesday, Dec. 5th, which was the last evening, we enjoyed the most glorious times. Eleven sisters were baptized in the church. All present were pervaded with a feeling of the solemnity and importance of the occasion, heaven seemed to be open over us, and all felt the presence of God. All praying hearts that were present, swam in emotions and happy sensations. After this solemn transaction, we held a love-feast, when our Heavenly Father poured out his blessings abundantly upon us. We then invited the mourners, to make the measure of our joys full; and in order to render the glory of this night perfect, God granted to some more mourning souls peace and pardon. His holy Name be praised for it! Now then see, what God has done.—Oh! where shall we find words to express it? If every stroke of the pulse were praise, it would not suffice! Reader! do thou also help us praise the Lord."

The old Lancaster circuit in Pennsylvania, which, several years before, had been declining very much, was at this time in a very flourishing condition again. Considerable revivals had taken place in different places, and 70 new members were added to its ranks during the year.

On Cumberland circuit, the work of grace still continued to prosper, especially at the Leathart Springs, and in Fishing-Creek Valley, as well as in several other places. Also Shenandoah circuit, in Virginia, enlarged its borders, and received a considerable increase during the year.

Some more circuits in the East and North, were somewhat enlarged; yet their increase was but inconsiderable.

This year the society of Buffalo, state of New York, was founded. Bro. Jos. Harlacher had, indeed, been stationed there the year before; but it was not until this year, that matters took a turn for the better. As the origin of this society may grow in importance for the future, and a full history of it be very interesting to posterity; we here insert an extract from a report of Brother H., which he published in the "Botschafter" at the close of his two years' service there. After a short introduction, he says:—

"When I first arrived at Buffalo, I preached to a society that styled itself '*evangelical;*' their preacher having left them and gone West. Although in possession of a spacious church, at first but few came to hear the word; for the society had fallen into discredit on account of the improper conduct of their preacher. But the news soon spread in town, that a new preacher from Pennsylvania would preach in G's church. This wrought on the curiosity of many, and thus the number of hearers increased from time to time; however, but few among them inquired after God. There were, indeed, some among them who professed to be converted; but there was reason to doubt the genuineness of their profession, and at last it became manifest that they had not built upon the true Rock and Corner-stone of the Church; for as soon as persecution arose for the sake of Christ, they fell away. Yet the word preached did not remain without its effects. Although but few were converted the first year, yet there were good prospects that the future would yield an abundant harvest. About the middle of the second year, the Lord commenced to pour out his Spirit abundantly upon us, soon there was a shaking of the dry bones, and sinners commenced to cry out, what they must do in order to be saved. They were pointed to Christ, who graciously received them, so that they could rejoice in his salvation, and praise him for their redemption. But persecution was not wanting either; for as soon as conversions took place, and the pardoned souls began to praise God for what he had done for them, those who had only the appearance and not the substance of godliness, rebelled, protesting against the praise of God and decrying it as disorder, and insisted that I should forbid that noise, as they called it. Here was literally fulfilled what Christ says: 'The last shall be first, and the first last.' For those who seemed at first to be my best friends, now became my bitterest enemies; and as I could not comply with their demands to stop the noise and disorder, as they called it, they finally locked the church against me. We then rented another house to hold our meetings in. On Christmas last, we held a general meeting, and many sinners were aroused from their lethargy, and the believers were confirmed and strengthened in their most holy faith. From the time of this meeting, the Lord wrought powerfully in our midst: sinners were converted, and the faithful rejoiced greatly in the Lord of their salvation. Although the leaders of the aforesaid society persecuted, calumniated, and abused us sorely; yet they could not impede the work of the Lord.

On Easter following, we had another general meeting. I had preached daily for a week before, and we enjoyed glorious times. The weeping, crying, and praying of the penitent souls, were general, especially so on Easter Sunday when we celebrated the Lord's supper. On Easter Monday I preached my valedictory sermon, and immediately took my departure. There was such a commotion among the people, as I had never witnessed before. Some wept tears of joy; others, tears of repentance and sorrow. We now have a society there of from 50 to 60 members, most of whom profess to have experienced a change of heart. O that the Lord would grant unto them his rich blessings, that they may persevere and continue steadfast to a happy end!"

The following two years, the city society was connected with the Buffalo circuit; but afterward it was changed into a regular station, which, during the first two years was under the charge of Fr. Krecker.

In the West, the work progressed likewise gloriously in several places. In a letter, dated Bucyrus, Sept. 25th, 1837, Bro. A. B. Shaefer writes of Crawford circuit, Ohio, as follows: "The work of conversion is still progressing on our circuit, and about 40 souls have already found peace with God.—Our camp-meetings were crowned with success. Our circuit has been greatly enlarged. We have received Brother Fr. Best for our assistant here, and hope to realize a plentiful harvest before we leave these borders."

Of Columbiana circuit, Bro. E. Stœver writes in a letter, dated Dec. 26th, 1837, as follows:—

"On this circuit, many souls have been converted to God this year, and they now rejoice with the people of God for what the Lord has done for them, viz., for having delivered them from the dominion and power of darkness, and translated them into the kingdom of his dear Son.

In old Harmony, Butler county, Pa., the work of God has spread wonderfully. In the town, a few years ago, matters looked very dark and gloomy, in a religious point of view; as experimental religion was a rare thing among the people. One reason of this was, want of instruction; but God, who will have all men to be saved and to come to the knowledge of the truth, has caused the light of the Gospel to shine unto these people also. A few years ago, when the servants of God came to this neighborhood, they were at once kindly received; and it seemed as if no one was filled with prejudices against them. Houses and hearts were opened to them, churches were at their service, and the societies and their pastors came to hear the word of life. Words almost fail to express, how attentively the people listened to the word preached. But, though only the fourth part fell on good ground, yet the divine seed of the word of God soon brought forth fruit. Many took the word to heart, and saw that the life they had hitherto led, was not good. They now came in contrition of heart to God, and by faith in Christ obtained the forgiveness of their sins, and joy in the Holy Ghost. Parents and children praise God for the glorious work which he has begun in and among them."

In this year a preacher of our Association visited for the first time the state of Illinois; although a number of our members from Pennsylvania had emigrated thither some time before. The first had gone to Chicago and vicinity, in the fall of 1836; and these were followed by some more, in the ensuing spring. At the same time some had also gone to Mount Carmel, Wabash county; where, as it appears from the records on hand, the first conversions took place by means of our ministry. Brother J. Butz writes in a letter, dated June 21st, 1837, among other things, the following: "Thus I am like a solitary bird upon the roof, and meet with sore opposition; but the Lord has thus far been with us. Three souls have been converted to God, who had been awakened by our instrumentality: two of them obtained peace in our prayer-meetings. The Lord alone be praised for it!"

These members had come from Lehigh county; but the others, who had settled near Chicago and vicinity, were from Warren, Pa. As the work mainly took its beginning in the last mentioned part of that state, and thence extended itself, we here insert a somewhat detailed report, received mostly from

Bro. J. J. Esher. He describes the emigration of the members of the Warren society, their journey, arrival in Illinois, as follows :—

"Late in the fall of 1836, some of the members of this society emigrated to the far West and settled in and around Chicago, then numbering but 4000 inhabitants. The following spring, a number of families followed them, who, at their arrival in Illinois, separated into three companies ; the first, which was the most numerous, settled along the river Des Plain, near Wheeling, Cook county ; the second, in and near Napierville of the same county ; and the third in Henry county, Illinois ; and thus the foundation was laid of the three societies at these places, which have existed to this day. Before their setting out from Warren, their preacher, Brother H. Bucks, had advised them, that as soon as they had arrived at their new homes and permanently settled, they should form themselves into classes and elect leaders, till a preacher would visit them. While on their journey, they did not in the least neglect their religious meetings, except when it was absolutely impossible. Prayer in the family, prayer and class meetings, and the keeping of the Sabbath, were as exactly and scrupulously observed by them, as before at home. That blessed prayer-meeting is still in fresh remembrance, which they held on board the steamboat. There were about 1100 passengers on board, many of whom crowded around them, and exclaimed with deep emotions: '*Truly, these people are Christians indeed!*' Thus these members of the Evangelical Association first emigrated to the state of Illinois, bringing along their sanctuary; therefore the Lord was also with them and blessed them.

In compliance with the advice of their preacher, immediately after their arrival, they formed themselves into classes, according to the directions of our Discipline, and elected leaders. The class at Des Plain consisted of 28 members, including a number of persons and families, named: *Esher, Ott, Trier, Schally, Kreienbuehl, Stanger, Strubler*, and *Luther ;* that at Napierville of about 15 members, named: *Esher, Wirth, Grass, Strubler, Knopf*, etc.; and that at Rock River of about 10 members, named: *Schuler, Arnet*, and *Rink*.

With regard to time, these organizations took place as follows: those at Des Plain and Napierville, in June, 1837; and that at Rock River, one year later. Thus, before a preacher had come to this part of country, the order of the Evangelical Association was introduced as completely as it was possible, without the presence of a minister. Prayer-meetings on Sabbath-day, and during the week, class and extra devotional meetings were regularly held, and, in general, great earnestness was manifested in the cause of religion. The only reasons which induced these people to emigrate from Pennsylvania to this, then but little known, and, to a great extent, still wild section of country, were the sterility of their farms near Warren, and their inability to purchase properties in settled districts of the country, where the soil is good. It was therefore a matter of necessity with them, to look out for homes in a wilderness. They were far from a desire to become wealthy; all they sought was, to make a living with a moderate share of labor.

The country where our emigrants settled, fully answered their expectations, with but few exceptions; although the greatest part was still uninhabited, and even the few settlements that had been made, had as yet received but few impressions of cultivation, almost every thing being yet in its primitive romantic beauty. The many wants and inconveniences, that are almost constantly incident to the lives of the first settlers in new countries, were shared by our friends, and that in a high degree, as the great bank swindling took place in those years (1836—1840), in the United States. But, great as these inconveniences were, the settlers made but little account of them, having expected nothing else. They felt, however, far more keenly the want of the privileges of the sanctuary, which they had enjoyed in their former homes. For, besides their own, in those days there was no other German Christian society in the whole northern half of the state of Illinois, nor in the territory of Wisconsin; and there was nowhere divine service held in those parts, in the German language. The prayer-meetings of our people were the first regular religious meetings in that language, in the West. Nor was the state of things in this respect any better among the English settlers. From these facts, it is easy to conceive in what condition, in a religious point of view, the scattered German settlers in and about Chicago must have been. The first effect of this state of things, was an entire disregard to the Sabbath; in consequence of which, ungodliness and vices of various descriptions, as intemperance, fornication, cursing and swearing, cheating, etc., multiplied to an alarming extent; so much so, that he who excelled in wickedness, was the lion of the day.

Under these circumstances, the panting of our small Christian band after their religious teachers, was continually increasing. They would speak of them day and night, and pray the Lord incessantly, so to order it that one of the preachers would visit them. God also heard their prayers, and as early as July of that year, Bro. *Jacob Boas*, who was stationed on Miami circuit that year, which extended as far as into the state of Indiana, made his appearance among them, to their inexpressible joy. On seeing Brother Boas, with whom they had already become acquainted in Pennsylvania, some of them were so greatly surprised, that they could scarcely believe their own senses, hesitating to decide whether it was his spirit or himself. Never before, we dare say, had there a man of God been more welcome, and never had a preacher of the Gospel caused more joy than Brother Boas by his appearance among these people. With tears of joy they thanked God, that he had answered their prayers, and not left them destitute, which they had already begun to apprehend.*

July 23rd, 1837, after a very difficult and dangerous journey of several hundred miles, Brother Boas arrived safe at Chicago, where he met with some of the young brethren and sisters, that were servants in that place; and the following day he reached Bro. Jacob Esher's, sen., at Des Plain, near Wheeling, Cook county, Illinois, where he was received with ecstasy.

*Brother Boas had been traveling the year before on Erie circuit, in Pennsylvania, to which Warren belonged; and had made a conditional promise to these people, that, should they move to Illinois, he would visit them there. But little did they expect that he would fulfill his promise so soon.

On the 25th, the third day after his arrival, the friends assembled at 11 o'clock, A. M., and Brother Boas preached at Bro. J. Esher's the first evangelical sermon in German, within what is now the Illinois Conference, from the words of Jesus: "*I will see you again, and your heart shall rejoice, and your joy no one taketh from you.*" John 16, 22. Great was their joy, caused by the good word of the Gospel; and the Lord blessed his children so abundantly, that they shouted for joy, and it was fulfilled what is written: "The wilderness shall be glad," etc.

Brother Boas, after having recovered somewhat from his long and tedious journey, went to Napierville, where he was not less welcome than at Des Plain. Besides these two societies, he also preached at Dunkley's Grove, a new German settlement, situated between Des Plain and Napierville; yet without any visible effects.

The first general meeting of the Evangelical Association in the far West, was held by Brother Boas, at Jacob Esher's, sr., near Wheeling, Cook county, Illinois, in September, 1837. This was a time of gracious refreshing for the two societies—that of Des Plain and that of Napierville. Some conversions took place, and, as usual, Brother Jacob Boas held a quarterly conference at this meeting; and, if the writer's memory serves him right, it was under a shady oak, on the banks of the Des Plain river. The members attending this conference were: J. Boas, preacher; Jacob Esher, sen., and Martin Esher, class-leaders; and Joseph Wirth, assistant. Bro. Boas now ratified the election of the class-leader, that had taken place before his arrival.

The efforts of Brother Boas, during his six months' stay there, were crowned with success; but as the charge of the Miami circuit, situated partly in Ohio, partly in Indiana, had been entrusted to him, he felt it his duty to leave them again, about Christmas, with the promise to do all in his power to induce the next conference to send them a minister next spring, for regular preaching; for he had satisfied himself at the first view, that this would be a very important field for the Evangelical Association. His efforts at conference were crowned with success; the state of Illinois was received as a circuit, and one year later the circuit was called *Illinois circuit.* In March, 1838, conference had allotted it to Bro. P. Wist; but as one of the other brethren of Ohio Conference was unable to travel on his circuit, Brother Wist had to supply his place in Ohio, and so was prevented from going to his new field of labor. Thus it came, that the infant societies in Illinois were almost a whole year, viz., from the close of December, 1837, to the beginning of September, 1838, without a preacher. This time was almost insufferably long to them, so much so that some of the members often spoke of returning to Pennsylvania, where they would have, at least, their preachers. So great was their desire, that when finally the glad tidings spread: "*The preacher has come!*" a certain man leaped, praising God with a loud voice; and this was not an isolated case, but the general feeling among them.

While the societies were without a preacher, the class-leaders had conducted the religious exercises, and managed all other affairs according to the best of their abilities; and the work of the Lord had prospered among them, and some conversions taken place. They were, however, not without persecution from the world; but making it a point to be conscientiously honest in all their business transactions, they were, nevertheless, highly respected wherever they were known. This prepared the way for the Gospel, and exerted a very salutary influence.

Brother Boas, in a report published in the "Botschafter," dated Cook county, Illinois, Dec. 2nd, 1837, states the following with regard to his visit to Illinois, and the prospects for our Association there:—

"In obedience to the order of our presiding elder, which was, at the same time, in accordance with my own feelings, I traveled last summer to the state of Illinois. I left my circuit in the beginning of July, and arrived safely on the 23rd at Chicago, the capital of Illinois. I soon ascertained where the brethren lived, and found them with but little difficulty. When they saw me, they greatly rejoiced, and we praised God together for his merciful dealings with us. I immediately gave out appointments, and commenced preaching; and the Lord poured his blessings abundantly upon us, so that we could truthfully say: '*The Lord has done great things for us, whereof we are glad.*'—There are a great many Germans in this state, but they are somewhat scattered over the country; yet very fine societies and circuits might be formed. There are as yet but few, and in most places no German preachers at all, although the people are so anxious to hear the Gospel preached unto them. The Germans in this state are, for the most part, Europeans, and are like sheep without a shepherd. Since my arrival, I have preached very often, and my labors have not been without effect, as some have obtained the pardon of their sins by faith in the blood of Christ; others have been powerfully affected, and some persecutors of the children of God and opponents of the truth have been aroused from their lethargy, so that they now acknowledge the work of God and withhold not their assent from it. But as my horse was sick most all the time I was here, I could not travel very far around, and consequently not make the circuit as large as I desired. There are now about seventy of our members here, and still more are constantly arriving. There are prospects too, that many of the inhabitants of this region will embrace religion."

From the preceding statement it appears, that the work in Illinois took its origin as it had done in the state of Ohio, by emigration from Pennsylvania; and this emigration was one of the principal causes of the rapid increase of the western Church. Some classes and societies mostly consist of members emigrated from Pennsylvania.

During this year, the Society lost three useful local preachers by death, viz., *J. P. Breidenstein*, of Lebanon county, *Andrew Yeakel* of Lehigh county, Pa., and *John Thomas* of Wayne county, Ohio. The last mentioned had for many years been a preacher of the Association, Mr. Albright himself having signed his first license to preach the Gospel. His death was caused by an accident—he was caught by a thrashing-machine while in motion, lost his arm, and mortification taking place, he died a few days after, in full assurance of eternal life, aged 54 years.

Father J. P. Breidenstein had been 30 years a member of the Association, and had served for 25 years in the capacity of a local preacher. He was a pious and devout man, and a true follower of the Lord. It is true, in his latter years he preached but seldom; yet his life and conduct among his fellow-men were a constant sermon, exerting a very salutary influence on many of them. He had taken an active part in furthering the interests of the connection, and had always been a strong pillar in the same. During his sickness he waited with calmness and composure for the hour of his final departure, which came January 22d, 1838.

Brother A. Yeakel had, in his earlier years, been a preacher among the Schwenkfelders, in Upper Milford, Lehigh county, Pa., and had been universally esteemed for his uprightness and honesty. But seeing the corruption of his Church, he, with some of his fellow believers, united with the Evangelical Association; on which account he met with great opposition from some of his former brethren. However, he did not suffer himself to be discouraged thereby, but was zealous in promoting the kingdom of God and the welfare of his fellow-men. He was a very conscientious, pious, and devout man,—a character of rare occurrence; he was both in conduct and doctrine a worthy example for the faithful; diligent and punctual in his official and domestic duties, as well as in his earthly occupation. He suffered for a long time from consumption, but was fully resigned to the will of his heavenly Father, and died in great tranquillity and in full hope of eternal life, April 6th, 1837, in the 51st year of his age.

The membership at the close of the year, was 7309, consequently an increase of 844.

The Year 1838.

Both conferences held their sessions again in March; the Western began its sessions on the 5th, in Jackson township, Wayne county, Ohio, and the Eastern on the 28th, at Orwigsburg, Pa. Seven of the itinerants located, and six were admitted on trial, viz., *Wm. Mentz*, *John Rosenberger*, *Fr. Krecker*, *A. Longsdorf*, *S. Krall*, and *Joseph Hummel.*

Canaan district, of the Eastern Conference, was divided, and the eastern part of it called *Philadelphia district.* A new circuit was also formed in the Eastern Conference, viz., *Womelsdorf circuit;* and two in the Western Conference, viz., *Franklin* and *Illinois* circuits.

This year was not only highly blessed, but it forms another epoch in the history of our Church, especially by the awakening of a missionary spirit and the founding of the first missionary societies in our midst. Both, the Missionary Society of the Eastern Conference and the Parent Board of Missions of the Association were founded this year, besides a number of societies auxiliary to the Missionary Society of the Eastern Conference.

It is true, the Association had cultivated a missionary spirit from its very beginning, and often sent out ministers, in order to visit spiritually neglected societies, to preach unto them the Gospel of peace, and to introduce the use of the means of grace among them. Objects of its solicitous care were also those societies, who indeed had *pastors*, but such as lived with their members in carnal security, sins, and errors, and were entire strangers to experimental religion. In this way the Association had done much already for the salvation of many souls. But this had been done only occasionally; when, for instance, there was an abundance of preachers; when a section of country was situated very conveniently near a circuit; or when members had removed to distant parts of the country, soliciting a visit from their ministers. But systematic arrangements for collecting missionary contributions, and sending out missionaries every year, had not yet been introduced. And, indeed, the necessary acquaintance with the cause of missions had heretofore been wanting with the greater part of our ministers and members; the condition of Pagan and non-Christian nations especially was partially known to but few; and even the true religious wants of the greater part of Christendom were not properly understood and laid to heart.

Nor had our Periodical as yet taken up the subject of missions, and missionary sermons were something altogether unknown in the Society. The *principal cause* of the introduction of the cause of missions into our Association *just at this time*, was the "*Basler Missions Magazine*," (a missionary magazine published in Germany). Brother John Seybert had purchased a considerable number of volumes of said work, from a certain person in Blooming Grove, Lycoming county, Pa., and presented them to the Printing Establishment for the use of the Editor. The perusal of this work aroused a missionary spirit in the Editor, and filled his heart with zeal for this sacred cause. The first volumes of said work especially, affected the Editor powerfully; and as his heart became full of this good cause, the subject often formed the topic of conversation in circles of friends, and the wish was ventured, that something might be done in this cause also by our Association. The influence of said magazine, and the many glorious reports of awakenings and conversions on the different fields of labor of our brethren, which were published at this time in the Periodical, induced the writer to pen the following article, which appeared in the last number of the 2nd Vol. of the paper, headed: "*Men ought to extol and magnify the work of God.*" This article alludes to, and encourages, such an enterprise, without, however, expressly naming the cause of missions. We quote a few sentences from it, as follows:—

"Christ says, that the angels in heaven rejoice when sinners repent; should not, therefore, all Christians and children of God also rejoice, and magnify and praise God, when they hear, learn, and see, that not only a few sinners here and there are converted to God, but that in some places whole crowds of them leave the paths of sin, and turn to the God of their salvation? Yes, truly, we ought to rejoice and thank the Lord, when we see how he carries on his work in our times. Some heathen nations, who but a few years ago sacrificed and bowed to dumb idols, sitting in darkness and in the shadow of death, now rejoice in the light of the Gospel and serve the true and living God of heaven and earth. And thousands of Christians, who formerly were satisfied with the mere form of Christianity, now enjoy its substance and reality.

United in faith and love, let us henceforth use every means and ability God has given us, in order to promote the honor of his name and the welfare of immortal souls. Why should we be disconcerted and discouraged? Has not God thus far helped us, and extended and enlarged his work among us, in spite of all opposition?—Arise, then, ye friends of Zion! unite your prayers for the spread of his work and kingdom among all the nations of the earth.

Ye watchmen on the walls of Zion especially, take courage, cry aloud, and spare not; lift up your voices like a trumpet, and show the people their transgression, and the house of Jacob their sins; give no rest till Jerusalem be established and be made a praise in the earth."

Just at the time when the Eastern Conference was in session, which founded the first missionary society of the Association, there appeared another editorial article on this subject, headed: "*The Christians and the Heathen*," which in the beginning gives a brief statement of the moral condition of the whole human family, and then inculcates the duty of the Christians *to preach the Gospel to every creature.* Here follow a few extracts from it:—

"Has not Christ commanded his disciples to teach all nations, and to preach the Gospel to every creature? Yes, this is as much the duty of every Christian, as it is the duty of every sinner to repent and to believe the Gospel. This command is given not only to the teachers, but to the Christian Church in general. The Church is in duty bound to make arrangements and to provide means to send out missionaries, and to do everything in her power to have the good news of man's redemption preached to all nations and races of the earth. But how little has thus far been done, to carry out this important command! It is true, there have in our days been missionary societies founded in different places, and provisions made to preach the Gospel to the heathen; and it is even probable, that at this time more is being done in this cause, than at any other time since the days of the apostles. But, if we take into consideration what could be done, if all Christians were filled with the proper spirit and zeal to save souls; all that is done in this important and necessary cause, in our favored and happy age, scarcely deserves to be mentioned.

In the days of the apostles, and for some time after, the Christians risked their property and even their lives, in order to extend and promote the doctrine and religion of their Master. But the Christians of our days, with few exceptions, seem to have lost all zeal and interest in the conversion of the world. Most of them seem to be far more anxious to accumulate wealth, and to secure the goods of this world, than to save souls. Whenever but the least efforts are to be made, to promote the spread of the Gospel and the kingdom of God, many are at once afraid that it may cost too much.

Jesus Christ left the seat of his glory and became poor, for man's sake; yea, he suffered and died the most ignominious death on Golgotha, for the salvations of the souls of men. The apostles forsook all they had, counting their lives not dear unto themselves, and labored day and night to save souls. And the Christians of the first centuries generally, spent, in many instances, all their property in order to promote the honor of their Master, and the welfare of their fellow-men. But where are we? Will we continue professing to be followers of Christ, without following him indeed, or obeying his commands? To us it appears, that it is high time for all Christians to pause, and to ponder this matter well. * * * * *

How do we expect to excuse or justify ourselves, when we shall have to appear with all nations and races of the earth before the tribunal of the righteous Judge of the universe, if we see our brethren according to the flesh, the heathen and heathen-like nominal Christians, in want, or know them to be in want, and shut our hearts against them?—Will they not accuse and condemn us before God? Christ declares, that one soul is worth more than the whole world, and we are not willing to spend even the little that we possess in this world, in order to send the Word of life to the many millions of souls, although we are commanded to lay down our lives for the brethren. Is it possible, that we are properly concerned for our own souls, if we have no pity on our fellow-men?"

This appeal and the many encouraging reports of revivals and the extension of the kingdom of God, that appeared from time to time in the Periodical—the many inquiries and demands for preachers of the Evangelical Association, in different places—especially also the many openings for ministers of our Church, in the principal maritime cities and larger inland towns, and other places, though they had not directly appealed to us, to proclaim to them the Gospel—all these causes combined, led to the founding of missionary societies and the systematic support of the cause of missions in the Association.—At the annual session of the Eastern Conference, from the 28th of March to the 4th of April, 1838, the first missionary society of the Evangelical Association was established. On motion of the writer of this history, said conference formed itself into such a society, for the purpose of making arrangements, and to provide means to promote and extend the Gospel of Christ and the kingdom of God; and a committee was appointed to draft a constitution for said society. The committee, after retiring for some time, reported the following constitution, which was adopted.

CONSTITUTION.

Article 1. This society shall be called: *The German Evangelical Missionary Society of North America.*

Art. 2. The object of this society shall be to make arrangements and provide means, to extend and promote the kingdom of God, by missionaries.

Art. 3. Every member shall annually contribute an optional sum, for the support of the society.

Art. 4. For the transactions of the business of this society, a *president* and a *vice-president*, a *secretary* and an *assistant secretary*, and a *treasurer*, shall be annually elected.

Art. 5. In addition to these officers, four members of the society shall be selected, who, with the officers, shall constitute a committee, to transact the necessary business during the interval of the annual meetings. The majority of this committee shall form a quorum, to transact business.

Art. 6. All superintending preachers of the Evangelical Association, shall be authorized agents to establish auxiliary societies, and to receive moneys in order to hand them over to the treasurer.

Art. 7. All demands on the treasurer must be accompanied with an order signed by the president and secretary.

Art. 8. The members of this society are to meet annually in the place where the Annual Conference session takes place, in the evening before the opening of conference.

Art. 9. This society shall be authorized, by a majority of votes, to alter or to amend this constitution from time to time.

The following officers were elected for the first year, by a majority of votes of the society :—

W. W. Orwig, President.
J. P. Leib, Vice-President.
J. Vogelbach, Secretary.
C. Hammer, Assistant Secretary.
Thomas Buck, Treasurer.

Select committee members: *P. Wagner, F. Hoffman, J. Schnerr*, and *J. Saylor*.

It was also resolved, that a voluntary contribution be taken up immediately, which was accordingly done, and amounted to $26,50.

The organization of this society, its object and constitution were published in the Periodical, with additional remarks, in reference to the sacred cause of missions, whereby a missionary spirit was kindled in many places of the connection, and in various directions societies auxiliary to the Conference Missionary Society were established, in order to support the good cause ; also from other directions contributions were received.

Thus *five hundred dollars* were contributed the very first year, although no missionaries were sent out or supported by the society, until the second year. The spirit of missions being thus roused in the Association, promising fields of labor were soon looked for, and at the next annual session of the Western Conference it was resolved to establish four missions, which resolution was forthwith carried out. The Canadians, whom several of our ministers had visited of late, sent a strong and very touching appeal in writing, for a minister of our Church. This appeal had been communicated for insertion in the Periodical, by a highly respectable and very influential man, named *H. W. Peterson*, and with a few introductory remarks by the Editor, was published in the September Number of 1838. We here insert both the introductory remarks, and the appeal itself.

"*A Macedonian Cry.*"

"And a vision appeared to Paul in the night; there stood a man of Macedonia and prayed him, saying, Come over into Macedonia and help us." Acts 16, 9.

The following communication we may call a '*Canadian cry,*' resembling somewhat the one quoted above, and can certainly not fail to affect every Christian and sympathizing heart; and it appears to me, that we may, like Paul and his companions, come to the conclusion that the Lord has assuredly made this appeal to us, in order that some one of our number might preach the Gospel unto them. Oh! that we may also, like Paul, immediately endeavor to go thither. (See Acts 16, 9–12.) We hope that this appeal will not be slighted; some of our brethren in the state of New York may, perhaps, be able to make a few visits to Canada, between now and our next Annual Conference, which, if at all practicable, will send them a minister.

This appeal ought to stir up the friends of the cause of missions among us anew to continued efforts, and to induce others to make arrangements on their circuits, to support this good cause.

Present state of Christianity among the Germans of Upper Canada.

Dear Brother in the Lord:—

I would like to call, if possible, the attention of your brethren in the ministry, and of your principal conference especially, to the present deplorable condition of many of my fellow-citizens here. In Waterloo township, where most of the Germans of Upper Canada live, and among whom there are so-called Catholics, Lutherans, Reformed, Mennonites, Dunkers, and United Brethren; the Mennonites and Dunkers are the only ones having their regular teachers, and consequently regular divine service. I also rejoice exceedingly, that these my brethren are provided with well-disposed pastors; but, at the same time, I regret very much, that others, who are also anxiously concerned for the salvation of their souls, but are excluded from the privileges of the Mennonite and Dunker societies, are entirely destitute of the services of a regular preacher. It is true, there is a man here, named *Bindeman*, who pretends to be an '*Evangelical*' minister, holding general meetings every three or four weeks; but I regret from the bottom of my heart, that we cannot repose that confidence in this teacher of morality, nor unite with him in intimate Christian brotherly love, as we should like and ought to do, as genuine Christians; the condition, therefore, of the United Brethren, Lutherans, Reformed, Methodists, and such as have not joined any church or sect, call for sympathy and even commiseration by every child of God. Many of us are almost like straying sheep, whose pastor is absent.

Compared with us, the United States are far better supplied with ministers of every denomination. How is this? Even the "Evangelical Association," whose ministers seem not to labor either for money or fame, has forsaken or at least forgotten or neglected us.

Dear Brother Orwig: I greatly mistake the principles of your Church or rather of your brethren in the *ministry*, if their main object is money or fame; for the three or four preachers, whom your "Association" formerly sent us, out of

Christian love, manifested both humility and self-denial; and I believe, that their labors here were not in vain. Bro. *Jacob Riegel*, especially, was well received by all among whom he labored. By dint of indefatigable labor, self-denial, persevering, enlightened zeal for the glory of God and the welfare of immortal souls, he, or one like him, might accomplish a vast amount of good among us. And as far as my information goes, some one of the dear brethren that have visited us, could make himself as useful in our midst, as our dear Brother *Riegel*. But alas! we are *poor*. We fear, we are not able to give him a sufficient support. But, dear brother! shall we, because we are too poor to give a teacher a sufficient support, shall we *on that account* be deprived of his services, and suffer and starve? Will ye Pennsylvanians not have pity upon us? Will you, who have plenty and to spare, will you let us suffer in the wilderness, without any pity? or will you pray for us, and if possible, send us a spiritual guide? Could you not contribute something toward his support the first year? or could he not visit us three or four times during the year? But it would be better if he could live among us.—Much money we cannot give him; but we will do what we can.

Under the wise guidance of a truly Christian pastor, who would adorn his *doctrine* by a *pious life*, there could, with the help of God, soon a considerable society be gathered in our midst. Perhaps you can spare us the dear Brother *Riegel*, provided he is willing to come. He would be the very man for us, because he can preach in English and German, and is, as far as I know, without a family yet. But whoever he may be, that comes to us as a laborer in the vineyard of Christ, in order to do good in the name of God, he must have proper certificates as to character, usefulness, etc.; otherwise I fear very much, that he could not accomplish much for a long time. And why? Whoever comes, will find that out soon enough.

The visits of pious German preachers, no matter whether Methodists, Evangelical, or United Brethren, would be exceedingly welcome to every individual that is concerned for the salvation of his soul; the number of these, however, seems to be but small, and is, alas! daily decreasing. Come, therefore, over, to help us. That our kind and merciful Father in heaven may soon send us a genuine minister of his word, is the heart-felt prayer of a

POOR SINNER.

Waterloo township, U. C., July 15th, 1838."

Thus the cause of missions took its origin in the Evangelical Association, in the year of our Lord 1838, which has since not only proved a blessing to many souls, but has also done much toward the more rapid increase and extension of the Association.

As one of the conferences had now made a beginning, by forming itself into a missionary society, and as it could be expected, that other conferences would follow this example in the future; some of the brethren felt it to be necessary to have a *Parent Missionary Society*, in order to secure a general co-operation in this good cause, instead of dividing the strength of the Church in the enterprise, by each conference acting for itself, independently of the rest. This matter was discussed time and again, and the necessity of forming such a society was felt more and more. There was, at last, on Christmas, in 1838, during a protracted meeting at New Berlin, Pa., a convention held in the house of the writer, which consisted of preachers and several private members; here the matter was further considered and discussed, and finally a resolution was passed to make a beginning. The following committee was at once appointed to draft a constitution: J. Seybert, G. Brickley, and W. W. Orwig.

On the 1st of March, 1839, a second meeting was held in this cause, at J. S. Dunkel's, in Buffalo township, Union county, Pa.; here the constitution that had been drafted by the aforesaid committee, was laid before the meeting, and, after a short discussion, unanimously approved and adopted. The constitution is as follows:—

Article 1. This society, called "*The Missionary Society of the Evangelical Association of North America*," has for its object to enable the Annual Conferences of the Evangelical

Association, in a more effectual manner, to extend their missionary operations in the United States and in other places.

Art. 2. Each subscriber, paying annually $2,00, shall be a member of this society; and who at any time pays $25, shall be a member for life.

Art. 3. The officers of this society shall be: *a president, 3 vice-presidents, a secretary, a corresponding and recording secretary, and a treasurer,* who, with fourteen managers, shall form a board to transact the business of the society. All of these must be members of the Evangelical Association, and shall be annually elected by the society.

Art. 4. The board shall have power to make by-laws for the regulation of its own business, and to fill vacancies that may occur during the year; it shall also lay before the society, at its annual meeting a report of its proceedings and funds, and likewise before the General Conference an exact report of all its proceedings and receipts and expenditures, during the past four years.

Art. 5. Ordained ministers of the Association, being members of the society, shall be, *ex officio*, members of the board.

Art. 6. The annual meeting of the society for the election of officers and managers, shall be held on the third Tuesday in April, at New Berlin, Union county, Pa.

Art. 7. The president, or in his absence, the one of the present vice-presidents standing first on the list, and in the absence of the three vice-presidents, any member that may be appointed by those present, shall preside over all meetings of the society and the board.

Art. 8. Twenty-one members shall form a quorum at all meetings of the society, and eleven at those of the board; the minutes of each meeting shall be signed by the president.

Art. 9. It is recommended, that within the boundaries of each Annual Conference, a conference missionary society be established, as a branch of this society, with auxiliary societies on the different circuits, under such regulations as the conferences may see proper to lay down. Each of these conference missionary societies shall annually send a copy of its annual report to the corresponding secretary of this society, and inform the treasurer of the same body of the amount of the funds collected for the support of the missionary cause; this amount shall be placed at the disposal of the treasurer of the parent society, under the provisions of the following article.

Art. 10. The treasurer of this society shall, under the direction of the board, annually or oftener, as the board may deem necessary, inform the bishop or bishops of the financial affairs, and of those amounts that may be drawn for the purposes specified by this constitution; and according to this information, the bishop or bishops shall be authorized to draw from the treasurer any sum within the specified amount, that may be deemed necessary by the missionary committees of the Annual Conferences for the support of the missionaries under their care; with this proviso, however, that no more be allowed to any missionary, than is allowed to the other itinerants for their support. And whenever a bishop draws money from any treasurer of one of the conference missionary societies, he shall at once inform the treasurer of the parent society thereof; each missionary shall also transmit to the corresponding secretary a quarterly report in writing, on the state and the prospects of the mission under his care. No missionary that has not been appointed by one or the other of our Annual Conferences or by our bishops, shall draw support from the funds of this society.

Art. 11. This constitution shall be subject to our next General Conference; and if the object of the society be approved, the constitution shall, in future, not be altered, except by the General Conference on a recommendation of the board.

This constitution having been approved, the convention proceeded and formed itself into a society, by the election of officers and managers for the present year, as follows:—

John Seybert, President.
James Barber, 1 Vice President.
Daniel Berger, 2 do.
George Brickley, 3 do.
S. G. Miller, Secretary.

W. W. Orwig, Recording and Corresponding Sec.
John S. Dunkel, Treasurer.

Managers: Chas. Hammer, Henry Thomas, Philip Schmidt, John Kaufman, Dr. I. Brugger, Martin Dreisbach, Martin D. Reed, John Rohland, Philip Wagner, Mich. F. Maize, Isaac Eyer, John Maize, Leonard Gebhart, Sebastian Mosser.

This was the origin of the missionary society in the Evangelical Association. Soon after it had been established, General Conference met in Centre county, Pa., and in conformity with the last article of the constitution, this document was laid before that body, who approved and confirmed the same as well as the establishment of the society. Thus, this society became the principal or parent missionary society of the Evangelical Association; and the missionary society of the Eastern Conference, that had been established a year before, altered its constitution at its next annual meeting, and, together with its auxiliary societies, united with this as a branch, which example was afterward followed by the other Annual Conferences. Subsequently there were important alterations made in the constitution, as may be seen by comparing the above with the present constitution of the society.

On Monday, January 17th, 1839, the board of the society held its first meeting at New Berlin, Pa., in order to adopt by-laws to the constitution, and rules to regulate its business transactions. It was also resolved, that notice shall be given of the founding of the society in the Periodical, and that its constitution, together with the circular, and an address of the board, drawn up by a committee, shall be published in said paper. These two documents are here inserted.

A Circular.

The board of the Missionary Society of the Evangelical Association, beg leave to inform all the friends of Zion in general, and the ministry and membership of the Evangelical Association in particular, of the existence of this society, and to lay before them both its constitution and address, and to express the heart-felt wish, at the same time, to secure the Association's active and zealous co-operation, especially by the founding of branch and other societies auxiliary to this body.

Although the missionary operations of the Evangelical Association are as yet new and very limited, yet we have signal proofs already, that they have met the Divine favor and approbation. Each step thus far taken in this good cause, seems to have been crowned with the approval and blessing of God. A little over a year ago, one of our conferences made a beginning in this matter, by forming itself into a missionary society, and also received help in different places from auxiliary societies, and the result is, that after all the auxiliary societies have paid in their contributions, more than $500 have been raised, and four missionaries have already been sent out by that conference. However small this work may as yet be, when compared with other institutions of the kind, it has, notwithstanding, made a glorious beginning, and we have reason to thank God for the same, and to invoke his richest blessings upon it for the future.

But as our ecclesiastical organization is intended to secure a general co-operation, it was deemed expedient also to take in the missionary cause such measures as to secure the prosecution of the work with united efforts. For this purpose the Missionary Society of the Evangelical Association has been founded at New Berlin, Pa., and confirmed by the General Conference as the principal or parent missionary society of the Evangelical Association. The sole object of this society is, according to the first article of its constitution, to support the different Annual Conferences in their missionary operations. It does not claim the power to send out missionaries, but leaves this to the conferences; its sole object is to assist the conferences in procuring means to send out messengers of peace.

For this reason the board, in the name of the whole society, solicit the co-operation of all the brethren, cordially inviting them, as well as other friends of Zion, to become members of the society. Should any be members of auxiliary societies already, this need not prevent them from becoming members of the parent society also. Not a few of our brethren already belong to two, and others to three of such societies.

Persons living at a great distance, may give their names and the requisite sums, to constitute them members, to any of our presiding elders, superintending preachers, or to the bishop of our Association, who, as soon as they have $10, may remit them with the names of the donors, per mail, to the corresponding secretary, W. W. Orwig, at New Berlin, Union county, Pa.; or if some should not receive as much as the specified sum, they may forward only the names and residences of the donors, and retain the money until a suitable opportunity presents itself to transmit it. Whatever may be sent at any time, must be accompanied with the name of the giver.

Although the constitution requires the annual payment of exactly two dollars, in order to become a member of this society, or the payment of $25, in order to become a life member; yet it by no means excludes smaller or larger sums, such as donations, legacies for the society.—Some have already signed $5, instead of $2, to be paid annually; and an unknown friend has sent us $25. Thus we see that the Lord inclines the hearts of men to promote and extend his kingdom; and we sincerely hope, that many of our friends will procure for themselves God's richest blessings, by supporting this and similar institutions. But as our cause is, undeniably, of great importance and excellency, it is taken for granted, that it needs no further recommendation, but that it will recommend itself to all true and genuine Christians. May God, who will have all men to be saved and to come to the knowledge of the truth, in his infinite goodness grant his richest blessings to rest upon this work, to the welfare of many souls, and to the honor and glory of his great and holy Name!

Signed in the name of the board, by

G. Brickley,
C. Hammer, } Committee.
W. W. Orwig,

New Berlin, June 20, 1839.

An Address, by the Board of the Missionary Society of the Evangelical Association.

Dearly beloved brethren and friends in the Lord:—Since it is God's wise counsel and earnest desire, that all his intelligent creatures should be really happy already in this life, and still more so in that to come, for which purpose he sent his only begotten Son into this world, who has abolished the enmity caused by sin, and reconciled mankind to his Heavenly Father, that henceforth all who believe in the Son, should not perish, but have everlasting life; and because the relation which we sustain to the whole human family, makes it our special duty, as professors of the Christian religion, which consists in love to God and to our fellow-men, to promote, according to the best of our ability, the temporal and everlasting welfare of all; therefore the board of the Missionary Society, in the name of the whole body, beg leave to call your attention, and that of the Christian public in general, to the glorious and praiseworthy subject of the cause of missions.

That the missionary cause, or the promulgation of the Gospel of Christ, is the work of God, which must be continued till all heathen, nations, and tongues of the earth shall have been brought to the knowledge of his name and salvation, seems to be plain from the prophesies, promises, and commands of the Word of God. But this great and glorious work, God designs to carry out through his Church. This is the command of the Head of the Church: "Go ye therefore, and teach all nations, baptizing them in the name of the Father, Son, and Holy Ghost; teaching them to observe all things, whatsoever I have commanded you," etc., Matt. 28, 19, 20.—Christ himself made the beginning in this glorious work, and commanded his disciples to continue it until its completion. The first Christians, or followers of Jesus, obeyed the injunction of their Master, and it is probable that they did all in their power to extend his doctrine and religion: they sacrificed their ease, property, and even their lives, for this noble work. Notwithstanding the powerful opposition and the barbarous and unheard-of persecutions, through which they had to pass, their Master's command was of greater importance to them than anything else in the world; and the Word of God increased mightily, and extended far and wide. For several centuries, the Church prosecuted this work with intrepidity and courage; and the consequence was, that in spite of the great opposition from Pagans and Jews, of hell and Satan himself, thousands, hundreds of thousands, and even millions of souls were converted by the preaching of the Gospel, from idolatry and the service of sin to the true and living God, of whom indescribable numbers continued steadfast in the faith, and now sing with the innumerable hosts of the blood-washed souls in heaven an everlasting hallelujah to the Lamb. But as this glorious work was some time after impeded by the cunning of the devil, and made but slow progress for many centuries, much still remains to be done by the Church of our day. Hundreds of millions of the human family are still in moral darkness, without the saving knowledge of the Son of God, living without God in the world, and hastening with rapid strides to everlasting destruction. And even among the Christians there are comparatively but few blessed with the pure and unadulterated doctrine of the Gospel. Unscriptural traditions, commandments of men, and superstitious rites and ceremonies, still rule over the greater part of the visible Church of Christ. Even of those who have been better instructed, we are compelled to acknowledge, that the most are dead, while they have the name to live. Even among those branches of the Protestant Church, that excel others in point of numbers and popularity, there are comparatively but few found, who come up to the standard of the Word of God; while others who, on account of their small numbers and peculiarities, are looked upon with suspicion, lack the substance of religion not less, although their outward appearance may be more conformable to the Christian religion.

The religion of the Bible, that imparts to its possessors the mind and spirit of Christ more and more, and effects inward and outward holiness of heart and life, is even in our blessed and enlightened age one of the greatest rarities. Sin and vices of every description, such as lying and cheating, atheism, rationalism, superstition, and various doctrinal errors and religious contentions, are still in the ascendency in what is called Christendom. The true followers of Christ are almost as rare as the righteous were at Sodom. This description and exposure of the true character of modern Christianity, are indeed no honor to us; but the thing is too true to be questioned by any one, consistently with truth.

With the full knowledge of all these facts, and for the purpose of bringing about a better state of things, and of helping to extend and promote the pure doctrine and religion of the Saviour of the world, the *Missionary Society of the Evangelical Association*, at New Berlin, Pa., has been established and formed. And the society hopes, therefore, that its well-intended and honest enterprise will not be regarded and envied by any impartial and humble fellow-Christian, as forward presumption or rash inconsiderateness; but that, on the contrary, every true Christian will rejoice in the enterprise, bidding us Godspeed, and helping us that this mustard seed may become a large tree.

Who that has felt in his heart the blessed effects of the Gospel, and the substance of the religion of Christ, and is acquainted with the condition of the world, with regard to the Christian religion, can remain inactive any longer in this glorious enterprise of the cause of missions? Behold, how much good has already been accomplished in the world by missionaries? Nearly all nations that are blessed with the Gospel, are, under God, indebted for it to missionaries. The German nation also received the Gospel first through missionaries. Now, since it has proved so great a blessing to us, should not we, on our part, also put forth strong and even self-denying efforts, in order to enable others to share in this great boon? Yes, of a truth, and all true followers of Christ, who love their neighbor as themselves, will be active in this glorious cause.

It is not, indeed, our object at present to send missionaries to the heathen, as we have too much to do yet at home, and especially among our German brethren, according to the flesh. Nor do we lose sight of the poor heathen; on the contrary, we hope that, before many years, they too shall experience our humble co-operation in the general work of the spread of the Gospel.

With such a glorious and praiseworthy object in view, we do not apprehend that our appeal to our brethren and friends, for their co-operation and support, will be in vain. Whose heart can remain cold, and whose hands closed, when he is appealed to for help in so glorious, important, and sacred a cause?

Because it is, in the next place, also the object of the society, to extend and strengthen itself through branch and auxiliary societies, and to enlist the co-operation of all Annual Conferences of our Association, measures have been taken in the constitution to realize this object, and we trust that each of our Annual Conferences will form itself into a branch-society of this, and establish auxiliary societies within its boundaries, wherever practicable. Come dear brethren, let us begin the work with united hearts and hands, cheerfully and courageously, in the name of the God of Israel, and let us entreat him fervently, to grant unto us and to all his people liberal hearts, to help in the support and promotion of his great and glorious work, with our temporal means. Let us, at the same time, pray daily in faith, that the kingdom of God may come, till the wilderness and the solitary place shall be glad, and the desert shall rejoice and blossom as the rose. May the Omnipotent God bless his Church abundantly, and send many faithful laborers into his vineyard, that the heathen may be given to his Son for his inheritance, and the uttermost parts of the earth for his possession!

Signed in behalf of the board, by

G. Brickley,
C. Hammer,
W. W. Orwig,
} Committee.

New Berlin, Pa., June 20, 1839.

These appeals, and some other remarks that appeared from time to time in the Periodical, as well as copious extracts from the missionary reports of the principal missionary societies of Europe and America, coming from the heathen world, that were also published in said paper; and then in the second year, the reports of our first missionaries,—all these things combined, exerted a very salutary influence upon the whole Association, and kindled the missionary spirit in our midst, more and more. The preachers generally took a deep interest in the matter, delivering missionary sermons, forming auxiliary societies, and laboring hard to enlist more and more friends in the good cause; and many of the lay members were also truly liberal in their support.—Yet, like all other good enterprises, so also the cause of missions encountered opposition in the connection. It was a new thing among us, and there were still people in our midst, who considered it safe to cling to the *old* measures, and who, therefore, opposed all new ones about to be introduced, especially such as came into contact with their purses. Others again, who were not so very apprehensive in this respect, yet were not able to see the necessity of such a laborious and expensive enterprise; least of all, the propriety of making arrangements to send missionaries among the heathen. They were of the opinion, that since the old brethren, or the first preachers and members of the Association, had not recommended this cause, and as God had owned and blessed the Association, being without such measures and institutions, the introduction of each and every one of these measures was but a step toward "*Babel*," as some used to express themselves; not considering that it is the duty of the children to continue the work begun by their fathers, and to use all proper means and measures, required by the times and circumstances, in order to prosecute it in the most successful manner;—notwithstanding, that the increasing affluence and wealth of our Association, as well as our nation's and the world's advance in arts and sciences, etc., impose new duties upon us.—Yet the cheering results of our missionary operations in the very first years, silenced all these objections and excuses in a short time. Of late, however, the first zeal for the good cause has, alas! abated with too many.

Another subject received the attention of the Eastern Conference this year, viz., the procuring of suitable parsonages for married preachers on every circuit, wherever practicable. Conference had before already passed resolutions on this subject, but thus far without any effect. But from this time there was something done in the matter; for the other conferences passed similar resolutions, and in many places suitable parsonages were secured; but in not a few places nothing has been done yet.—This is a great defect of our organization, which proves injurious to many a circuit, and to many preachers it causes much loss of time and great inconveniences; besides involving them in heavy expenses. Although this subject has time and again been acted upon by the conferences, and been strenuously recommended to our laity; many, and even wealthy circuits have not yet done anything in the matter, while others have secured very uncomfortable or inconveniently situated houses. The object of conference was, to secure on every circuit, if at all practicable, a plain, yet comfortable and conveniently situated house, large enough, if possible, for two families, as two married preachers were often stationed on the same circuit.—The want of such houses for the itinerants, has injured the good cause in many respects; for it has induced many a preacher to buy a house himself, in consequence of which he could no longer be sent to any place; and in the second place, the stationing of the ministers has become more difficult, since many a circuit cannot every time be allotted to those preachers who would have suited best, and would also have been stationed there, had parsonages been provided. But not only this; many otherwise very useful ministers have been, by the unpleasant situation of their families, in consequence of the want of suitable residences, not only impeded in their efficiency, but even *discouraged*, to the great injury of their fields of labor. Whether they did right in thus yielding and suffering themselves to be discouraged under existing circumstances, and for the reasons stated, we leave to the judgment of the reader; but would remind him, at the same time, that, strictly speaking, ministers are not angels.—The greater, however, the measure of grace and of the love of God is shed abroad in our hearts, the easier such inconveniences and cases of self-denial are borne.

Another resolution of this conference was as follows: "Resolved, That the general use of tobacco, as it is customary in our days, is a great evil, and that we unanimously protest against it."

However improper and extravagant this resolution may have appeared to some in those days, yet similar resolutions have since been passed by several other ecclesiastical bodies. Our Periodical raised at that time, and still more after the passage of the above resolution, its voice in earnest against the evil, and not without success. Many were convinced by the sound arguments urged against the prevailing use of tobacco, and renounced it, some of whom have remained faithful to their resolutions, while others, alas! relapsed into the evil practice. In subsequent times, some of the other conferences passed similar resolutions, and quite recently the subject has been taken up again. But many members of the Evangelical Association, as well as of other Christian denominations, still indulge in this bad practice; and while many papers, that are devoted only to the secular improvement of mankind, are almost constantly protesting against it, the religious press is almost entirely silent on this subject. One of the principal reasons, why this evil has thus far not more effectually been combated in the Society, is, because *many* of our preachers are still addicted to it themselves. And as in many other things, so also in this, many appeal to the old brethren, the fathers of the Association; not considering, that in their times that amount of light was not thrown on this subject, nor on the cause of temperance, which we enjoy in our days; and that our ancestors are, consequently, more justifiable in these things than we. Moreover, some of the best men of the Society have always been opposed to this evil, in word and deed; and of these none has, at any time, whether formerly or lately, combated these two evils with more perseverance and resolution, than Brother Seybert, especially the evil of intemperance, or the use of intoxicating liquors as a beverage. Privately and publicly, in sermons and lectures, he has opposed this monster evil. Another inexorable opponent of the use of tobacco within our Society, has been, and we trust still is, Father H. Niebel, now in Ohio, one of the oldest surviving preachers in our Church.—Some of the older members probably still remember, how he in his sermons sometimes dealt with those that were addicted to the misuse of tobacco—and he generally did it with good effect. Hence he was greatly feared by them; and it was but seldom that one suffered himself to be caught by him in the act. Some followed his example in attacking the evil, but none perhaps could do it as wittily and with as good grace, as he generally did it. The writer recollects being present at general and camp-meetings, where H. N. painted the misuse of tobacco in such horrible colors, that many of the guilty, during the sermon, threw away their pipes, cigars, and blocks of tobacco, and at once forsook the evil. These *sudden* conversions, however, did not always prove lasting.—This conference also resolved, that none of our preachers shall deal in tobacco, similar to the Discipline rule of our Church forbidding the traffick in intoxicating liquors and in slaves.

The work, as might be expected from the awakened missionary spirit in the connection, extended itself during the year in many directions; and in some places, where it had formerly begun and taken a solid footing, glorious revivals took place. All things considered, this was one of the most blessed years up to that time. The camp-meetings, especially, were, on the whole, very productive of good, as well as some of the quarterly and protracted meetings. For the confirmation of what has been said, some extracts from reports of camp-meetings, held during that year, are here inserted. Brother D. Berger reported through the Periodical of a camp-meeting, that took place on Centre circuit, among other things as follows:—

"On Monday, September 3rd, our camp-meeting began, in George's Valley, Centre county, Pa., on the land of Brother J.

Falget, and lasted till the following Monday. The number of tents was 32, and the beginning of the meeting was very good. As early as the second day, conversions took place, and the meeting was constantly increasing in interest. At every invitation penitents came forward, in order to plead for mercy and the pardon of their sins, and God imparted his blessing abundantly.

The sermons were quite remarkably blessed and full of unction. The servants of God were in such a degree filled with courage and power, that I can say, to the honor and glory of God, that I had never before attended a camp-meeting, where the preaching was, from first to last, so plain and powerful as at this: many of the hearers have said the same. Others that embraced religion during the meeting, afterward confessed that they often thought their hearts would burst under the mighty power by which God accompanied his word. * * * * * *

On the last evening, the manifestations of God's power were such, that sinners broke down and cried for mercy; and without being invited, mourners came forward to the altar, in order to pray and to be prayed for. And when the time of the evening sermon had arrived, a number of penitent and contrite sinners lay round the altar on their knees and faces, crying to God for mercy and the pardon of their sins, so that another sermon was considered altogether unnecessary. The mourners were then conversed and prayed with, till most of them found peace and were translated into the glorious liberty of the children of God. Now followed a scene of heavenly shouting of the children of God, to which the words of the German poet can justly be applied:—

> '*Hier freut sich ein Juengling, der Jesum gefunden;*
> *Dort singet ein alter Verehrer der Wunden;*
> *Hier lobt eine Seele mit stillem Vergnuegen;*
> *Dort jauchzet ein Andrer und mœchte wohl fliegen.*'

Shortly before parting, all that were desirous to join the Society, were invited to become members, on condition that they were resolved to renounce all sins, and to lead holy lives, in accordance with the Word of God: twenty-seven persons came forward, and had their names recorded in the book of the Church.—The exact number of the new converts at this meeting, we cannot give; but as far as we could ascertain, it was about 50. To the Lord alone be all the praise!"

Of another camp-meeting, held on Mansfield circuit, in the state of Ohio, Bro. A. B. Shaefer reported as follows:—

"Our second camp-meeting began on the 20th of August, on the land of Bro. Henry Kiplinger, in Wayne county, Ohio, and was the second that was held at the same place. Eight itinerant and ten local preachers, eighty families that dwelt in about forty tents, and a considerable number of friends from a distance without tents, in all about 210, were present, most of whom were on the spot at the beginning, and had come, as I believe, in the fear of God, in order to do his work with solemnity. Although the meeting was very numerous, and increased daily, yet the attention and conduct of the people were remarkably good, so much so that not the least disturbance took place. It almost appeared as if all were on the side of God. The effect was general, from beginning to end: after almost every sermon, the mourners were invited, and each time more or less came forward. At the first invitation, about twenty-five persons presented themselves at the altar, and at every subsequent one between 40 and 50. On the last evening, 68 came forward at the first invitation, and afterward many among the crowd fell on their knees, crying to God for mercy. It is impossible for us to give the exact number of the new converts at this meeting, but it may have been between 60 and 70, most of whom united with us forthwith. Others have since declared, that they would join us at the first opportunity. We can indeed say, '*This was a time of the Son of man.*'"

Several other camp-meetings of this year were also remarkably blessed and efficacious, as may be seen from the reports of them in our Periodical.

Old York circuit, that had been thoroughly tried by a variety of vicissitudes, was refreshed this year, under the pastoral care of J. Sensel and W. Heim, with an almost general revival, especially in Canadochley and near Loganville; in point of newly received members, it ranked highest in the East. Cumberland circuit was still progressing. Centre circuit also enjoyed revivals in different parts, principally in Sugar Valley, and in several other places.—Columbia circuit, under the charge of the Brethren J. Barber and B. Epley, was blessed with an almost general revival, especially in the neighborhood of New Columbia, Union county, Pa., at Loyalsock, etc. On Lycoming circuit, too, glorious revivals took place. In order to enable the reader to pass a fair judgment on the amount of good accomplished in some places by our ministers, we here insert two reports, from some parts of the last two mentioned circuits, that were written by brethren residing in said places, for publication in the Periodical in 1839; they are as follows:—

"*Report of the Work of God in Loyalsock, Pa.*

Dear Brother Orwig:—Encouraged by the cheering news of the work of God, through the columns of the 'Christliche Botschafter,' I take up my pen in order to inform you of what the Lord has been pleased to do for us in this wilderness.

When we take a retrospective view of the condition we were in, before the servants of God came to us, we can truly say, '*The Lord has done great things for us.*' The people here are of different denominations, and ungodliness had almost reached its climax: cursing, swearing, lying, tippling, desecrating the Sabbath, etc., were the order of the day, and true Christianity a rare article. We indeed had preachers, but they were such as the prophet Micah, 3d chapter, describes: They were concerned for the wool, not for the sheep. In vices and immorality they took the lead. In short, our condition was lamentable, till about six years ago, the Lord had pity on us, and sent us his servants. Brother Seybert was the first who preached here; from that time the servants of God have labored very earnestly among us. At fisrt it seemed as if all were anxious to fall in with the good work, till about three years ago conversions took place, when the devil was aroused and rushed upon the children and servants of God with all his might, the priest being the leader. And when the Brethren

Berger and Sindlinger formed a class here of ten members, Satan commenced anew, through his servants, to calumniate, scold, and rail against us, as if we were reprobates; the cause of this was what Peter writes, 1. epistle, 4, 4.

From that time we have held prayer-meetings, and endeavored to work out our souls' salvation. The work of conversion stood still for some time, but the slander and persecution of the children of God went on without interruption; but blessed be God, who knoweth how to deliver those that are his.—Last summer, under the superintendence of the Brethren Barber and Epley, the work began again to extend itself rapidly. We also held two general meetings, at which Brother Seybert assisted us. Several of the strongholds of Babylon gave way, and a considerable number of precious souls were converted to God, so that we now have a society here of 23 members, who are determined to work out together their souls' salvation. Many others are in the net of the Gospel, the light shines with increased brightness, and ungodliness of every kind, especially drunkenness, has considerably decreased. A tavern-keeper said, that where he used to sell 5 barrels of liquor, he now sold scarcely one any more. Thus our country has been greatly improved, since the pure doctrine of the Gospel is preached here. We can say of a truth, with the poet:—

'Ob Teufel und Hælle gewueth't und gekracht,
So wurden doch Seelen zu Jesu gebracht;
Ob Belzebub Pfeilen mit Macht auf uns schosz,
So fielen doch Sæulen von Babylon los.'

May the Lord grant us grace to remain faithful to him till death! Amen.

J. G. Bertsch.

Loyalsock, Feb. 16, 1839.

Dunstown, Feb. 18th, 1839.

Dear Brethren in Christ!

Grant me the privilege to inform you, through the columns of the 'Botschafter,' of what the King of kings has done for us in our new settlement. It was five years last September, that I came from Germany to this settlement. There were then but few converted persons to be found in this neighborhood; but the Lord, in his infinite mercy, has been pleased to rouse some of us out of our lethargy, and to lead us to true repentance.—We have now heaven already here on earth; our class consists of 37 members, 12 of whom have been converted this year. We have frequently glorious times together; the wilderness and the solitary place have been made glad. Fathers and mothers, some of whom are already ripening for the grave, who but 4 or 5 years ago came from Germany, have been accepted in the 11th hour. Yes, dear brethren and sisters, we have reason to thank God for having sent his faithful servants in our neighborhood, who have thus far visited us so regularly. I have no doubt, but that many of this region will yet thank them in eternity, for their toil and care. We thank God also, that the 'Christliche Botschafter' has found its way to our part of the country; for it has already effected a vast amount of good, as many a house has been opened to it already, where it can teach and preach; and I hope, that many more houses will follow the example.—My dear brethren and sisters in the Lord, pray for us that our merciful Father may grant us grace to persevere steadfast to the end. The Lord's work prospers in our region; our meetings are blessed, the Master himself is often in our midst, so that old and young rejoice together in praising the Lord. May our Heavenly Father be our guide during life, and eventually bring us, with all blood-washed souls, to his everlasting kingdom, is my prayer for Christ's sake. Amen.

I remain your brother in Christ,

JOHN BROBST."

These are two out of the many instances of the great success that attended the labors of our itinerants. Wherever they found admittance, great moral changes for the better were effected by their simple preaching of the unadulterated truth, owned and blessed of Almighty God. But, notwithstanding these glorious results of their labors, they were formerly decried almost in every place where they began to labor, by cold teachers and hardened and ignorant nominal Christians, as false prophets and deceivers, that ought to be guarded against.—

Had the opposition on the part of the clergy not been so powerful, the fruit of their labors would have been still more abundant. In some parts of the country, the people had been filled with such strong prejudices against our preachers, by their pastors, that for a long time they had but few hearers; and only when the effects of their labors became visible by the thorough conversions and evident reformation of individuals, who had been great sinners, people commenced to attend in greater numbers, and to hear and judge for themselves. But as soon as this was done, glorious changes for the better generally took place, and some of the most respectable and influential Church-members of those cold teachers, were generally among the first converts and friends of the itinerants. By and by the influence of our itinerants became so strong in some places, that all railing and slandering of their enemies could harm them no more. It was then that the other preachers commenced to imitate their method and manner of proceeding to some extent, in order to prevent the people from leaving their churches. In our times, scarcely any one ventures to oppose us in so rude and ruthless a manner, except perchance a rationalist, but lately come from Germany, who, although blind in spiritual things, is anxious to convert the *ignorant* Americans; but men of this description generally soon lose all influence by these very acts, and are consequently harmless.

For the confirmation of what has been said, we here give a report of a work of the Lord in Galen, then Lake circuit, in the state of New York, which appeared at that time in the Periodical. It is as follows:—

"In Galen, Wayne county, Lake circuit, the work of God is in a flourishing condition, and there are prospects for a rich harvest. About three years ago a class was formed in this neighborhood; but meeting with great opposition from the devil and his servants, the work was somewhat impeded, till finally God wrought so powerfully that the enemies of the cross of Christ could hinder us no longer.

We have held four general meetings during the year, in this part of the country. At the first, God manifested himself already in his power; at the second a work of reformation was begun, which has been progressing ever since, so that sinners have been awakened and converted from time to time, and the fire is still burning. To the Lord alone be all the praise! Last spring, when we arrived on this circuit, we found a class of 29 members; since that time this number has been more than doubled. We have also established a missionary society, named: "*Galen Missionary Society;*" it consists of 26 members, and has subscribed $35."

In the eastern part of the state of Pennsylvania, the work continued to extend itself, especially in the counties of Lehigh, Northampton, and Bucks. In Allentown things went on very well, and our church-edifice there was built and dedicated during this year; and another was built in Upper Milford. In Philadelphia the work progressed finely, and continued to become more firmly established. The society at New Berlin, having had to complain for a long time of spiritual barrenness, was visited this year with a gracious visitation, to the awakening and conversion of a considerable number of precious souls, who were added unto the Lord. The old members also were quickened anew, and filled with more courage to prosecute their journey to heaven.

In compliance with the urgent requests from citizens of Upper Canada, for preachers of our denomination, Bro. C. Holl, who was stationed that year on Buffalo circuit, in the state of New York, paid them a visit toward the close of June, remaining there to the end of August following. He confined his labors mainly to Waterloo township, where he found many warm friends of the truth, who expressed a great desire to have a preacher of our denomination permanently located in their midst.

In the Western Conference, especially on the circuits of Mansfield and Sandusky, some conversions took place during this year. At Liverpool, Medina county, Ohio, where in 1834 the first class had been formed by Brother Bucks, consisting of ten members, which, however, had afterward been almost dissolved again, it pleased God this year to bless the labors of Bro. A. B. Shaefer, who was stationed on the circuit, so abundantly that the work was powerfully revived, and many souls were converted and added to the Church. The year following, when the Brethren A. Yambert and J. Holl were stationed there, the society was visited with another out-pouring of divine grace, during a general meeting in September, at which nearly thirty souls were converted.—Though this society has since that time been subject to a variety of trials and siftings, yet the Lord has still his faithful witnesses there, who serve him in spirit and in truth, and their conduct proves their conversion to have been a genuine work of God. This society has also furnished a number of candidates for the ministry, whose labors have been owned and blessed of the Lord.

From a report of Sandusky circuit, where Bro. P. Gatez was stationed this year, it appears that even as late as that time, the preachers of the Evangelical Association, especially in the West, had to labor harder in many places and to submit to greater inconveniences, than in our days. The report in question is as follows:—

"Our camp and general meetings during this year have, on the whole, been greatly blessed, and the grace of God has accompanied our labors to such an extent, that a considerable number of persons have been converted, who are now working out their souls' salvation. Yet, I am of opinion that more good might have been accomplished, if the circuit were not so large.—Some time ago, a communication appeared in the Botschafter from Brother Zinser, having reference to the difficulties and inconveniences of such extensive circuits, which I read with great delight; for I can say from my own experience, that the remarks of the brother are true. The circuit on which I have been traveling this year, contains 300 miles in circumference, with 35 appointments. Thus the journeys are necessarily long, and also very difficult, owing to the country being new and the roads bad, so that the horse has sometimes to wade up to his knees in water and morass. The distance from one appointment to another being often from 20 to 30 miles, and the roads bad, the preacher is obliged to travel the whole day, and often does not arrive until the congregation has assembled and is waiting for him. And think you, that after such a long and fatiguing journey, he is fit to preach? Since I have been traveling in these parts of the country, I frequently was compelled to spend the day on the road in the severest cold, and when I reached my appointment, I had scarcely any time for secret prayer, and no other closet than the snow-clad wilderness. And still some find fault with the preacher for not visiting them, although he frequently does not find time enough to read two or three chapters of the Bible, during the whole week. I do not wish to complain, but think matters could be greatly improved. Many of our old preachers would, undoubtedly, be in the field, were they not compelled, by the want of an adequate support, to stay at home. O that our boundaries of Ohio could be supplied with the necessary number of ministers! Now, though a married preacher on such an extensive circuit visits his family, that is from 100 to 200 miles off, but 2 or 3 times during the year, yet much time is lost thereby, and the circuit does not receive its proper attention. The consequence is, that not by far that amount of good is realized, which could be accomplished if the arrangements were better and the number of ministers larger."

It is true, not all the circuits in the West, and along the extreme borders of our sphere of operations, were as extensive as this; but some were still larger, and even in our times there are such circuits in new settlements, in the western states and territories.

Our small societies in Illinois had to pass through another severe trial this year, being deprived of the services of a minister for about eight months. But notwithstanding this, they kept up their religious services, although under great discouragements. The second preacher of our Association who visited that state, was Brother M. Hauert. In a report of these circumstances and his visits, published in the Periodical, he writes as follows:—

"As Bro. P. Wist, who had been appointed for these parts, could not, for certain reasons, enter that field, the children of Zion in the far West were for eight months deprived of the services of a minister. In their longing after the preaching of the word of God, they laid their case before the throne of grace. The Germans in these parts are generally very eager to hear the Gospel preached. The prayers of our friends were answered. Agreeably to the order of my presiding elder, I set out for these distant parts, and arrived, with the help of God, on the 3rd of September, safe and sound within 30 miles west of Chicago. My arrival caused great joy among the dear friends. The Lord assisted me powerfully while preaching his word, so that his children were encouraged and edified, and sinners awakened and convinced of the truth, some of whom found pardon in the blood of the Lamb, to the comfort and joy of their hearts. Hallelujah! I also traveled 117 miles to the Rock river, where I found some of our friends: tears of joy flowed freely, and we had a precious time. Thence I traveled to the Illinois river, where many Germans live, who alas are, for the most part, like sheep having no shepherd. I preached to them as often as I could; but on account of sickness some could not attend. Oh, that we as a German organization may soon come to the rescue of these straying sheep in the far West! We could, undoubtedly, gather many a sheaf for heaven. It is heart-rending to see that so many of our Germans live without God in the world. Oh, how many of them do yet stand idle in the market! and not a few are already in the 11th hour of their pilgrimage! The harvest is great, but the faithful laborers are few."

Brother Hauert, on his journey to Rock river, in Henry county, and farther South, organized the small class in said county, as Bro. Boas had not come thus far, and they had, therefore, up to that time, been without a preacher. Meanwhile the Des Plain society, under the direction of their class-leader, established the first Sabbath-school of the Evangelical Association in the far West; it consisted of the superintendent, 3 male and 2 female teachers, and 15 scholars. There being no permanent locality for the school to meet in, and the scholars and teachers living at a distance of 3 or 4 miles from each other, the enterprise was attended with great difficulties. Moreover, there was also a great want of suitable Sabbath-school books, and they had to shift as well as they could with Bibles, hymn-books, old catechisms, etc. Yet they were not discouraged, and their labors have been crowned with abundant success; the school has continued ever since, exerting a most salutary influence on the young of the whole neighborhood, and thus been a great blessing to the society.—On motion of the class-leader, it was also resolved by the society to erect a church, and this resolution was carried out during the months of April, May, and June, 1839. A man, then yet unconverted, named *Nicolas Miller*, presented to the society an acre of ground for a church and a grave-yard. A building of hewn timber, 21 by 23, was erected by the united efforts of the society; yet the class-leader did most of the work himself. This, then, was the *first church* of the Evangelical Association, west of the state of Ohio, directly one mile and a half east of Wheeling, Cook county, Illinois. Brother Hauert labored with very great success during his five months' stay among these people. Not only were the young societies more thoroughly established and richly comforted, but powerful conversions also took place.—The new circuit then consisted of 4 regular preaching places; as, Des Plain or Wheeling, Napierville, Dutchman's Point, and Sharon in Henry co. Although the appointments were but few, a round on the circuit amounted to *three hundred miles*—the distance from one preaching place to the other, was in one instance 130, and in another 150 miles; and as the preacher was *German*, and the population for the most part *English*, he could take up no new preaching places.—The northern half of the state of Illinois was in those days, for the most part, an almost impassable wilderness and very thinly settled. The distance between dwelling houses, even along the main roads, was often from 15 to 30 miles; and even these few inhabitants were but poorly prepared to accommodate strangers, so that traveling in those parts of the country was then extremely difficult. Where now fields in a high state of culture, and respectable farm-houses, greatly delight the eye of the beholder, the solitary traveler saw in those days nothing but a blooming wilderness, where wolves, cranes, bitterns, and partridges, swarmed by hundreds and thousands in perfect security.

Toward the close of the conference year, at the end of February, 1839, Brother Hauert took his leave to attend the session of the Western Conference, leaving the young circuit in a highly flourishing and promising state, numbering 78 members, 15 of whom are designated in the record of conference as new converts, and 18 as newly received. Notwithstanding their great poverty and the many difficulties they encountered, they had raised $74,32 for the support of the preacher, though he had labored but 5 months among them.

This year, Bro. S. Altimos moved to the state of Michigan, and settled in Monroe county. He preached in different places, both in Michigan and the northern part of Indiana, and in several places met with members of the Evangelical Association, who had emigrated from the state of N. York, and formed them into classes. Thus he laid the foundation of the operations of our Church in Michigan and in the northern part of Indiana. In the counties of Adams, Wells, and Allen, along the St. Mary's river, he met with many Germans and preached to them. Also in Fort Wayne, Indiana, he was hospitably received by Brother Stetzel, and preached there with great success. He also paid a visit to Detroit, and preached there in the German language. This was the beginning of the operations of our Church in the southern part of Michigan and the northern part of Indiana.

From this description of the condition of the Society in those days, it appears that it had arrived at a very important and eventful epoch of its history. The germ of the inward power of the Association, that had thus far but slowly expanded, now began to develop itself more rapidly. As a stream swollen by a heavy and long continued rain, overflows its banks, thus the Church now began to go beyond its former limits, in every direction.—The provisions for the better support of the ministers, their more rapid increase in point of numbers, their growth in outward and inward culture and qualification generally, the introduction of protracted meetings, Sabbath-schools, and the cause of missions, but above all the establishment of the German Periodical (the Christliche Botschafter) and of the Printing Office, exerted a very salutary influence on both the Association and the Public at large, contributing largely to the prosperity and growing usefulness of the Church. The Society began to command more respect in general, and even some of its former most inveterate enemies commenced, at least in appearance, to show it more respect, although they had no more sympathy for it than ever before. The Periodical had been instrumental in placing the Society, its principles, object, and mode of operation, with many in a more favorable light; in rousing and bringing to public notice the talents of its more gifted preachers; in fostering, in general, a spirit of inquiry, and setting their combined strength in a more effectual manner to work. But, as already remarked, not only within the Society, but also out of it, the Periodical exerted a very salutary influence, especially in later times, when its circulation had become greater. It was not only *read* by many who were no members, but also *regularly subscribed for*. To its usefulness many subscribers and agents bore witness from time to time, as some of the following extracts will show. One of the subscribers, in a letter addressed to the Editor, dated Feb. 18th, 1839, writes among other things as follows :—

"We also thank God, that the Christliche Botschafter has found its way to our part of the country; for it has here already accomplished a vast amount of good. It has gained admittance into many a house, where it found opportunity to teach and preach, and I trust that many more houses will be opened to it."

Another subscriber, some few months later, makes the following remarks with regard to the Periodical :—

"Perhaps no observer has failed to see, that the establishment of the Christliche Botschafter has proved an epoch in the history of the Evangelical Association, a fact that secures it a high rank in the esteem of every true friend of the principles of our Church, although it still admits of many an improvement. The expectations that were entertained at its start, have been more than realized, and a correspondent of the Botschafter, instead of addressing 50 or 100 hearers, has the satisfaction to speak at once to at least 4000 or 5000 hearers. A means through which all the members of the connection can be addressed at once, is of incalculable benefit; for thereby (to mention but one thing) an eminent object, that is indispensably necessary for the continuous prosperity of the connection, is secured, viz., *an identity of views throughout all the societies.* I am also very much pleased to perceive, that the usefulness of the Botschafter is to be materially enhanced, by being enlarged and oftener published. It is presumed that none of its present subscribers will be induced by the slight increase of the subscription price to discontinue the paper; while on the other hand, it is confidently expected that it will receive many new subscribers, and that its agents will not rest satisfied until it is taken by every family within the Association, and also by many others."

The historian has to chronicle the death of but one preacher during this year, as far as he has been able to learn, viz., of Bro. *Benjamin Ettinger.* When called to depart, he resided in Scott township, Sandusky county, Ohio, and was 45 years of age. Brother E. found the Lord in his youth, and soon after united with the Evangelical Association. Afterward he served about 5 years as an itinerant, and the remainder of his life as a local preacher. On his death-bed he professed to have uninterrupted peace, and to enjoy the hope of a blessed immortality.

The membership at the close of this year, was 7859; the increase during the year, 550.

NINTH SECTION.

FROM THE SEVENTH GENERAL CONFERENCE IN 1839, TO THE EIGHTH GENERAL CONFERENCE IN 1843.

The Year 1839.

Seventh General Conference.

This was the first General Conference that had been appointed by the one preceding, and took place in the church of the Evangelical Association, about three miles south-west of Millheim, Centre county, Pa., commonly called Mosser's Church. Its session began March 25th, 1839. The following members were present:—

Eastern Conference.

Thomas Buck,	Charles Hesser,
George Brickley,	Solomon G. Miller,
Francis Hoffman,	Philip Wagner,
Charles Hammer,	John Sensel,
Michæl F. Maize,	Joseph Harlacher,
Daniel Berger,	John Young,
James Barber,	John Seybert,
Daniel Kehr,	John P. Leib,
John M. Sindlinger,	W. W. Orwig.

Western Conference.

Joseph Long,	Absalom B. Shaefer,
Henry Niebel,	Samuel van Gundy,
John G. Zinser,	John Lutz,
Henry Bucks,	Peter Wist,
Elias Stœver,	Peter Gates,
Jacob Boas,	Aaron Yambert,

John J. Kopp.

As the Society had as yet no bishop, *H. Niebel*, the presiding elder of the last General Conference, opened the session by reading a part of the Word of God, singing, and prayer. *Thomas Buck* was then elected chairman, and he appointed *George Brickley* secretary.

Hitherto the Discipline of the Church contained no provision, either defining or limiting the power of General Conference, so that this body had, in fact, an unlimited power. It could make alterations of, and additions to, the *doctrines* and *government of the Church*, as it deemed best. But this Conference adopted a constitution, defining the power of future General Conferences. This constitution, however, can be altered under certain conditions, with the exception of the *articles of faith*, and has been changed somewhat since. This was a very necessary measure, and ought to have been taken fifteen years before.

This conference limited also very materially the power of the bishops, especially with regard to the appointments of the preachers, and their transfer from one place to another, during the interval of the Annual Conferences. Heretofore, a bishop was authorized, with the assistance of two presiding elders, to assign, at the Annual Conferences, both to the presiding elders their districts, and to the preachers their circuits, and in the interval of the Annual Conferences to transfer both presiding elders and preachers, according to his option. Attempts have since been made to restore this power of the bishops, especially with regard to the transfer of preachers from one conference to another; but not being supported by a constitutional majority (three-fourths) of the General Conference, it proved a failure. As, however, the connection had no bishop from the publication of its Doctrines and Discipline up to this time, this power vested in the bishop, was never exercised by an incumbent. But as this conference elected a bishop, it was therefore considered expedient to circumscribe his power. Brother *John Seybert* was elevated to this highest office of the Church, and thus became the first *regular bishop* of the Association, according to the rules of the Discipline. As to Mr. *Albright*, he was elected to this office before the Doctrines and the Discipline had been adopted, for which reason he can hardly be considered one of our former bishops. His case was in every respect an extraordinary one; for even before his elevation to the superintendency of the Church, which happened but a short time before his death, he exercised, from the very organization of the Association till his death, all episcopal power, transferring preachers and arranging everything in the Association, as it seemed best to him, yet not always without consulting his brethren. He was, therefore, in the full sense of the word, the *bishop* of the Association from the time of its organization to his death, exerting a power and influence upon it, such as no bishop has done after him and probably none ever will.

Together with these changes of the Discipline, some more were made, and a number of new clauses and rules introduced, especially in the chapter of "*Temporal Economy.*" Of these new laws and rules, the following are the most important: "*Of selling and using spirituous liquors;*" "*Of slavery;*" the above mentioned constitution or rules, touching the power of the General Conference, and the section: "*Of the support of Missions.*" With these new regulations new clauses were introduced in different places; for instance, the addition to the duties of the superintending preachers, making it obligatory on them to establish Sabbath-schools wherever practicable.—The chapter on the temporal economy of the Association was considerably changed, especially the section of our Printing Establishment, and that of the support of the preachers. The unequitable rule which diminished the small salary of the married preachers still more, increasing thereby that of the single men, which the General Conference of 1835 had introduced, was repealed and the former rule re-introduced. With the limitation of the power of General Conference, and the change of its routine of business, the *delegate system* was introduced, which makes the General Conference consist of *one* member for every *four* members of each Annual Conference. As before stated, each elder was heretofore entitled to a seat and vote at the General Conference. This change was evidently for the better, as General Conference is now composed of the most experienced and generally most talented members of the ministry.

The new Printing Establishment claimed and received the particular attention of this conference. Its present arrangement was not only sanctioned, but various measures were also taken to increase its efficiency. It was resolved, that the "*Christliche Botschafter*," beginning with the following year, be published *semi-monthly*, instead of once a month, and be enlarged somewhat, at the slight addition of 25 cents to the former subscription price. This gave a powerful impulse to the paper, but at the same time more than doubled the amount of labor in the Establishment. From that time the Periodical made rapid progress and exerted a constantly increasing salutary influence on the connection. Arrangements were also made to publish a considerable number of Sabbath-school and some other books, especially the well-known stereotyped *German pocket Bible* of the Association. This latter work was, indeed, a great enterprise in those days, as it cost almost or fully as much as the Establishment itself; but it being published for subscribers at a high price, the undertaking succeeded, though not without some difficulty. The first edition nearly covered the costs of the plates, and the price was then reduced to less than one-half. The little school-book, called "*Anfangsbuch*" (primer), was in manuscript approved by the conference, and 6000 copies were ordered to be printed. Two new committees, one called the *Book Committee*, the other the *Committee for examining new works that may be offered for publication*, were elected; also a third one, to select and prepare Sabbath-school books for publication.

This conference also took the first measures toward publishing a history of the Evangelical Association. The following editorial article that had shortly before appeared in the Periodical, was the occasion for this action of conference.

"*A History of the Evangelical Association.*"

"Almost every branch of the Christian Church has a history of its origin, progress, and the most important and memorable events connected therewith. This can hardly fail to be appreciated as a dear legacy by their descendants, especially in those branches whose founders have built upon the true foundation, and were themselves in possession of genuine religion; since, as the History of the Church Universal teaches, very remarkable events generally take place under such circumstances, as well with regard to awakenings and conversions, as to opposition and persecution from the kingdom of darkness.

The Evangelical Association has not, indeed, attracted much attention in the world, when compared with other Christian denominations; yet it is by no means inferior to any other Church of the country, in proportion to the time of its existence and other circumstances. No other branch of the Church has, in our days, given more and stronger proofs of the power and approval of God, than the Evangelical Association, as well with regard to many remarkable and ordinary conversions, as to sore and malicious persecutions, for the sake of the truth and righteousness. It is, therefore, our opinion that it ought to have a minute and correct history of its origin, progress, and all memorable and interesting events, to transmit to its descendants. This subject has lately been considered and discussed by some of our ministers; but has, as far as we know, not yet received public attention. It is high time, however, that this should be done *now*, if it is to be done at all; for at present it *may* yet be done, but in a few years hence it will no longer be possible. Some of our first preachers and members are still living, who are fully acquainted with the history of our denomination from its very start, and can, in all probability, give an accurate account of all memorable facts and events, both from memory and from the notes taken in their journals. But before many years will have passed away, these fathers who have witnessed the mighty power of God, when he commenced, 35 or 40 years ago, through the instrumentality of an *Albright* and his fellow-laborers, a glorious revival of genuine religion among the neglected Germans of North America, which has continued to increase ever since, despite all opposition from the powers of darkness, — these fathers we say, will, in a few years, have followed their brethren to their rest, and then there will no one be left to relate these glorious works of God. As for ourself, we have often listened with exquisite pleasure and delight to some of our fathers, while they recounted the glorious victories of the Lord in past times; but soon there will no one be left, that can say with the apostle John: 'That which was from the beginning, which we have heard, which we have seen with our eyes, which we have looked upon and our hands have handled, we declare unto you.' No, we shall then have nothing left but hearsay; the history will lose its originality, power, and purity, and the descendants will forget their fathers, perhaps also their principles and method of operating.

It is true, this subject may not be of equal interest to each and every one of us, especially those who are acquainted with our whole history. But after 40 years more shall have passed away, what will be the state of things then? There will then, in all probability, no one be left who was personally acquainted with the first preachers and members of our Society. Would not then our descendants find fault with us, for not having left them a historical account of the origin, progress, and the most remarkable events of our connection? They would certainly find fault with us, and that justly. But we trust that measures will be taken to have such a work compiled and published.

The work in question ought, in our opinion, to contain the following points:—

1. A chronological and geographical account of the origin and progress of the Evangelical Association, embracing the names of all our first preachers, with short sketches of their lives and labors in the vineyard of the Lord; an account of the time and place of the first class, the names of its members and class-leader; likewise of the second, and third, etc.

2. An account of the first regular circuit, its territory, name, and that of its first minister, and so on of the next following.

3. When and where the first conference was held; who its members were; the order in which it was held. Who the first ordained preachers, deacons, elders, and presiding elders were; when the first district was formed, its name, territory; when and where the first general and camp-meeting was held, the first church built, etc.

4. When and where the first General Conference took place;

when an approved Discipline, containing the articles of faith, was introduced, etc.

5. An account of the spread of the Association in the several states of the Union; what preachers were first sent to this and that state; when and where the first class, circuit, and district, were formed there, etc.

6. When the second conference was formed; its territory.

7. Of the remarkable revivals in the several counties, cities, and parts of the country; when they took place, and which preachers were the instruments, etc.; also of the most extraordinary persecutions and oppositions from ungodly men, and of all memorable events.

8. Some notices of the Printing Establishment, etc.

These are some of the most important points the work should embrace. But on a thorough investigation, perhaps a great many more important items will be found.

But the question may be asked: how is a correct information of all that has taken place within 40 years, to be obtained? We answer: in a variety of ways. An agent may be appointed, whose duty it is to travel through all the parts of the Association, and to inquire of the old preachers and members after these things, and then to record them. Or, each Annual Conference may appoint a committee, to collect the necessary materials, afterward to be arranged by some one, in regular order.—We sincerely wish that such a work may soon be published; and it is our firm belief, that it will be welcomed by all the members of the Association, that take a deep interest in its welfare."

The conference resolved, that a history be compiled, according to the plan devised in this editorial, and be published in the following manner: Three brethren were appointed, one for each conference; viz., Charles Hammer for the West Pennsylvania, Thomas Buck for the East Pennsylvania, and John Dreisbach for the Ohio Conference; of whom it was required to gather the necessary materials, which the writer was then to arrange and collect into a book. But this resolution was not carried out, as only a few sheets of written matter were produced. The appointed brethren found their task much more difficult than the conference had anticipated; nor did they receive that assistance from the ministers, on which they had calculated. Thus the matter remained till the next General Conference.

The writer was re-elected Editor for four years, and the Establishment received an additional officer, the General Agent, the duties of which office had hitherto been attended to by the Editor. Bro. Charles Hammer was appointed to this office. This was a necessary and highly beneficial improvement.

As the two Annual Conferences had increased considerably for several years, and became pretty numerous, they were divided into *three*, with the following names:—1. *East Pennsylvania Conference*, consisting of the districts: Philadelphia, Canaan, and Moriah. 2. *West Pennsylvania Conference*, consisting of the districts: Zion, Salem, and Carmel. 3. *Ohio Conference*, consisting of the districts: Tabor, Sandusky, and Ohio. The territory of East Pennsylvania Conference embraced the part of Pennsylvania east of the two branches of the Susquehannah, a great portion of the north-western part of the state of New York as far as the city of Buffalo, and subsequently extended over a great part of Upper Canada; that of West Pennsylvania Conference embraced Pennsylvania west of the two branches of the Susquehanna, and extended into Maryland and Virginia; that of Ohio Conference embraced the greater part of Ohio, and some parts of Indiana and Illinois. This, then, was the field of labor of the Evangelical Association in those days. As to the cause of missions, it received the full attention and warm support of this General Conference, for not only was the lately founded Missionary Society sanctioned, but a section on the *Support of Missions* was introduced into the Discipline of the Church.

As the cost of living is generally more expensive in cities than elsewhere, this General Conference authorized the Annual Conferences to increase the salary of their preachers and missionaries in these places, beyond what the Discipline allows, to any amount they may deem necessary.

On the whole, this conference was characterized by great zeal for the cause of God. It was animated, not by that timid, diffident, faithless, and fainting spirit, which never dares do or undertake much for God's kingdom, but by a bold enterprising spirit, that took hold not only of the majority of the ministry, but also of some of the societies and members. It was particularly the missionary spirit which filled the whole Association in those days; and this spirit called forth and fostered, as it always does, a deep interest in all the enterprises having the glory of God for their object. A great many new churches had been erected of late, and their number increased annually. Wherever the societies were not too weak, both in towns and in the country, churches were built; and frequently even there where they were really too weak, in consequence of which they became involved in difficulties. These difficulties, however, had generally their origin not so much in the inability of the societies, as in mismanagement. The building was often commenced before the necessary arrangements had been made, or proper efforts put forth to collect the necessary funds.

The Western Conference held its annual session this year in the church of the Association in Green township, Stark co., Ohio, beginning March 4th; the Eastern in the borough of Lebanon, Pa., beginning April 11th. Over the former H. Niebel presided, over the latter the newly elected bishop. Heretofore the Annual Conferences had elected their presiding officers from among the presiding elders; but now the bishop presided over both the Annual and the General Conferences. Seven of the preachers located, and twelve new ones were received into the itinerancy. The Western Conference created a new presiding elder district, which was called *Sandusky district*, and six new circuits, partly by dividing the larger ones, partly by extending its sphere of operations. The Eastern Conference formed a new station, called "*Pottsville and Minersville station*," and founded four missions, two in Upper Canada, one in the state, and one in the city of New York, viz., the *city of New York mission, Jacob Borkert* missionary; *Mohawk mission, Christian Hummel* missionary; *Waterloo mission*, in Upper Canada, *Christian Holl* missionary, and *Black Creek mission* [ibidem], *Michæl Eis* missionary. These, then, were the first regular missions of the Evangelical Association.

The General Conference having, as before stated, created *three* new conferences out of the two old ones, the names of the latter were, as a matter of course, dropped, and "Eastern Conference" and "Western Conference" disappeared from this time out of the annals of the Church. Therefore, when the "Eastern Conference" met for the last time, it was made optional with the preachers to choose one of the two conferences, or to receive an appointment within the limits of either. Some chose their conference, others gave themselves up unconditionally. Thus, in 1839, the Association numbered *three Annual Conferences*, consisting of 80 itinerants, 36 circuits, 2 stations, and four missions, which were divided into nine presiding-elder districts.

The Association enjoyed great prosperity in this, as she had also in the preceding year. The work extended considerably, and glorious awakenings occurred in different places. Most of the new circuits in the West and the four missions in the North gained firm footing, and the old fields of labor were extended and strengthened.

As the founding of the Evangelical Association and its labors had, in former days, been considered superfluous and pernicious, by some of the older ecclesiastical organizations; so its present attempt to found home missions was also found fault with, especially in those places where said denominations had regular churches and preachers. They saw in this attempt an insult offered to their churchly character, and a declaration on our part, that they were heathen. It is true, there were in most of the existing Churches praiseworthy exceptions, but there were still whole districts and parts of country, where the conduct of many members of said denominations was not a whit better than that of heathen; and as this was the case then, so it has been ever since, in almost all parts of the country. Other denominations, again, were in appearance not so rude and godless as those just spoken of, and many of their members were well disposed, and conducted themselves becomingly; but the great majority of the members of even these Churches had only the appearance of godliness, while they denied its power. This was the condition of the greater part of the German Churches of this country even in those times, and many of the *English* were not much better. In order to prove this, we here insert a few truthful reports on the state of morals in some parts of the Union and Upper Canada. Bro. Berger, in a report of Lehigh circuit, in Lehigh county, Pa., in the year 1839, writes among other things as follows:—

"The attendance, on the whole, was good (he refers to a camp-meeting); but some of those present manifested their so-called faith by pelting the congregation with rotten eggs and stones.—We cannot as yet say much of awakenings and conversions; but there is no lack of opposition and persecution from the devil and his servants; and the great ignorance and unparalleled impiety of the people have astonished me this year more already than ever before. I have, before this, been in places where the people were wicked; but nowhere found such shameful wickedness as in this part of the country. Here the words of our Saviour are fully applicable: 'Behold! I send you forth as sheep in the midst of wolves.'"

Bro. J. G. Zinser, in a report of some camp-meetings in 1839, in the state of Ohio, writes of certain parts in Pickaway county, Ohio, as follows:—

"The light of truth has not yet everywhere dissipated the uncommon spiritual darkness which envelops many of the German inhabitants of these parts of the country. It is true, the Gospel of Christ has in various places achieved many a glorious conquest, and not a few have been brought to a saving knowledge of the truth; yet it will require many more mighty struggles, before a great reformation can be brought about among these so very degenerate professors of religion."

In order to show the moral condition of the Germans of Upper Canada at that time, we here insert a condensed report of Bishop Seybert. They were mostly Catholics, Lutherans,

Reformed, Mennonites, Dunkers, etc. The members of the last two denominations were not as bad as the others, as they observed more outward decorum; although most of them were strangers to the new birth and life in God. But the others were totally enveloped in moral darkness and in viciousness. Some of their pastors were notorious inebriates, drinking to excess at every opportunity; yea, sometimes when they baptized children, they could scarcely go through the form of baptism. After the ceremony, however, drinking began in earnest, and the minister, sponsors, and all present, were frequently so full, that they had to stagger home as best they could. Near Pushlinch, one of these pastors became so intoxicated after performing a wedding ceremony and christening a child, that he fell from the chair on the floor and was unable to rise alone, whereupon the lady of the house indignantly said: "*Why did you not let him alone?*" At another time, when a would-be Lutheran preacher intended to celebrate the Lord's supper at Hamburg, on Easter Monday, he met on his arrival a portion of his parishioners on their way to a dance. One of the party was carrying a cask of beer on his shoulders, and another had a violin under his arm. They requested their pastor to put off the Lord's supper to some other time, and to give precedence to the frolick, and he complied with their request. At Waterloo, after the dedication of a church, the whole assembly went to a tippling-house where cups and goblets were busily plied. These are only a few of the many examples of the wickedness of the clergy and their parishioners in general. But there were also some better disposed persons among them, who lamented this sad state of things, but were unable to remedy the evil. This was the moral condition of the greater part of the Germans of Upper Canada, when the Evangelical Association in 1839 established two missions there.—In this connection it must be stated that about ten or twelve years before, the United Brethren had occasionally preached at Waterloo, Berlin, and in the neighborhood, and made some efforts to organize societies. They had already a good beginning, and their prospects for the future were fair, as quite a number of souls had been awakened and some really converted; but the preacher they afterward sent thither, turned faithless and fell away, and thus the enterprise was frustrated in its very start. Discouraged by this sad turn of affairs, they abandoned the project, and sent them no more missionaries. The little band that had been gathered, was thus left alone, and afterward partly dispersed. But, as already stated, some families that had moved from Waterloo, in Upper Canada, to the state of Ohio, called by letters the attention of their friends at home to the Evangelical Association, and thus created a desire in them to have preachers of this denomination in their midst. At this time it also happened, that one of our brethren, *Jacob Vogt* by name, who lived near the Niagara Falls, had occasion to go to Canada, where he became acquainted with some pious German families, near Sodom, Niagara district, who attended the meetings of the Methodists, for their edification. When these good people learned from Brother Vogt, that there were German itinerant ministers in the United States, who preached the pure Gospel with power, they expressed a great desire to become acquainted with them. Brother Vogt imparted this information to the preachers, and then it was that J. G. Zinser, as already stated, paid them a visit, and preached at Martin and Christian Shaub's. Thus the Evangelical Association was induced to turn its attention to Canada, and commence operations there.—Whether the Association, under such circumstances, was justified in founding missions in Canada, or not, we leave with the candid reader to decide.

The two missions in Canada succeeded well from the beginning, and thus fully justified the expectations raised by the repeatedly expressed desire for the preaching of the pure Gospel, the preparatory labors of the United Brethren at Waterloo, and the visits of some of our brethren in those parts where the missions were founded. The Periodical, too, had been instrumental in preparing the way for the missionaries. On Waterloo mission, shortly after the arrival of the missionary, a camp-meeting was appointed, which was held in August following, consisting of fifteen tents, and was highly blessed. It is worthy of remark, that on this mission class-meetings were introduced, a Sabbath-school established, and a camp-meeting held, before a class or society had been organized.

In order to give an insight into the success of our first missions, we here insert in full the first reports of the four regular missionaries, who were sent out by the Society, and such extracts from the following reports during the first year, and other information, as may be necessary for this purpose. Brother Holl's first report of *Waterloo mission* is as follows:—

"Much beloved Brother Orwig:—In the name of Christ I take my pen in hand to inform you of the condition of our mission. By the help of God we arrived safely at Berlin on the 9th of May. The friends were in good health; but their spiritual condition was such as might be expected under the existing circumstances: being without a preacher, without regular services and the means of grace, etc. Some were also disappointed in the person of the preacher; yet a hearty welcome was extended to me and my family. Here I found a vineyard without fence, greatly neglected and grown wild; and my own experience verified the adage, that *every beginning is difficult.* Some of the friends were quite disheartened, apprehending that much could not be accomplished. This, of course, was not very encouraging to me. Yet my faith and courage did not fail me, and I clung the more firmly to God who has said: '*Fear thou not, for I am with thee; be not dismayed, for I am thy God; I will strengthen thee; yea, I will help thee; yea, I will uphold thee with the right hand of my righteousness.*' After I had preached for about two weeks, I was delighted to see that darkness and unbelief were giving way. The friends soon took courage to press forward; our public services increased in interest; our class and prayer-meetings were blessed with conversions, and nearly all the friends seem now to be in good spirits and determined to fight the good fight of faith, and to serve God with a perfect heart. I can truthfully say, that things are going on finely. The Lord be praised for it!

Some time ago, four families, myself, and a few other individuals, had intended to go to a camp-meeting, to be held on Buffalo circuit, in the state of New York, at a distance of 115 miles, and anticipated great joy from this meeting of the children of God. But shortly before the time we were informed that it would not take place; the reason I did not learn. This sad news induced us to propose holding a camp-meeting ourselves in the neighborhood. The proposition met the hearty approval of all the friends, and we resolved at once to hold a camp-meeting on the land of David Erb, two miles north of the village of Waterloo, to begin August 23d. I know already of fifteen tents to be pitched, and have reason to believe that this number will still increase.

We have also commenced a German Sabbath-school; it opened with 41 scholars, and the number has been increasing every Sunday. At a class-meeting on the 18th inst., I applied to the friends of the school for assistance, and they contributed $34; several were not present who are also expected to contribute their share.

The friends salute Brother Seybert, and would be very happy to see him on our camp-ground; his presence would indeed cause universal joy.*

I greet our missionary society, all its branches and auxiliary societies, and all other friends, begging of them to remember me in their prayers.

CHRISTIAN HOLL.

Berlin, Upper Canada, June 24, 1839."

Extract from the second report of Brother Holl, concerning that mission:—

"On August 20th we were greatly rejoiced by the arrival of the Brethren J. Sindlinger and M. Eis in our midst. Though much fatigued by their long journey, yet Brother Sindlinger preached for us at Berlin that very evening, from Rom. 8, 1. The sermon was plain and pointed, and to judge from its ef-

*Brother Seybert is just on his way to New York and Canada, and his intention is, as he told us, to attend the camp-meeting in Canada.
EDITOR.

July 22d, 1839.

fects, must have been taken to heart, for tears both of sorrow and joy flowed freely. Late in the evening of the 21st., our joy was still increased by the arrival of our dear Brother Seybert, accompanied by the ministers of Buffalo circuit in New York, and some friends from Williamsville. The courage and faith of our friends waxed strong. On the 23d our camp-meeting began. The opening sermon was delivered by Bro. Seybert, from Rom. 2, 4—7; heaven seemed to open, and showers of blessings descended upon us. On Saturday the meeting increased in feeling and interest. Toward evening some rain fell. On Sunday morning crowds of people came from every direction, and the conduct of all present was admirable—all were filled with wonder and astonishment. In the evening awakenings and conversions broke out, and shouts of praise and thanksgiving ascended to heaven, because the Lord is merciful and his goodness endureth forever. During that night and the following day, powerful storms, interspersed with heavy peals of thunder, and accompanied by copious showers, passed by in quick succession. On Monday *showers of blessings* came down upon the assembly, and sinners were converted to God. In the evening the meeting became uncommonly interesting; the cries of sinners for mercy, and the shouts of praise and thanksgiving of the children of God resounded from the camp ground. I myself felt like singing with the poet:—

'O! dasz ich tausend Zungen hætte
Und einen tausendfachen Mund,
So stimmt' ich damit um die Wette,
Vom allertiefsten Herzensgrund,
Ein Loblied nach dem andern an
Von Dem, was Gott an mir gethan.'

On Tuesday we celebrated the Lord's supper, and 54 communicants partook of the sacred emblems. In the evening we had another blessed waiting upon the Lord. Our parting on Wednesday morning was uncommonly touching and affecting; God's presence was so powerfully manifested, that his children praised him and shouted for joy. Before the meeting was closed, an invitation was given to join the Church, whereupon 26 persons had their names recorded; thus the foundation of our society here was laid. Since that time some more have joined us. The prospects to gather a people here to the Lord among the Germans, are very good."

The first report of the Black Creek mission in Canada, is as follows:—

"Dear brethren in Christ:—I feel it my duty to send you a report of this my distant missionary field. I can say to the praise of the Lord, that he takes the lead and prepares the way for me. Last year when I arrived in this wilderness and commenced to preach, weak in body and in spirit as I was, I found open doors and was kindly received by some children of God. But the religious condition of these people in general is indeed wretched. Their religion mostly consists in the observance of some rites and a plain dress. Yet I can say, that a great change has already taken place, and many begin to inquire what they must do to be saved; and already some profess to have found peace with God. My meetings are generally well attended, and light from on high begins to penetrate the dark places. Though the prince of darkness is enraged and sets opposition and persecution on foot, yet there is every reason to believe that the Lord will gather himself a people here.

In the beginning of June I traveled about 60 miles upward along the shores of lake Erie, and found a large settlement of Germans. I offered to preach for them, and permission was readily granted. I then preached on Sunday to a large congregation, and God was pleased to own and bless his word. These people, that have for years gone astray like sheep in the wilderness, manifested a great longing after the word of God. They wept for joy that they were privileged once more to hear the pure Gospel preached in their vernacular tongue. At the close of the meeting, some men came forward with tears in their eyes, entreating me to preach once more for them; they confessed that they must change their lives, or else they could not go to heaven. I made some private calls, and found the people greatly interested in their souls' salvation. My heart was filled with joy and gratitude to God for the missionary arrangements of the Evangelical Association. whereby it has become possible to preach the Gospel of Christ to these far-distant perishing souls. Brethren in Christ! let us work while it is day, for the night cometh when no one can work. All our labors, our property, yea our lives ought to be consecrated to the Lord; and the main object of our labors ought to be, to save souls and thus help in building the house of the Lord. Dear brethren, remember in your prayers your brethren who labor in the distance, that the Lord may protect and assist them, in order that his kingdom may be extended through their instrumentality and many souls be saved. Pray that the word of the Lord may have free course and be glorified everywhere. Lord, grant each and every one of us grace! Amen.

MICHAEL EIS.

June— 1839."

This mission prospered exceedingly the very first year, and at its close numbered 84 members; for this reason it was changed into a regular circuit the second year, and received two preachers.

Mohawk mission, in the counties of Herkimer and Montgomery, N. Y., along the Mohawk river, prospered likewise greatly and at the close of the year numbered nearly 60 members. The second year it was also converted into a circuit, and received two preachers who labored very successfully, and at the expiration of the year reported 84 new converts, altogether 166 members. The following is the first report of this mission:—

"Much beloved brethren in the Lord:—It affords me much pleasure to send you a report of our missionary field and its prospects for the future. My journey to this place was long and tedious; for my horse was sorely rubbed by the saddle, and I had to lie still time and again, for several days. Yet with the help of God I arrived here at last in safety; and the reception I met with, was kind and cordial, especially on the part of Father and Mother Dunkel.—As to true religion, there are scarcely any vestiges left, though there are many here who once had some experience. But most of them have retained only an outward *form* of it, while they have lost its *substance*. This is the effect of their not having been fed with the pure milk of the Gospel; but thanks be to God, that the prospects for the future are encouraging. I have already obtained ten preaching places, and in several other places the people desire my services. I preached twice in Utica in a church which the Germans have rented, and there is reason to believe that many can be gathered here to the Lord. Yea, I am confident that with the grace of God, which I am determined to seek more and more for myself, my labors on this field will not be in vain. I can truthfully say, that since I have been at a distance from my brethren in the ministry, my interest in the salvation of immortal souls has been greater than ever before.

It is to be regretted that the work once here begun by our brethren, was not continued. Many souls that are still walking in darkness, might have been saved. But thanks be to God, that it is not too late yet, and there is reason to hope that some good will be accomplished here. The congregations are generally pretty large, the attention is good, and there seems to be a real hunger and thirst after the bread and water of life. O brethren and sisters! remember us in your prayers, especially in your prayer-meetings for the cause of missions, that God may be with us and many souls be saved through our instrumentality. And pray, at the same time, the Lord of the harvest, that he would send forth more laborers into his harvest; for there are yet so many going astray, like sheep without a shepherd.

I will now close this epistle, hoping that in my next report I may be able to say more of the work of the Lord. Remember me in your prayers. I remain your brother in the Lord.

CHRISTIAN HUMMEL.

Frey's Bush, Montgomery co., N. Y., June 21, 1839."

The mission in the city of New York was established from the conviction that a strictly evangelical mission among the Germans of that city was highly necessary, for which reason conference did not deem it necessary to wait till an invitation was sent from that quarter, as had been the case with the three other missionary fields. The following is the first report of that missionary field :—

"Since it is the duty of the missionaries to lay quarterly reports of their missionary fields before the Church, and as it is believed that these reports will be read with some interest by all the readers of the 'Botschafter,' but especially by all the members of the Evangelical Association, who by their contributions to the cause of missions have exhibited so deep an interest in the welfare of these sheep going astray without a shepherd in the wilderness, we will lay the first report of our mission before the Church in as few words as possible.

I arrived here in safety on the 3d of May, and the following day I looked about for a convenient preaching place and succeeded. On the 12th, I preached the first sermon on this mission to *seven* hearers. Some thought it was not worth while to preach to so small a number; but I told them it was well worth while, etc. My text was Rom. 1, 16.; the hearers were quite attentive, and some have come regularly ever since. The number has since increased, and I have reason to believe that some of the seed of the divine word has fallen on good ground. May the Lord grant his divine blessing, that it may spring up and bear fruit for everlasting life!

I hope and feel confident, that our labors in this place will not be in vain; yet the work is connected with many and great difficulties, and many a strenuous effort will be required, before much can be accomplished. For here we have to contend, not only with great immorality and wickedness, but also with a settled unbelief, both rationalism and atheism. This mission is also more expensive than the friends have probably been aware of. For the preaching place I have to pay $25 per quarter, where I deliver three sermons on Sunday. But I have some hopes of finding ere long a cheaper preaching place, where I may also preach during the week. Living, too, is very expensive here, as all kinds of provisions are very high; but I shall be as economical as possible.

Since I have offered my services to the Church as a missionary, I have often been solemnly impressed, especially when meditating on the importance of my position and the trials I must pass through. It is true, that every laborer in the Lord's vineyard has his share of difficulties and sufferings; yet there is, after all, a great difference between being almost alone, and living in a place where the children of God encourage and comfort one another. But I hope to God, that out of the great number of Germans in this great city, many will yet be awakened, enlightened, and converted to God. For this I labor, hoping the Lord will bless my humble efforts, in answer to the intercession and prayers of his children. I would ask a special interest in their prayers, when they meet to pray for the cause of missions.

JACOB BORKERT.

New York, June 14, 1839."

This mission had to contend with great difficulties, and at first made but slow progress. During the first year there was no effort made to organize a society. In the second year a class consisting of 12 members was formed, which increased considerably in the third year. During the first three years it seemed sometimes as if the mission would fail and have to be abandoned; but toward the close of the third year, it gained a firmer footing, and the prospects became brighter.

The glorious success of the first missions of the Society, exerted a most salutary effect upon the whole membership, by kindling a universal missionary spirit: and in a few years the Church had a number of missions, and was permitted to see much fruit of its labors.

There are no records extant of special revivals during this year; yet the work extended considerably. It made good progress at Philadelphia, Reading, and Pottsville; especially at the latter place. In the counties of Bucks and Montgomery, more hearts and doors were opened to the pure doctrine of the Gospel, and the society in Upper Milford was in a very flourishing condition. At Orwigsburg a new church was built during this year, the old one having become too small and dilapidated. It was dedicated in January, 1840, and a glorious revival took place; about twenty persons were translated into the glorious liberty of the children of God.—During this year there was a highly blessed camp-meeting held in Brush Valley, Indiana county, Pa., on the land of Bro. *John Oberdorf*, which resulted in the hopeful conversion of from 40 to 50 persons, among whom was Brother Joseph Truby, who has labored to this day with great success as an itinerant in the vineyard of the Lord.*

During a general meeting held the same year at Brother Jacob Miller's, a glorious revival took place. In this valley our ministers commenced preaching in 1822, at Nicolas Enders' and George Baumeister's, who had removed thither from Virginia. The Brethren Jacob Baumgartner and Joseph Long were the first preachers of the Society in that part of country, and formed a class of seven members in said year. Subsequently a number of families removed thither from York co., Pa., named Oberdorf, Miller, and Frey; and in 1832 the first camp-meeting was held there, attended, with others, by the Brethren Seybert, Hesser, and Boas. Many persons have since been converted in that valley; but some of them have removed to other parts of the country, while others, alas! have backslidden.

Miami circuit of the Western Conference, embracing part of the state of Indiana, extended considerably during this year as far as the centre of that state, and had a considerable addition of members and classes. Brother A. B. Shaefer writes in his report of the beginning and progress of our work in the state of Indiana this year, as follows:—

"The work of conversion made but slow progress on this field of labor, till several families from Pennsylvania settled here, who, by their deep interest and exemplary lives, confirmed the truth of the word preached, and thus gave the cause a new impulse."

The societies of the Evangelical Association in the state of

*He died April 25th, 1856.

New York and Ohio had been founded mainly by emigrants from the state of Pennsylvania; this was also the case in the states of Indiana, Illinois, and the western states and territories generally, where our societies were for the most part, and in some places exclusively, founded and sustained by Pennsylvanians; and even to this day some of our best societies in the West consist almost exclusively of Pennsylvanians; while those societies in which the European element predominates, were formed out of converts, generally made during revivals.—There is a striking resemblance between the progress of Christianity during the first centuries and that of the Evangelical Association. Primitive Christianity extended from the East westward, and so has the Evangelical Association ever done from its start; it has extended almost entirely westward. It has made no efforts yet to reach the eastern or New England states; and it is but a few years since some of our preachers have found entrance in some of the northwestern counties of New Jersey. The West is, therefore, under great obligations to the East; and the East ought, for the same reasons, to continue to take the deepest interest in the prosperity of the West. Yet, notwithstanding these sacred ties, too many local prejudices, both in the East and the West, have appeared already, which can only produce mischief, and will certainly disturb the peace of the Association, except its *leaders* and the *officers of the Printing Establishment*, and the ministers generally, oppose this evil with energy and keep themselves free from it.

This year the infant societies in the state of Illinois had to pass through another sore trial; for their preacher, *L. Einsel*, soon after his arrival among them, was attacked with a fever, which disabled him for the greater part of the year, so that he could preach but little. He had made a good beginning among them, and had raised the brightest expectations. One of his first official acts in Illinois was the dedication of the lately completed small church, which was the *first* of our connection in the far West, on June 20th, 1839. Soon after he visited Sharon, in Henry county, Rock Island, and the vicinity of the present Cedarville in Stephenson county, and preached there. He had also preached a few sermons in Chicago, and taken it up as one of his regular preaching places. But on his return from Stephenson county to Wheeling, his health gave way to the influence of the new climate, and becoming very sick, it was with the greatest difficulty that he reached the latter place, where he was confined to a bed of sickness for the greater part of the year, treated all the while with the kindest attention by the friends, but especially by Brother Esher's family.—Several families from Penn's Valley, Centre county, Pa., all members of our Church, settled in the neighborhood of Cedarville in the spring of 1839; before they set out from Pennsylvania they had been organized into a regular class by Brother Seybert, and had elected a class-leader according to the Discipline of the Church, so that they arrived as a regular class in Illinois. According to the advice of Brother Seybert, soon after their arrival in their new home, they introduced the order and discipline of our Church, sustaining them also till they received the regular services of our ministers. The following are the names of some of the heads of said families: *C. Epley*, *John Falget*, *Sill*, *Warrig*, etc. Thus not only individual members, but whole classes of our Church emigrated to the *far West*, as Illinois was then called. In this manner the East subsequently lost many members every year, while the membership in the West increased the more rapidly.

In the beginning of December of this year, Bro. *John Lutz* was appointed to assist Brother Einsel, or rather to take his place, as he was still sick. He arrived at Wheeling, and soon after set out for Napierville, accompanied by Bro. J. J. Esher, who was then a layman yet. The distance between the two places being 30 miles, and the way over trackless prairies, a guide was absolutely necessary for strangers, in order to find the place. A deep snow was lying on the ground, with an icy crust, so that traveling on the unbeaten path was extremely difficult, and they did not arrive at their destined place until midnight, almost entirely exhausted and benumbed, as it was extremely cold. They were very kindly received by Brother

C. Gross, and soon recovered under his hospitable roof. Bro. Lutz labored with great success at Wheeling and Napierville during that winter, also in Stephenson county. In the latter place, near where Cedarville now is, his labors were blessed with a glorious revival in the month of February, the first important instance of the kind by the instrumentality of our preachers in Illinois. The class of emigrants was thereby considerably increased and greatly encouraged. Brother Lutz also undertook an exploring tour to Milwaukie and vicinity in the territory of Wisconsin, and met with many Germans who received him kindly. While Brother Lutz was thus acting the part of a bold pioneer, preaching the word of life to the inhabitants of the impervious north-western counties, Brother Einsel labored as much as his enfeebled state of health permitted, along Des Plain and at Napierville, and God's blessings rested upon his labors.

In the beginning of May, 1840, the two brethren returned together across the lakes to Ohio, in order to attend the session of the Ohio Conference; they reported 18 newly received members, and a membership of 93 on the circuit. Although, as a matter of course, the work did not, under existing circumstances, progress rapidly, yet it gradually gained strength and influence; and had the infant societies and the other preaching places been regularly attended to from the beginning, the work would undoubtedly have increased much more rapidly. But small as it then was, tares were already making their appearance among the wheat. At Napierville appeared premonitory symptoms of a bad movement, which afterward resulted in ill feelings and divisions, to the great grief of the children of God and the injury of his work. But while this fatal leaven was at work, an occurrence of the most pleasing character took place in another place of the circuit, at Dutchman's Point. While the preachers were at conference, the class-leader of the Des Plain society, moved by the Spirit, visited said place on a Sunday, where there had indeed been preaching, but as yet no conversions taken place, in order to hold the first prayer-meeting with the people. The grace and power of God manifested themselves to such a degree during this meeting, that some persons were deeply affected and called upon God for mercy, till they had obtained peace and pardon. The work of grace began in this prayer-meeting, extended farther and farther, till all the Germans of the neighborhood came under its influence and professed to have found peace with God. This was the first revival in Illinois, in a country where there had been no members of the Society before, and the new class that was formed, consequently consisted altogether of new converts, and afterward prospered remarkably well.

During this year there were four watchmen called from the walls of Zion, viz., *Samuel van Gundy* and *George Dressel*, itinerant, and Father *John Hammer* and *Henry Miesse*, local preachers. All of them had been esteemed, pious, and useful members of the Church, and three of them as yet in the prime of life.

S. van Gundy was an excellent, promising young man, a highly gifted preacher, of a noble, prepossessing appearance and genuine piety, for which reasons he was universally esteemed and beloved. In 1834 he was received by the Western Conference into the itinerancy, and became the assistant of Bro. Charles Hammer on Canton circuit; the following year he was J. J. Kopp's colleague on Mansfield circuit. In the spring of 1834 he was ordained deacon and appointed preacher in charge of Lancaster circuit, W. Bergheimer being his colleague. The following year he was stationed for the second time on Canton circuit, and H. Heiss became his colleague. In 1838 he was ordained elder and became the preacher in charge of Columbiana circuit, H. D. Grunder being his assistant. In the spring of 1839, in March, he attended the General Conference in Centre co., Pa., where the writer saw him for the first and last time. Shortly before his conference had stationed him alone on Harmony circuit, in the western part of Pennsylvania; but soon after his return from General Conference, he was attacked by bilious fever and died after an illness of three weeks, on the 26th of April at 4 o'clock

P. M., in the 27th year of his life. He had to pass through some hard struggles on his death-bed, but finally died in the triumphs of Christian faith, and entered into the joy of his Master. The writer knows of no extraordinary revivals brought about by the instrumentality of this brother; but as he was conscientious and scrupulous in the discharge of his duties, there is no doubt that many were instructed and edified by his short ministry of five years. He was, as already stated, universally beloved, and had prospects of great usefulness before him; the Church lamented his death as that of one of its most talented and promising men.

After S. van Gundy's death, *George Dressel*, who was then the superintending preacher on Canton circuit, was appointed as his ssecessor, till another preacher could be obtained for the place, or different arrangements be made. But shortly after his arrival he was seized with the same fever that had finished van Gundy's career, and died of it after a protracted illness of a few weeks, on the 27th of June, 1839, in the 30th year of his earthly career. Brother Dressel is likewise said to have been a very talented and apparently still more promising man than Brother van Gundy. He had lived in a state of grace for about five years, and served as an itinerant for sixteen months, when he was already called to those regions from whence no traveler returns. He was very much composed on his death-bed, and died in a firm hope of life everlasting.

The loss of these two promising young men, whose deaths were announced in the Periodical, filled all that had been acquainted with them, with grief, and cast a universal gloom over the Church. The notice of their departure was accompanied by the following remarks:—

"These are, indeed, mysterious dealings of Providence. Both these brethren were young, and, as we have been informed, highly promising men, such as we do not often find. Why was it, that these two useful men were called in their youth from out of the small number of faithful laborers in the vineyard of the Lord? This is to us a mystery; but we will humbly submit: God is just, and all his dealings are righteous."

Some were of opinion, that they had not received proper medical treatment; but this cannot with certainty be proved. Even granted, that many a man's life has been shortened by improper medical treatment; yet the deaths of the two brethren in question may have been the work of Providence, for holy and wise purposes, which eternity alone can and will disclose.

Father John Hammer, of Orwigsburg, Pa., died also this year, on the 6th of Nov., in the 67th year of his age. He had been one of the pillars of the Orwigsburg society, and done much to build it up. Many of the itinerants had become acquainted with him, and found a pleasant home under his hospitable roof. Till the 50th year of his life, he had been a respectable member and for a long time an elder in the Lutheran Church, yet without having experienced a thorough change of heart. But when the great revival, of which mention has been made, broke out at Orwigsburg and vicinity, about sixteen years before his death, he and his whole family learned to see that a mere profession and form of Christianity are not sufficient for salvation; and he therefore at once commenced to pray with more fervency, and some time after, believing in the Son of God, he obtained the pardon of his sins and perfect peace of mind. He then soon joined the Evangelical Church and remained a consistent member till death. He served for some time as class-leader, discharging his duties faithfully and conscientiously, and in every respect he set an example worthy of imitation to those entrusted to his care. Subsequently he was licensed to preach, and served as a local preacher the remainder of his life. In his sermons he did not aim at systematic exposition, but generally gave utterance to those thoughts that filled his bosom, in demonstration of the Spirit and power, feeling deeply his responsibility, and manifesting a heart-felt concern for the salvation of his hearers. He was always ready to assist his neighbors by word and deed, and took the deepest interest in the universal welfare of the human family. The scorn and contempt of the world and enemies of Christ, of which he as a follower of the Lord also received his share, he bore with exemplary courage, counting it an honor to be deemed worthy to suffer for Christ's sake. But God also granted him the pleasure to witness the conversion of many of his neighbors and of his whole family—of his wife and eleven surviving children. His faith in this respect had been so strong, that he had often said with positive assurance: "*My children will all yet turn to God!*" For the last six years of his life he suffered much from arthritis, to which came, about four weeks before his death, an inflammation of the liver, which accelerated his death. He bore his sickness and pain with Christian fortitude and perfect submission to the will of his Heavenly Father. Death, grave, and corruption, had no terrors to him. Once he said: "*Why should I be afraid of the grave; has not my Lord and Master sanctified it?*" At another time he said: "*It is my desire to have no will of my own, but to be fully resigned to the will of God.*" Again he said: "*I am about to set out on a long journey to a great city, that is as yet unknown to me; but I know the Lord of this city, whereof my heart is glad. I also have good fellow-travelers, who know the road well and will conduct me in safety thither!*" And again he said: "*As soon as I arrive there, I shall, first of all, prostrate myself before the throne of the Almighty, to thank him for what he has done for me!*" While he lay on his death-bed, his pale lips whispered many a word of affecting exhortation, that caused his visitors to sigh, and at times to weep bitterly. Thus he was a blessing to humanity while living, and now his memory will not less be a blessing to those who were acquainted with him, and follow his pious advice and example.

Brother *Henry Miesse*, son of Jacob Miesse, formerly of Berks county, Pa., departed this life in Fairfield county, Ohio, in the house of his brother, Dr. G. Miesse, on the 20th of January, 1840, in the thirty-first year of his earthly career. About ten years before his death, he embraced religion, and joined the Evangelical Association, remaining a consistent member till death. He was for some time a local preacher, but could not preach much on account of his bodily weakness. From his youth he was subject to great sufferings, caused by a scrofulous disease, and but rarely enjoyed good health. Subsequently he was taken with pulmonary consumption and a violent inflammation of the tonsils, which closed his earthly career. He was fully resigned, and died in the triumphs of faith. His brother, Dr. Miesse, writes about him as follows: "For him we ought not to mourn, because his departure from this world was attended with joy and great faith; he left us many very beautiful and consoling exhortations, and testified even in the struggle of death, that it is good to die a Christian."

Thus almost every year some itinerant and local preachers died, besides lay-members, who testified by their joy and blessed hope of future glory upon their death-beds, and even in the struggle of dissolution, the genuineness of their Christian experience and the evangelical faith, to the great comfort and encouragement of their fellow believers. And such a testimony speaks louder for the creed and doctrine of any Christian denomination, than all apologetical works that have ever appeared, and all other arguments that may be advanced. *That* faith which changes the heart and life, produces a pious and consistent conduct, and gives comfort and joy in death, must certainly be the *true and saving faith*. This faith is professed, advocated, and recommended by the Evangelical Association; and it recognizes all those who possess and show this faith by their actions, irrespective of names, forms, and differences in non-essentials, as fellow citizens of the kingdom of God, and heirs of eternal life, extending to them the right hand of fellowship.

The increase during this year was only about 200; and the whole membership at the close of the year, 8050. The Eastern Conference has no record of its full membership for this year, for which reason the precise number cannot be given.

The Year 1840.

This year there were, for the first time, three conferences held; to wit, the East Pennsylvania Conference at Schuylkill Haven, Schuylkill county, Pa., beginning the 25th of March;

the West Pennsylvania at New Berlin, Union county, Pa., the 8th of April, and Ohio Conference in Walnut township, Pickaway county, Ohio, from the 13th to the 20th of April. A considerable number located again, as usual; some on account of bodily infirmities, others on account of family concerns. Yet there was also a fine number of young men willing to travel. The East Pennsylvania as well as Ohio Conference had enough preachers and to spare; but the West Pennsylvania Conference had not sufficient. A great number of their itinerants had located during the year, others located at conference, while yet others went over to the East Penn., and some to Ohio Conference. For this reason the various circuits of West Penn. Conference were but scantily supplied. Many of the circuits that had always had two preachers, received but *one* this year. The conference requested, therefore, the friends on the respective circuits to exercise patience, and to send up their believing prayers to the Throne of Grace, that more laborers might be sent to his vineyard. It appointed also a day of fasting and prayer, enjoining its strict observance upon all the ministers and members of the conference district, and to implore God to own and bless his word and to extend his kingdom, etc. It also ordered a pastoral letter to be drawn up by a committee, and to be published in the Periodical; and as this is, as far as the writer knows, the first and only pastoral letter that ever went forth from a conference of the Evangelical Association, and may be useful to our readers, it is here subjoined.

Pastoral Letter, addressed to the Members of the Evangelical Association of the West Pennsylvania Conference.

Dearly beloved brethren and friends in the Lord:—The undersigned having been instructed, in the name of the conference to address you, through the columns of the Botschafter, we commence with the apostolical greeting: "Grace be with you, and peace from God our Father, and the Lord Jesus Christ!"

1. When we retrospect the loving kindness of God, our Heavenly Father, which he has manifested in the gift of his

only begotten Son, the revelation of his will and word by the preaching of the Gospel and the influences of his holy and good Spirit, we feel constrained to exclaim with the psalmist: "Come, let us sing unto the Lord: let us make a joyful noise to the Rock of our salvation. Let us come before his presence with thanksgiving, and make a joyful noise unto him with psalms." The Lord has indeed done great things for us, who have tasted his pardoning grace and love, whereof we are glad. Is it not, therefore, our solemn duty also to be thankful to him, and to consecrate ourselves entirely to his service? Yea, ought not each and every one of us to feel it as his duty, whatever his calling or position may be, to labor conscientiously with the talents entrusted to him, in order to promote the honor and glory of God as much as possible?

It is true, last year we had not as many revivals of religion as might have been desirable. But, if we take into consideration the infinite value of *a single soul*, we have great reason to rejoice and thank the Lord for having owned and prospered our humble efforts, and to look upon ourselves as more than sufficiently rewarded for our labors. We are likewise encouraged by the bright prospects in some parts of the Church for the future, and therefore hope that this year will be greatly blessed and fruitful.

2. Our conference, it is true, is at present somewhat embarrassed by the paucity of itinerants; but our help is with the Lord, and we humbly trust that, guided by his Spirit, and assisted by the prayers and co-operation of our friends and brethren, we shall see glorious results at the close of the year; but should this not be the case, the fault will be ours and not God's. For, although everything depends on the blessing and grace of God, yet it is altogether with us, whether they shall rest on our labors or not. Great awakenings and revivals of religion generally follow the combined efforts of his children, when wrestling with him in believing prayer for an outpouring of his Spirit. It is a fatal error to believe that no revival can take place in a neighborhood or city, except at a particular time appointed by God. No, brethren, God is willing at all

times to grant us his Spirit if we ask him, and according to our faith it shall be done unto us. God calls on the sinner to hear his voice *to-day;* and if all preachers and Christians were properly united in faith, and in the power of God, in the use of the means of grace and the proper efforts for the extension of his kingdom, we should hear of greater revivals and conversions, than is generally the case. The kingdom of God would come with power, and scores of sinners would be converted and brought to God. God generally works by means of his children and servants; and if they consecrate themselves exclusively to his service, pray, preach, and labor in faith, and walk as lights of the world, revivals of religion will never be wanting.

3. Now, if this principle holds good, it is evident that revivals and the conversion of sinners depend mainly on the professors of religion. How very important and absolutely necessary it is, therefore, dear brethren, that we should be mindful of our duties, discharging them faithfully, lest by our carelessness souls be neglected! Should we be found guilty of so heinous an offence, our damnation would be certain. For the purpose, then, of extending the kingdom of Christ, and of promoting the salvation of immortal souls in the most effectual manner, we call upon all our brethren and friends to act in concert, and to assist us with their combined efforts, to carry forward the work of the Lord, by humble supplication and prayer to him that he would abundantly pour out his Spirit, by preaching and exhorting, by a holy and godly walk, by a constant use of all the means of grace, and by supporting all the institutions of the day, having for their object, and being calculated to promote, the best interests of mankind.

4. In the first place, we appeal to our brethren, the local preachers, and entreat them, one and all, to come to our assistance in promoting the prosperity of the different circuits and classes within our conference district. We calculate on your assistance, dear brethren! and hope that you will do all you can in order to carry forward the work of the Lord, by preaching and exhorting, as well as by observing and enforc-

ing our Discipline, and in every other possible way and manner. This is the more necessary, because the number of our itinerants is so small, and the circuits, on the whole, are so scantily supplied this year. If you take a deep interest in the work of the Lord generally, and the prosperity of our conference especially, as we are confident you do, we expect *much* from you, under the present circumstances. If you do not consider it your duty or call, to give yourselves entirely to the service of the Lord, or if your delicate state of health prevents you from doing so, we expect you to preach at least on Sundays as often as your strength and circumstances will permit, and to lend us a helping hand whenever necessary.

5. In the next place, we also call upon our brethren, the class-leaders and exhorters, to labor with us faithfully in the vineyard of the Lord. Dear brethren! there is indeed an important post in the Church of God committed to your care; souls purchased with the blood of Christ, are entrusted to your keeping. And if by a neglect of duty on your part, one of these souls should be lost, how would you answer for it on the great day of accounts? Next to the ministry, your office is the most important, and much depends, accordingly, on your fidelity toward God and your brethren. You can be of great service to your brethren in the ministry, and lighten many of their burdens. Will you, then, in unison with the local preachers, assist us in the good work entrusted to our care? Will you endeavor to set an example, both by word and deed, worthy to be imitated by your brethren; to reprove and suppress vice of every form and shape, and to labor with us in order to bring about a general revival of religion? If you do this, success will crown our united efforts.

6. In the third place, we address ourselves to all our brethren and sisters indiscriminately, who have, indeed, no particular office committed to their charge, but are nevertheless called as laborers in the vineyard of the Lord, and as members of the mystical body of Christ have certain duties to perform. You, beloved friends, can do much to further the cause of God, as well by your prayers for your ministers and those

that are placed over you in the Lord, as by your conversation, and the influence you exert upon your neighbors and acquaintances. You can do much in building up the kingdom of God, by private instruction, good example, earnest prayer, and by assisting your superiors in the suppression of vice and the promotion of peace, love, and harmony, etc. Oh, how it gladdens the heart of a faithful teacher, when he sees that the professors of religion committed to his care, are active in the work and service of the Lord, and are at all times willing to do the will of God! For such a people he labors with joy and not with grief, nor can his labors in the Lord be in vain. But if he must see that they are cold and indifferent toward him, that they take little or no interest in the cause of God, or even oppose the teacher in his efforts to carry out the Word of God and the Discipline of the Church, in reproving vice and insisting on inward and outward holiness; he cannot but labor with heartfelt grief in their midst, and his labors cannot be crowned with much success.

Therefore, dear brethren! if you have espoused the cause of God and his kingdom, come to our assistance by your prayers and intercession, by word and deed, as much as you possibly can. Pray for us that the door of the word may be opened to us, to speak the mystery of Christ, and that the word of the Lord may have free course and be glorified. Pray for awakenings and revivals in general, but especially in your neighborhood. Let your light shine before the world, that they may see your good works and praise your Father who is in heaven.

7. Finally; let us all be united in carrying forward the work of the Lord, and in promoting the best interests of humanity, as far as we possibly can. Let us be earnest and punctual in the discharge of our duties, each in his calling and position, and above all seek first the kingdom of God and his righteousness, as Christ has commanded us to do; constantly bearing in mind that here we have no continuing city, but that it is our duty to seek one to come. Let us never forget, that this world with all its pleasures and glory passes away, and

that all the treasures and riches of this world, together with all the honors of men, are *nothing* when compared with the inheritance of the saints in light. We say *nothing*, except that they are nets and snares, wherein thousands are entangled and ruined forever. Let us, therefore, lay up for ourselves treasures in heaven, where neither moth nor rust does corrupt, and where thieves do not break through and steal; for where our treasure is, there will our hearts be also. Let us consider the danger to which we are exposed, to lose our souls; and let us lay to heart the great and sacred trust that is committed unto us, to work out our souls' salvation with fear and trembling. One day we shall be called upon to give an account of our stewardship. and Oh how important that day will be! We shall either be found as faithful stewards, and then be permitted to hear the words: "Come, ye blessed of my Father, inherit the kingdom prepared for you from the foundation of the world," or we shall hear the terrible words addressed to us: "Depart from me, ye cursed, into everlasting fire, prepared for the devil and his angels." If all would take these solemn truths to heart as they ought, they would undoubtedly feel, with Paul, like "forgetting those things which are behind, and reaching forth unto those things which are before, and pressing toward the mark for the prize of the high calling of God in Christ Jesus." Dear brethren, let us ponder these things well, and endeavor to live exclusively for God and eternity; to save our own souls, and to do what we can to promote the everlasting welfare of our fellow-men. Let us, in order to realize this glorious end, take hold of and improve every opportunity and means within our reach. Above all, let us count sacred the closet and the family-altar, or, in other words, conscientiously attend to secret and family prayer. Let us attend prayer and other meetings regularly, improving them for our instruction, edification, encouragement and consolation. Let us daily read the Bible and other useful books, that we may become wiser unto salvation and better fitted for the service of the Lord. One of our first and most sacred duties in this life must be, to remember the Sabbath-day, and to keep it holy;

nothing under heaven must induce us to desecrate the day of the Lord. As professors of the religion of Christ, we must not forget to be merciful as our Father in heaven is merciful; to do good unto all, especially to those that are of the same household of faith; to be cheerful givers, to assist others to do good and to communicate; for with such sacrifices God is well pleased.

In accordance with our professions, we ought likewise to be very active in the support of such institutions as have for their object the suppression of vice and infidelity, the spread of the kingdom of Christ and the furtherance of the best interests of humanity, and are calculated to realize these ends, viz., Sabbath-schools, missionary, tract, Bible, and temperance societies, etc. The cause of Sabbath-schools has especial claims on our attention; for experience has long since taught, both elsewhere and in the Evangelical Association, that they are a great blessing to the young, and powerful helps to keep the Sabbath holy, to train the rising generation, to inculcate and develop sound principles of morality, and thus to further the cause of true religion. Sabbath-schools may justly be regarded as nurseries of the Church, where thousands of youthful minds receive the first impressions of the fear of God and religion, which generally strike deep roots and are not easily erased. And even if not all Sabbath-school scholars are converted to God in their youth, there is still more hope that they will turn in subsequent years, than those who are not taught in their youth to remember their Creator—a duty which is too generally neglected by parents, and often even by those who profess to have tasted the love of God. Let us, therefore, pay our full and undivided attention to this powerful lever, to promote the honor of God and the welfare of mankind, and establish and keep up Sabbath-schools wherever practicable.

8. In conclusion, we would call the attention of all to the day of fasting and prayer, which our conference has appointed to be observed on the 4th of July, within its boundaries. We hope and trust that all our brethren and sisters, who take an interest in the work of God and the salvation of their own

souls, will unite with us to keep this day with fasting and prayer. The object of it is, to offer up to God, unitedly and simultaneously, an offering of thanksgiving and praise, for the many favors conferred upon us, both in a temporal and spiritual point of view; to humble ourselves before him, by confessing our sins, both of omission and commission, and above all, to implore him to let his kingdom come, to extend his work over the whole world, to multiply the number of faithful laborers in his vineyard, and especially to bless this conference district with awakenings, conversions, and a universal revival of religion. This being the object of said day of fasting and prayer, which of you, dear brethren and sisters, will stand aloof and neglect this duty? We trust, not one. We are confident also, that each and every one, who does prepare himself for and celebrate this day properly, will reap the richest personal blessings, and this ought to be one of our main objects in view; for the more we grow in grace and consecrate ourselves to the service of God, the greater our usefulness will be, both in doing all manner of good unto others, and in advancing the best interests of the kingdom of God.

We now close this our pastoral letter, and humbly trust that God will own and bless it to his honor and glory, and to your edification and encouragement in the work of the Lord, dearly beloved brethren and sisters in Christ!

In the name and by authority of the conference,

G. Brickley,
C. Hammer, } Committee.
W. W. Orwig,

New Berlin, Pa., May 8, 1840.

These special measures of conference exerted a very salutary influence, and were crowned with great success. With regard to the day of fasting and prayer, Bro. H. Bucks, then presiding elder on Carmel district, remarked as follows:—

"We have also the joyful prospect, that our district will furnish this year several laborers for the vineyard of the Lord. Our day of fasting and prayer, observed on the 4th of July last, has contributed its share toward this happy result. It is my sincere desire, that it may become customary with us to appoint such a day annually."—Whether this would be best, we are not prepared to say; but to observe such days at certain times and under particular circumstances, would undoubtedly always be very salutary. From this time the West Pennsylvania Conference made very rapid progress, and a few years after had outrun the two sister conferences considerably, with regard to the number of memberships. But all the conferences made more rapid progress at this time than ever before, and it almost seemed as if they were vying with each other in carrying forward the work of the Lord. The number of itinerants increased very much every year, and the boundaries of the conferences extended in many directions. The newly awakened missionary spirit gave a powerful impulse to the work, promoting the more rapid spread and influence of the Association. Brother G. Brickley, in a report of his district, at the close of the conference year, writes, with regard to the salutary influence of this missionary spirit on the Association, as follows: "I believe that the cause of missions in our connection is a powerful help to promote the best interests of the kingdom of God, and I have not the least doubt that if our ministers had introduced this sacred cause at an earlier date, the Church would have increased much more rapidly. But we greatly rejoice that the cause is now going on, and we trust that God will prosper it to his honor and glory! O ye friends of Zion, let us all have faith and take courage to labor for the glory of God—yea, let us not be weary in well doing; for in due season we shall reap, if we faint not."—Such was the general feeling of the ministry in those days, with regard to the cause of missions, and would to God this were the case still in our days! But alas! with too many this spirit of activity and zeal for the cause of the Lord began to languish in later years.—Brother Bucks says in a report of his district: "At every camp-meeting a missionary sermon was delivered, which was always attended with good success; at two of them we gave an opportunity to subscribe, and although money being so very scarce, considerable amounts were subscribed, and part of them paid on the spot. May the Lord bless this good cause, to the salvation of many yet sitting in darkness and in the shadow of death! Who would not be willing to pray for it in faith and earnest?" Brother A. B. Shaefer, in a report of Lancaster circuit, Ohio Conference, at the beginning of 1840, among other things writes thus: "The cause of missions progresses finely; the three auxiliary societies that were announced in the Botschafter some time ago, have increased considerably, and we have since established one more. * * * Many of our friends speak favorably of the matter, and I have reason to believe that some more will help to support and advance this cause with their abundance of means, in order that many more of those souls yet sitting in darkness or having a false gospel preached unto them, may be saved." These auxiliary societies belonged to the Parent Missionary Society of the Association; as it was not until at its subsequent session that the Ohio Conference formed itself into a missionary society with which then these auxiliary societies united. Similar reports of the zeal of many members for the cause of missions, were received from almost every direction. It was only in a few places where the cause met with opposition, and this was owing to their want of knowledge as to its necessity, scope, and object. In order to a better understanding of the state of the cause of missions in the Evangelical Association in those days, we here insert the first report of the parent board which was read at its first meeting on the 21st of April 1840, in New Berlin, Pa.

"*Annual Report of the Missionary Society of the Evangelical Association.*

With great joy and sincere gratitude to God, our Heavenly Father, we lay before our friends to-day the first annual report of our missionary society.

Our hearts overflow with feelings of praise and gratitude to God, for having accepted our humble efforts, and crowned them with success beyond our most sanguine expectations. We would, therefore, call upon the friends of our Zion, to join with us in praising the Lord, '*for he has done excellent things; let this be known in all the earth.*' He has not despised our insignificance, nor rejected our enterprise in the cause of missions; to his name be all the glory!

But *one* year has elapsed since the formation of our missionary society, and small as its beginning was, it soon found many warm friends, advocates, and supporters. The receipts of the society amount to $1434,31, including the $500 which the conference missionary society, that had been formed a year earlier, paid over into the parent board's treasury, when it united with it. The expenditures of the society during the last year, we cannot exactly state, not having as yet received a full report thereof; but thus much we know, that our treasury will be nearly, if not altogether, empty, at the close of the year.

The number of branch and auxiliary societies of the parent board, as far as we have been able to learn, is already over 30; and we have learned with pleasure, that many of our friends in various places are only waiting for an opportunity, to form themselves into auxiliary societies.

But our society has not only found many warm friends and supporters, but God's blessings also have rested on the labors of its missionaries, of whom it employed four during the first year, all of whom labored on different fields and met with more or less success.

Brother Borkert labored in the city of New York, and has been sent there again for this year. It is true, his labors met not with as much success as might have been desired, and many of the friends undoubtedly did expect; yet it would seem, that his labors were not entirely lost, and we humbly trust the Lord will yet gather out of the Germans there a people unto himself, zealous of good works.

On Mohawk mission, in the state of New York, God has done great things in the awakening and conversion of many a precious soul. The mission has already been formed into a circuit, and received two preachers.

Black Creek mission in Upper Canada, has also succeeded remarkably well, and has likewise been formed into a circuit, and supplied with two preachers. The membership, most of whom were converted during the last year, is already over eighty persons, and the prospects for the future are very favorable.

Waterloo mission, in Canada, has also been owned and blessed of the Lord; sinners have been awakened and converted, and a small society of about 30 members has been organized. According to Brother Holl's report, the prospects for the future are very encouraging there also.

The whole membership of the four missions is 166, 125 of whom are reported as having been converted during the last year. Truly, the Lord has done great things for us, whereof we are glad! Two of these missions of last year having been changed into circuits, there remain only two; but a new mission has been established this year in the city of Baltimore, Md. It is highly probable that the brethren of Ohio Conference will likewise send out some missionaries among the many Germans of the West, who are like sheep without a shepherd.

Having such evidence of God's approbation, and the prospects of future success being so brilliant, we feel encouraged, and are resolved to continue the work in the name and to the honor and glory of God. We also call on all friends of Christ to take a deep interest in this glorious enterprise, and to support it with their prayers; for we are fully persuaded that without the blessing of God all our labors and efforts will be in vain.

We close our first annual report with the deepest gratitude to God, the giver of every blessing; leaving our cause with him, and confiding in his promises for all time to come.

W. W. Orwig, Corresponding Secretary."

Ohio Conference, as had been expected, established at its session in May following, also a mission, partly in the state of Illinois, partly in the territory of Wisconsin, appointing Bro. Lutz their missionary. Thus the connection had four missions again this year. The mission in the city of New York made but slow progress, as before stated; but Waterloo mission, in Canada, was crowned with glorious results. At the close of the year, the latter numbered 96 members, 71 of whom had been received during the year. Classes had been formed in Waterloo, Pushlinch, and Wilmot, and preaching places been taken up in various other places, which were highly promising. When Brother Joseph Harlacher, the missionary, wrote his fourth and last quarterly report of the mission, he was almost in a state of ecstasy, on account of what the Lord had done through him. Among other things he makes the following remarks: "I feel to call upon all my brethren and sisters, to praise the Lord with me, and to exalt together his holy name. Yea, 'let every thing that has breath, praise the Lord;' for he has done wondrous things."

The first mission at Baltimore, Maryland, began on a very small scale, and although it soon found friends and patrons, there were not wanting those who were displeased with and persecuted it. In the second quarter, a small class was formed, and regular prayer and class meetings were introduced. Bro. Boas rented a small church from the Methodists, on corner of Cove and Fayette streets, where he preached twice every Sunday, but to very small audiences. In the third quarter, matters took a more favorable turn—the church became crowded, conversions took place, and a considerable number of the members of Otterbein's Church there, seceded for certain reasons, and joined the small mission society; in this way the number of members rose already to 100, but was afterward more than doubled during the conference year. The little church was bought during the third quarter, but was soon too small, and even before the close of the first year, arrangements were made to build a new and spacious church in a more convenient part of the city. Those from Otterbein's Church, had been, to a great extent, members of the best standing and greatest influence in that society; and the work of grace in the mission society seems to have been genuine, and thus the society had a solid foundation. Bishop Seybert, who visited the mission at that time, expressed himself in a letter addressed to the writer and dated York, Pa., February 16th, 1841, as follows:—

"On Friday, the 5th of this month, I arrived at Baltimore in the evening, and found the brethren engaged in holding a love-feast, during a protracted meeting that had already been in progress for ten days. The friends spoke with great freedom of what the Lord had done for them. There were also a number of convicted and penitent souls in the meeting, who, without waiting for much entreaty, followed the invitation of Bro. Hesser, who attended the meeting, to come forward to the altar to pray for mercy and the pardon of their sins. Thus we had a happy waiting before the Lord, while the mourners obtained peace and pardon, and were thus enabled, with others, to shout and praise the Lord. I remained at Baltimore till the 11th, during which time we had affecting meetings, and several souls were made happy in the pardon of their sins. I was told that about sixty souls had been converted during this meeting, among whom there are members of different religious denominations, also a few Catholics. The society consists already of more than 150 members, and is divided into seven classes. The lately purchased church—30 by 35 feet—is already too small to contain all those who desire to attend; it is therefore proposed to build a new and larger church in a more central part of the city, if practicable.

With one trait of the public services I was especially pleased during my stay at Baltimore, which is, that our friends there are lively in their services, and you do not see sour faces and knit brows, when any of God's children praise him aloud and shout for joy, under the influence of God's Holy Spirit. I also observed, that the new converts were willing to lay aside all gorgeous attire—another trait which I was highly delighted with.

O ye friends of Zion, who have thrown your mite into the missionary treasury, behold how richly God has blessed your gifts—praise the Lord for it."

As this was one of the most successful and prosperous missions ever established by the Association, we lay the last quarterly report of Brother Boas in full before our readers, hoping that it will be encouraging and instructive to them.

"Fourth Report of Baltimore Mission.

'*It is honorable to reveal the work of the Lord!*'

Brethren:—It is difficult to find words in the human language, that will adequately set forth what the Lord has done in our midst. Yea, language is altogether insufficient to express properly what God has of late been doing for us on this mission. The amount of good that has been accomplished by the grace of God among the Germans of this city, through my humble instrumentality, will become fully known only before the throne of God; yes, only there will he be perfectly happy, who here has supported the cause of missions by his prayers and gifts. The Lord has richly, yea abundantly rewarded our efforts in this good cause. And who should not feel encouraged thereby, to continue in the support of so holy and blessed a cause? About *one hundred* souls have learned to know the Saviour as willing and able to blot out sin, and with the Psalmist can now, with hearts full of heavenly joy, call on all that fear God, to come and hear from their lips what the Lord has done for their souls.

Since last New Year, some have been willing to pray for pardon after almost every sermon, and *every* invitation to come to the altar of prayer, has been accepted by some.—Here they waited for the Lord, and he inclined unto them, and heard their cries; he brought them out of the horrible pit, out of the miry clay, and set their feet upon a rock, and established their goings; and he put a new song in their mouths, even praises unto our God. Psalm 40.

When I arrived here as missionary, we had but two members; now we have *two hundred and fifteen. Many, O Lord, my God! are thy thoughts which are to usward: they cannot be reckoned up in order unto thee: if we would declare and speak of them, they are more than can be numbered.*

We also met with opposition from various directions; but in every instance the Lord frustrated the designs of his enemies, and granted us glorious victories. We will wait for the Lord in prayer, in the firm assurance that he will continue to prosper the good work begun on this mission, till many—very many will yet say to their acquaintances, friends, and relatives, as Moses said to Hobab, the son of Reguel, the Midianite, his father-in-law: 'We are journeying unto the place of which the Lord said, I will give it to you; come thou with us, and we will do thee good; for the Lord has spoken good concerning Israel.'

'Darum, Zion, unbetruebet!
Die Erquickungszeit ist da,
Und des Herren Huelf' ist nah.'

As our present church, under existing circumstances, is entirely too small, we were compelled to make arrangements to build a new one; it is to be plain, substantial, and spacious, and with the grave yard which contains about two acres of ground, will cost about $7000. But in order to meet these outlays, we shall be obliged to call upon our liberal friends in the country for help. We cherish the hope, that all of our friends who take a heart-felt interest in the work of God, will contribute something of their abundance toward this object. We must have a large house, if the work of God shall continue to prosper. I merely intended to touch upon this subject, as it will probably be laid fully before the Association in the columns of the Botschafter. I greet all the friends, and would entreat them to remember me and the Baltimore Mission in their prayers. J. BOAS.

April 13, 1841."

As the society in Baltimore was engaged in building a new church, and had many other heavy expenses, it was thought best to continue it as a mission for another year; after this it was changed into a station, supporting its own minister.

The Illinois mission, that was partly in the neighborhood of Milwaukee, Wisconsin, partly along the Cedar creek, in Stephenson county, Illinois, was very inconveniently situated, the missionary having to travel on every round about 250 miles in order to fill 6 or 8 appointments, and to re-cross a distance of 90 miles, besides being often exposed to great privations. Bro. Lutz labored on this mission this year with truly apostolic self-denial. At the close of the year he formed a small class in Wisconsin, in the vicinity of Milwaukee, the members of which were scattered in every direction, about twenty miles in circumference, to the North, South, and West of Milwaukee. This was the first society of the Evangelical Association in Wisconsin. John G. Esslinger (class-leader), his wife, the first person converted in Wisconsin through the instrumentality of our preachers, Jacob Martin and wife, the Eckert family, Martin Shulz and others, were its first members.

In the East Pennsylvania Conference the work spread considerably in some places, especially in the state of New York and in Upper Canada. This year the northern district numbered more newly received members than the two other districts of the conference together. The work had prospered there for several years previous to this, and has made progress ever since. J. M. Sindlinger labored then on the district with great success. Filled with great zeal to extend and enlarge its boundaries, he pushed forward with his preachers wherever there was an opening for the word, taking great pains at the same time to advance the existing societies in piety and true godliness. On Mohawk circuit, under the charge of Christian Hummel and G. Ramige, important awakenings took place in different parts, and the number of newly received members during the year was 124. On Lake circuit also, where M. Lehn and D. Fisher labored, the work prospered exceedingly in some places. The society in the city of Buffalo, under the charge of Fr. Krecker, was visited with some glorious revivals during this and the following year, thus gaining a solid footing. Likewise Buffalo circuit, under the charge of P. Schwille during this and the preceding year, extended considerably, and thus rose in influence. In North Bush a glorious work took place; H. Knob and P. Trautman were the first there who opened their houses to our preachers, and soon after gave their hearts to God. Father G. Sheuer and others soon followed, and thus a class of seventeen members was formed there in a short time. P. Troutman was the first class-leader in that part of country.

This year the brethren also commenced to labor in the city of Rochester, N. Y. Brother S. Muck made the beginning, and afterward the brethren on Lake circuit took up the city as one of their regular preaching places, and preached there as often as they possibly could, without neglecting the other parts of their very extensive field of labor. At first they preached in a private house, afterward in a school-house; and when this was denied them, they preached again in a private house. January 10, 1841, a small class was formed there, who elected Brother Voos as their leader. But the good cause had to pass through great difficulties, and made but slow progress. In 1842, the society built a small church; but not being able to keep it, they had to submit to its being sold. This was a heavy blow which almost annihilated the work commenced; but by and by it recovered, a better church was built, and the society is now apparently in a prosperous condition. Simultaneously with the first efforts made by the brethren in Rochester, they found entrance in Fairport, six or eight miles east of Rochester, where subsequently a flourishing society was organized.

Glorious revivals took place during this year at Orwigsburg, Schuylkill Haven, and Pottsville, whereby these societies were considerably increased. During a protracted meeting at Lebanon, 50 souls are said to have found pardon and peace. In Adamstown, Lancaster county, where our preachers had labored for several years, a glorious work of grace broke out during this conference year, which continued the whole of the following year. W. Heim and J. P. Kræmer were stationed there this year, and H. Fisher and C. Holl the next year. The society of Manheim was also blessed with a revival, and received a considerable addition during the year.

Philadelphia station had to pass through a severe trial this year. Jacob Vogelbach, who had labored there already the year before with apparently good success, fell out with the society in the very beginning of this year. After having had a trial, he left the connection and subsequently went over to the Lutheran Church. This occurrence proved very disastrous to the society; for, although the popular Brother Hesser became Vogelbach's successor, yet not much could be done any more for the remainder of the year, and it required several years to heal the wound. The circuits of Reading, Milford, and Lehigh, made but little progress during this year, and their accessions were small.

In West Pennsylvania Conference no particular revivals occurred during this year, except in Baltimore and on Centre circuit; yet the work progressed more or less on all the circuits. Several of the camp-meetings were particularly blessed—some of them extraordinarily. One of these was held on the land of A. Orwig in Buffalo Valley, Union county, Pa., where a considerable number of precious souls were awakened and converted, and many more came to the knowledge of the truth. This meeting was greatly blessed and victorious, from beginning to end. The presiding elder, who superintended the meeting, writes at the close of his report of it: "If the appearance and professions of some who were present, are a correct criterion, this meeting was a great blessing to the country and the whole neighborhood." Another meeting was held on the land of D. Shreffler in Penn's Valley, Centre county, Pa., where many sinners were convicted and converted, and at its close thirty new members were received into the church. Some of the new converts had already left the camp-ground, else the number would in all probability have been much larger. At this place a most remarkable phenomenon occurred, which was published in the Periodical as follows:—

"On Sunday, the 23d of August last, a remarkable phenomenon took place during a violent storm, in the upper part of Penn's Valley, Centre county, which cannot fail to convince every one of the particular providence of Him who possesses all power in heaven and on earth. It was as follows: In the woods of Daniel Shreffler, about three miles south-east of Old Fort, a place had been prepared during the week for holding a camp-meeting, to begin on Thursday following. The preachers' stand and several tents were already erected, and on the Sunday in question there was preaching on the camp-ground in the morning. In the afternoon the friends of the vicinity, with some of their neighbors, repaired to the camp-ground for the purpose of holding a prayer-meeting; while they were engaged in the first prayer, a terrible and devastating tornado came on, which they did not perceive until it was too late to make their escape out of the forest. Some, however, took refuge in a house close by; but others, wanting to follow, were terrified and prevented by the crashing and breaking of the trees. The consternation now was great; while some screamed for fear, and others endeavored to calm them by holding forth the duty of trusting in God, others again shouted and praised God with a loud and joyful voice. But the most surprising thing was that the camp-ground and the meeting were not in the least injured by the storm; although in every direction around the camp, trees were broken down by scores. On the west side, whence the storm blew, the tops of the fallen trees touched the camp-ground; on the south and north sides, trees lay in heaps along the ground; and on the east side, the ground was almost covered with trees and branches; but not one tree on the large camp-ground, nor the tents, nor any thing that was on the ground, was in the least damaged or injured. This fearful destruction of the woods around, from which only the camp-ground formed a providential exception, astonished all who saw it. Some did not credit the report till they visited the ground and saw the miracle for themselves. This occurrence made a deep impression on many of the inhabitants of the neighborhood, and was probably one of the main causes why so many became awakened and converted. The trees here were generally very tall; yet many of the tallest and thickest were broken off about 10 or 15 feet above the ground, while others were torn out by the roots." In another report of this event, the writer among other things says: "There was a tree of uncommon size, measuring 18 feet in circumference, near the camp-ground, which, as it could not be uprooted on account of its deep roots, was broken off near the ground. By this the uncommon violence of the tornado may be estimated."

On Carmel district, situated for the most part on the Alleghany mountains, the camp-meetings were likewise victorious and crowned with conversions. The presiding elder, H. Bucks, writes thus: "We had three camp-meetings in June, all of which were crowned with awakenings and conversions of sinners, and glorious revivals among the people of God.—At the last of these meetings in Brush Valley, Indiana county, we had on the last day, during the celebration of the Lord's supper, and afterward at an experience meeting, glorious times; it seemed as if heaven had opened over us, and the grace of God were descending upon us in showers so abundantly that the praise of God flowed from many lips, and some actually fell down, overcome by the love of God."

This year Centre circuit seems to have surpassed all the other circuits of this conference, in point of activity and increase. It held three camp-meetings; one in Penn's Valley, the other in Brush Valley, and the third in Nittany Valley, all of which were crowned with success, and a number of general and protracted meetings, some of which were remarkably victorious and blessed with many conversions; two protracted meetings especially, that were held in Nittany Valley, one at Jacob Best's, the other at Jacob Waky's, were times of great refreshing. At the close of the third quarter of the conference year, Bro. H. Thomas, the superintending preacher of the circuit, remarks in his report as follows: "On the whole, we have had during the year many conversions on this circuit, and many more souls are deeply wounded and near the kingdom of God. Let all honor and praise be ascribed to God alone!"

Bishop Seybert, in a report during this year, makes the following remarks touching the West Pennsylvania Conference:—

"Notwithstanding the great scarcity of preachers in this conference, matters prosper in general, and in some parts succeed remarkably well. Most of the camp-meetings have been richly blessed with awakenings, conversions, and revivals. This shows that God is still with his people, however dark the prospects seemed to be. '*Truly, God is good to Israel, even to such as are of a clean heart.*' I lately attended a camp-meeting in this conference, which was the seventh held this year on Salem district. It was held on the land of J. Krebs, in Perry township, Union county, Pa.; and as the presiding elder was prevented from being present by sickness, the brethren requested me to take charge of the meeting. The Lord was in our midst, granting his servants grace to preach his Gospel with power. We also had, all the time, very orderly and attentive hearers, many of whom became convinced of the necessity of repentance and a change of heart. On Monday and Tuesday, the last two days of the meeting, the ice broke, as the saying is, and every thing seemed to be prepared for a revival. The hearts of the children of God were filled with his love; parents commenced to pray for their unconverted children, as the woman did, Mat. 15, 21–28, and others for their relatives. Hereupon such a power of repentance descended on the meeting, that sinners commenced crying out for mercy, and thus a glorious victory followed and some were filled with the Holy Ghost. During the last night we again had glorious times, sinners were converted, and the praise of God could be heard at a distance."

This year Ohio Conference received more new members than either of the two other conferences. Its boundaries were extended in various directions, especially toward the West, in Indiana and Illinois. Miami circuit, situated for the most part in the state of Indiana, was considerably extended and made good progress under the charge of A. B. Shæfer. During this year the first camp-meeting of the Association was held in the state of Indiana, on the land of John Dill, in Wayne county: it was abundantly blessed, and thus proved a benefit to many. Brother Shæfer writes of this meeting: "This was indeed a time of the Son of man. * * * * From this time the work of conversion became more known in this part of the state, and found its advocates." In the preceding year, the city of Dayton, Ohio, was taken up as one of the preaching places of Miami circuit, and at the end of this year a class of twenty-one members was formed there. As this circuit had become very large by the industry and activity of the preachers, that portion of it lying in Indiana, was formed into a mission at the next session of Ohio Conference, and called *White Water mission*, with two preachers stationed there; two years after, it was made a circuit, and called *White Water circuit.*—Dayton was now served by the preachers of Miami circuit, until 1843; it was then received as a mission, and a small church was built and dedicated as early as September of the same year. From that time the work has been progressing finely in Dayton, yet not without manifold oppositions and trials. Some time after, the small church was converted into a parsonage, and a new, spacious, and highly respectable church erected there. In Cleveland also, a preaching place was established this year, by the preachers of Lake circuit, (Ohio Conference). The Brethren A. Stroh and John Holl traveled on Lake circuit this year, and in a report of their circuit, they speak of the beginning and progress of their labors in Cleveland as follows: "We have commenced since last spring, to preach in the city of Cleveland also, and in spite of the rage of the devil, in spite of our having been pelted with stones by his servants, and denounced by the priests of Babel, the Sun of righteousness begins to shine into many a heart. Some have already been translated into the liberty of God's children, while others are almost persuaded to become Christians. We have a small class here, holding weekly prayer-meetings regularly, and we humbly trust that the Lord will also here gather himself a people zealous of good works."

Brother C. G. Koch communicated the following more minute report of the first labors of our ministers in Cleveland:—

"It was in the year 1840, that the Schnuerer families, father and son, moved from Buffalo to Cleveland, at the instance of some relatives. Having arrived at Cleveland, however, they felt quite forsaken, finding neither members of the Society, nor other believers among the Germans, with whom they might meet for their edification, and hence they thought at times of returning to Buffalo. But, while they were laying their case before God, seeking his guidance with earnest prayer, the now sainted Bro. A. Stroh felt a strong inward desire to seek an opening somewhere in Cleveland, in order to preach the Gospel to its German population. Following this impulse, he rode to Cleveland, crossing its streets, when a member of the Schnuerer family recognized him by his simple dress and costume as an itinerant, and accosted him. This was a moment of joy and gratitude, and both parties saw in this meeting the guiding hand of Providence and the answer to their mutual prayers. After this there was regular preaching in Cleveland during the year, as this appointment was then added to the circuit. The word proved efficacious, and as early as the first year arrangements were already made to build a church. A certain man, favorably disposed to the cause, granted them a building lot near the shore of the lake, for temporary use, without charge.

With the aid of the friends of Lake circuit and others, a small church, 28 by 38 feet, was erected and dedicated as early as the beginning of August, 1841. In the spring of said year, Cleveland was taken up as a mission, and L. Einsel appointed its missionary. He received nine persons during the year into the church, but was also obliged to expel several. The following two years, Bro. H. Heiss was the missionary; but the work progressed slowly, having to struggle with many difficulties. In 1844 and 1845, N. Gehr was missionary there; but the progress of the mission was still very slow and feeble. In the fall of 1845, the small frame church was moved from the shore to a lot owned by the society, about a mile southward, at the south-western corner of Eagle and Erie streets; which was a real improvement, as thenceforth the number of hearers increased considerably, and the prospects for the future became better every year. Under Gehr's administration, the Sabbath-school was already in a flourishing condition, and subsequently improved still more; yet not without vicissitudes. But the society, in general, increased but slowly, and its membership remained small."

J. J. Kopp mentions in a report of his district, a large and highly blessed camp-meeting, held this year on Canton circuit, on the land of John Mattinger. It numbered 50 tents, and more than 200 communicants celebrated the Lord's supper. Matters went on very well in different parts of Lake circuit, as well as in various places of several of the other fields of labor of this conference, in the states of Ohio and Indiana.

On Illinois circuit, which had seven regular preaching places and 400 miles in circumference, the Brethren Isaac Hoffert and Daniel Kern traveled this year; they labored with a great deal of self-denial and also success; for, although their labors were not blessed with great awakenings, yet by their strictly evangelical walk and conversation, they exerted a very salutary influence upon the societies, and thus prepared the glorious success of the work in subsequent years. They turned their special attention to Chicago, and preached there in private houses, in a carpenter's shop, especially in the northern part of the city, called *New Buffalo*. About 12 or 15 persons were converted during the year, and the brethren formed them into the first class of the Society in Chicago. The Brothers Willemer, H. Beste, Silke, Schenk, and others, were the first converts. According to the census of 1840, Chicago then numbered 4853 inhabitants, and being a conflux of emigrants from every direction, it was a very immoral place. But there being as yet no other services there in German than those of our preachers, they were very well attended, although there was preaching only every other Sunday. Our labors among the Germans soon attracted the attention, as well as the respect and interest of the religious portion of the English population of the place, and even many Germans respected our Church, on account of the uprightness and honesty that characterized our first members of the West in their business transactions. But the small society had no lack of persecution, either. A great deal of reproach and slander was brought on by the strange phenomena, that took place at times in their meetings; as sinners frequently during the sermon and elsewhere, fell suddenly to the ground as if struck dead, screaming for mercy, and then all at once jumping up, shouting, and praising God for the pardon of their sins. This kind of exercise was pretty general, both in towns and in the country of the West. Yet such *bodily exercise* is of little account, if only the heart and conduct are right.

The Evangelical Association attaches no importance to these strange bodily exercises, and is far from recommending them; although it has always been, and still is, in favor of a lively and animated service of God. As in New York, Philadelphia, Baltimore, and in other large cities, so also in Chicago many souls were converted from time to time, without, however, increasing our society proportionably in numbers; for many of the members annually moved into the country, strengthening the old societies as well as forming even new ones there.

In the fall of this year, Illinois was for the first time visited by one of our presiding elders. Bro. J. G. Zinser, whose district embraced the far distant West, paid the societies there this welcome visit, in the months of September and October, and assisted the brethren in holding several general meetings. This first visit of the presiding elder in the West, imparted to our work there a powerful impulse, both the preachers and the infant societies being encouraged thereby, and because the claims of the West, which were now fully understood by him, were, by an influential minister, laid before the Ohio Conference. Both the Illinois circuit and the Illinois mission were, at the close of the year, in a promising condition; and the brethren who labored there during the year amid many hardships and trials, are indeed worthy to be held in grateful remembrance, since it is questionable whether any of our preachers were at any time exposed to greater privations than they.

The Printing Establishment was at this time in a prosperous condition. The demand for books, especially Sabbath-school books, constantly increased in the Association, and the preparations made for the publication of the German pocket Bible, took a more favorable turn, and secured the carrying-out of the enterprise. The patrons of the Periodical increased likewise, and its sphere of action extended more and more. During this year its columns were especially filled with articles discussing the claims of the cause of missions, with missionary reports, both from home and foreign missions. This had a tendency to increase the interest of the Society in this glorious cause, which was thereby greatly promoted. A practiced and influential minister remarked in this year, with reference to the Periodical:—

"The Christliche Botschafter seems to become more popular every day; and there is reason to hope that the number of its subscribers and its sphere of usefulness will increase more and more, provided its agents and friends do their duty, recommending it as it deserves. It always has something for the heart, and is like a friend coming from a distance and bringing a large amount of good news, and imparting instruction on different subjects."

The cause of Sabbath-schools likewise became more popular every year in the Association, and its glorious results began to show themselves at this time in the awakening and conversion of many of the scholars of our Sabbath-schools. They were, however, not yet generally introduced, and there was room left for many improvements even where they existed; and this, alas! is still too much the case at present.

This year death again took its victims from the ranks of the preachers. Four of them fell by this "*king of terrors*," who, however, comes without terror to the faithful servant and real child of God. These who had finished their earthly career, were: Father *Michæl Maize*, *Leonard Zimmerman*, *Solomon Altimus*, and *Wm. Bergheimer*.

Father M. Maize, residing two miles east of New Berlin, Union county, Pa., was one of the first who, west of the Susquehannah, received our preachers, and became a member of the Society. Its first two preachers, *Albright* and *Walter*, already found a home under his roof, and ever after his house was a pleasant home for the preachers, till his death. At first, he, as well as those of his neighbors who set out at that time to serve God, had to suffer a great deal of opposition and persecution from the world and the unconverted nominal Christians. But, formerly, he was hated more than others, on account of his zeal for the honor of God, and of his liveliness during divine service. He lived and died a worthy member of the Society, serving as an officer, both as class-leader and local preacher, nearly the whole period of his Christian career; although he never preached a great deal. He also had the honor of having the first camp-meeting of the Association held on his land, in the month of May, 1810. After having served the Lord for about 35 years, he died in the 72d year of his pilgrimage, on the 4th of March, 1841. Father Maize raised a numerous family, and most or all of his children followed the faithful example of their father, thus verifying the words of the wise man: "*Train up a child in the way he should go, and when he is old, he will not depart from it.*"

L. Zimmerman, a resident of Manheim township, Lancaster county, Pa., died on the 17th of December, 1840, aged about 58 years. He was converted in his younger years, by means of Mr. Albright's preaching, and is said to have had a very severe struggle, so much so that even Mr. Albright declared he had never seen the like before. In 1811, when the connection numbered but 3 circuits, 8 itinerants, and 740 members, Brother Zimmerman was received into the itinerancy and served till 1821, when he was obliged to locate on account of bodily infirmities. For the rest of his life he was an active and useful local preacher. Being a tall and stout man, moving and speaking slowly, somewhat bent, very plain in his dress, of an humble, yet fearless appearance, he filled the hearers with respect wherever he rose to preach. Though naturally not a gifted orator, yet when he became excited, his countenance brightened, his delivery became fluent, his voice powerful and piercing, and a great commotion of the audience was the usual result. This was especially the case, when he preached at camp or other extra meetings. Sometimes, while preaching, he was so filled with the power of God that he leaped, shouted, and praised God with a loud voice in the pulpit: this, however, he did with the greatest decorum and with good effects on the hearers. Once, it is said, he preached in a place where the people were very wicked, threatening to put down the small band of believers, and everything looked gloomy in the meeting. All at once, Brother Zimmerman commenced to praise God, to shout and to leap; and when he was asked how he could do so under so discouraging circumstances, he replied: *"Oh, I did it to spite the devil!"* He, with all the first preachers of the Evangelical Association in general, had to suffer a great deal of persecution, scorn, and contempt, for the sake of the truth: but bore it all as a brave soldier of his divine Master with Christian fortitude, rejoicing that he was counted worthy to suffer reproach for the sake of Christ. The first two years of his itinerancy he spent on Northumberland circuit—the first year under John Erb, the second as the superintending preacher with two preachers on trial for his colleagues; the third year he traveled on York, and the fourth on Lancaster circuit; the fifth on Schuylkill, and the sixth again on York circuit; afterward he traveled on Columbia, Centre, Lancaster, and lastly on Franklin circuit. Brother Zimmerman was sickly for a number of years, suffering at times great pains, but bore it all with exemplary patience. His death was sudden, caused, as was supposed, by apoplexy. Thus this soldier of Christ finished his warfare, and entered into the rest and joy of his Master.

Solomon Altimus was received in 1833 as an itinerant on trial, by the Eastern Conference, and stationed with Bro. D. Kehr on Lake circuit, in the state of New York. The next year he was appointed preacher in charge of Shenandoah circuit, in Virginia, and labored there with success. The third year he was preacher in charge of Indiana circuit, in Pa., and had J. Boas for his colleague; the fourth year he superintended Armstrong circuit, which then belonged to Western Conference. But being subject to epileptic fits, that often caused a great deal of alarm when he was from home, and increased in violence from time to time, he took no more appointments from the conference, but traveled about in the country according to his pleasure, preaching in different places with good effect. This he did mostly in the counties of Bucks, Lehigh, and Northampton, Pa., in 1837. Afterward he moved to Michigan, traveled in that state and the northern part of the state of Indiana a great deal, preaching often and forming here and there small classes, as already stated in this history. In

1839 he came to Pennsylvania, attended the session of General Conference in March, and laid a report of his labors and the prospects of the north-western regions before that body. Notwithstanding his disease becoming worse, he did not quit preaching, but traveled about as much as he possibly could. Although he was somewhat odd and singular, probably the consequence of his disease, he was, nevertheless, a talented and powerful speaker, fearing neither the power of hell nor of the world. He attacked sin and vice of every shape without fear, and with great seriousness and zeal insisted on immediate conversion. But his career and warfare were not long.—His death was announced in the Periodical of May 1, 1841, in the following words: "Solomon Altimus is no more—he died on the 18th of March, at his home in Ash township, Monroe co., Michigan, of his old disease (epilepsy). He had nineteen fits in succession, and then fell asleep to awake no more till the voice of the archangel will raise the dead. He was about 8 years a preacher of the Evangelical Association. By his death the Church has lost a faithful shepherd, his neighbors a sincere teacher and servant, and his wife and two children a kind husband and father. Still they need not mourn like those who have no hope."

William Bergheimer departed this life July 23, 1840, in the 26th year of his age. The writer knows not much of him, except that he finds his name in the list of itinerants of the Western (now Ohio) Conference, from 1836 to 1840. The first year of his regular itinerancy, he spent on Lancaster circuit in Ohio, under the superintendence of Bro. S. van Gundy; the second on Indiana circuit, Pa., under D. Kehr. He was then ordained deacon, and appointed preacher in charge of Armstrong, and the fourth year of Maumee circuit, and thus finished his itinerant and soon after also his earthly career. From the notice of his death in the Periodical of August 15th, 1840, we learn that he was converted in his youth, and died of consumption, after a lingering disease and confinement to his bed for about two months; that he had been kindly treated, and had died, in the house of John Brecht, in Fairfield county,

Ohio; that he bore his disease with great patience, and expressed at all times a lively hope of eternal life. Some of his last words were: "*The work will soon be finished!*" and thus he ended his career.

The membership of the Society at the close of this conference year was 8992, and the increase during the year about 900. On account of the incomplete report of the East Pennsylvania Conference of last year, the increase of this year also can not be stated precisely.

The Year 1841.

The East Pennsylvania Conference held its annual session this year in the Evangelical Church in Fayettetown, Seneca county, N. Y., beginning the 17th of March. This was the first Annual Conference of the Society held in the state of New York, which greatly encouraged the northern brethren, and also afforded pleasure to the ministers, although most of them had come from a great distance. Two of the ministers located on account of bodily infirmities, and two brethren were received into the itinerancy. This time the salary was *full*—an unmarried minister received $60, a married one $105, and $15 for each of their children under 14 years of age, besides reasonable traveling expenses. This being the first time that all the brethren of a conference received the full salary allowed them by the discipline, was a very encouraging novelty for the brethren, who felt thankful that matters had come thus far at last. Not only *full salary*, but there was also some balance left in the treasury, which was divided among the brethren to make up, in some measure, for their inadequate support the preceding year. The conference congratulated itself on having finally reached this point, and expressed its gratitude in the following words: "*This is a clear proof that our friends become more and more liberal, and do not desire their brethren in the ministry to lay down their sacred office, for want of a sufficient support.*" Is it not a wonder that the itinerancy of the Evangelical Church has not long ago ceased to exist? This would certainly have been the case, had not the majority of the ministers been animated by an ardent desire to save souls, combined with a truly apostolic sense of self-denial. For even the *full salary* was no adequate support for a man with a family, except he received a great many presents, etc., besides. Thanks, however, to God, that this reproach and curse are, in part at least, removed from the Society! The present salary, as fixed by Discipline, with table expenses, is sufficient for a minister, provided he receives it in full; and there is reason to hope that this will soon be the case in most places. Our membership now consists, not only of *many* wealthy, but also enlightened and liberal men, who undoubtedly will hereafter give their ministers an *adequate* support, and a genuine minister of the Gospel does not want more.

West Pennsylvania Conference held its annual session again at New Berlin, Pa., beginning April 7th. Some itinerants located, and five were received into the itinerancy.

Ohio Conference met in Lafayette Church, Wayne county, Ohio, May 12th. Four itinerants located, and just as many were received into the itinerancy. Canton and Columbiana circuits were united and received three ministers, and Illinois circuit was called *Des Plain circuit* (in Illinois). Three new missions, viz., *White Water*, *Fort Wayne*, and *Cleveland* mission were established, and Illinois mission was continued, although changed as to its limits.

From this time the West took the lead in the cause of missions, the strong current of western immigration opening doors almost everywhere for the establishment of new missions, more than could be supplied for want of men and means. But as missions in the West were generally far less expensive than in the maritime cities and other large places of the East, many of them being from the very start nearly and ere long altogether self-supporting, Ohio Conference was able to establish more missions than either of the two other conferences; moreover, the cause of missions was proportionably better supported in the West than in the East. At this time the Society began to extend more rapidly than it had ever done before; but at the same time, felt also more keenly than ever, its want of a sufficient number of properly qualified men and of means, for the successful prosecution of the work of the Lord. The Germans who had emigrated from Europe or from the middle states to the West, were, in very many places, entirely destitute of all the means of grace. The older German Churches did little or nothing for them, and in some places the people had, as long as they had lived there, not heard a single sermon in German, and English preaching they did not understand to their satisfaction. Such was the condition in which our preachers found many Germans in the states of Indiana, Michigan, Illinois, and in the territories of Wisconsin and Iowa. Some, it is true, had their pastors, but such pastors!—most of them were outcasts and scoundrels—drunkards, voluptuaries, etc., proving rather a curse than a blessing. In this way our preachers took the lead in many places of the West, and retained it also in many of them; but they would have done a great deal more, had their number been larger.

This was a very prosperous and successful year to the Society. Never before had its increase been so large, and never were its general prospects so bright as now. The work of the Lord progressed not only on all its fields of labor, but in every part and corner in the East and West, South and North. The ministers were, in general, filled with the proper spirit to carry forward and extend the work of God; and the many cheering reports of its glorious success and prosperity, which filled at that time and afterward the columns of the Periodical, tended greatly to increase their zeal and activity. Whoever will take the time to peruse the many cheering and encouraging reports of the work of God, that appeared in the Periodical of 1841 and 1842, can easily satisfy himself of the truth of this statement. In an article on revivals, published this year, we find among others the following remarks, touching the subject in question:—

"In spite of the devil's and his servants' rage, and the charges of *disorder, fanaticism*, and *excess*, of such as, either from envy or malice, seem unable to bear that the so-called '*Albrights*' meet with so much favor and find so many followers;

the boundaries of the Evangelical Association extend more and more, and the increase of its membership grows more rapidly from time to time. The false prophets who in the beginning predicted its speedy failure, have long since been confounded; and the strong prejudices of the common people have, to a great extent, disappeared, since the principles, doctrines, and Discipline of the Society have come to be better understood; so that many who used to look upon the *little* band with contempt, have commenced to fear it. In most places it will not do any longer to attack them by bands armed with clubs and stones, sometimes led by a Rev. gentleman, or to denounce them, *indiscriminately*, as fanatics, deceivers, and deceived wretches."

Another writer remarked:—

"This conference year is a highly blessed one to our Society. The work of the Lord extends mightily; men are awakened and converted to God by scores. On all circuits and stations yet heard from, revivals of religion have taken place. Hence it is evident, that the more the Evangelical Association is spoken against, the more it extends, and the more glorious is its progress."

At this time there were once more violent attacks made on the Society, from different quarters; its manner of proceeding with mourners, its active and lively services, were the main points of attack. Pains were taken to prove that these things were fanaticism and disorder. Some periodicals especially busied themselves in this way, in order to prevent the rapid extension and increase of the connection, and to break down its influence. And as it fearlessly and boldly attacked the wickedness and immorality of many nominal Christians, and disapproved and rejected their dead and hypocritical services, it was also accused of fault-finding. In order to check the frequent desertion from their ranks to ours, some clergymen of different denominations took great pains to cast reproach upon us, and to fill their people with prejudices against us. Both from the pulpit and in the family-circle they labored for this end; while others wrote libelous pamphlets to blacken our character. Our Periodical of 1841 says with reference to such pamphlets: "The libelous pamphlet of pastor ——— against the Evangelical Association, deserves, in our estimation, no notice. Such *ignes fatui* generally vanish in a short time, doing little or no harm; on the contrary, they sometimes rather serve to stimulate the people to read our books and tracts, in order to become acquainted with our doctrines; and in this way they do us more good than harm. We would therefore advise Brother K., not to trouble himself with writing a refutation of those false and shameless charges."

Our Periodical, however, was not remiss in those days in defending the Society against attacks of this kind. With what fervor and intrepidity it discharged its duty in this respect, appears from the following article which appeared in its columns at the close of this conference year; this article also confirms what has been said on the great prosperity of the connection at that time. It is as follows:—

"At no previous time have so many and so great awakenings and revivals taken place in the Ev. Association, as has been the case for some years past. The missionary spirit that has animated the Society at large, and its ministry in particular, for a number of years, seems to have contributed largely toward this glorious result; but more especially the increased efforts to bring about revivals by protracted and other meetings, seems to have exerted a powerful influence.

Notwithstanding the great want of itinerants, and the many oppositions and impediments, the Evangelical Association extends with increasing rapidity. Its membership enlarges by thousands, and the work runs from town to town, from state to state. For these reasons the Society is in these days more envied, slandered, and abused, by various corrupt Churches and proselyters, than ever before; though the persecution is not as rude as formerly. Churches, preachers, and editors, some of whom seem to be rationalists and infidels; drunkards, swearers, and Sabbath-breakers, etc.; moralists and formalists —who bite and devour each other, differing as widely in their religious sentiments and rites, as the languages at the building of the tower of Babel, seem to have united for the purpose of rushing upon the hated '*Albrights*,' as they call us, with their slanders, abuses, and calumnies, and of branding them as the most pernicious, dangerous, and selfish of all. Pilate and Herod, at other times enemies, here make common cause, and become friends. But they generally find no occasion against us, except concerning our mode of worship, (Dan. 6: 4, 5.) which they find too disorderly, noisy, and sectarian, etc. That our members lead wicked or immoral lives, or that we admit drunkards and profane swearers to the Lord's supper, they do not say a word; but of our *disorderly services*, our proselyting, fault-finding spirit, etc., they complain most bitterly. They know too well where the shoe pinches, and hence their silence on certain points. Yet, if the poor fellows knew how little we care for their boisterous scolding, and how little harm they do us thereby, they would certainly be silent.

But the Evangelical Association will not suffer itself to be disturbed by such little souls, even if they should discharge their whole infernal battery against us, but will go on in its endeavors to lead as many souls to Christ as possible. And if it continues to enlarge its boundaries, and to increase its membership in this way, which every Church has a right to do, no one need or will find fault with it, except only envious sectarians and proselyters.—If any of our members think they can enjoy and edify themselves better in some other Church, they are at perfect liberty to leave us and join the same; and if their standing in our midst has been good, we give them a certificate to that effect. And members of other denominations should have the same liberty to join us. Let every Church preach the pure Gospel with power and unction, keeping up lively services in the sanctuary, and enforcing the Discipline, and there will scarcely any room be left for complaints of deserting members; then those that leave, will generally be such as are no blessing to any Church. But that people should leave churches which are so corrupt as to retain profane swearers, dancers, gamblers, drunkards, etc., as members from year to year, and to admit them to the Lord's supper, none but hirelings and arch-sectarians will find fault with."

It is true, this is strong and unsparing language; but whoever is acquainted with the abominable and mean attacks on the Society, will readily excuse the same and ascribe it to a holy zeal for the truth and honor of the Lord. In order to give the reader a better insight into the missionary operations of the connection, we here insert also the second annual report of its missionary society, although it mainly has reference to the preceding year. It is as follows:—

"*Second Annual Report of the Missionary Society of the Evangelical Association.*

With feelings of gratitude toward the great Giver of every good and perfect gift, and with rejoicing over his rich blessings which have rested upon our enterprise during the past year, we to-day lay the second annual report of our society before the friends of the sacred cause of missions.

Already in our first annual report, we felt constrained to call upon our friends to praise the Lord with us for the success of our enterprise; and during the year just closed, it was his divine pleasure again to accompany the same with his rich blessings, and to show thereby his approbation of our intentions.

Of the four missions we had the last year, two were remarkably successful, viz., those of Baltimore and Waterloo missions. Illinois mission was likewise blessed; and, although there has as yet no society been organized in the city of New York, yet from the last report of the missionary, it appears that even there our efforts have not been altogether in vain. On Baltimore and Waterloo missions, during the past year, not less than 276 members were received; some time ago the latter was converted into a circuit, and supplied with two preachers. The society in Baltimore is already engaged in building a spacious church, which will cost a great deal, for which reason the missionary there is to be supported another year out of the missionary treasury.—The receipts of the society during the past year amount to $1073,65¾. There was not much done in founding new auxiliary societies, nor was the support on the whole as liberal as it might have been; yet this may have been owing more to the general scarcity of money, than to a want of interest on the part of our friends. Yet we think more ought to have been done. We are pleased, however, to be able to state, that our treasury was not yet embarrassed; and we humbly trust that with the opening of new doors for missionary labor, the Lord will also open hands and hearts to support this holy cause.—All the Annual Conferences of the connection have now formed themselves into branch societies of the parent board; and we may reasonably hope that all our members will be enlisted in this holy cause, provided the itinerants do their duty. May He who commanded his first disciples to *go and preach the Gospel to every creature*, inspire, fill, and animate us with the same spirit, with which he had qualified them for rearing the superstructure of his Church; and may our humble institution also be one of his honored instruments to save the world from the power of darkness, and to change it into a paradise.

In conclusion, we would yet call upon all our friends, to support our enterprise with their faithful prayers and intercession; being more firmly convinced than ever, that all depends on the blessing of God. We might, indeed, in different places, gather societies of nominal Christians and carnally-minded professors, without the help of God; but, if we desire to do something toward the salvation of the world, and the preparation of souls for heaven, we need the help and blessing of God, which he has promised to all that ask him. Our Lord has also taught us to pray that his kingdom may come. May he grant us the spirit of prayer!

W. W. ORWIG, Corresponding Secretary.

New Berlin, Pa., May 22, 1841."

This year we had six missions; four in Ohio, one in East Penn., and one in West Pennsylvania Conference, which were all crowned with more or less success. New York mission especially succeeded beyond all expectation, after almost all hope as to its final success had been abandoned; sore trials, however, had not been wanting. Brother M. Eis, who had been appointed missionary there at the last session of the East Pennsylvania Conference, was, on account of his failing health, obliged to bid farewell to the mission toward the end of September. Brother C. Meyers was then appointed his successor, and arrived there in safety Oct. 29th, to the great joy of the little band. In his first report he remarks thus: "The brethren and sisters were greatly delighted with my arrival, and thanked God with tears of joy for having sent them another minister. Although they were about four weeks without a preacher, yet they had remained firm in the service of the Lord. It is true, the enemy had not been idle during this time; the world had rejoiced and said, that everything would now be frustrated again; and some individuals had even taken the pains to visit those who had received the truth, in order to turn them away from us. But hitherto their efforts have failed, and our small society, instead of decreasing, has had an addition of one member.—The prospects of this mission are at present very bright."

Brother Meyers had been a local preacher for several years in Philadelphia, and this year set out as an itinerant. His thorough acquaintance with the German character and city life, gave him great advantages and qualified him eminently, before many others, for the important post he was now called to fill. He justified all reasonable expectations; the affairs of the mission took a more favorable turn, and at the close of the year it numbered 57 members.—But now the want of a church and graveyard was deeply felt, without which two requisites no enterprise of the kind can permanently prosper. Several plans were, accordingly, devised, but alas! none carried out. The sainted Brother *Hesser* proposed the following plan for the erection of churches in larger towns, and wished to have it applied first to the city of New York, viz., that each member of the Association should lay by *one cent a week* for this purpose, whereby between four and five thousand dollars would have been raised annually at that time. Bro. John P. Leib was of opinion, that this plan, although very good in itself, would scarcely do for New York, as it would work too slowly, and the necessity for a church there was very urgent. He therefore proposed the well known *ten thousand dollar plan* for New York; which was, that 1000 persons should obligate themselves to pay $10 each. Strong efforts were made to realize this plan, and much was written in the Periodical respecting it, but all to no purpose. A third plan, devised by a sister in Ohio, to raise $1000 by as many subscriptions of $1 each among the sisters, was but partially carried out; and there were not quite $2000 raised by means of the two latter plans, that of Bro. Hesser having been dropped altogether.—Thus the infant society in the city of New York was indeed greatly disappointed in their expectations; but, nevertheless, the preparatory step toward erecting a good church finally succeeded; it progressed, however, slowly, and not without great difficulties.

This year Baltimore mission prospered as well as the first; the society increased considerably, and the commenced church edifice was completed and dedicated to the service of God, December 12, 1842. At the close of this year the society numbered between 250 and 300 members, and was in a highly prosperous condition; but strange as it may seem, it never exceeded this number considerably, but was often a great deal below it; notwithstanding some great revivals and many conversions, its membership seldom reached 300. The deaths of many of the old members, the removal of others, as well as the expulsion and egression of considerable numbers, prevented an increase of the numerical strength of the society, while in other respects a great many improvements were made.

Ohio Conference had four missions this year, which, however, on account of their great extent, could not properly be attended to, that of Cleveland alone excepted. Illinois mission had more than 300 miles in circumference, and but one preacher, Brother J. Hoffert, and his health was very delicate. Yet he labored not in vain. He had thirteen regular appointments, of which the region of the present Cedarville and Sharon, Henry county, were the principal places. In each of these two places there was a class of 20 members—the only classes of his mission which lay. for the most part, fallow and extended beyond the Mississippi. Hence the travels of the missionary were not only connected with great hardships, but even with danger, especially in winter and spring, when the waters were high.

On Fort Wayne mission, situated for the most part in the state of Indiana, around Fort Wayne, and extending over parts of 7 or 8 counties, Brother J. Hall labored amid great difficulties and discouragements. He explored and occupied an extensive territory, formed also several small classes, and thus prepared the way for the future. Many parts of the country were very thinly settled in those days, the people were generally poor, and the roads bad, so that after a day's journey man and beast were often considerably worn out, and had then to content themselves with scanty food and bad lodgings. In the following year the Brethren J. Hall and J. Nicolai labored on the mission, but without great success; yet their labors were not altogether in vain. They encountered great opposition by would-be pastors, and still had to deny themselves in many things. In 1843 this mission was allotted to the Brethren D. Kern and G. A. Blank; it made fine progress this year, conversions took place, new preaching places were taken up, and between 60 and 70 members received. The following year Brother Blank, again, and S. A. Tobias were appointed the missionaries there. But Brother Tobias had to return home, was taken sick, and Bro. Blank was thus left alone for a great part of the year. He was, however, assisted a great deal by his presiding elder, A. B. Shæfer, who labored with indefatigable perseverance and great self-denial as a pioneer in the state of Indiana, and was also permitted to see much fruit of his labors. Honor, to whom honor is due.—It may be observed here, that when Ohio Conference was divided, this mission fell to Illinois Conference, and in 1844 consequently belonged to the latter.

Of White Water mission mention was made in the preceding year, and consequently is passed over here.

The remaining fields of labor prospered pretty generally this conference year. Some of the camp-meetings especially were highly blessed. In a report of Salem district, West Pennsylvania Conference, it is said at the close: "Our camp-meetings seem to have caused a revival over the whole district."—By means of one of them, on the land of A. O., the work was introduced into the village of Hartleton, Union county, Pa., which had lain waste for a long time. Some were converted at this meeting, and others deeply convicted, so that they commenced to seek the Lord. This number afterward increased, and a class was formed, which has existed to this day.

On Carmel district also some highly blessed camp meetings were held; and one of the most blessed took place on York circuit, Zion district, where more than 400 members are said to have been present at times, and about 50 persons to have found the pardon of their sins. There were 46 tents on the ground, occupied by about 80 or 90 families. This circuit was many years renowned for its large and good camp-meetings; almost every family tented, both rich and poor, and the result was always good. But afterward many lost their courage or inclination to tent. Whether they now regard such meetings as not so necessary any more, there being plenty of churches everywhere, or whether their interest in the cause of God has abated, we will not presume to decide. These remarks apply to many other circuits in all conferences, especially the older. Of the camp-meeting on Lycoming circuit, Bro. B. Epley remarks: "Our camp-meeting last fall was blessed beyond all expectation, with awakenings and conversions."

Bishop Seybert mentions a camp-meeting held in Fairfield county, Ohio, on the land of Bro. Brecht, as follows: "The very first evening we had blessed times. On Friday the meeting grew in interest, many hearts were touched, and praying and wrestling with God followed. On Saturday afternoon everything seemed favorable for a revival. At first a solemn silence pervaded the assembly, followed by a powerful commotion of both saints and sinners. Many tears were shed by the children of God, while praying for the conversion of their friends and relatives, till sinners cried to God for mercy and pardon. Toward evening a gang of ruffians and Belial's children had come to the camp-ground, for the avowed purpose of breaking up the meeting; but the Lord frustrated their design, by sending a heavy storm with lightning and powerful peals of thunder, whereby the ruffians became so frightened and tame, that we could continue our exercises in peace, without further disturbance, praying with and instructing the mourners."

In Dry Valley, Union county, Pa., a glorious work of grace took place during this year, under the superintendence of G. Shæfer and J. Truby; it began with a protracted meeting, held in the house of Isaac Eyer, toward the close of October. A considerable number were converted, and joined the Church. Old Union circuit prospered throughout, this year.

In East Pennsylvania Conference many glorious revivals took place this year. The number of the newly received members within this conference district amounted to nearly 1000, and its boundaries were greatly extended, especially in the North, in the state of New York, and in Canada.—In Schuylkill Haven and Pinegrove, glorious revivals took place, under the pastoral labors of Bro. F. Hoffman. The society of Schuylkill Haven was considerably increased, and that of Pinegrove founded this year. Also at Lebanon and Millerstown, five miles above Lebanon, cheering awakenings took place, under the pastorage of Brother D. Berger. At the last mentioned place a protracted meeting was begun January 28th, which is said to have resulted in the conversion of about 100 souls. The number of mourners at the altar was sometimes from 30 to 35, and on one evening 31 souls are said to have found peace and consolation. Many of the new converts united with us, and arrangements were made forthwith, to build a church; but the society being so very small yet, the enterprise did not succeed without great difficulties.

This year the Philadelphia society commenced to prosper again. Brother Hesser remarks in a report of the society as follows: "On Christmas we commenced a protracted meeting, which lasted twelve days. The Brethren Leib, Maize, and

Boas, had come to our assistance. Between 20 and 30 souls were converted during the meeting, most of whom joined our society. The work is still progressing, and almost every week we have some conversions. * * * * * Our society is, on the whole, quite revived and in fine spirits; my prayer is, that harmony, love, and peace, may prevail more and more.—In the vicinity of Germantown also a glorious work of grace has begun, and our prospects here are, on the whole, very good. I also take great pleasure in being able to state, that most of them who with Vogelbach had left us, have come back, and are glad that they are at home again among their brethren. * * * Our Sabbath-school is likewise in a highly flourishing condition, numbering about 200 children. Considering the powerful opposition we have to encounter, we can truly say: "*The Lord has done great things for us, whereof we are glad.*" Brother Leib, in a report of his district, fully confirms Brother Hesser's statement, giving it still stronger colors.

On Milford and Lehigh circuits, matters went better again this year, especially at Allentown. Brother M. F. Maize, the preacher in charge of Lehigh circuit, writes in November, referring to Allentown: "The Lord has commenced a glorious work here, during a protracted meeting; a considerable number have been converted to God, and many more have been awakened. We expect a rich harvest this winter." Bro. Leib writes, referring to these two circuits: "In spite of all opposition, the Lord has done wonders. Although we have not occupied a very large field, yet I venture to say that we have not been idle in cultivating what we have. The work of God is still progressing on these circuits." In Springtown and Williams township, as well as in the neighborhood of Mauch Chunk, the work extended and gained a solid footing this year. On Lancaster circuit, Turkey Hill, the society increased considerably, and in Adamstown the work of the Lord progressed finely. This year the first protracted meeting was held here by our ministers.

On Lake circuit in the state of New York, the work of grace progressed finely in general, but especially in Grove, Alleghany county, where a glorious revival took place, and the society increased considerably. In Sparta, Livingston county, they were also blessed with a revival. When the Lord's supper was celebrated there, Evangelicals, Lutherans, Methodists, and Baptists, partook of the sacred emblems together, and there was a general union of the believers of all these denominations. M. Lehn and M. Sindlinger traveled the circuit. On Buffalo circuit, N. Y., the number of believers also increased considerably, especially in Boston, Erie county, where the membership was almost doubled.

The Canada circuits prospered and made rapid progress. Two camp-meetings were again held there, which were highly blessed; one on Waterloo, the other on Black Creek circuit. As early as this year four men were admitted there on trial into the itinerancy, and a church erected, viz., at Berlin. Joseph Harlacher and Jacob Dereich traveled on Waterloo, and P. Schwille on Black Creek circuit.

On Canton and Columbiana circuits, in Ohio Conference, which had conjointly three preachers this year, under the charge of E. Stœver, conversions took place in different places, especially at Greensburg where the society increased considerably. Erie circuit prospered also, as well as Mansfield, Marion, and some others. But in the absence of the necessary documents, we cannot say which parts enjoyed the most glorious outpourings of the Spirit of God.

Des Plain circuit, in the state of Illinois, did admirably well this year. The Brethren Adam Stroh and Christian H. Lintner labored there with great success. The circuit extended from Chicago and Napierville, in Illinois, as far as 10 miles north of Milwaukee, in Wisconsin.—This year Brother Stroh also commenced to preach in the city of Milwaukee. In different places considerable awakenings took place, of which the most important were those near Wheeling in Illinois, and at Eckert's, six miles south of Milwaukee. The one at Wheeling continued from Christmas almost all winter, and about 50 souls were converted. The revival near Milwaukee took place principally during a protracted meeting in Brother Fr. Eckert's barn, and the conversion of about 30 individuals, for the most part heads of families, was the glorious result. In Chicago also the brethren labored with great success. They generally preached in the *City Hall*, a large room in what then was the City Hotel, corner of Clark and Randolph streets, where the "Sherman's House" stands at present. There were about 100 new members received during the year, and the whole membership was 186. Illinois mission numbered fifty members, seven of whom were received during this year.

During this year Bishop Seybert paid his first visit to Illinois and Wisconsin; and the first camp-meeting of the Evangelical Association in the *far West*, as it was then called, was also held this year on the land of Father Jacob Esher, two miles south-east of Wheeling, Cook county, Illinois, and 20 miles north-west of Chicago, beginning July 15th. There were 18 tents on the ground, which were crowded. Some of the friends had come from a distance of thirty miles on wagons drawn by oxen, through bad roads and deep waters; and others as far as 70 miles on foot. To all except the preachers, camp meetings were a novelty. Bishop Seybert superintended the meeting, and besides him the following preachers were present: J. Hoffert, A. Stroh, and C. H. Lintner. "That the meeting was highly blessed," says Brother Esher in a report of it, "I need scarcely mention. God was not only *feelingly*, but even *visibly* present with his people; for one evening, when a heavy storm was gathering around the camp ground, some profane persons present, exultingly predicted that now the meeting would be broken up; but lo! all at once the storm divided just in front of our camp, and while the rain fell in torrents on all sides, scarcely a drop fell on the camp-ground! Even the unconverted saw in this the finger of God, but his children praised him with thankful hearts for this wonderful exhibition of his protecting power. Most of the witnesses of this event are still living, and can at any time confirm what I have just written."

The meeting was victorious from beginning to end, and crowned with awakenings and conversions. "Many," says Bishop Seybert, "passed from death unto life." At the quarterly conference held during this camp-meeting, there was also the first preacher of the "far West" received on trial, namely Brother *Christian Ebinger*, one of our first converts in the West. Thus the first visit of the Bishop, the first camp-meeting of the Society, and the first reception of a minister by it, in the West, took place here together. By Brother Seybert's visit, both the members and the preachers of the "far West" were greatly encouraged and strengthened; and the Bishop himself, having become fully acquainted with the importance and wants of the West, has ever since been the warm friend and advocate of the same. Fully satisfied of the immense importance of the West, in a political and religious point of view, he exerted his whole influence to call the attention of the Church in its operations to the same. In the East he sometimes spoke so favorably of the West, that he was often charged with arousing and fostering the spirit of immigration to those beautiful *prairies* and *flowery groves*, to the injury of the East, as far as the Evangelical Association was concerned. But the Bishop's object evidently was, to promote the honor of God and the best interests of the Association. The emigration had already commenced, and increased every year. Hundreds of our members, often the greater part of classes and societies, and even preachers, emigrated to the West. Most of them improved their temporal affairs considerably; some gained both in a temporal and spiritual point of view; while others gained in temporal things only, but lost spiritually. The work had now gained a broad and solid basis in the West, and the prospects for the future were bright.

From what has been said, it appears that the year under consideration was a highly blessed and fruitful one. It ought to be added yet, that the willingness of our members to build churches, which had been manifested for some years past, was still on the increase, especially in the eastern conferences. Churches were built in many places of the country, but especially in country towns, though also in some of the maritime towns. The difference between the churches that were built now, and those that had been built in former times, was also remarkable, both with regard to the external appearance of the buildings, and their internal arrangements and costs. Our first churches were small, low and plain, for the most part in remote corners, especially in towns, either on account of poverty of the members, or out of humility, the sincerity of which we would not question. The costs were generally from $300 to $500, and in some instances a little more. One story 12 or 15 feet high, an aisle through the middle, seats on both sides, a proportionably high pulpit, generally on one of the sides, no altar—this was the general style of our first churches. Those built in the next period, were somewhat larger, generally 30 by 40, or 40 by 45, a little higher, the pulpit lower, frequently two instead of one aisle, generally with an altar, which cost from six to seven hundred dollars, sometimes $1000. Of this kind there are still some built in our days, especially in the country; and they also answer their purpose.—At this time our people commenced to erect larger buildings, in some places of two stories, especially in towns, the costs varying from $1500 to $3000, in the large cities from $6000 to $7000, without the lot. There was, thanks be to God, no occasion till then for complaining of extravagance in the erection of churches in the Evangelical Association, and, as far as the writer knows, there is no such occasion yet, except that by mismanagement more money is often spent than is necessary. But, though there was generally more done in this line than ever before, it was still rather necessary to encourage than to discourage the church-building spirit, or to warn against extravagance; and this, alas! is in too many places still the case. Instead of seeking also in this respect, first the kingdom of heaven, many of our people seek first to provide grand and convenient houses for themselves, contenting themselves with small, inconvenient, and insignificant houses of worship, to the great injury of the good cause and their own disgrace. Such conduct is, undoubtedly, as displeasing in the sight of God as extravagance and pride in church edifices.

The Printing Establishment was in a flourishing condition, and the book trade prospered beyond all expectation. The press was almost constantly in motion, and yet the demands for books could not all be met. The publication of the German pocket Bible, before alluded to, was completed this year, and one-half of the 3000 copies that were printed, were bound and sent off. But there being very few rail-roads in those days, the forwarding of books was rather inconvenient; the boxes had either to be sent for hundreds of miles by private conveyance, or some person had to be employed to ship a number of them, to be distributed among the preachers. Especially books for the West had to be sent this way. In order to give the reader a correct idea of these things, we mention here an order for books, that was received this year, and the manner of forwarding them. Bishop Seybert ordered in the course of this year, for the different districts of the Ohio Conference, *twenty-three thousand seven hundred and twenty-five* books, with the intention to forward them to the West himself. At the close of his order he remarked: "You will probably think I have entirely overshot the mark, in ordering so many books; but, if you were as well acquainted with the scarcity of books in the West, as I am, you would judge differently." A great portion of these books consisted, of course, of little Sabbath-school books; yet their whole weight was 2500 pounds, and their costs, including a small quantity for Illinois, amounted to *four thousand, four hundred and six dollars, and twenty-five and a half cents.* This was the heaviest order for books our Establishment ever received, and the General Agent, Bro. Chas. Hammer, remarked: "Should such a large order be sent us again, we ought to have it a year before the books are wanted, in order to have time to get them ready." The scarcity of German books in Illinois, Wisconsin, and Iowa, was in those days so great that the Christliche Botschafter and the smaller hymn-book were used in some Sabbath-schools to instruct the scholars.

As to a liberal education and higher institutions of learning, we can only say that they were still too much underrated and neglected by us as a denomination; although some of our members learned to see and feel their importance. The time had evidently not yet arrived for the Association, to establish higher institutions of learning; nevertheless, more might certainly have been done for the promotion of science and general culture, than really was done. The great abuse of learning, and of higher literary institutions, both in Europe and America, with its consequent injurious results, had filled many of our members, not only with indifference, but even with prejudices against every thing of the kind; and that the abuse of a good cause never proves anything against the cause itself, these friends did not take into consideration. But the increased book trade, the many good books, written by pious and learned men, that came into the hands of the preachers, in which Bishop Seybert manifested a particular zeal and activity, the *Christliche Botschafter*, and the spirit of the times, diminished this indifference and these prejudices more and more! and as the Association was frequently charged with being, as a body, hostile to learning and literary institutions, we were, at length, compelled to express ourselves in public on this subject. Meanwhile the Periodical would sometimes venture to express the views of a great part of the membership and ministry on the subject. We here insert a few specimens of these articles. At the close of this conference year, the following article appeared in the Botschafter:—

"'*I have no Time for Study.*'

This miserable excuse which is made by many to justify their ignorance, is in most instances without any foundation whatever. Although all may not have time to go through a regular collegiate course, yet most persons can surely find time enough, amid the duties of a proper calling, in the course of a few years, to store their minds with a large amount of useful information. If every one would but devote the time to study which is frequently spent in idleness, useless employments, unnecessary visits, over-indulgence in sleep, etc., they would have sufficient time for this useful employment. But, alas! most men do not consider the value of their time. Many spend one or more hours daily, sometimes even half days, in some useless manner, without ever considering that it is just as wrong to squander their time, as their money.

Redeem the time, is an apostolic injunction, and whoever heeds it, will have plenty of time for studying. He will daily find more or less time to read useful books, and to store his mind with knowledge. There is reason to fear, that those who imagine they have no time for studying, have no real inclination to do so. They have no desire to learn, and for this reason they misspend their time in useless pleasures. Others lack the spirit of enterprise and perseverance necessary in order to overcome the difficulties that present themselves in the pursuit of science. They wish to reach by one effort the pinnacle of science, and as this is an impossibility, they become discouraged and throw aside their books. But this is not the way that leads to scientific attainments. Resolution and perseverance are indispensable prerequisites. To those, therefore, who have been under the impression, that they have no time to study, we would give the advice, hereafter to set a higher value on their time, and to avoid misspending a minute, either in idleness, sleep, useless talk, visiting, etc., and our word for it, they will have one or two hours a day left for studying, without curtailing their business time in the least. By doing this, they will in a few years cultivate their minds, and store them with useful knowledge. And if they succeed thus to master one branch of science—a thing by the way, that can very easily be accomplished, by dint of resolution, application, and perseverance—their spirit of enterprise and courage grows, so that they will take up another branch, and finally conquer all difficulties that may present themselves in the way to the pinnacle of science. By studying thus privately, many have already accomplished more in the sciences and languages, than others who have spent a number of years in higher institutions of learning.

In New England, it is said, there lives a man who is but 33 years of age, works daily 8 hours at the anvil, and has already mastered more than fifty languages. He works daily 8 hours for the support of his family, studies 8 hours, and sleeps

8 hours. Many other examples of a similar nature might be given. Now, if others accomplished so much by private study, no one ought to despair of mastering one or two of the modern languages, and of storing his mind with the most necessary knowledge. But let no one flatter himself, that he can master his grammar in a few days, weeks, or months; but let him study it a year, or even two or three years, until he perfectly understands it; after having mastered one branch, let him take up another. Let him take care, however, not to take up many things at once, or else one will be in the way of the other, and he will accomplish nothing."

A month after, the following Editorial appeared in the Periodical:—

"*Learning of the Clergy.*

There is, perhaps, nothing that has been more misjudged by men, than the necessity of learning for a proper discharge of the duties of the Gospel ministry. While some are of opinion, that human learning is an indispensable condition, and almost the only qualification for the sacred office, so much so that no one is properly qualified to be a herald of the Gospel, who has not been for years in high schools and gone through a classical and theological training; there are others, who look upon learning in a minister of the Gospel not only as something unnecessary, but as something positively hurtful and dangerous, in whose eyes all higher institutions of learning are, consequently, detrimental to the cause of religion. Each of these two classes is in the wrong, and both are, perhaps, equally far from the truth.

That human learning, even the highest order of it, cannot, without the unction and calling of the Holy Ghost, qualify a man for a proper discharge of the duties of the Gospel ministry, must be evident to every one who has but the least acquaintance with the nature of this divine and sacred calling. But that solid learning, in connection with the unction of the Holy One, is very serviceable to a minister of the Gospel, rendering him more useful in his high and responsible calling, even common sense teaches, apart from the testimonies of the

History of the Church and the Bible. Every unprejudiced, sensible reader can, therefore, plainly see, how improper and wrong it is, to find fault with human learning, so as to denounce it as dangerous and hurtful, just because some have abused it to their own injury and that of others. If the abuse of a thing would justify or oblige us to discontinue its use altogether, and to denounce it as useless and dangerous, we could, on this ground, reject every good cause in the world. What has ever been more basely abused by Christians, or to the destruction of more men, than the Bible? And should it, for this reason, be discarded as useless and dangerous? We dare say, that no Christian would draw this inference. And the same might be said of singing, prayer, preaching, going to church, and of every other means of grace. Are not all these things grossly abused and desecrated by thousands, to the dishonor of God and to their own destruction? And does this abuse justify us in neglecting and rejecting them? Certainly not.

But we do not wish to be understood as saying, that no one can be a successful preacher, who is not a learned man. No—for experience has taught, that men and youths, without having gone through a classical course, have been called of God to the Gospel ministry, and the glorious success that has crowned their labors, is sufficient evidence that God owned them as his servants. These facts cannot be denied or questioned. Yet it is equally true, that of the men thus called, those who apply themselves to close study, and the reading of books written by good and learned men, in order to store their minds with useful knowledge, in addition to the divine unction, are generally more useful and efficient laborers in the vineyard of the Lord, than those who unfortunately are filled with prejudice against learning, and consequently do not feel their want of a better education.—

Nothing is more improper and more despicable, than that an unlearned man should despise learning. A blind man might just as well speak of colors, or an ignorant sinner of conversion or regeneration.

What student of Church History does not know, that when

the Church was sunk deepest in error, vice, and superstition, the clergy were most ignorant, so much so that many could not write their own names?—Should any one feel disposed to appeal to the case of the apostles, to prove that learning is neither useful nor necessary for a preacher of the Gospel; we have the same right to say that it is necessary for every preacher to be possessed of miraculous powers, such as raising the dead, healing the sick, speaking in unknown tongues, etc.; for all of the apostles were possessed of these powers, and thereby they established their divine mission. Would to God that all modern preachers were as great philosophers and linguists as the apostles were, and had also the same measure of unction, divine wisdom and zeal, to prosecute the work of the Lord—the Church and the world would then soon present a different aspect, in a moral point of view. It is true, the apostles received their learning not in a regular, but rather in an extraordinary manner. But why did God give it to them? No doubt, because it was needful and necessary for them. Why was the learned Saul, afterward called Paul, awakened, converted, and called to the apostleship, in so extraordinary a manner? Was not his learning of the greatest service to him, in defending and spreading the Christian religion? Is it probable that he could have accomplished as much good in the many great cities he visited, if he had not been a learned man? What would he have done, when he was asked by a certain centurion: "*Canst thou speak Greek*," if he had not been a linguist? See Acts 21, 37. And was it not of service to him in one of his defences, in order to attract the attention of the people, to be able to speak *Hebrew*? Acts 22, 2. His intimate acquaintance with the customs, manners, and literature of the different nations, was likewise serviceable to him in finding points of connection for the Gospel he preached, and in founding Christian societies in their midst. From his letters also, which he addressed to the different Churches, it is evident that human learning is of great value.

Although we admit that God can make use of unlearned men in his vineyard, yet it is our firm conviction that he needs learned men also in order to defend his word and religion against infidels, scoffers, and skeptics, and to build up his kingdom on earth. We deem it especially necessary for every preacher of the Gospel, to study the manners and customs of the nations of antiquity, to which the inspired penmen allude so often, as well as geography, chronology, astronomy, etc., in order to be able to expound the Bible. Without being acquainted with these sciences, the preacher is not prepared to explain many of the best texts of the Bible correctly. Josephus and Church History ought also to be diligently studied by every minister of the Gospel.

Now, whoever has either no opportunity or no means to acquire this knowledge in properly conducted institutions of learning, may acquire it by private study, though perhaps not so advantageously, if he buys the right kind of books, and is enterprising and active. But the first of all, is, he must study and learn that he knows nothing.—This article is mainly intended for the preachers of our denomination."

At the same time a translated article on "*learning*" appeared in the Periodical, from which we insert the following extracts:—

"It is the will of God that Christians be well instructed, that they become wise and intelligent. Solid learning is very serviceable to the cause of religion: the best informed and wisest Christians are the most persevering, and can be the most useful. If a man is a child in knowledge, he can easily be carried about with every wind of doctrine, and is a play-ball in the hands of selfish and cunning men. The better informed a man is, the safer he is in this respect. If our circumstances are such as to place the facilities of but a limited education within our reach, we ought to improve the same to the fullest extent. An imperfect education is, after all, better than none at all. He who cannot realize every thing he would like, ought to endeavor to realize as much as possible. If total ignorance is an evil and dangerous thing, every degree of learning lessens both the danger and the evil. * * * * * Every Christian ought to study philosophy, because he will learn from it: 1. That he who is so wonderfully made, so wonderfully supported, and so abundantly provided for, ought to surrender himself unreservedly to his God, and devote all his powers to the service of his Creator. 2. If atheistical notions assail him, some meditation on the great wisdom displayed in creation may be the means for him to discover the subtle snare of a deceitful enemy and to escape it. 3. By the study of nature, seconded by divine grace, the mind is enlarged and prepared to bear a more comprehensive, deeper, and better defined image of the divine perfections."

These three articles and a short one on *mental culture*, in Vol. 5. of the Periodical, were all that had appeared, up to this time, in its columns, on *learning*, *science*, and *mental culture*. The subject was almost entirely new in the Association; no one wrote on it; no one recommended it in public, although many of the older preachers frequently called the attention of their younger brethren to the reading of good books, in order to store their minds with useful knowledge, etc. The fact is, the brethren were afraid to make mention of the subject, partly because they were themselves unlearned men, and partly because they were afraid of giving offence.—Many of the members of the Society had come from denominations, in whose ministers they had clearly seen that higher institutions of learning and an educated ministry without the unction of the Holy Spirit, are useless; and as they now felt far happier, after having been converted to God, under the guidance even of a comparatively *unlearned ministry*, and saw, on the whole, more of the fear of God, more spiritual life and Christianity, than in their former Churches; it is not so very strange that they mistook the advantages of solid learning, in connection with true piety, and were filled with prejudices against it. And as the ranks of the ministry were constantly filled and increased from the laity, it was reasonably to be expected that they brought these prejudices into the ministry. Moreover, a considerable portion of our membership, and even several of our ministers, had come from the Mennonites and Dunkers, whose ministers, as is well known, are unlearned. Under these circumstances, no other feeling on the subject of learning and higher institutions of learning could reasonably be expected; and any movement which had for its design a change for the better, would, as a matter of course, create an excitement and encounter opposition. To this, however, must be added that many of our ministers and lay-members had, by meditation and observation, become satisfied of the advantages of a liberal education long before this, and would have been ready to aid in establishing institutions of learning, if they could have satisfied themselves that the time had come for the Evangelical Association to engage in an enterprise of the kind. But, as even the warmest advocates and strongest supporters of the cause of learning did not believe that this time had already come for the Association, and consequently not without reason doubted the practicability of an enterprise of the kind, the matter was put off to a more favorable time, and this was certainly the wisest course. But at this time it was deemed necessary to make a beginning in the matter, in order to accelerate the arrival of that wished-for time, and to prepare everything for it.—The given extracts from the Periodical were the beginning of these preparatory labors. Afterward more light was thrown on the subject, by freely discussing it, and when it came up before General Conference which was held the next year in the state of Ohio, it met with favor and was strongly supported, as the sequel of this history will show.

This year the following two ministers died: Bro. *Samuel Witt*, of Somerset county, Pa., and Bro. *Simeon Keil*, of Wayne county, Ohio.

S. Witt became a subject of converting grace about 1816, and joined the Society. The Annual Conference of 1818 received him on trial into the itinerancy, and appointed him the colleague of Bro. J. Barber on Somerset circuit. The following year he was stationed on Bedford circuit, and at the next conference he located on account of family affairs. He subsequently served 22 years as a popular and esteemed local preacher. By the Special General Conference, held in Somerset co., Pa., in November 1836, he was ordained deacon, not having had, as it would appear, an opportunity before, as the sessions of the Annual Conference, to which he belonged, always took place at a great distance from his residence. He was consumptive for a number of years, but died at last of bilious fever, on March 17th, 1842, in the 53d year of his age. On his death-bed he was composed and departed in firm hope of eternal life. He left a widow and nine children.

S. Keil died of consumption, April 6th, 1842, aged 22 years, 7 months, and 14 days. About 4 years before his death, he found the Lord and was a consistent member of the Church from that time to his death. In the spring of 1841 he was received by the Ohio Conference on trial into the itinerancy, and appointed colleague of Jacob Fry on Pickaway circuit; but his health soon failing, he had to quit traveling; he grew worse and died before the close of the conference year in the firm hope of a blissful immortality. A. Stroh preached his funeral sermon, to a very large audience.

The increase during this year was 1514, and the whole membership at the close of the year was 10,506, the number of itinerants 104, and that of local preachers 109; divided among the three conferences as follows: East Pennsylvania Conference, 3439 members, 35 itinerants, and 19 local preachers; West Pennsylvania Conference, 3429 members, 30 itinerants, 34 local preachers; Ohio Conference, 3638 members, 39 itinerants, 56 local preachers.

The Year 1842.

East Pennsylvania Conference held its session this year at Allentown, Lehigh county, Pa., beginning March 2nd; West Pennsylvania at New Berlin again, beginning April 6th; and Ohio Conference in Walnut township, Pickaway county, Ohio, beginning May 11. Nine ministers in all left the itinerancy, and 17 were received. The East Pennsylvania Conference formed a new circuit in the state of New York, called *Jefferson circuit*, and established a mission in the city of Rochester, N. Y., and another at Germantown, Pa. West Pennsylvania Conference founded a mission at York, Pa., and a second in the co. of Baltimore, Md., near and around Baltimore. Ohio Conference established two new missions in Illinois: *Rock River* and *Mount Carmel* missions. In the East Pennsylvania Conference the preachers' salary was full again, but the two other conferences fell considerably short.

This year was still more prosperous than the preceding one, and the increase of membership exceeded every former year. Each of the three conferences received considerably more members this year, than in any previous one, and the work extended and increased extraordinarily. Never before nor since have so many and extensive awakenings and conversions taken place, as this year. Not only in some places, but almost everywhere crowds of sinners were converted, and the believers encouraged and advanced. Some of the preachers stated that they had never witnessed the like before. On some of the circuits nearly all the classes received additions, and in many other places new classes were formed. The usual number of 30, 50, 70, or even 100 on a circuit or station, were far exceeded this year in most places. Some circuits reported as many as 150, 200, and even 250 new members. Some of the preachers remarked in their reports, that they could not give a particular report of the work of grace on their fields of labor, as it was general. People of every rank and age, old and young, rich and poor, moral and immoral, became the subjects of converting grace. But not only in our Society, but also in every other denomination insisting on a scriptural conversion, such frequent and great revivals took place; and this happened even in several denominations, where this had never been the case. A. Ettinger, then the presiding elder of Zion (now Baltimore) district, in a short report of his district among other things makes the following remarks:—

"As to the work of God on my district, I would, indeed, send you a glowing report, but for want of time and opportunity, I cannot go into details. May it, therefore, suffice to say, as to the generality of awakenings and conversions, that I have never seen or heard anything similar to it before. Everything appears to be in commotion; wherever you turn your eyes, you see new and powerful revivals. Here in York, at Baltimore, and on the different circuits, scarcely a meeting is held, without more or less mourners coming forward to the altar, many of whom wrestle in prayer till they receive the blessing. Even in Churches, where only a few years ago everything was dark and gloomy, in which the cries of penitent sinners for mercy and the shouts of praise of the new converts, were rejected and despised as *imbecility*, *exaggeration*, and *fanaticism*, you now see scores of persons coming to the "anxious bench," falling on their knees and crying to God for mercy; and where they are not frightened and intimidated by the soul-murdering cries of *order*, *order*,—there—astonishing—even *in the strange land*, the *praise of the Lord* is heard here and there. But, alas! only too soon the harps are again hung on the willows."

In a report from J. C. Reisner and his two colleagues, J. Dereich and P. Schwille, of Lancaster circuit, East Pennsylvania Conference, the following remarks are made:—

"On the whole, we are doing exceedingly well on this circuit. There is no class that has not received additions, and some classes consist of new members altogether. More than 200 persons have found peace with God during this conference year, and over 150 have joined our Church. And had we been able to hold all the general meetings that were desired by the friends, the number would have been much larger.—On Turkey Hill about 70 persons are said to have found peace during two weeks. Yes, the Lord works so powerfully, as has never been witnessed here before. Persons were wrought upon by the grace of God, both in their houses and in the streets; and a certain man is said to have found his Saviour while in a well, 60 feet under the surface of the ground! Hallelujah!"

Reporting from York circuit, West Pennsylvania Conference, the Brethren H. Thomas and J. Etger, among other things, remark as follows:—

"During the last few months more souls have been converted to God than we have ever seen or heard of before in so short a time. The houses are too small, the nights (it was in the midst of winter) too short, and our strength is entirely inadequate to the labors which the mourners require. Some of the friends are exhausted by their incessant labors, while others have laid their secular business almost entirely aside, in order to labor exclusively for the salvation of their fellow-men."

In his report of Cumberland circuit, Brother Boas states:—

"Of a truth the Lord has this year visited old Cumberland circuit with the outpouring of his Spirit. * * * * Parents and their children, young men and young women, rich and poor, have given their hearts to the God of all mercies, choosing rather to suffer affliction with the people of God, than to enjoy the pleasures of sin for a season. * * * More than 200 new converts have joined our Church during this year."

During a meeting in Kutz's Church, three miles east of Carlisle, which lasted 4 weeks, between 50 and 60 persons are said to have been converted, 48 of whom have joined our Church. There was a meeting near Mount Rock that continued 16 days, and resulted in the conversion of 30 persons, 28 of whom united with us. During a seven day meeting, in a school-house in the Pines, near Shippensburg, between 30 and 40 persons found peace with God, and 32 of them united with us. In Fishing Creek Valley, Perry county, and in several other places of that circuit, glorious conversions have also taken place. These are some specimens of the heart-refreshing reports of the brethren during this year.

In East Pennsylvania Conference, most of the other circuits as well as Lancaster circuit just mentioned, were blessed with glorious revivals. On Lebanon circuit, in Fishing Creek Valley, Dauphin county, a considerable awakening took place during this year; also in Millerstown again, Lebanon county, where about sixty are said to have found peace; and in Lebanon, so writes Bro. Jacob Saylor, a large number have been converted to God. On Schuylkill circuit the labors of the Brethren D. Berger and S. Neitz were likewise abundantly blessed. At Schuylkill Haven about sixty persons are said to have been converted during a protracted meeting, at Pine

Grove 30, and at Orwigsburg about 20. On the whole, there were 119 members received during the year on this circuit. On Leikens circuit the Brethren J. Sentzel and G. T. Hains labored, and the work of the Lord extended farther and farther. At Millersburg a glorious revival took place. Bro. H. Bucks reported, that the work progressed finely in Pottsville, and the society there was in a flourishing condition. In Philadelphia Bro. M. F. Maize's labors were also greatly blessed. The new mission in Germantown and neighborhood, where Bro. J. M. Saylor was stationed, succeeded remarkably well, and the society resolved the first year to build a church, which resolution was also carried out the second year. The circuits of Mohawk, Lake, and Buffalo, in the state of New York, numbered many converts, especially the former two.

In the West Pennsylvania Conference the work was, with very few exceptions, a general one. Glorious awakenings took place on Columbia circuit, situated then for the most part in Union county, and embracing what is now Buffalo circuit. In New Columbia between 30 and 40 were converted, and arrangements were then made to build a church. A meeting of nine days was held in the house of J. Rohland, in Buffalo Valley, and nearly 40 persons were converted, 30 of whom joined our Church. The work progressed also in other places of the circuit. The preacher in charge, Bro. G. Shæfer, writes at the close of his report thus: "I can truly say, that this year the Lord has done great things for us, as from 100 to 150 persons have become the happy subjects of redeeming grace. My colleague, Bro. D. Rishel, and myself are still resolved to continue in the work of the Lord." Lycoming circuit, which then included the greater part of what are now the circuits of Clinton and Blockhouse, in charge of the Brethren A. Longsdorf and S. M'Lehn, was in a most flourishing condition, and was blessed during the year with many awakenings and conversions, especially in Nittany Valley. During a protracted meeting there, held in the house of Jacob Niess and John Rissman, about 70 persons are said to have found peace. Also in Sugar Valley and in many other places, large numbers were converted. There were 147 new members received during the year. In Millheim, on Centre circuit, a glorious revival took place at the dedication of the new church. H. Rohland and A. Wolf labored on Union circuit, and their labors were crowned with more than ordinary success; nor was New Berlin an exception to the general rule, about 30 souls were converted to God, and the society was powerfully revived and strengthened.

In the town of York, Pa., where the year before a spacious, convenient, and fine looking church had been built, but alas! not paid for; and where a mission had been established by the previous conference, a considerable awakening took place this and the following year under the charge of G. Brickley. When the mission was being established, there were 12 members there, and after the lapse of two years the society numbered more than 100 members. After this, the mission was changed into a station, and seemed to do tolerably well for some time; but afterward it commenced to go backward, and continued to do so, until finally it failed almost entirely, and had not the conference interfered by appointing a collector and paying their debts, it would, in all probability, have failed altogether, and the church would have been sold. This failure was mainly attributed to the church which had been built contrary to the directions of our Discipline, and without any reasonable prospect of paying for it; and after it had been built, the financial affairs were miserably managed for several years. This was *one* of the great causes why the work there did not prosper better. But even after the church-debt had been canceled, there were still other causes at work in the society, which precluded the possibility of its success. May it fare better for the future!

Baltimore county mission, where L. Eberhart was stationed, did remarkably well the first year, and at its close numbered nearly 100 members. Also at Jarrettville, Md., a glorious work was commenced this year, a considerable society was gathered, and afterward a church built. There was likewise a good beginning made in Whiteground, west of Baltimore, and subsequently a church built there. The missionary had found still more openings near Baltimore; but the following year the mission was changed into a circuit in charge of M. M'Lehn, when it began to stagnate and go backward. Afterward the circuit was dropped altogether, but finally taken up again, and, it is hoped, will prosper hereafter.

The Baltimore society was this and the following year in charge of Bro. C. Hammer, and gained in point of solidity and strength, but not much in numbers.

In Virginia, where the sainted M. Bower labored, several important awakenings took place, one of them in Quaker Hollow, and another in Black Creek Valley. This circuit that had lain fallow for a number of years, now began to recover and bring forth abundant fruit. G. Dellinger reported of Gettysburg circuit, that the Lord had commenced a glorious work near Baalhill; a considerable number were converted, and a class of 27 members formed. Also at Warren the work made glorious progress.

In Ohio Conference the increase of membership was not as large as in either of the other two conferences, yet larger than ever before. Many conversions took place on Wayne circuit, in charge of E. Stœver, especially at a protracted meeting in the house of John Bender, in Wayne county. Brother Stœver writes of it: "This was one of the most blessed meetings that we have attended for a long time. The cries for mercy and the shouts of victory were heard at a great distance. Here 34 new converts joined the Church. We are, however, confidently looking for a still richer harvest, as the prospects on this circuit are very promising." On Canton circuit the work of God prospered greatly, and brought forth much fruit, especially at Greensburg, where another great revival took place. Brother Long, preacher in charge of the circuit, writes in one of his reports thus: "During this meeting from 25 to 30 penitents came to the altar at every invitation, and many of them found peace." He further remarks: "About two miles south of this place, where about eight years ago a small number of our people were ruined by Mormonism, a new class can now be formed again. These unhappy persons lost, through that imposition, not only the correct knowledge of God and his word, which they had acquired, but also their property, and some even their lives; for, after they had come to Nauvoo, their former class-leader, B., was shot by a mob, and, with three others, buried in a well." On this circuit the largest camp-meeting, at least in point of the number of tents, that had at that time ever been heard of in the Evangelical Association, was held during the year, on the land of J. Rau; the number of tents was 56. In a report of his circuit, J. J. Kopp writes of this camp-meeting: "It was blessed with awakenings, conversions, and a general revival of religion, from beginning to end. The exercises were continued without interruption from 8 o'clock of Monday morning till Tuesday morning. During the last night of the meeting between 30 and 40 penitents cried for mercy at the altar, most of whom were also pardoned." Glorious awakenings likewise took place on Lake circuit, in charge of P. Gates; a meeting near Vermillion Furnace was especially richly blessed and resulted in the conversion of a fine number of souls. Another glorious work of grace broke out in the north-eastern corner of Seneca county, Ohio, which resulted in the formation of a fine class there during the year. Bro. Gates writes at the close of one of his reports: "I can say to the praise of God, that, upon the whole, we are doing well on this circuit. There appears to be a great excitement among the people on the subject of religion. Protracted meetings are being held by different denominations, which are protracted not only for weeks, but even for months, and hundreds of souls are said to be converted. I am at times of opinion, that by Miller's prediction of the nearness of the second advent of Christ, about which a great deal ado is made in this part of country, some men are saved through fear." The circuits of Lancaster, Pickaway, Sandusky, Crawford, Mansfield, Bristol, and Columbiana, fared as usual. We have no reports of extraordinary works of grace there during the year.

In the states of Indiana and Illinois, the fields of labor of our brethren extended more and more, although the increase of membership was but small in most places during the year. Mount Carmel mission, however, made an exception; it had been established by the last conference, did admirably well the first year, and at its close numbered nearly 100 members. As had been done on Waterloo mission in Canada, so the brethren did here, i. e., they held a camp-meeting the first year, namely on the land of P. Dundor, who had emigrated to the West as a member of the Society. It consisted of 13 tents and was richly blessed, although the missionary, Bro. C. Augenstein, had no help in the pulpit, but a local preacher and an exhorter. The following year, C. Lintner and A. Nicolai were sent there, and the following year C. Nicolai and G. G. Platz. The mission continued to extend, and in 1845 its western part was converted into a circuit, called *Mount Carmel circuit*, while the eastern part, situated in the state of Indiana, was continued as *Dubois mission*, and also brought forth abundant fruit.

The former Illinois mission was now called *Rock River mission*, in charge of L. Heiss. On Des Plain circuit, traveled by F. Wahl and G. A. Blank, a second richly blessed camp-meeting was held this year on the same spot, where one had been held the year before. It would seem, however, that the circuit did neither increase nor extend much during the year.

From what has been said, it is evident that Ohio Conference had for the last few years extended its borders remarkably, and was in a highly flourishing condition.

The extraordinary revivals of religion and many conversions that took place in the years of 1842 and 1843, in the different Churches of the country, seem to have been, to some extent at least, the effects of extraordinary causes, some of which may have been the following: 1. The hard times, caused by the *complete prostration* of commerce and the great scarcity of money all over the country, in consequence of which thousands became bankrupt, and tens of thousands were thrown out of employment, whereby many were reduced to abject poverty and even to want. 2. The prophecy of the Baptist preacher *Miller*, which was promulgated by himself and his followers with the greatest boldness all over the country, that the *second advent of Christ* would speedily take place. The former of these two causes damped the reigning spirit of worldliness and speculation to a great extent, and thus made room for serious thoughts on the subject of religion with many; the second, by working on the principle of fear, may have induced many to seek the salvation of their souls. But the final consequences of this excitement were of a disastrous nature; *Millerism*, as a matter of course, falling into disrepute and contempt, its adherents were greatly perplexed; some became skeptics and infidels, and vast numbers of those who had been induced, at least in part to reform their lives, by means of this new and greatly exciting doctrine, relapsed into the service of sin and Satan. The general excitement caused by Millerism, was followed by an almost equally general indifference and apathy of most of the Churches, a consequence which, alas! the Evangelical Association also shared, at least in some places.

Our Printing Establishment also was affected by the great financial crisis in the country. The German pocket Bible, the cost of which amounted to about $5000, became ready for delivery at that time; but as many of the subscribers were not prepared to make immediate payment, and as some of the other dues of the Establishment were not paid, no dividend could be made at the close of the year, for the several conferences.—The stewardship of the Establishment also, passed into other hands at the opening of this conference year. Charles Hammer, who had filled that post for three years, resigned his office, and Thomas Buck was elected his successor. Thus Brother Buck entered upon the duties of his office while the Establishment was in rather critical and unpleasant circumstances, which greatly discouraged him. Like all others who never before had the office, so he found the duties of his new post far more onerous and difficult than he had imagined, and soon regretted having accepted it. The prospects of the Establishment appeared to him rather gloomy, and he entertained strong doubts as to its future prosperity. These apprehensions, however, were owing to his want of acquaintance with the true state of things, and the business routine of the Establishment; real causes for them there were none, as the sequel proved.—But Brother Buck's cares and difficulties as General Agent were of but short duration. In May, 1842, he entered upon the duties of his new post, and on the 26th of October following he died. The stewardship was then given to the writer for the second time, which he held, together with the editorship of the Periodical until the session of the next General Conference, in the fall of 1843. The general financial difficulties of the country, and the want of proper arrangements and experience in collecting the moneys due for the Periodical and books, were the real causes of the embarrassment of the Establishment; but they soon changed for the better, and at the close of the following year a dividend of $1200 could be distributed among the several conferences. Touching these difficulties of the Establishment, the last number of Volume VI. of the Periodical contains the following remarks:—

"This has indeed been a year of trial for the Botschafter and our Establishment generally. For we have not only had to struggle against great difficulties, arising out of the financial crisis of the country, that involved us in heavy losses; but death also appeared in our midst, and called one of our number from time into eternity. Yet we do not wish to murmur against Providence, but rather hope that everything will work for our best interests. We have, after all, great reason to thank God, the wise and gracious Ruler of all things, for the prosperity and success, that our Establishment has been permitted to enjoy from its very start, five years ago, to this hour. The business capital has increased tenfold, and more than $3000 have been divided among the several conferences."

This year the Association again lost four of its ministers by death, all of whom had been useful men, some eminently so. The deceased were: *Thomas Buck*, *Adam Stroh*, *John Shæfer*, and *Abraham Frey*. All of these brethren were, with the sole exception of Brother Buck, in the prime of life, and might have served the Church many more years. But thus far only comparatively few of our itinerants have attained to old age—most of them who have died, departed as young men and in the prime of life, yea, many of them in the very first years of their itinerancy. Others who indeed lived longer, generally impaired their health for life in the same period of their ministerial calling. The causes of these disastrous consequences were various: irregularity with regard to diet and lodging; the frequent change of climate; exposure to every kind of weather; and the fatigues of difficult travels and almost daily preaching, to which our itinerants were then more subjected than at present. For a man that is not accustomed to a life of such hardships, and in the absence of necessary instruction and care, to get along for any length of time without ruining his health or even losing his life, before his constitution becomes hardened, is almost a miracle. In this way the itinerancy of the Society formerly lost many of its most promising men in their prime of life, and still meets with more or less similar losses. Some of the enumerated evils were, indeed, and still are unavoidable; but, at the same time, it can not be denied that by proper attention and more care, these injurious consequences might have been avoided, at least to a great extent. Preachers ought not to overdo themselves by preaching or in any other way, but ought to use the utmost care, when they have to change diet and lodging so frequently, and to avoid, as much as possible, exposing themselves in a state of perspiration, to the cold or damp night air, etc. May at least some be benefited by these digressive remarks.

Of the exact time and circumstances of Brother Buck's conversion and calling to the ministry, the writer knows nothing, although he was long and intimately acquainted with him, from 1828 to his death in 1842. Brother Buck was one of the most influential men of the Association of his time, and ranked as high as G. Miller, J. Dreisbach, and H. Niebel of former days, and J. Seybert, J. Long and others of later days. In penetration, resolution, and energy, he was inferior to none of them; superior, perhaps, to most of them. He was of a highly choleric temper, stern gravity, had an uncommonly sharp sparkling eye, a penetrating look, and was rather reserved in ordinary conversation, and his whole appearance commanded reverence and respect; bashful and timid persons were rather afraid of him, especially when he found it necessary to examine or censure them. At times he was very reserved, then again very social and affable, and in his conversation with those who enjoyed his confidence, very frank. But woe to those in whom he placed no confidence; in that case his remarks were often too harsh and even insulting. But whenever he learned that his judgment was wrong, or that he had treated any one with too great severity, he hastened to heal the wound in some way or other, or to render satisfaction. What the writer says on these and the following points, he does so from his *personal knowledge* and from what he has often *seen* and *heard.* His sermons were generally pointed, powerful and overwhelming, especially in his younger years. His favorite subjects were: the word and the commandments of God, faith, freedom from sin, and perfect holiness of heart and life. His discourses were for the most part, and often almost altogether, argumentative; and at times he became highly excited and severe. He generally drew the attention of his hearers, and but rarely failed to make a deep impression on them. Gainsayers were often filled with anger while he preached, and left abruptly, as many of old did, when our Saviour preached; others again were powerfully shaken and humbled. He was fitted in an eminent degree to preach to professors of religion. Watching and praying, growing in grace, undefiled brotherly love, the duties in the family, plain dress and a simple mode of living, liberality, and, above all, *holiness* or *Christian perfection,* were generally the subjects of these discourses. But he belonged not to the number of those who believe that the Christian is *fully sanctified* simultaneously with being justified, but he preached the necessity of a *further cleansing* from indwelling sin, without which no one can see the Lord. For the confirmation of what we have just said of his views on this most important subject, we here quote a paragraph from one of his reports of his district, which he wrote about 11 months prior to his death; it is as follows:—

"Pleasing as it is to see, that sinners are converted and extend the hand of fellowship to the children of God, in order to travel with them to the heavenly Canaan; so lamentable it is, that it is so rare a thing for Christians to seek and obtain the sanctification of their souls. On reading the lives of preachers of former days, especially those of J. Nelson and B. Abbot, one is almost ashamed and led to believe, that in our days neither preachers nor members follow holiness, as they ought to do."

Whoever is but partially acquainted with the literature of the Methodists, knows that Nelson and Abbot fully agreed with Wesley and the first Methodist peachers generally, on the doctrine concerning holiness. The same view was held by Bro. Buck, and, in fact, by all the preachers of the Evangelical Association, as far as the writer's information goes.

In enforcing the Discipline, Brother Buck was very exact, and, in the opinion of some, too severe. He but seldom showed favor to transgressors, especially if they were preachers; and as his influence in the conference was great, he was much feared by those who sometimes took wrong steps, or were carried away by levity. He was possessed of an extensive knowledge of human nature, yet sometimes mistook persons, at first acquaintance with them, and thus was in danger of passing an unfavorable judgment—he scarcely ever overrated persons. Unsteady, noisy persons, conducting themselves improperly during divine service, were sometimes sharply reproved by him in public; but lively, powerful services, conducted in the spirit, he advocated to the utmost of his power. With regard to cleanliness in every point of view, he had but few equals. His person, his dress, everything on and around him, had to be clean. But he preached cleanliness not only by his example, but often inculcated it in private, and even in public, as necessary to godliness. Cleanliness, order, and punctuality, were three prominent traits of his character, which he also recommended to the preachers under him, and to all with whom he came in contact. Wherever he lodged, he left everything in the very best order, so as to save the family the trouble to clean or sweep after he had gone. In short, he was courteous, and knew how to conduct himself in any place. In his religious private duties, such as praying, reading, studying, fasting, etc., he was very exact and scrupulous; as long as his health and strength permitted him to do so, he fasted regularly.

From his time of serving as presiding elder to the election of a bishop, he was elected chairman of his Annual Conference nearly every time, and he was also eminently fitted for that office. His love of order, vigilant eye, strong judgment, his respect, commanding appearance and conduct, and his peculiar business tact, entitled him to that dignity before many others. His decisions touching questions of discipline were almost always acquiesced in. In conducting camp and other large meetings, he had but few equals.

Brother Buck was received into the itinerancy on trial by the Annual Conference of 1823, convened at Strasburg, York county, Pa., and appointed the colleague of John Dehoff on Somerset circuit. He was at that time a widower, and already over 30 years of age. At first he is said to have been but a weak preacher, but improved rapidly. In 1824 he and C Kring became the colleagues of P. Wagner on the circuits of Union and Centre. In 1825 he was ordained deacon, and appointed preacher in charge of Lancaster circuit, Pa.; in 1826 he traveled on Schuylkill, and 1827 on York circuit. In 1828 he was elected presiding elder, and stationed on Salem district, consisting of the circuits of Union, Centre, Somerset, and Lake, the latter in the state of New York. This year the writer became acquainted with him, while traveling with Bro. Barber on Centre circuit. The next year he was transferred to Canaan district, consisting of the circuits of Schuylkill, Lebanon, Lancaster, York, Franklin, and Berkley, the latter in Virginia, and served two years there; in 1831 he was transferred to Zion district, consisting of the circuits of York, Franklin, Berkley, and Somerset; and after two years, he was re-transferred to Canaan district, but served there only one year; for he married again during this year, and located at the next session of conference, on account of family circumstances, after having served the Church five years as a circuit preacher and six as presiding elder.—In 1837, three years after his location, he re-entered the itinerancy and was stationed on Schuylkill circuit. The year following he was re-elected presiding elder, and stationed on Canaan district, where he served three years up to the spring of 1842. Thus his itinerancy lasted 15 years. The General Conference of 1839, in Centre county, Pa., elected him its chairman, and in 1842, when he could not take another appointment on account of bodily infirmities, his conference retained him in the itinerancy, and gave him permission to travel and preach according to his convenience. Soon after he attended the session of West Pennsylvania Conference, beginning April 6th at New Berlin, and was, as already stated, elected General Agent of the Printing Establishment. In May following he removed with his family from Millersburg, Dauphin county, Pa., to New Berlin, and entered upon the duties of his office in high spirits; but finding more trouble and greater difficulties in the discharge of his new duties than he had imagined, his health which had been poor before, declined fast. He, however, did not complain much, but endeavored to fill his post as well as he possibly could, till on the 9th of Oct. following he was seized by a severe cardialgy, which caused an inflammation of the bowels, and after severe suffering, terminated his earthly career, October 26th, between 3 and 4 o'clock, A. M. At that time the writer was traveling in the West, but learned after his return that Brother Buck had spoken but little during his sickness, had said nothing about his spiritual condition—probably because no one had asked him about it —and he died, as it were, unexpectedly. He was, as above stated, rather taciturn, especially so when he was unwell, or where he was not intimately acquainted. This and his severe sufferings, as well as his extreme weakness and the heavy doses of stupefying medicines, that are said to have been administered to him, were doubtless the causes why he did not speak more during his sickness of his faith and trust in God; yet his tranquillity of mind, his entire freedom from any fear of death, and his whole conduct, proved abundantly that all was right with him. Thus died, in the firm hope of eternal life, and in the 53rd year of his life, one of the most efficient, and, in some respects, most useful preachers of the Association, whose memory is still cherished by many of his friends and acquaintances, and ought never to be forgotten.—The day following his death, at 2 o'clock, P. M., his remains were buried in the grave-yard of the Evangelical Association at New Berlin, Pa., and Brother Barber preached his funeral sermon from Luke 2, 29. 30.: "Lord, now lettest thou thy servant depart in peace," etc. Brother Buck left a widow and 4 infant children by his second, and three grown ones by his first wife.

A. Stroh was a vigorous and promising young preacher, talented, industrious, active, and very successful in his ministerial labors, but died at the early age of 25 years, 7 months, and 17 days! About 8½ years before his death, he was converted, when Brother Buck traveled Wooster circuit in Ohio Conference. About two years after he felt himself called to the Gospel ministry, but waited almost a whole year before he obeyed this call. After he had traveled with Bro. D. N. Long about five months on Bristol circuit, Ohio, he attended the conference for the first time, was received on trial, and stationed with G. Dressel on Canton circuit. In 1840, while yet a probationer, he was appointed preacher in charge of Lake circuit, Ohio, with John Hall for his colleague. This year he was led by an inward feeling to seek entrance in the city of Cleveland, for preaching the Gospel there; he made the attempt, and succeeded in a rather extraordinary manner, as already stated. In 1841 he was ordained deacon, and appointed preacher in charge of Des Plain circuit, in Illinois, with Christian Lintner for his colleague; his labors there met the approbation of the people, and were crowned with success. Referring to his farewell sermon there, before a very large and solemn audience, in the spring of 1842, Bro. J. J. Esher writes thus, among other things: "Brother A. Stroh's valedictory discourse, which he delivered here, from Acts 20, 32: '*And now, brethren, I commend you to God,*' etc., will never be forgotten of most of them who heard it. As if both the preacher and his audience had been aware, that this young and excellent watchman in Israel would so speedily be called from the walls of Zion, a preternatural, heavenly solemnity pervaded the whole assembly." Ohio Conference, held in May, 1842, appointed him preacher in charge of White Water mission in the state of Indiana, with F. R. Tobias for his colleague. But here his health failed. His biographer, N. Gehr, writes: "He had scarcely labored four months on his new field of labor, and become acquainted with his people, when he was seized by a violent fever, which terminated his ministerial career and laid the foundation of a fatal disease. When the fever had apparently left him, the malady took another turn, passing into consumption, as his physician said. In this state of health he returned with his wife to his and her parents, and with the latter spent the greatest part of the remainder of his life. I visited him, and conversed with him. He expected to recover, and others who saw him, entertained the same opinion. But what are our earthly hopes! How short, how uncertain is our life! The work of the fell destroyer progressed rapidly, his vital spirits fled, and soon—almost unexpectedly, his immortal spirit left its tenement of clay."

During his disease he looked forward, with composure and calmness, to the day of his departure, and left this world in the enjoyment of *that* hope which maketh not ashamed. He died April 2d, 1843, in Green township, Summit county, Ohio, leaving his parents, brothers and sisters, and an afflicted widow with whom he had lived but 10 months in the bonds of matrimony. Thus a young and useful laborer in the vineyard of the Lord finished his earthly career, whose services were still so much needed by the Church. Why did he die so soon? This question eternity will probably answer. His remains were buried in the grave-yard of the Evangelical Association near Greensburg, and Bro. E. Stœver preached his funeral sermon from 2. Tim. 4: 7, 8.

J. Shæfer died March 8th, 1843, at Erie, Erie township, Pa., in the 27th year of his age. The time of his conversion is not known to the writer; but the minutes of Ohio Conference show that he was received by that body in 1840 into the itinerancy on trial, and appointed the colleague of Bro. Jacob Frey on Bristol circuit. The following year he traveled with P. Gates on Erie circuit. By the conference of 1842 he was ordained deacon, and located on account of bodily infirmities. He consequently served but two years as an itinerant, and suffered much during the greater part of this period, on account of his shattered health. He impaired his health the very first winter of his ministerial career, by preaching while he had a severe cold; in this way, as is supposed, he became consumptive, of which disease he died. We know nothing of his talents as a preacher, except that he is said to have been useful in the Lord's vineyard. On his death-bed he was composed and full of hope of eternal life. Bro. A. Niebel preached his funeral sermon, from Phil. 1, 21: "*For to me to live is Christ, and to die is gain.*"

A. Frey, a resident of Richland county, Ohio, died of fever, January 29, 1843, in the 33d year of his age. He was brought up in Union county, Pa., and was converted there about 1830. In 1832 he was received by the Eastern Conference into the itinerancy on trial, and appointed the colleague of E. Stœver on Indiana circuit; the next year he became the colleague of D. Brickley on Somerset circuit; the third year that of C. Hesser on Cumberland circuit; and the fourth year he traveled with J. Lutz and G. Seger again on Somerset circuit. At the close of the third year he was ordained deacon. Subsequently he traveled yet two years in the Western Conference, and served the remainder of his life in the capacity of a local preacher. He was not a very gifted orator, yet labored with success. On his death-bed he expressed the full assurance of being a child of God, and died in this happy frame of mind, leaving a widow and two children.

The increase during this year was 2519, and at the close of the year the whole membership amounted to 13,025. The increase within the East Pennsylvania Conference was 933, within the West Pennsylvania 1007, and within the Ohio Conference 579. The number of the newly received members, however, was much larger; for the East Pennsylvania Conference had received 1361, the West Pennsylvania 1384, and that of Ohio 850 members, altogether 3595.

TENTH SECTION.

FROM THE EIGHTH GENERAL CONFERENCE OF 1843, TO THE CLOSE OF THE YEAR 1845.

The Year 1843.

Eighth General Conference.

We open this section, as we did the last, with the General Conference and its proceedings, although it held its session after the Annual Conferences.

This was the first General Conference consisting of regularly elected delegates; it was also the best attended one that has ever been held in the Evangelical Association, and transacted the largest amount of business. It convened at Greensburg, Summit county, Ohio, and held its session in our first church there, from October 23d to November 2d late in the evening—11 days. The number of delegates was 32:—

East Pennsylvania Conference.

John P. Leib,	Charles Hesser,*
Wm. Mentz,	Francis Hoffman,
John C. Reisner,	Michæl F. Maize,
Joseph M. Saylor,	Henry Bucks,
Michæl Lehn,	Henry Fisher.

West Pennsylvania Conference.

Wm. W. Orwig,	Charles Hammer,
Philip Wagner,	George Brickley,
Adam Ettinger,	Jacob Boas,
Daniel Kehr,	Henry Rohland.

Ohio Conference.

John Dreisbach,	Jacob Frey,
Joseph Long,	Adam Kleinfelter,
Samuel Baumgartner,*	Elias Stœver,
John J. Kopp,	Henry Longbrecht,
Henry Niebel,*	Lewis Einsel,
John G. Zinser,	Aaron Yambert,
Absalom B. Shæfer,	George Mattinger.

The delegates marked with a star (*) were not present, but were represented by their alternates. Bishop Seybert was present, and after conference had been opened by reading a portion of the word of God, singing, and prayer, he appointed A. B. Shæfer secretary, who chose H. Fisher and C. Hammer as assistants. After conference had been regularly organized, and the question disposed of, whether there was any charge against any of the delegates, it was unanimously "Resolved, That out of respect for Brother *Charles Hesser*, who, on his way to conference has died by an accident, no business be transacted on the following Wednesday afternoon, and that the bishop shall then preach the funeral sermon of the deceased." This resolution was carried out, and great solemnity and deep feeling characterized the exercises.—The news of Brother Hesser's death on the day before the opening of conference, had filled the delegates with grief and tears, especially those who had been intimately acquainted with him, and hence felt the loss the more deeply.

After these exercises and other various preliminaries, including the adoption of a routine of business, conference was ready to commence its regular, various, and, to some extent, very difficult business.

The amendments of Discipline as recommended by the Annual Conferences, were generally adopted, viz.: An amendment of the section defining the power of General Conference, of the rules for the admission of preachers, additions to the duties of class-leaders and local preachers, etc. In the chapter of the temporal economy many alterations were made, to wit:

The salary of a single preacher was raised from $60 to $100, and that of a married one from $105 to $200, with $25 for every child under 14 years, besides reasonable traveling expenses: the salary of the officers of the Printing Establishment was increased by $50 each; better arrangements were made for the support of superannuated poor itinerants and their families, and many new rules were introduced into the Printing Office. The Annual Conferences, it was resolved, shall for the future be independent of each other, with regard to the support of the preachers. Thus far all the preachers of the different conferences had received the same salary; as in former years the conference that had collected the largest contributions, had to assist those which had fallen short; and in the years immediately preceding this conference, these short coming conferences had drawn the more from the "Chartered Fund" and the avails of the Book Establishment. But after this, each conference had, in this respect, to take care of itself.—These were important and necessary changes, which contributed largely toward the improvement of the itinerancy. Although these increased allowances to the preachers did not secure to them the full amount allowed, yet it was a change for the better, and their salary has since increased, almost annually.

Another very important action of this body was its resolution that the Association shall hereafter pay more attention to the English portion of our population, endeavoring to preach the Gospel unto them, and to labor for their spiritual interests; as well as that it shall be lawful to form English conferences, and to publish an English paper as soon as practicable. It was also resolved to enlarge our English hymn-book. This was very encouraging to the English portion of our preachers and members, and contributed, as a matter of course, toward the more rapid increase of the same. It was especially the West Pennsylvania Conference, which progressed more rapidly from that time, and in a few years it exceeded all other conferences in membership. But it was by no means the intention of General Conference, that the German population should be neglected; it was, on the contrary, its firm conviction, that the Evangelical Association was called of God to take care of the Germans of this country, who are so grossly neglected by so many Churches of this country.

This conference ventured also, to express its views on the literary qualifications of the clergy, to recommend learning highly to all ministers and candidates for the ministry within its connection, and to lay down a plan of studies for our young preachers. This was a strong move in a cause that had been neglected too long—not, indeed, from indifference, much less from contempt, but rather from the conviction that it was still too early for the Evangelical Association, to establish higher institutions of learning, numbering as yet but *thirteen thousand members*, and from an apprehension to give offence to some of our members and preachers, who, for reasons already given, underrated literary qualifications in the ministry too much. The latter looked upon the establishment of higher schools of learning as a dangerous innovation, full of mischief; yet their motives were, probably, as pure as those of the others who wished that the time might soon arrive to establish such institutions. Referring to this subject, the Periodical, soon after the adjournment of conference, contained the following remarks: "Not one word was said about the establishment of a higher school of learning or college, which some seem to apprehend so very much. We doubt, whether a single member of General Conference expected that something would be done by that body in this matter, as every one could easily satisfy himself that the proper time for us has not yet come." Four years after there was, indeed, an attempt made, but failed, as was to be expected. Yet this step was by no means in vain, as the subject was thereby kept before the people and discussed. The manifesto of General Conference on this subject was as follows:—

"As the Evangelical Association is charged by many, though unjustly, with looking upon learning, or rather a classical education of the ministry, as altogether superfluous and useless, yea even as dangerous and injurious, and despising, for this reason, all higher institutions of learning; this body feels itself called upon and under obligation, to declare and express its views on this subject in public, and to repel thereby this false charge.

It is indeed true, that this conference believes and teaches, that *all* human wisdom, learning, and knowledge, without a divine call and the unction of the Spirit, qualify no man for the Gospel ministry; and that a man, called of God to this office, and filled with the Holy Ghost and with power from on high, without *great* human learning, or as a comparatively illiterate man, can be a preacher of the Gospel and accomplish much good, if he fears God and is conscientious in the discharge of his duties. But notwithstanding this, the conference acknowledges and maintains, that learning in the common acceptation of the term, or a classical education, is in many respects of great use to a man who is called of God to the Gospel ministry, and endowed with the Holy Ghost, and enhances his usefulness; or in other words, that he who has the divine unction, and great learning, can, in many instances, and even generally, accomplish far more in the vineyard of the Lord, and toward the conversion of the world and the spread of the Redeemer's kingdom, than the unlearned man, though he may possess the same measure of divine unction and grace.

Entertaining these views of the advantages of learning in a minister of the Gospel, this conference recommends to all its candidates for the ministry, and to all its ministers generally, to take proper measures to store their minds with as large an amount of useful information, as they possibly can, or to endeavor to become *learned* and *literary men*, who have also the unction of the Holy Ghost.

John Seybert, } Bishops.
Joseph Long, }
Absalom B. Shæfer, Secretary."

Some time before the meeting of this General Conference, an editorial appeared in the Periodical, headed: "Our General Conference," which contained, among other things, some remarks on the subject in question; they are here inserted to throw light on the subject, and are as follows:—

"We also indulge in the hope, that General Conference will take measures to raise the literary standard of our ministers; for it cannot be denied that this is as yet very low. Although there is now, in this respect, a better spirit at work among us, than was formerly the case; yet too many of us do not yet take that interest in their mental culture, which the subject requires, while others do not yet know the proper use of learning and a thorough mental training.

We, indeed, do not mean to say that a high school or college is now to be established forthwith by us—for this step we are not yet prepared; but measures ought to be taken to furnish our young ministers, and all those who feel themselves called to the Gospel ministry, with the necessary books, and to give them instructions how to use them for private study to the best advantage.—Many buy books that are of no use to them; and then having no system in their studies, much of their time also is misspent. But, if they were supplied with the right kind of books, and if a proper plan of study were laid down for them, they would acquire more useful information and make better progress in a few years, than they do in their present way, and in a comparatively small number of years we might have men in our midst, who would favorably compare with regular graduates. For experience has taught, that self-made men are often the most thorough scholars.

But, although we think highly of private study and self-made men, yet we do not wish to be understood, as if we regarded higher institutions of learning as superfluous and useless—far from it. Such institutions, provided they are conducted by pious men, are unquestionably a great blessing to the Church and the world; for, if there were no learned, pious men, who were educated in such institutions, our holy religion would not have been defended so triumphantly and spread so victoriously, since the extraordinary gifts of the Spirit have been withdrawn from the Church.

God also made use of learned men, in order to bring about the glorious reformation of the sixteenth century, and still makes use of such men for the defense and spread of his kingdom, and the overthrow of idolatry, superstition, and infidelity; although he can also, for the same purposes, make use of less informed or even comparatively unlearned men; yet it admits of no doubt, that the pious and educated minister of the Gospel has, in many respects, great advantages over his less informed brother, and can accomplish far more good.—It is, therefore, a matter of course, that we are in favor of higher institutions of learning, such as are conducted and managed by pious men. Their manifold abuse, both in this and the old country, is by no means a proof that they are useless and injurious; no more so than the abuse of religion proves that it is useless and injurious. Every reasonable man admits, that the abuse of a thing is no proof against its proper use. All arguments for the uselessness and injuriousness of such institutions and of learning in general, are, therefore, without the least force or foundation."

All these articles and remarks on this subject, brought and kept it before the Church, elicited discussion both in public and in private—and the more it was discussed, the more favor it found.

The subject of the History of our Church that had been acted upon by the last General Conference, but had scarcely begun to bud during the four intervening years, was resumed by this conference, and met with somewhat better success. Bro. John Dreisbach was now appointed to write said history, to be assisted by the two bishops and all the presiding elders of the Church, by collecting and forwarding to him all materials within their reach. Brother Dreisbach went to work, and the result of his labors was 15 sheets (of common foolscap paper) of written matter, which no other man in the whole Church could have accomplished as well, he being better informed about the origin and first twenty years of the Association, than any other man living. These writings were laid by in the Printing Establishment, and have now been made use of in compiling the first part of this history.

Another measure of General Conference, was a resolution ordering the compiling and publishing of a catechism, containing the fundamental doctrines of Christianity, as they are taught in the confession of faith of the Association, for the instruction of the young. This work was assigned to the compiler of this history, but was not completed till 1846, and shortly afterward published. The appearance of this catechism filled some of our sister Churches with no little astonishment, as they had erroneously put the Evangelical Association on an equal footing with some other denominations, who regard all catechisms and catechetical instruction as remnants of Babel, and, consequently, as dangerous and injurious.—The origin of this wrong opinion has already been accounted for in a former part of this history.—The catechism was afterward published in English, but alas! chatechetical instruction has, hitherto, not been generally introduced into the connection. Many of our members are still prejudiced against it, on account of its abuse in some other Churches; and too many of our preachers are too careless and negligent in recommending and introducing it. Others, having witnessed its salutary effects in the thorough conversion of many of their catechumens, while they were under instruction, are so much in favor of it, that they regard its neglect as a remissness, that ought not to be overlooked any longer.

Conference also ordered a new edition of G. Miller's "*Practical Christianity*" (German) to be prepared. As the original was greatly defective in style and arrangement, the writer of these pages was instructed to revise and improve it. This little work had been highly esteemed in our Society, and deserves to be so still. It was written by G. Miller, one of our first ministers, in 1811, but did not appear in print till 1814. It is the only devotional book hitherto written by a minister of our Church; it discusses practical Christianity in a very satisfactory manner, and ought, therefore, to be found in the library of every family of our connection.

Furthermore, Conference ordered that our two German hymn-books be condensed into one, to be called "*Evangelisches Gesangbuch*"—(Evangelical Hymn Book), which was to be stereotyped with the small types of our pocket Bible; but, *fortunately*, this resolution was not carried out. To condense the two books into one, might perhaps not have been out of place; but to stereotype it in the manner indicated, would, at that time, have been a great error. The new officers of the Printing Establishment, A. Ettinger and J. C. Reisner, were appointed a committee to compile the new book from the two old ones: the "*Saitenspiel*" and the "*Viole,*" and to prepare it for the press. But as the committee had not carried out its instructions at the meeting of the next General Conference, other arrangements were made, and the two books ordered to be published in their present form. And as it is always easier to find fault than to make better, there were not those wanting who were displeased with the new editions, as soon as they left the press; but, on the whole, they were favorably received. The books had underwent a thorough change; many stanzas and parts of hymns, and even whole hymns that were particularly esteemed by some, were left out; and as the revising committee was not able to assign the reason of every change, omission, and addition, and was, moreover, not infallible, nothing else could be expected than that some would find fault with the books. They have, however, ever since sold so readily, that the demands for them could sometimes not be met.

The writer of this history had been the Editor of the Periodical since the erection of the Printing Establishment, and also the General Agent since the death of Brother Buck. But this conference elected A. Ettinger as Editor, and J. C. Reisner as General Agent, and gave them Wm. Bersch for an assistant. This brother having been employed for a number of years in the Establishment, his services had become almost indispensably necessary, and have been retained to this day. His connection with the Establishment is regarded by himself as providential; for, soon after his conversion to God in the city of Philadelphia, he relinquished his business there, and removed, at the suggestion of Brother Hesser, who was then stationed at Philadelphia, to New Berlin, with the expectation of finding employment in our Printing Establishment, which had just been started. Upon his arrival at New Berlin, the writer received him, assigned him some rooms in the building of the Establishment for his dwelling, employed him at his own expense, in packing the Periodical, reading proof, etc., and gave him Fletcher's Appeal to translate into German. In this way he became acquainted with the business, and was, after a few years, employed altogether in the Establishment. By this time he has become thoroughly acquainted with, and practiced in all the branches of the business, so that his services can scarcely be dispensed with, especially at the frequent change of the officers of the Establishment. Ettinger and Reisner held their offices only four years, and the next General Conference elected new officers.

The following report of the value of the Establishment, including the capital, was laid before General Conference :—

"The building, materials, Bible-plates, etc.	\$7000,00
Printed books, bound and unbound, paper, etc.	7800,00
Money due for Bibles	3469,07¼
Accounts of the Establishment against preachers	6391,48½
Money due for the German Periodical	3072,59
	\$27,733,14¾"

From this report it appears that the Establishment had succeeded well, and its prospects were bright at that time. Six years before, it was founded with a few thousand dollars that had been collected, and now its value amounted to nearly \$28,000, exclusive of the \$3000 which had been distributed among the several conferences.

The territory of the Association having become too extensive for *one* bishop to travel over, this conference resolved to elect two bishops, and, accordingly, John Seybert was reelected, and Joseph Long, for the first time, elevated to this highest office in the Church. The episcopal dignity in the Ev. Association, however, is scarcely enviable, and indeed is only nominal. The influence of a bishop of this communion depends, therefore, not on the office itself, but on the incumbent's qualifications for the office, the interest he takes in all institutions and enterprises of the Church, combined with his fidelity and zeal in the discharge of his duties. If he commands, in all these things, the general respect of the ministers and members, the way is open for him to exert not only a very extensive, but also a very salutary influence on the whole connection. But if he fails in one or the other of these items, his influence is proportionably less and his usefulness diminished. His salary is that of an itinerant—*one hundred dollars*, if unmarried! Of his power in the Society no one need be afraid, as it is in many respects far more limited than that of several other officers of the Church. The same is the case with his privileges. At the conferences he has to act as chairman, without expressing or even intimating his views on any subject, unless he is requested to do so. Neither has he a right to vote, except when there is a tie. Whoever, therefore, seeks the office of a bishop in the Evangelical Association, desires indeed "*a good*," but by no means *desirable* "work." The two brethren in question have been re-elected to this office by every succeeding General Conference.

Ohio Conference, whose territory had become very extensive, was divided, and that part of it which lay in the states of Indiana and Illinois, was formed into a new conference, called *Illinois Conference*. This was now the fourth Annual Conference, and since then more have been formed. By this division of Ohio Conference, it became a great deal easier for the ministers to attend its sessions, and the work in the far West received a powerful impulse, as now two presiding elders devoted their whole time to it, and the preachers in general became much sooner acquainted with all parts of the work.—The time also for the sessions of the Annual Conferences and the *figurative names* of several of the presiding elder districts were changed. The names: *Canaan, Zion, Salem, Carmel*, and *Tabor*, were changed into: *Harrisburg, Baltimore, Susquehanna, Alleghany*, and *Columbiana*. A delegation of the Methodist Episcopal Church, that had been appointed by the General Conference of that denomination in 1840, waited on this conference and made proposals tending to the establishment of relations of closer friendship between these two bodies, so that they might be enabled to lend each other mutual aid, fight with better success against the enemies of the Cross, and labor for the temporal and spiritual welfare of the neglected Germans of this country. Said delegation consisted of the Revd. Brethren *J. F. Wright*, *N. Callender*, and *Wm. Nast;* but only the last two attended our conference, delivered addresses on the subject of their mission, and also presented a statement of their object in writing, praying, that a reply to it in writing might be given them. We here give an extract from their written address, as it was published in the "Christliche Apologete."

"*To the Bishop and the General Conference of the Evangelical Association.*

Dear Brethren:—From the official extract from the protocol of the General Conference of the M. E. Church, held in 1840, and from a certificate drawn up by one of its secretaries, which two documents we hereby present to you, you will see that we are the delegates appointed by the proper authorities, to your General Conference.

It is our first duty to present to your body the Christian salutation and sincere friendship of our General Conference, which represents, as you know, all the preachers and members of the M. E. Church; and we would entreat you to take our expressed assurance of high regard and esteem not as a mere compliment, but as the language of the heart, of a heart feeling the sacred influences of true friendship and religion.

You will also permit us to express the hope, that this will be only the beginning of a lasting friendly relation between the two bodies, whereby the best interests of both may be promoted, and other important advantages secured. We are fully persuaded, that a firmly established friendship between the Evangelical Association and the M. E. Church will be attended with the blessed effects of opposing the common enemies of true Christianity more effectually, and of promoting the interests of a pure and undefiled worship with greater success.

We agree in doctrine, and our disciplines, constitutions, and customs, resemble each other so much, that the Evangelical Association was, in many places, called by the people, for a long time, the "German Methodists." Our faith and our institutions have, for this reason, the same enemies. We likewise firmly believe, that we have the same ends in view, viz., the glory of God and the salvation of immortal souls. We, therefore, extend to you the right hand of fellowship, and beg of you to unite your strength with ours in some way or other, that we may discuss and agree upon, in order that the great cause of our Redeemer may be promoted.

However desirable it might be, that all Germans, who are *Methodists* in doctrine, experience, discipline, and customs, should enter into the same organization and bear the same banner; there are, at present, undoubtedly, too many impediments in our way to become *one in name;* but we see no solid reason, why we should not be *one* in truth and in deed, so that we may strengthen each other's hands, to wit:—

1. By a publicly recognized relation of friendship, similar to that which has existed in some places between the Lutherans and Reformed, and has led to the use of a common Hymn Book. Such an understanding would be attended with blessed effects, and especially prevent our interfering with each other in our fields of labor.

2. By acting in concert in publishing the standard works of Methodist theology, as for instance the sermons of Wesley, a systematic statement of our articles of faith, and a commentary on the Bible. We doubt not that arrangements could be made, by which we might lend each other effectual aid in publishing books, without any disadvantage arising therefrom to either party. Providence has led several individuals into our ranks, whose services in the performance of the necessary literary works would be important; yet as the number of our German members is too small, and hence our support too limited, we would not be prepared as yet to venture upon the publication of any of the named larger works.

For the last eight years the M. E. Church has directed its attention with tender concern and increasing interest to the German immigrants, who are swelling the population of our country. This field is already white to harvest, and an important object of our mission is, to seek the assistance of your Revd. body, or to ask leave to offer you our assistance, in cultivating this important missionary field. Our Church has entered upon that field, in obedience, as we believe, to a direct call of God who, by the most remarkable openings of his Providence, has led us from step to step. and, as it were, compelled us by the force of circumstances. The eminent success which has crowned our labors, fully justifies the belief that the hand of God is in the work, and his blessing resting upon us.

Since the fall of 1838, the number of our German members has risen from 24 to 2000, and there are now 24 German itinerants laboring in our midst. We have already built 14 (German) churches. Multitudes of precious souls meet there from time to time, worshiping God according to our customs, and offering up their prayers and thanksgiving in the German language. Many of them were once Papists, and paid Roman priests for the forgiveness of their sins; "but having been justified by faith, they now have peace with God, through our Lord Jesus Christ, and rejoice in hope of the glory of God." All this has been accomplished in the short period of eight years. "This is the Lord's doing, and it is marvelous in our eyes."

We now have, dear Brethren, discharged our solemn duty, as delegates of the General Conference of the M. E. Church, by laying before you the great enterprise, upon which we have entered. We now leave our proposals with you, hoping that you will take them into careful consideration; and whatever may be the result of your deliberations on them, we would respectfully ask you to return us an answer in writing, in order to lay it before our next General Conference, which will meet in the city of New York, May 1, 1844.

Our prayer is, that the Great Head of the Church may be with your General Conference, and his Spirit guide you in all your deliberations, so that all your resolutions may meet his approbation, and be crowned with his blessing. May you and all members of your Church be led in safety through the toils and sufferings of this life, and finally be received into heaven with all believers of every name and description, to inherit eternal life through Jesus Christ! Amen.

We remain, in the bonds of love and with great respect,

Dear Brethren,

Yours in Christ,

J. F. Wright,
N. Callender,
Wm. Nast."

To this address, our General Conference returned the following reply, as drawn up by a committee for that purpose.

"*To the Delegates of the General Conference of the M. E. Church.*

Dear Brethren:—In compliance with the request expressed in your written address, we return you the following reply:—

We feel ourselves under obligations to you for your friendly salutation and expression of fraternal regard for us, and do sincerely wish that you may not be disappointed in your expectations that this will be but the beginning of a lasting friendly relation between your Church and ours. We fully agree with you, that there are strong reasons why we should endeavor to unite our mutual influence as much as possible, in fighting against the enemies of the Cross, and in laboring for the reformation of the Germans of this country. We also entertain the same views you have expressed on the character and condition of the German immigrants in general, and are, therefore, perfectly willing and ready, to extend to you the right hand of fellowship, and to do, on our part, what we possibly can, in order to secure their temporal and everlasting welfare. Although we neither go by the same name nor belong to the same organization, yet it will afford us pleasure to enter with you into friendly relations, so that we may labor together in harmony and love, without hindering each other in the least, in carrying forward the great work which the Lord has assigned us. But in order to realize this end, it will be necessary for us to use the utmost care, to act harmoniously in enforcing the Discipline of the Church, and in reproving sin of every shape and description. We are of opinion, that it will be especially necessary for us to be on our guard, not to take the advantage of each other, wherever the two Churches may meet in the prosecution of their work, nor to receive members that have been excluded by the other Church for immoral conduct, until such individuals have become reconciled to their Church and bring a testimony to that effect. Whether it would be best for both of us to build, like the Lutherans and the Reformed, union-churches, and to introduce a common Hymn Book, we do not presume to decide; we doubt, however, that any real advantage would be gained thereby for the realization of our great object.

A union for the purpose of publishing good German books, would be highly desirable; but our book establishments being at so great a distance from each other, we do not see how this could be effected in any other way, than by a mutual agreement to exchange and take each other's books on commission. We are willing to take from you as many good German books of every description, that we may not have, as we may need, provided we can get them on reasonable terms.

We rejoice that God's blessings have rested upon your labors among the Germans, and wish that this may be still more so hereafter. It will likewise afford us pleasure to contribute hereafter, in Christian fellowship with you, much toward the amelioration of the condition of the Germans, by the blessing of God resting upon our united labors. Our earnest prayer is, that the Great Giver of every good gift may fill us all with his Spirit, sanctify and lead us into all truth, and finally take us with all the elect into his heavenly kingdom, for his Son's sake! Amen.

Respectfully,

Your Brethren.

Summit county, Ohio, Oct. 25, 1843."

The public initiative toward this official conference on the subject in question, was a resolution of the General Conference of the M. E. Church on it, which was published in the "Christian Advocate and Journal," and copied with comments in the

Christliche Botschafter. The resolution in question was as follows:—

"Since some of the leading men of the Evangelical Association, commonly called '*Albrights*,' have expressed a wish to maintain a friendly intercourse with the M. E. Church, and taken a deep interest in our plans and efforts to advance the best interests of the many German immigrants that settle in our country; therefore,

Resolved, That a delegation of three be appointed by the bishops of this conference, whose duty it shall be to attend their next General Conference, and impart to them our fraternal salutation and sincere friendship; and that the said delegates be likewise authorized to confer with that body on the prospects of circulating our German periodicals and other works among them, and on any other subject that has reference to the great interests of the European or native Germans of our country."

From the comments of the Botschafter on this resolution we quote the following:—

"The respect and friendship shown us by the General Conference of the M. E. Church in the above resolution, deserve our consideration, and ought to be regarded and treated by us as a token of their Christian and fraternal disposition toward us; and, whereas their doctrines, ecclesiastical polity, and mode of operation, have, from the beginning, been essentially ours, for which reason we have felt a stronger attachment to them than to others; and as they have of late also commenced to labor among the Germans, we ought now to endeavor the more to maintain a friendly intercourse with them, and to take all proper measures, in order that we may labor in unison with them for the spiritual interests of the many thousands of German immigrants and others, who have hitherto been neglected, and thus help to build up the kingdom of God. Such a friendship and union between them and us, appear to us, under the present circumstances, to be indispensably necessary. We shall, in all probability, in our future labors among the Germans, meet in some places; and as we have the same doctrines and mode of operation, it will be the more necessary to guard on both sides against overreaching each other; because from such conduct of professed Christians the cause of Christ has been, at all times, and still is suffering very much."

The correctness of the views here expressed, has since been abundantly established; but the desired friendship and mutual foresight and peaceableness have, alas! in many individual cases, been too frequently violated. Time and again, when the ministers of the two Churches happened to labor on the same field or in the same place, especially in the West, collisions have taken place, which caused unpleasant feelings. We express, however, the sincere wish that nothing of the kind may take place again. There is still a peaceful relation between the two Churches, and we hope it will ever be sustained.

The resolution of the General Conference of the M. E. Church, induced some to think that the object was to bring about a formal *union* of the two Churches, although the document itself was silent about it. Whether this opinion was well founded or not, we are not prepared to say; but certain it is, that many members of both Churches have already expressed their regret that no stronger efforts were made to bring about a union, at a time when its realization might have been possible. And some would still be in favor of such a union, if they could only see how it might be done.

These were the main acts and proceedings of this General Conference, although it passed, in all, 107 resolutions, many of which required a great deal of time for discussion, and much labor for their actuation. The result of most of these resolutions has been very good.

The Annual Conferences of this year took place as follows: East Pennsylvania Conference met in Lebanon, Pa., on March 22d; West Pennsylvania Conference in the Leathart Springs Church, North Middleton township, Cumberland county, Pa., April 5th, and that of Ohio in the church in Thompson township, Seneca county, Ohio, May 10th. Three itinerants located, and 17 were received on trial. Eleven were ordained as elders, and 14 as deacons. Some of the larger circuits were divided, and a number of new circuits and stations formed; several missions were changed into circuits, and new missions established at Pittsburg, Dayton, Chicago, and Milwaukee. The rich harvest of the previous year had extended the limits of the Association considerably, and greatly increased the labors of the itinerancy.

This year the work again extended considerably, and in some places great awakenings took place; but, although nearly 2400 new members were received during the year, the net increase was not quite 800; the Society must, consequently, have lost 1600 members this year—a fact we can hardly account for. This heavy loss was, undoubtedly, to a great measure owing to the re-action of Millerism, which, however, cannot have been the sole cause. The fault must lie somewhere else; and it is probable, that want of proper attention to the new converts, is one of the main causes of the heavy loss of members, that takes place annually. The *decrease* exceeds the *increase* almost every year; this year it amounted to two-thirds of it. In the frequent changes of our ministers, we opine to find another cause of this deplorable phenomenon; for it often happens that the most conversions take place, and the greatest number of new members are received, toward the close of the preacher's ministerial labors on a circuit or station, many of whom are ensnared again by the world or by Satan, before the arrival of the new preacher; while others, not feeling as strongly attached to the new minister as to the old, by whose instrumentality they were converted, grow cold again by degrees, so that ere long scarcely any fruit is left of great awakenings; especially if the succeeding minister is careless about making pastoral calls, and attending to the lambs of the flock. This is a disadvantage connected with the itinerant system, which cannot be questioned. By greater carefulness, however, more regular visits, and a deeper interest in the welfare of immortal souls, this evil might be remedied to a great extent; especially, if every minister, on entering upon his new field of labor, would make it his special duty to call on the new converts, in order to become acquainted with them, and to gain their confidence, and, on the whole, treat them with marked attention and distinction. In this respect, it must be confessed, many ministers of both the Evangelical Association and other denominations have from their very start been too negligent, and the evil seems to be rather on the increase.

But, although the increase of this year was far inferior to that of the year before, yet the boundaries of the Association were considerably extended, a number of new preaching places were taken up, a large number of new classes formed, and many of the old ones were considerably increased. The missions, especially, did very well. In the city of New York and at Germantown, within the East Pennsylvania Conference, the work gained a solid footing; although it had, in the former place, to struggle against great difficulties, arising mainly out of the building of a church. The missions of the West Pennsylvania Conference at York and Pittsburg, were abundantly blessed of God. L. Eberhart was our first missionary in the city of Pittsburg, and labored there for two years with great success. He arrived there on the last day of April, 1843, immediately commenced his labors among the Germans, and as early as the following Whitsuntide an attempt was made to organize a society. He shortly after rented a large hall in the old court house, and preached there three times a week, and once in Alleghany City. The number of hearers increased from time to time, and the prospects of the enterprise were bright before the close of the first year. Bishop Long visited the mission in December, and made the following remarks with regard to it: "The prospects of this mission are very promising; it is, however, to be regretted that we have no church of our own. * * * * The hall in the court house is too small already for the number of hearers who would like to attend our meetings." A considerable number of precious souls had, at that time, been converted to the Lord already, and at the end of the conference year the society numbered 32 members. The next year they built a small church in Hand-street, but became thereby involved in debts, and great difficulties were the consequence; and yet the new church was neither large enough, nor conveniently located. But as a number of extensive revivals took place from time to time, the society increased and acquired strength by degrees.

The new mission at Dayton in Ohio Conference, and several of the others in the far West, especially the Mount Carmel and Fort Wayne missions, prospered greatly. At Chicago and Milwaukee the work advanced gradually, although no considerable awakenings took place during this year.

Thus far the annual contributions had covered the missionary expenses; but as their number now began to increase rapidly, the treasury of the missionary society soon became involved in debts, against which it had to struggle for a number of years. But, as the conferences which contracted the debts, also held themselves responsible for their payment, this matter was of no importance, and caused the parent board no further troubles. It ought to be stated here that, although all the Annual Conferences had formed themselves into branch societies of the parent society, yet each conference kept its contributions in its own treasury, and applied them also. This was, strictly speaking, not in accordance with the constitution of the parent society; but, as it bade fair to be most liberally supported, and to promote the good cause most efficiently for the time being, it was not objected to. But in the course of time a change of this state of things will probably become necessary, especially when more foreign missions will be established. —In the East Pennsylvania Conference the circuits of Lancaster, Leikens, Womelsdorf, and, above all, Lehigh, seem to have prospered most. The particular places and parts of country, however, where the greatest success attended our labors, are, with a few exceptions, not mentioned in the published reports of those circuits.—A rather extensive revival took place in Mahantango Valley, in the neighborhood of Hepler's; another in Meyerstown, Lebanon county, where arrangements were then made for the erection of a church. In 1837, D. Klapp removed from Orwigsburg to Meyerstown, and our ministers preached regularly in his house. In 1839 a fine class was formed there, and from that time the work gained a solid footing.—

Upon the whole, the work in the North did not progress as finely as it had done in the preceding years; yet it advanced gradually, especially in several places.

In the West Pennsylvania Conference the following circuits had most success: Centre, Perry, Cumberland, York, Virginia, Bedford, Clarion, Lycoming, Gettysburg, and Somerset. On Centre circuit the number of new converts was 116. Glorious awakenings took place at Millheim, Penn's Valley, and Rebersburg, in Brush Valley and vicinity, and other places of the circuit. Perry circuit reported 90 newly received members: it had the services of but one preacher, Bro. J. Dunlap. The principal work of grace seems to have taken place at Milford, where arrangements were forthwith made to build a church. In Kingston, on Cumberland circuit, the work had begun the year before, and this year already a church was built; another was built at Leesburg. On York circuit a camp-meeting was held this year, which numbered 59 or 60 tents, and not less than 40 souls were converted, most of whom joined our Church. —The camp-meetings that were held this year, during the latter part of summer, were, on the whole, highly blessed and victorious; while those that were held in the forepart, were not as good as usual.

In Ohio Conference the Fort Wayne mission reported 66 newly received members, the Mount Carmel mission 50, Pickaway circuit 54, and that of Sandusky 51. All the other circuits & missions fell short of 50; Canton, Mansfield, Crawford, and Miami, however, nearly came up to this number. On the whole, this conference held this year the second rank among the three conferences, in point of newly received members. But, as the reports that were published in the Periodical, speak, as a general thing, only in general terms of the circuits and of individual meetings, and as but little more information was received from that quarter, the writer is unable to furnish a more detailed description of the work there. The Des Plain and Rock River circuits in the state of Illinois, the former traveled by Chr. Kopp, and the latter by L. Heiss and J. G. Miller, together reported 79 newly received members, and in all 298.

But a new district having been formed this year from these two circuits and the missions at Chicago and Milwaukee, ministered to by Samuel Baumgartner, there were brighter anticipations indulged in for the future, and also realized. This year our second church was built in the state of Illinois, viz., at Napierville, Dupage county, and the first commenced in Wisconsin; this is also said to have been the first German Protestant church in that state. At Chicago likewise a church was built this year and dedicated, which was also the first German Protestant church of that city, and for a number of years the only one. Our society is likewise the oldest German Protestant congregation there, and was the only one for about five years.

At that time certain would-be Lutheran ministers forced themselves upon the Germans of Wisconsin; but they deserved not that name, on account of their immorality, bigotry, and intolerance, and, together with the advocates of infidelity assisted in making the people still more immoral. Under these circumstances, our ministers and societies had a difficult task to solve, and this the more so as they were the only Germans there in those days, who fought the battles of the Lord.

Bro. *Charles Hesser* was the only minister of the Association, who died during this year. His unexpected death, in consequence of an accident he met with on his way to General Conference, caused, as before stated, great grief and many tears among the delegates of conference, and was deeply lamented by all who had known him, as well by members of the Society as by others. His death was caused in the following manner: On the 6th of October, he and the Brethren H. Fisher, J. M. Saylor, and M. F. Maize, started in a two-horse carriage, in order to attend General Conference, to be held in the state of Ohio. The following day they dined with Bro. D. Zartman in Jackson township, Northumberland co., Pa.; and thence starting, they drove down hill, when the tongue of the carriage came loose, and, touching the horses, caused one of them to kick so furiously as to hit and break Bro. Hesser's leg, who drove. A fever ensued in consequence of this wound, and in five days he died, October 12th. His remains were taken to Orwigsburg, his native place, and buried there the following Sunday, October 15th, in the burying-ground of the Association; Bro. John Sensel preached his funeral sermon to a very large and deeply affected concourse of people, from Luke 2, 29. 30: "Lord, now lettest thou thy servant depart in peace, according to thy word; for mine eyes have seen thy salvation." He left a widow and four children.

Brother Hesser was converted about 1824, during the great revival at Orwigsburg and vicinity. A few years afterward he was licensed to preach, entered the itinerancy in 1831, and was stationed with Bro. P. Wagner on Centre circuit, where he preached with much applause and with marked success. The following year he traveled with S. G. Miller on Union circuit, and was universally beloved. In 1833 he was stationed for the second time on Centre circuit, as the superintending preacher, with John Young for his colleague. In 1834 he traveled Cumberland, and in 1835 Lebanon circuit, and labored successfully and with acceptance on these two circuits, although no special awakenings took place during that time. In 1836 he traveled again on Cumberland circuit, and in 1837 he was sent, for the first time, to Philadelphia, where he labored for two successive years with glorious results, and rendered general satisfaction. In 1839 and part of 1840, he traveled on Schuylkill circuit; he was then stationed again at Philadelphia, and in 1842 and 1843, to the end of his earthly career, he traveled on Lehigh circuit. Thus he served the Church as an itinerant a little over 12 years, and died at the age of 35 years, 11 months, and 7 days.

Brother Hesser was universally regarded and beloved; he was well built, about 5 feet and 8 inches high, rather slender, with regular features, sharp clear eyes, of rather dark complexion, cheerful disposition, and nearly always of pleasant mien. His manners in the pulpit were very pleasing, his voice was piercing and lovely, and his discourses were always touching. In almost every sermon, part of his audience wept, and the impressions they received, were often lasting. He was a talented orator, but not deep in his scriptural expositions or explanations of texts. His strength did not lie in this direction, but rather in his touching appeals, his expressions of sympathy, and in his pleasant conduct toward every body. His biographer says of him among other things:—

"He was one of those few who have almost no enemies, and every body for their friend. As a private citizen, he was strictly moral and without blemish in his conduct; as a Christian, he was courageous and resolute, to suffer for Christ and the truth; and as a minister of the Gospel, he was well qualified and full of unction. He filled his office with credit and dignity, and blew the trumpet of the good news of the great salvation in Christ Jesus with clearness and indefatigableness. His discourses were strictly evangelical, animated, instructive, and greatly calculated to engage the attention of the audience; and there is no doubt, that a vast amount of good has been accomplished by his labors in the vineyard of the Lord."

Cheerful and courageous, as he had been in life, so he was also in death; and thus he fell in the triumphs of faith as a conqueror on the field of the Gospel. His dying words were: "*Glory be to the Lamb for ever and ever!*" and thus he died happy in the Lord.

The increase during this year was 883; and at the close of the year the whole membership amounted to 13,908.

The Year 1844.

The Annual Conferences were held this year as follows: East Pennsylvania Conference convened at Orwigsburg, February 28th; West Pennsylvania at Millheim, Centre county, on the 13th of March; and that of Ohio in the Lafayette Church, Wayne county, Ohio, on the 8th of May. Eight preachers located and nineteen were received into the itinerancy.—In West Pennsylvania Conference none left the itinerancy this year, a phenomenon of rare occurrence in every conference. This conference formed two new circuits at its annual session, viz., *Westmoreland* and *Loyalsack*, and a new district, called *Potomac district*, consisting of parts of Bahimore and Alleghany districts. The East Pennsylvania Conference likewise formed two new circuits, viz., *Northampton* circuit, consisting of parts of Lehigh and Milford circuits, and that of *Dauphin*, consisting of parts of Lebanon and Lancaster circuits. This conference established missions at Reading and Syracuse. Ohio Conference changed some of its missions into circuits, and established new missions at *Chillicothe*, *Peoria*, and *Galena*.

This was, on the whole, a successful year, and the increase was more than twice as large as in the previous year. Great awakenings took place in different places, and the work extended more and more on most of the fields of labor. On Leikens circuit, in East Pennsylvania Conference, glorious awakenings and revivals took place; especially at Berrysburg, beginning at the dedication of the church, and on some other circuits, as Lehigh, Northampton, Lebanon, etc. The new mission at Reading did very well from its very start, and our church there was built in the first year of the mission, the basement was finished, and divine service held in it. The mission at Syracuse, N. Y., also prospered greatly, and a church was built there during the year.

In West Pennsylvania Conference the work prospered most on Union, Perry, Cumberland, and Warren circuits, where considerable awakenings took place in various parts, especially one near Selinsgrove, Union circuit, in charge of the Brethren J. Barber and C. Link.

Of the work in Ohio Conference, the reports in the Periodical of that year are very meager. Some camp and protracted meetings, however, are spoken of as having been eminently blessed, especially a camp-meeting on Canton circuit, and a protracted meeting at Greensburg, on the same circuit. In a report of the camp-meetings held on Columbiana district, Bro. E. Stœver remarks among other things as follows:—

"The third we held on Canton circuit, from the 15th to the 21st of August, consisting of 60 tents, the most of which were occupied by two families each. There were between 300 and 400 friends present, and our audiences were large and attentive. On Sunday thousands of people had met, who conducted themselves, generally, very well. This meeting was highly blessed from beginning to end, and many will long cherish its memory. The preaching of the cross was well received, and at every invitation penitents came forward to the altar. It is estimated that between 40 and 50 individuals were converted, 34 of whom joined our Church. * * * Among the children of God joy and happiness prevailed, and their praises and shouts were heard at a distance."

The *new Illinois Conference* consisted of two districts, viz., "*Indiana*" and "*Illinois*" districts; the former ministered to by Bro. A. B. Shæfer, and the latter by S. Baumgartner, both sturdy pioneers in the western wilds, who were not easily discouraged by difficulties or inconveniences, or frightened away from their posts. The conference extended over large portions of the states of Indiana and Illinois, as far as Wisconsin and Iowa, and was about 500 miles long and nearly 400 wide, numbering 14 preachers 763 members, 3 circuits, 6 missions, 5 churches, 5 Sabbath-schools, and about 50 preaching places, some of which were from 60 to 80 miles apart, and almost inaccessible on account of the unbeaten, trackless prairies, swamps, and unbridged rivers. The preachers frequently missed the right direction on the pathless prairies, lost their way, and wandered about till late at night, yea sometimes had to spend even the night there. The sainted Brother Lintner told the writer a few months before his death, that once he wandered about on such a prairie for a whole day and a night, and part of the following day, during a severe and very cold snow-storm, without meeting with a house or human being, in the certain apprehension of death. Fortunately he saved his life. At another time, he and his horse almost froze to death. Many of our first preachers in the far West, suffered similarly. These were trials, such as our ministers had often to pass through. But their labors in the Lord were not in vain; hundreds and thousands of precious souls were converted to the Lord by their instrumentality, who now praise him for the salvation brought to them by these faithful messengers of God.

Brother Shæfer and the preachers under his care on Indiana district, labored with glorious success. Hearts and doors were opened before them, and their fields of labor extended more and more.

On Illinois district, presided over by Brother Baumgartner, the work made, upon the whole, likewise glorious progress; the circuits and missions were considerably extended and the membership increased, partly by conversions, partly by members coming from the East. At Chicago a glorious awakening took place, and the society was considerably increased. Milwaukee mission, too, grew stronger, both from without and within; from without by taking up a number of new preaching places, and within by the conversion of a goodly number of precious souls. During this year the brethren commenced to preach at Racine, Wisconsin, and formed a small class. This year Bro. John Niebergall moved with his family, all of whom belonged to the Society, from Lyons, N. Y., to that place, and opened his house to the preachers. He held the first German service in that city—a prayer-meeting with his wife and a brother, named H. Young, who had, meanwhile, come thither. During this prayer-meeting a soul was awakened and became penitent. Brother Hauert preached the first German sermon there in September of the same year. This was the beginning of the labors of the Evangelical Association at Racine.

The Galena mission was very large from the beginning, extending over about 300 miles, and increased still more from time to time. The missionary, J. G. Miller, labored amid many difficulties and discouragements with indefatigable zeal, and was permitted to see the fruit of his labors.

Bro. Baumgartner and Bishop Seybert also bore their share of the burden of the work in the new country, and set their younger brethren an example of application and perseverance, that could not fail of making very salutary impressions upon them. The bishop took so deep an interest in the prosperity of the West, both in a temporal and moral point of view, that he traveled, preached, visited, and underwent the greatest difficulties, in order to promote its best interests.

But all the efforts of the bishop, the presiding elders and preachers generally, were not sufficient to meet the spiritual wants of the West. The harvest was too plenteous—much too plenteous for the small number of laborers.

This year the Association likewise lost but one of its preachers by death, viz., Bro. *Daniel Focht*, of Schuylkill county, in the East Pennsylvania Conference. In connection with the great revival at Orwigsburg, mention has already been made of Brother Focht, and his character and usefulness have been described to some extent. We therefore insert here but an extract from his biography, which appeared in the Botschafter, as follows:—

"Brother *Daniel Focht* died happy in the Lord, March 16, 1844, at his old residence, Brunswick township, Schuylkill county, Pa. His disease was a nervous complaint, which caused him for about four years almost unendurable sufferings. Yet great as his sufferings were, God strengthened him and granted him a victorious faith, in which he died calmly. Shortly before his final departure, he said: 'I have examined myself, and through the blood of Christ I see my way open to heaven.' Subsequently he was so abundantly blessed and strengthened, that he said to his family, he could scarce wait for the time of his dissolution, but would soon go to heaven, requesting them to tell this to his brethren and sisters, and to all men. Thus departed this just and pious man in the faith and firm hope of a blessed immortality.

Brother Focht was converted about 25 years ago, through the instrumentality of our preachers, joined the Society, and was for the greater part of his subsequent life a local preacher, which office he filled with great zeal and faithfulness, to the conversion of many souls and the edification of the children of God. His age was 60 years, 2 months, and 1 day, leaving a widow and 9 children, to lament his death."

The increase of members during this year was 1010, and the whole membership at the close of the year, 14,918.

The Year 1845.

The Annual Conferences of this year took place as follows: East Pennsylvania Conference convened at Philadelphia, Feb. 26; West Pennsylvania at York, March 12; that of Ohio in Emanuel's Church, Greenfield township, Fairfield county, O., May 14th; and that of Illinois at Des Plain, Cook county, Illinois, June 11th. Nine itinerants located, and 13 were received on trial. Several of the circuits were divided, and others changed; but only one new mission was started, viz., at Albany, New York, and a few more by Illinois Conference.

Although the boundaries of the Association extended considerably during the year, and nearly 2300 new members were received, yet the net increase did not even amount to *one hundred!* The loss of membership was greater than in any former year. The East Pennsylvania Conference received 736 new members, and yet its increase only amounted to 43; the West Pennsylvania Conference received 812 new members, and yet sustained a decrease of 91 members; that of Ohio had 486 new converts, and yet had a decrease of 15; while that of Illinois received but 224 new members, and had an increase of 160. However incredible this report may appear to some of our readers, it is nevertheless true, according to the protocols of the several conferences. It is, therefore, no wonder that the increase of the membership of the Association was so very slow. Our views of the causes of these heavy annual losses we have already given; and as the evil still exists to a great extent, the Annual Conferences ought to take it into consideration, in order to remedy it as far as possible. It can, indeed, not be expected that in a denomination enforcing Discipline and excluding the transgressors, the increase of membership should be as rapid as in those where this is done but to a limited extent or not at all; but notwithstanding this, the annual losses of the Evangelical Association are proportionably by far too heavy. We repeat it, that, in our opinion, the want of proper treatment of awakened and newly converted persons is the principal cause of these losses, viz., neglect of regular family visits, want of personal acquaintance with every member of the Church, of familiar conversation with the members generally on the subject of religion, and the great neglect of class-meetings by both preachers and class-leaders. For it cannot be denied, that the Discipline, on these points, has at all times been too much neglected by very many, yea there is reason to fear, by the majority. And that the Annual Conferences, when examining the preachers, pass so lightly over these points, does not disprove what we have said, but rather shows the alarming extent of the evil. Formerly some of the preachers excused this neglect of duty by the plea that their circuits were too large, that they had to preach almost daily, and hence had neither time nor strength left for making calls or holding class-meetings. Had this plea been well founded then, it would, for the most part, not hold good any more in our days. But that the plea was, in most cases, entirely unfounded, appears from the fact that a small number of preachers, some of whom were of very delicate health and feeble, always attended punctually to these duties, and also saw their labors crowned with the happiest results. But, even admitting that the preachers are excusable in these respects, it does by no means follow that this is the case with the class-leaders and exhorters also. From these and other neglects of duty, that have existed in the Evangelical Association as long as the writer has been acquainted with the same, it appears that even the best discipline is worth but little if not enforced.

At this time the first zeal for the cause of missions had considerably cooled in many places. Some of the auxiliary societies had already dissolved, others relaxed in their efforts, and the number of new societies did not increase as fast as before. By the efforts of the Annual Conferences, however, matters afterward took a better turn again. But on the whole, the Association has never yet paid as much attention to the cause of missions as it ought to have done, according to its means and circumstances; yet, taking all things into consideration, it must be admitted that the cause has a good start and bids fair for the future. The Association progresses in all its enterprises, rather slowly, but generally steadily and perseveringly. This was the case with the Printing Establishment, with the cause of missions, and is now the case with the educational cause.

Of extraordinary awakenings this year, there are no reports extant, although about the usual number of new members was received. In East Pennsylvania Conference, the circuits of Northampton, Monroe, and Leikens, and the Albany mission, had the best success. Awakenings took place at Weisport, in Beach Wood, in Williams township, and at Springtown; and a considerable number of souls was also converted to the Lord.

In West Pennsylvania Conference the circuits of Columbia, Cumberland, York, Lycoming, Perry, and Clarion, and in Ohio Conference the circuits of Wayne, Sandusky, and Marion, and the Ann Arbor mission, made the best progress, as far as the receiving of new members is concerned.

Illinois Conference was in great want of ministers, and its extensive fields of labor could therefore be supplied but sparingly, not to mention that nearly all the ministers were inexperienced young men. This proved a great impediment to the rapid extension of the work.—But notwithstanding all this, new preaching places were established in new parts of the country, and the boundaries of the conference considerably extended. There are no reports extant of great awakenings.

At this time a discussion was carried on in the columns of the Periodical, on the subject of a learned ministry. A communication by Father Dreisbach, headed: "*Teachers and Preachers should not be ignorant*," gave rise to it. Father D. expressed himself in said article in favor of a learned ministry, and admonished such preachers and candidates for the ministry, as had not received a proper school training, to study privately and store their minds with useful knowledge, as being highly necessary to a successful minister of the Gospel. He declared that a classical education was, indeed, not absolutely necessary to a minister of the Gospel, but allowed that it was no disadvantage, either. But human learning, sanctified by the Spirit of God, he represented as highly advantageous to a minister for greater usefulness in his calling. Above all other things, he inculcated that preachers should strive to master the language in which they officiated, etc.—This communication of Father Dreisbach was soon followed by an article on the subject in question, headed:—

"*A learned Ministry.*"

"The communication: '*Teachers and Preachers should not be ignorant,*' which appeared in the last number of the Botschafter, is, in my opinion, worthy of particular attention, both on account of its author and its contents. The views of so old, experienced, and universally known a brother as Father Dreisbach is, when expressed in public, on any important subject, must necessarily carry great weight, and are calculated to mould and confirm the position of the Association with regard to that subject. It must, therefore, be self-evident to every unprejudiced reader, that much, very much depends on views flowing from such sources, and that it is highly necessary to prove their correctness or the contrary. Now, if the views of our author on the subject in question are correct, they ought to be supported, confirmed, and carried out; but if incorrect, they ought to be refuted, rejected, and abhorred.

That opposite views on the subject in question are held by us as a body, is a well known fact, and needs no proof. Some are of opinion, that a classical education is not only useless for a minister of the Gospel, but rather dangerous and injurious. This opinion, in all probability, originated in the observation that many of the learned men of all times were godless, and did a great deal of harm in the world, not considering that the abuse of a good cause is no valid argument against its proper use. Admitting that most of the learned men of all times were carnally minded, they ought to consider that this is no more a proof against the usefulness of learning, than the carnal-mindedness and wickedness of the great majority of professed Christians prove that the Christian religion is false and useless. Others are of opinion that learning is very useful and advantageous to a pious and faithful minister of the Gospel, and that every one ought to strive to acquire as large an amount of useful information as his time and circumstances permit.

These, indeed, do not think that an unlearned minister—in the common acceptation of the term—is unfit to preach the Gospel, provided he is called of God, is pious, and studies as much as he possibly can; but yet they are of opinion that the educated minister, with the same measure of grace and unction from on high, is far more useful in the Lord's vineyard than his unlearned brother. These seem to be the views of our author on the subject, if I understand him right. Although he does not regard the highest degree of school learning as indispensably necessary to the functions of a Gospel minister, yet he recommends a higher degree of learning and culture, than most of our so-called learned men have. He insists that the preacher should not only understand theology, but also grammar, philosophy, geography, etc. In short, he is in favor of *a learned ministry*, furnished with the grace, wisdom, and unction of the Holy Ghost, necessary to the discharge of the duties of his responsible office.

It also seems to follow from the remarks of our author, that he is not against higher schools of learning, but that he regards and endorses them as useful. This I infer from the following extract of his communication: 'It is true, some have excellent natural talents, so that, by observation and practice, they can comprehend and do things more readily than others; but how much would their usefulness be enhanced, if they would take a systematic course of instruction!' I rejoice to see that the Botschafter seems to be ready to open its columns for a full discussion of the subject under consideration, and this is, in my view, indeed necessary. Let the two sides state and support their views as well as they can, and the reader judge which party is in the right. If I should have misunderstood or misrepresented my author in any point, I shall be pleased to be corrected. I hope that the brethren will not disregard this subject, but give it all the attention it deserves. The views of the Editor on the subject would, in all probability, be read with universal interest."

In the same number of the Botschafter, there appeared an Editorial, censuring the views expressed in the article in question, on the difference of opinion in the Association on the usefulness of learning, and asserting that such a difference did not exist in the connection, etc.—This elicited further discussions on both sides, from which it appeared but too plainly that all were not in favor of a learned ministry. To deny this, would be nonsense. *Many*, both preachers and members, regarded a classical education not only as entirely useless, but as dangerous to the ministry.—Although such an error cannot be creditable to us as a Church, yet truth requires us to record that it was held by many of us. Many of the old surviving ministers and members know these to be facts, and they are also honest and humble enough, to acknowledge them.

Subsequently the subject on "*learning of the ministry*" was again discussed in the Botschafter; but the discussions led to no desirable results, but rather unpleasant feelings, as the difference of opinion on the subject was as yet too great. The party which maintained that there was a difference of opinion on the subject in the Association, and was, at the same time, in favor of a learned ministry, charged the origin of the dispute and the unpleasant turn of the discussions on the Editor, who, in his turn, repelled the charge, maintaining that the other party was in fault.

But, although these discussions did not lead to the desired result, yet the subject was thereby kept before our people, was discussed both in public and in private, and thus made progress.—A year afterward, the West Pennsylvania Conference formed itself into an *Educational Society*, for the purpose of supporting pious and poor young men in their studies, and of procuring a library for the use of the conference. And two years afterward the subject came up before General Conference, which at once took measures to establish a higher school of learning ("*Pflanzschule*") which, however, were never carried out. Yet, notwithstanding its failure, the project was a progressive movement. The prejudices and the opposition to high schools in the Association, gradually gave way, and many who had formerly been opposed to them, were now in their favor; and thus it has come to pass that the Association now has two promising seminaries, which have many friends.

The number of newly received members during this year was 2,258, but the increase only 97, and at the close of the conference year, the whole membership amounted to 15,015.

Thus we have come to the close of the History of the Evangelical Association up to the end of the year 1845. We are fully aware, that many things therein are very imperfect and defective, partly owing to the scarcity of reports and documents, necessary to compile such a history, and partly to the want of the proper qualifications for so difficult a task, on the part of the compiler. Had he foreseen all the difficulties, the trouble and labor he had to undergo, he could hardly have been induced to take the matter into his hands. But having, at least, made a beginning and furnished a sketch of the History of the Association, he consoles himself with the hope that his labors will not be without some value to the Church in future. And if a more detailed History of the Evangelical Association should never be written, the compiler hopes that many will find in the short description of it contained in this Volume, abundant cause to recognize and praise the grace of the Lord, in founding and conducting this branch of his Church, and be encouraged thereby, always to submit to his guidance and to trust in his Providence. He especially indulges in the hope that the ministers and members of the Association of the present time, will learn many salutary lessons from the example of their brethren and sisters of former days, and be animated thereby, to prosecute faithfully the work commenced by them, with the help of God.

Not to see the hand of the Lord in the work, from its beginning, would indeed indicate spiritual blindness on our part; and we should be guilty of ingratitude and faithlessness, if we did not strive according to the utmost of our ability to prosecute the work, under the guidance of the Most High. But, at the same time, we must not lose sight of the greater responsibility resting upon us, arising from the more favorable circumstances into which we are placed, and the better prospects of the Association, considering that more has been committed to our trust, than was the case with our fathers. With all due respect for their accomplishments in their day of small things, we, living in a different time and under different circumstances, must bring greater sacrifices, and make better arrangements for a more effectual prosecution of the work. In this respect we must not follow the steps of our forefathers—we must do more than they were able to do. But their singleness of heart, fidelity, and activity, we ought always to copy faithfully, and be incited thereby to discharge our duties conscientiously. As to our duty as a branch of the Church of God in days to come, we cannot guard too carefully against indifference and lukewarmness; nor can we be too cautious about taking the proper measures and using the proper means for the purpose of doing our part in erecting the great structure of the kingdom of God on earth. We trust that thus far the Lord has graciously winked at our short-comings, in this respect—but in future he will require more at our hands. We therefore need, for the time to come, more spirit of enterprise, more courage and more faith, in order to a conscientious discharge of our duties. Although the Lord has done great and glorious things for *us*, yet we have, thus far, done comparatively but little for *him* and *his cause*. We are yet far from doing what we can do, far from doing what is our duty to do. The spirit of persevering, faithful, and earnest prayer for the coming of the kingdom of God. and the spirit of liberality in the support of all proper means tending toward a more rapid spread of it, are not yet abundantly poured out upon us, although the Lord has, in these respects also, done great things for us.

Thus we have, on the one hand, great cause to rejoice in God, and to be thankful; on the other hand, however, we have just as much cause to humble ourselves, and to repent of our short comings.—And now may this History have its desired effect on all of us, and create in us a deeper interest in our own salvation, as well as in the welfare of all men, and the honor and glory of God! Amen.

Short Statistic Report of the Evangelical Association at the present time (1856).

Since 1845, the Evangelical Association has extended more rapidly than ever before, and nearly doubled its membership. At that time it numbered 15,000, now it numbers about 30,000 members.* Then it consisted of *four*, now it consists of *eight* Annual Conferences. The conferences formed subsequently to that time, are: New York, Pittsburg, Indiana, and Wisconsin Conferences. The number of its ministers is about 500, nearly one-half of whom are itinerants. It has about forty home missions, mostly in the western states; and *one* foreign mission, in the kingdom of Wuertemberg, Germany, which was established in 1845, and has two missionaries.

The Printing Establishment of the Association at Cleveland, Ohio, is in a prosperous condition, and progresses every year.

The Association has also under its care and patronage two promising seminaries; the one at New Berlin, Union county, Pa., and the other at Greensburg, Summit county, Ohio, in which the sciences and languages are taught.

*At this time (January, 1858,) about 32,000.

INDEX.

FIRST SECTION.

SECOND SECTION.

THIRD SECTION.

FOURTH SECTION.

FIFTH SECTION.

SIXTH SECTION.

SEVENTH SECTION.

EIGHTH SECTION.

NINTH SECTION.

TENTH SECTION.

CPSIA information can be obtained
at www.ICGtesting.com
Printed in the USA
LVHW040938020323
740706LV00007B/484

9 783375 149369